"An absolutely ... about Lucky Girl is remarkably precise in its meditations on art, youth, sacrifice, and obsession. It is a tart, manic, and exhilarating read. Tagle-Dokus has created a haunting account of Hollywood horrors told with the thrill of a reality show binge."

—KILEY REID,
author of *Come and Get It*

"What a completely fabulous debut! Allie Tagle-Dokus delivers us a witty coming-of-age story, with original characters and pitch-perfect dialogue. Lyrical and darkly funny—I adored it."

—ANNIE HARTNETT,
author of *The Road to Tender Hearts*

"At once shimmering and gritty, breezy and heartbreaking, *Lucky Girl* is pure pleasure from beginning to end. It's so much more than a showbiz satire: it's a meditation on art and work, the slippery difference between the two, and how easily a gift can become a curse. Above all, it's a family drama full of prickly, uneasy love, and it bursts with feeling. Tagle-Dokus writes with such a light touch, and the story moves along so fast, you'll feel like you're flying—and falling—right along with Lucy as she dances. We're so lucky to have *Lucky Girl*."

—JAMES FRANKIE THOMAS,
author of *Idlewild*

"*Lucky Girl* is a moving, witty, original, and timely novel about a young girl's search for fame, belonging, and home in the most unlikely places. I would follow Lucy Gardiner to the ends of the earth, whether that means a reality TV dance stage, the absurdly large home of an aging pop star, a high-school time warp TV show, or even the dark underbelly of the Internet. This book is as funny as the most viral TikTok and as profound as a Greek tragedy."

—MARIA KUZNETSOVA,
author of *Something Unbelievable*

lucky girl

lucky girl

a novel

Allie Tagle-Dokus

Tin House

A **zando** IMPRINT

NEW YORK

Tin House

The characters and events in this book are fictitious. Any similarity to real persons, living or dead, is coincidental and not intended by the author.

Copyright © 2025 by Allie Tagle-Dokus

Zando supports the right to free expression and the value of copyright. The purpose of copyright is to encourage writers and artists to produce the creative works that enrich our culture. Thank you for buying an authorized edition of this book and for complying with copyright laws by not reproducing, scanning, uploading, or distributing this book or any part of it without permission. If you would like permission to use material from the book (other than for brief quotations embodied in reviews), please contact connect@zandoprojects.com.

Tin House is an imprint of Zando.
zandoprojects.com

First US Edition 2025
Manufacturing by Kingery Printing Company
Cover and text design by Beth Steidle

The publisher does not have control over and is not responsible for author or other third-party websites (or their content).

Library of Congress Cataloging-in-Publication Data is available.

978-1-963108-62-0 (paperback)
978-1-963108-63-7 (ebook)

10 9 8 7 6 5 4 3 2 1

Manufactured in the United States of America

For Stephanie Weymouth

Act I: Breakout

Kimberly

Things you give up being a dancer: toenails, weekends, childhood, growth plates, prom, friendships. One friend, Kimberly, is my marker for what life would have looked like had I not gone down this path. Glancing at Kimberly's social media today, I find she has recently moved into a brick Cambridge walk-up with her boyfriend of seven years. LinkedIn suggests she graduated a year early from high school and is currently pursuing her PhD in American Studies, dissertation tentatively titled "Modern Slavery: Tracing the Fissures of the American Carceral System, 1920–Present." Kimberly's Instagram boasts two rescue dogs, Skipper and Porkchop, as well as countless hikes, beer gardens, paint-and-sip nights, trips to vast cultured European cities. What would she think of me now? Though I have tried to see if she's commented or liked any articles about me, my search remains futile.

We had been friends, best friends, since Kimberly was born; my mom and Kimberly's mothers were coworkers at the hospital. Our conceptions could not have been more different. Kimberly's parents, two high-powered surgeons, spent years genetically evaluating each embryo before selecting her. Meanwhile, I was an oopsie baby upending my family's already frayed ecosystem. My brothers, Joel and Micah, were preteens by the time I could walk and often played heavy metal to drown out my toddler tantrums. If Mom ever needed a break from the slew of testosterone in her own house, she took me thirty minutes down Route 2 to Kimberly's mothers' place, a brick house covered in ivy, out of a fairy tale. Our moms sat at the kitchen counter, drinking kombucha before it was in the popular zeitgeist, discussing sarcoma cells and politics and shitty coworkers. Kimberly and I were left to each other.

Mostly, we paced Kimberly's wood-paneled basement and narrated fabulous stories about what would happen if we were in the *Attack on Titan* anime universe. See us hunched over a small table in Kimberly's basement, drawing ourselves among the cast, creating comics that we laminated and stapled and hid beneath Kimberly's bed. Kimberly's mothers thought they were too violent, but that was because their home was synonymous with heaven.

For a time, Kimberly and I were the same, and we had no one else. I could tell what Kimberly was thinking by the way she blinked or drew breath, and I saw all things in terms of what could make Kimberly happy and what would not. Being with her was as comfortable as being by myself. It was not so with other people. In school, I found talking to strangers cumbersome, so I stayed quiet, observed, and blended in with a group of similarly ambivalent girls. Kimberly had it worse. Her dial was stuck at one level: Kimberly. She introduced herself by detailing exactly how she was created in a test tube. During a trip to the Burlington Mall, we bought matching lace stockings and fishnet gloves from Hot Topic, which I kept buried in a drawer, but Kimberly wore hers openly. She sent me Snapchats and my heart clenched seeing how sincerely she carried herself beyond her fairy-tale house, red Mikasa scarf draped over her chest, the Scout Regiment's cape shrimpy against her back. *Ready to save the world*, I'd snap back. Still. I knew how Kimberlys were treated at my school.

It didn't make sense. In contemporary dance, you go full out, bare your naked soul to the audience, move with your entire heart. I believed this vulnerable soul nakedness to be my strength, what made me special. Mom says she realized this when I first took to the stage. Usually, kids bluster around. In the rarest of occasions, a toddler remembers their choreography. Once a decade, a child will reveal genuine talent, and even rarer will they display the sort of talent that alters the trajectory of their life, the talent that makes them go from regular kid to a kid that will one day claim a Wikipedia page, a kid that will forever be in pursuit of this moment right here, the moment they were first deemed so marked. My first solo, at five, was set to the *Glee* version of "Don't Rain on My Parade" and I don't remember a lick of it. There's not even a version on YouTube to watch. There's only Mom's recollection to go on. As soon as the lights went on and the trumpets rang out, my tiny body became possessed by sound itself. My à la secondes hit every beat, my roundoff back tuck reached double my height, and my face animated to each joyous lyric. It wasn't a perfect performance; Mom later recounted: "You fell out of your turns at the last eight count." By then she was a professional dance mom and knew all the French terminology down to the last extended neck, but in the beginning, she didn't couldn't tell a plié from a pirouette. But you didn't need to know that to know I was breathtaking. That I let go. That on the stage, I was seen.

But through Kimberly, I learned there was a limit to what you could show the world, the audience. Perhaps only a fifth, maybe just an eighth. Mom confided to me that girls spread Kimberly-germs and boys played keep-away with her fishnet gloves, dipping them in the toilet and rioting with laughter when Kimberly would still put them on. Her mothers were considering pulling her out of public school.

In fact, I knew it was much worse than what adults saw at school. For years, Kimberly had been writing an *Attack on Titan* fan fiction, a deeply complicated and Kimberly-earnest tale of our characters in the *AoT* universe. This was her elementary magnum opus, and she had finally bitten the bullet and published the first few chapters on a popular fanfic site. It wasn't like she expected anything. She just liked to play sandbox in a universe of her own making. But the fic fell into the wrong forums, and vultures came for her. Dramatic YouTube readings created around an exchange of clunky dialogue. These messages stung Kimberly more than her trials at school. These were people who shared her obsession, and here they were rejecting everything about her, even going so far as saying anyone who butchered the characters this badly should die.

Kimberly told only me. Meanwhile, my life had swelled. I had joined a preprofessional dance company in Boston. As I began to trust my teammates to catch me falling backward off a prop, as I found myself enjoying easy and friendly rivalries within the studio, as my room became a shrine of first-place plaques from Jump, Nuvo, Starpower, and Radix Dance Convention, I stopped thinking about *Attack on Titan*. Always I was practicing penchés in the garage and making up dances in the backyard. My legs and hips were never flexible enough, feet never arched enough, core never strong enough. My morning routine involved 4:00 AM Pilates. Nights filled with analyzing dances on YouTube, memorizing all the national and Best Dancer–winning solos. My body bore the impact of dance: purpled knees, skinned elbows, blistered toes, and peeling feet. Yet any pain fled the moment the music began.

When I came in eighth place in the middle of my first year as a junior, I felt like my life was over. I was eleven. Understand: You aren't a dancer for very long. *Your body is a bag of sand with a hole!* Convention instructors shouted this in ballrooms, ballet instructors would corner you in the hallways and tell you: *Act fast, this will all be over soon.* I'm not sure when I crossed some sort of line, but suddenly I was a steel version of myself stepping onto the stage. And then I was this steel version all the time. And still there was Kimberly Snapchatting me at all hours, begging every weekend for a sleepover full of sugar cookies and anime. I had no idea how to fix her problems, I did not know how to tell her to stop wearing fishnets, to shut up and go incognito. That would hurt her feelings even more. Instead, I texted back plain platitudes. *Just be yourself. That's all you can do.*

thank u, Kimberly chatted back. Then: *What about next weekend?*

It was Kimberly's eleventh birthday in May—which coincided with Jump Anaheim—that ended our friendship. For my eleventh birthday, in December, she'd created a twenty-minute-long fan edit of my dances to the *AoT* soundtrack. (Confession: Sometimes I still watch it. She hasn't unlisted it on YouTube; is that a sign she still thinks of me?) She had been planning her eleventh birthday, her Harry Potter birthday, as she called it, for years. We would have a three-course meal at the Melting Pot, walk around the Burlington Mall, and then . . . I can still hear her voice: "Are you ready? You're going to die. We. Are. In. For. It. We've got . . . Nature Nick."

Then I had to react. Nature Nick was a well-known animal guru in our area. My brothers loved him. He would show up to kids' birthday parties in his big green van, the back stacked high with white crates of alligators, baby ostriches, skinks. The kids would sit on camping chairs in the driveway, and Nature Nick would throw boa constrictors around their necks like it was nothing. Nature Nick was awesome. And because it was just going to be Kimberly and me, we'd have all the time in the world to cuddle the blue-tongue skinks, the white foxes. Hell, he might leave behind a kangaroo. After Nature Nick, we would get down to the regular birthday stuff, ice-cream cake with Oreo crumble and eleven candles and a wish, then we'd buckle down in her basement with bowls of popcorn and we would finally watch the last season of *Attack on Titan*, the one that we had been saving exactly for Kimberly's eleventh birthday. I think she built this all up not only to get her through the bullying and the online hate, but also in the hope that once we got giggling in the Melting Pot, once we shoplifted from Hot Topic, once we conquered a gator together, once I returned to her wood-paneled basement, once we had that hot laptop blaring, I would come back to her.

But Jump Anaheim. I had to win because it was the last chance I had to qualify for the Dance Awards, *the* dance nationals. But the competition was another level, plus the exorbitant cost, plus hotel fees—a million lines Mom did not want to cross. She had not noticed how far gone I was with dance, suddenly feral like my older brother Joel with wanting, wanting, wanting. But I wanted to be just like Joel, whose portfolio had gotten him a scholarship to RISD, who everyone had said was going to be famous. Then suddenly, this year, everyone acted like he'd died, even Mom. So she said, in no uncertain terms, that Anaheim wouldn't be possible.

"I'm not taking out another mortgage just for you to agonize over placement for the rest of the year," she said.

I can still see Mom's face, stone. We were driving—we were always driving to and from dance practice—and I was in the back seat, trying to match her stone gaze through the rearview mirror. I told Mom I wouldn't agonize over placement because I was going to win.

"Really?" she said lightly, merging onto Route 2.

"Let me show you how good I've gotten," I whined.

"The price alone—"

"Joel can get us free plane tickets. And I have that scholarship with free hotels at the convention venue from last year; otherwise, it's going to expire."

At the time, Joel was loading and sorting baggage at Logan. These sorts of gigs never lasted long with Joel: All too soon he would be back to his odd hours, the closed door, the flashing red-blue-red-blue lights against my bedroom window, the whispering parents. But this one was holding out, Joel sporting an orange vest, calling himself the "baggage bitch." Already he had made friends with the "ticket bitch" and boasted he could go anywhere in the continental US free of charge.

In the car, I announced that I'd win the biggest regional competition, and I'd qualify for the Dance Awards, and then I'd win the title of Best Dancer.

"And then what?" Mom asked.

"And then I'll get a professional job," I added without hesitation. "And you won't have to take me to any more competitions because I'll be working commercially—getting money. And then I'll go to Tisch and then I'll drop out when a contemporary company picks me up and at first it will be somewhere random like Wisconsin but as I get more famous I'll work my way back to the East Coast so you can watch me. And when my body starts to go I'll choreograph Broadway or something."

All this I said in one long mounting breath.

"Hmm," Mom said dryly, circling the Concord Rotary. "I think your professional job is being eleven."

"I'll kill myself if I can't dance," I said without thinking.

Not skipping a beat, Mom pulled over. "Lucy," she hissed.

Then I was crying, and then I was crying because I was crying, and I never cried. Between shuddering gasps, I got out: "I need to do this, Mom. Before it's too late."

Lucky Girl • 9

Through all of this, the radio was blasting with the latest summer hit. Bruise was singing "HEART$TRINGS"—a bop about being cheated on, but later making more money than her ex. I remember thinking, through my tears, that it was super ironic that this jubilant song was overlaying my mental breakdown.

A truck passed, the driver laying on the horn. Mom flipped him off. When she turned back, her eyes softened. When I got older, I would know more. About Joel and how my threat sounded like code to Mom. Like she was a bad mom for ignoring me to save him. "All right," she finally said. "Okay, Lucy."

So we signed up for Anaheim, and Joel's buddy got us plane tickets, and we used my previous dance scholarships for the hotel, and still I didn't tell Kimberly I was going to miss her birthday. I didn't want to hurt her, so I put it off. And then time passed. And then it was too late. These are excuses. I was eleven. I delayed the conversation, replying vaguely but enthusiastically as Kimberly Snapchatted me. When she asked me what kind of animal she should ask for from Nature Nick, I said a tiger. It wasn't malicious—I simply allowed myself to believe both were possible until I was sitting in the Logan terminal at four in the morning, blearily watching yellow-vested men hurl luggage into the airplane. Because I knew Kimberly was sleeping and wouldn't respond, I sent her a quick Snap telling her happy birthday.

I put my phone on airplane mode, stuffed it in my dance bag. During the flight, I watched the clouds tinge orange-red with dawn and thought about my solo, running the choreography over and over in my head.

When we landed six hours later, only nine in the morning in Los Angeles, I stupidly powered back on my phone without thinking. A Snapchat from Kimberly.

So excited! When are u coming over?

I didn't reply. We took an Uber all the way to Anaheim, to the hotel where the convention was happening. On the way, I kept my face pressed to the window, watching what seemed to me an alien world. California was flat and dusty and full of palm trees, which I had never seen. I kept pointing out each cactus to Mom.

When are u coming over?

Lucy? When are u coming over?

She tried calling. I didn't answer. Mom and I checked into our hotel. When we got to our room, I stretched between the beds. Mom immediately called Joel, and then Dad when she got Joel's voicemail. "Did he go to outpatient? Cody, you can't just take his word . . . ." My solo was going on at 2:26 PM. Since I was eleven, I was at the bottom of the junior age category, and no one there knew me. My chest hummed with anticipation. Four hours later, Kimberly Snapchatted me again.

The melting pot reservations are in ten minutes. Are you meeting me there?

You can just imagine her, can't you? You can see the girl in her fishnet gloves and lace stockings, alone in the Melting Pot booth on her birthday because her mothers work the night shift at the hospital. In LA time, I strode alone into the busy convention, weaving among the packed teams warming up with jumping jacks, ducking past the room moderators to spy on the Teen Room, a ballroom of girls aged thirteen to sixteen learning a lyrical combo. Watching them, beautiful and slick and gazelle-like as they leapt across the floor, I knew I was in the right place, watching who I would become. But even still, my brain could not shake Kimberly, wondering what she was doing and how she was feeling, like we were still tied together, somehow linked.

2:06, Los Angeles.
The room moderator spots me, forces me back out into the main hall, sardined with stretching dancers.

2:13, Los Angeles.
In the wings of the competition stage, I watch my competition. Contemporary solo to static. Contemporary solo to howling wind. They're flexible, vacant. I realize I will lose.

2:17, Los Angeles.
My solo's called "Cosmic Love" and the choreography is basically just turns, which I do well. But it's too kiddie to go up against what I just saw. I find a quiet corner, plug in headphones, rehearse my solo, marking the leaps and kicks, going through the motions.

5:06, Boston.
Kimberly, alone in her big booth, looks at vats of bubbling broth and fountains of bright yellow cheese, too big for one. She stares into her phone, the screen black, urging it to light with a text.

5:13, Boston.
A waitress swings by and tries to clear the extra plate, and Kimberly says no, someone might be coming.

5:17, Boston.
Kimberly checks her phone. Only Tumblr hate. She plucks a Ritz cracker and crumbles it over the frothing and belching cheese.

2:20, Los Angeles.
Mom in the audience, sitting away from the other moms, frowning. Almost time. I return to the wings, breathing hard. Other girls stare at me without seeing me.

2:24, Los Angeles.
The last solo before me. I grip the railings going up to the stage. My lungs ring. The girl before me sashays off stage left. Darkness. Then, spotlight. The announcer calls my name.

2:26, Los Angeles.
My ears are inside a bowl. I walk with cold, flat feet to the middle of the stage, sink to my knees, and wait.

2:26, Los Angeles.
At the music's first chime, I rise slowly, hands reaching.

5:20, Boston.
In a flash, Kimberly rises. Maybe my phone died. Maybe I was dropped off at her house, waiting to go together. She leaves the restaurant without paying. The waitress, feeling bad, doesn't stop her.

5:24, Boston.
She embarks on the walk from the Melting Pot to home. It's not a long walk, just a few minutes along the busy road and then she can cut through the park, where home's nestled on the other side.

5:26, Boston.
As Kimberly walks alongside the busy road, car after car buffers her body with solid wind and noise. The ghost of an impact is sharp through thin stockings. She already knows I won't be at her house.

5:26, Boston.
Kimberly's feet stray to the edge of the sidewalk, and

then to the shoulder of the main road. The cars, heedless, roar. One more side step and her pain could be visible to anyone.

2:27, Los Angeles.
Thinking of her, I improvise. Snapping my body to each drumbeat, spinning loose as the singer's notes wind up and down.

2:28, Los Angeles.
Am I calling to Kimberly through dance, or through dance am I Kimberly? I'm angry at the world. Why can't Kimberly be Kimberly and be okay? Why can't she have other friends—right now I could be in a basement with her. I'm stupid for choosing this, I want to take it back, want to go back to that basement, but it's too late. On stage, I twirl, fall, crawl, look over my shoulder, hurl my body away in a half calypso, then another, careening like a struck animal, until I return

5:27, Boston.
But then, the whale call of a van, and her body, an animal of its own accord, leaps back to the safety of the sidewalk.

5:28, Boston.
For the rest of her life, Kimberly will feel like in that leap back on the sidewalk she crossed an enormous chasm, and on this side, she discovered a more certain and brighter world. Walking into the park, she sees everything—the oak trees, the pines, the baseball diamond, the red mulch—as if for the first time because she is still alive to see. In the baseball diamond, boys call back and forth to each other. Tree trunks scratched with initials. The pines exhaling pine. It is the

to center stage in a half dance, half run, opening my arms to the judges, asking for forgiveness.

2:29, Los Angeles.
No one claps. I walk off, forgetting to bow or even smile.

2:32, Los Angeles.
People looking over their shoulders at me. I don't care. Don't remember if I even pointed my feet. All I know is I want to go again.

2:45, Los Angeles.
Mom finds me wandering in the hallway outside the ballroom. She hands off my dance jacket. "That was different," she says. "What do you think?" I press. "Just different," she says again.

2:58, Los Angeles.
Almost time for awards. I'm

first summer evening, the kind of night as a child she believes is magical because its arrival promises many more nights like this.

5:29, Boston.
Walking the rest of the way home, Kimberly remembers she forgot to pay at the Melting Pot. She laughs to herself.

5:32, Boston.
Home. She fishes the spare key out of the fake rock and lets herself inside.

5:45, Boston.
She boots up the desktop and, without hesitation, deletes all social media. Her actual writing she keeps, hidden in a Word document. She knows she'll keep at it, if just for herself.

5:58, Boston.
Nature Nick arrives early,

ushered back to the competition stages, where I sit among a sea of other junior dancers. Most are clustered with their competition team, but I sit alone. I peek at their faces and wonder if I'm better than them.

3:02, Los Angeles.
It takes forever for the announcer to read through the adjudicated scores before he gets to overalls. The scores are between 0 and 300, and that score is translated into bronze, gold, high gold, and if you score above a 297, a You Rocked Jump! award. "Cosmic Love" receives a You Rocked Jump!

3:14, Los Angeles.
I walk past the rest of the top ten and receive the first-place trophy.

the green van backing into the driveway. She comes out and meets him. "Just you?" he asks, expecting a birthday party. "Just me," Kimberly deadpans. "No one else came." In my adult reimagining, Nature Nick's heart breaks. He skips the skinks and goes straight for the velvety boa constrictor.

6:02, Boston.
Kimberly holds a baby koala to her chest, feels his rapid heartbeat against her collarbone. She can't believe half an hour ago she wanted to die. Nature Nick tells her that since baby koalas can't digest eucalyptus at first, they have to nuzzle their mother's assholes to get their systems used to the enzymes. "Like middle school," Kimberly says, and Nature Nick solemnly nods.

6:14, Boston.
Kimberly runs her hand along the creamy underbelly of an alligator.

3:23, Los Angeles.
On the elevator back up to our hotel room, Mom's silent. When the elevator dings, she says without looking at me, "All right, Lucy. If this is what you want. We'll go full out." I nod. "No holding back."

5:27, Los Angeles.
To celebrate, Mom and I take an Uber to an Anaheim Chili's. We're homesick already for suburb mediocrity. Over the shimmering menus, Mom says, "It's Kimberly's birthday. Did you text her?"

10:31, Los Angeles.
I can't sleep. Mom snores. The hotel looks out onto the parking lot, and everything's purple with light pollution. In the hotel bathroom, I try Kimberly's number. No answer. So I send her a Snapchat explaining myself. Why I had to go. I tell her that as a dancer, you know,

6:23, Boston.
Midway through Nature Nick, her mothers come home early, having gotten their hours covered. They ask where I am. Kimberly, cradling a raccoon, says that I had something come up.

8:27, Boston.
Her mothers bring out the slab of birthday cake, eleven candles flickering in the dark. They sing, badly. One mother tears up; the other laughs. Kimberly makes a wish.

1:31, Boston.
She can't sleep. So she creeps downstairs to the basement and boots up the *Attack on Titan* season 1 finale. Midway through, her phone beside her thigh lights up. Me, finally. She lets a pillow smother the vibration and finishes watching the episode. She'll respond later. In the

it's always now or never. The peak of your career is sixteen, seventeen, eighteen max. She must understand. I tell her I'm sorry. I tell her I thought of her while I danced, and I won. *Kimmy,* I write. *I love you. You know that.*

morning, she'll read it once. She'll feel nothing. She'll respond, and then block my number. She'll transfer to a new school. She'll go by Kim. She'll make new friends.

Around three in the morning, my phone glowed. Kimberly.

She said, *I hope you win big at nationals or whatever. I hope you get to become a dancer, a famous one. But you're not a good friend.*

I read it, put my phone on my chest, and closed my eyes. I already knew that.

Micah

When I Google-Image *lucy gardiner at twelve* and zoom into the eyes, it's too grainy to gauge emotion. If I could go back in time and interview my twelve-year-old self, I would ask a lot of questions. Like: Hello? Can you hear me? Go back before it's too late!

But past-Lucy just smiles and chirps: "I'm from a small town in Massachusetts . . . I can't believe I'm here now!"

Here's what I wish I'd said:

I am from Leominster, home of the inventor of Tupperware. But that was back when the industrial revolution seemed like a good thing, when the brick buildings composing Main Street were not vacant corpses of an era long past. My two older brothers' regular Friday nights involve sneaking into the flaking factories by the river, panning flashlights off the graffitied walls and rusted machinery. They bring back flasks, belts, and knives left by vagabonds, and once, a soft yellow book with two ripped-bodiced women on the cover, which they passed back and forth over the next month, giggling and never letting me have a look.

My brothers are my half brothers. We share a dad, not a mom. My father was born, raised in, and has barely left Leominster.

Briefly he went to the University of Vermont, his tenure resulting in an honors thesis on the mating habits of marbled salamanders and a baby out of wedlock. But that was back when my father rolled with the punches, so he married the baby's mother, had another baby, and they had an okay life. They would have kept on if not for a bright August day when my father's first wife took the boys on a backpacking trip in the deep Maine wild. From what I've heard, this first wife was a free spirit, though unpredictable, quick to laugh, quick to cry, quick to up the ante, so it wasn't surprising when she led the boys off-trail on a spontaneous adventure. It wasn't out of character for her to zip ahead while the boys wrestled and whined and hurled sticks at each other. Likely she would have relished the last image of herself, a picture my oldest brother snapped: a snatch of red parka through the thick overgrowth, her face tilted back toward the boys. As my brothers later recounted to me: One moment she was just barely visible, and the next moment she melted into the forest. Just vanished. The boys spent the rest of the afternoon calling, *Mom, Mom, Mom* and stomping blindly ahead until the light thinned and they got scared. My oldest brother made the call to turn back. By some miracle, he managed to lead them down the mountain, converging with a busy road, where they flagged down help.

Their mother never reappeared: Eight months later, hunters found a ruined campsite rife with their ruined belongings, withering camelbacks and wrappers and sleeping bags engorged with wet rot—an empty notebook bloated and half-buried in the dirt, nothing written inside. A body was never found, and so you're left to wonder if she's still alive, if she meant to leave her boys behind or simply got lost, if she's still trying to find her way back or dissolving in some untraveled gully. My brothers will always wonder. Their mother's name is or was Lacy, incredibly close to mine, but just a coincidence. Mom loved the name Lucy.

Mom is a good stepmother because she does not care. To this day, photographs of the vanished wife line the stairwell entering our house, Lacy's Jordan Marsh decor remains untouched—a style unlike Mom's, but then again, Mom cannot be bothered to hang a painting. Family photos of that bygone era crowd the mantel and my father's bedside table. To my brothers she made it clear she was not Mom, but Denise. Still, she goes to bat for each boy when he needs her, and everyone needs Denise. When Micah required drop boxes during his solo attempt through the Appalachian Trail, she dutifully drove alongside the mountain range, waiting hours in the waning sun to make sure he got his cache of freeze-dried chili and corn. If Joel got picked up for breaking into another abandoned house, Mom would grab the dead wife's final photo and arrive at the police station with some story about how he was searching for confirmation of his missing mother's restless spirit. So, if the boys were weirded out when she named her only child nearly after their mother, they let it slide.

Their antics wreathed my childhood. I remember playing Barbies with Micah, lying on our bellies on the living room's rough carpet, and I remember Joel decapitating each Barbie one by one, freezing the heads in Dixie Cups of water so he could strategically place the ice-suspended heads in Market Basket's frozen section. I remember that if Mom brought pizza home from work, it meant something really brutal had been wheeled into Worcester County ER. I remember driving to Friendly's to celebrate my first time winning a dance competition, Mom calling Dad as she swung into the parking lot: "Cody, we've got another live one on our hands." I remember campaigning to get the bedroom in the unfinished basement, because it was the cleanest part of the house; from the window I could see Joel and Micah and their friends hanging out. I spent many nights fighting sleep to eavesdrop on the teenage tableau in the driveway. From my basement window, I could see them in the orange streetlight—boys in a semicircle, sometimes passing a basketball among themselves, talking about anything: space travel, music, celebrities, ghosts, teachers, crushes, climate change, car engines, and college, and I remember drinking in those conversations, inhaling them so deeply, because it was through them I learned about the world.

The last time we were together as a family and it wasn't about me, I had just turned eleven and I was still friends with Kimberly, and that Christmas, Mom took four days off work so we could all go to Sugarloaf Mountain. Though we didn't have a lot of money, one of her old acting friends had scored a time-share that we half shared. A lot of my mom's old acting friends, as deferred in their dreams as she had been, often gave my family free stuff like hand-me-down skis, almost like a conciliation prize to a piddled-out friendship, a consolation prize for a piddled-out career in the arts. Crossing into Maine, it began to snow for the first time that winter. At first the boys were quiet, contemplative. But inevitably someone booted up the Pinbox TV that sat in the center of the van, where they played combat video games. It was only a two-player, so once again I was left gazing into the blurry rush of woods for a moose. Squeezed into the back seat with Joel and Micah, I kept my watch resolute despite being barraged by elbows and curse words that blackened my ear drum, something a mean Russian ballet instructor told me once and I believed 100 percent.

"Motherfucker," Joel said. "If you don't stop button mashing like an ape, I'll kill you."

This was the year Joel had been kicked out of art school, and his fall from grace found him pacing the Leominster house like a caged, malnourished tiger.

"I'm not button mashing," Micah protested. "There's technique here."

On the tiny screen, his character thrashed his sword wildly. Joel's character snuck up behind him, grabbed his scruff, and hurled him off-screen.

"That, my boy, is technique." Joel whistled. Micah growled, his character lobbing *shuriken* after *shuriken*. Meanwhile, once again, Joel's character snuck behind Micah's, hurled him off the edge.

Throwing off his seat belt, Micah reached across me to swat at Joel. They grappled at each other, huffing and puffing. Practiced, I buried my head in my lap, letting their sharp boy elbows fly over me.

Then Joel went, "Moose! Moose!"

Dad slowed the van, and everyone, including Mom, usually not one to marvel, pressed our faces against the cold window. We were strangely hushed, oohing and aahing over the moose, except me, so buried that nothing could be ascertained over my brothers' big backs.

"Look, look!" Micah added. "She has a baby! It's so cute!"

Then, Joel: "Idiot, Lucy can't fucking see!"

His arms shot out, yanking Micah back and finally giving me an unobstructed view. The moose, who had been grazing the dry grass amid the dusting of snow, glanced up. I tried to lock the image into memory forever. Even the fleshy droop of her neck seemed regal, her amber eyes tracking us warily as the car passed, picking up speed. Just as the car slipped around the white bend, I finally glimpsed the baby moose, cautiously picking its way through the bramble on brand-new legs.

"Hey," Joel said once the moose were out of sight. "Let Lucy have a turn."

By the time we got to the cabin, the world outside was dark, and we were hungry. The lodge was closed, so we rummaged through the cabinets to see what had been left behind by the previous vacationers and ended up having a dinner of microwave popcorn and Ritz while watching a third of *The Shawshank Redemption* because it was playing on the cabin's singular channel and it happens to be my father's favorite movie. Around nine, both our parents fell asleep on the couch, woke with a snorting start, and then slumped into the master bedroom and shut the door.

Joel switched the TV off, put on his coat, and started for the door. Micah leapt in his way.

"Where you going?"

"Out," Joel said. "Maybe skiing."

"The mountain's closed," said Micah.

Joel shook his head. "Not till ten."

"I'll go with you," Micah said, not a question.

"We can't leave Lucy alone."

"She'll come with us," Micah said, shooting me an apologetic look. "Right, Lucy?"

Faintly, I nodded. We suited up and went outside into the bitter dark night, following Joel through the cluster of cabins and down the road, which was tightly packed with snow. By the time we reached the shuttle station, it was 9:30. A hazard sign announced there would be no more outbound shuttles.

"Well," Micah said. "That's that. Let's go back."

Joel was undeterred. Back then he was always jittery. Now I can look back and see the signs, but in the moment it just seemed like he was cursed by some wizard and if he stopped moving, he would turn to stone. "The night is young," he insisted, throwing ungloved hands to the sky, which, to his credit, was spackled with stars and a fresh moon. And it did seem like a shame to end the night here, in a space so liminal and possible as the empty Sugarloaf shuttle station at night, which was a bench protected by those plastic bus shelters. Beside the parking lot, there was a mound of plowed snow the size of which, to my kid eyes, could challenge the very mountain.

"We could build a snowman," I offered.

"Right on, prodigal sister," Joel said. He pulled Micah back, hissing, "Did you hear Lucy? We're making a snowman!"

"That's fine," Micah said evenly. "Remember the thing we made in middle school?"

"The principal getting taken down by gnomes?" Joel was approaching the mound, eyeing it like a sculpture. "Right by the flagpole, right? That was gutsy."

"Denise was called to the office," Micah added, his voice careful. "And she made a scene, crying about how we were just expressing our pain."

"Wasted talent," Joel murmured.

"Did you hate the principal?" I asked, hating when they reminisced about life before I was alive. Also, it was very possible this principal was still around, and after all I did share their last name.

Micah glanced at Joel. "He thought we would turn out to be losers who sneak out to make vacation about our angst instead of our little sister's birthday. But look at us now. Right, Joel?"

Joel clapped once, very sharply. "Let's make this snowman!"

So we got to work on this snowman, which turned into a snow dragon atop the mound, snow princess clutched in its talons. For narrative's sake, we added a snow army facing off the snow dragon below, snowmen and snowwomen spilling out into the parking lot. This took a lot of man power, mostly the boys heaving and stacking chunks of ice and snow around the parking lot, Joel pointing out that we could give the snow army spears from the abandoned ski poles we had found scattered between the cabins, that we could add a wig to the princess because Mom kept hair extensions for dance competitions in the back of the car. This was Joel at his best, making art no one asked for, because it was fun. When he had left for college, his side of the room became an unguarded treasure trove that I spent many nights digging through. To my ten-year-old eyes, the well-loved sketchbooks seemed the greatest works of art yet unknown to man, though I'm sure today Joel would be dismissive of their worth. And yet. A charcoal self-portrait. A comic panel of a woman running away from her demons. A bonfire, warped with small cities and mountains inside each wisp. A hand unraveling, revealing a metropolis in the veins and bone and marrow. Renders of Micah, renders of my father, none of me or Mom. Still, I kept those sketchbooks with me for a long time, flipping through them late into the night, their strangeness satisfying an unarticulated itch in my brain.

When our entire family shuffled out the next bright morning, bundled and bewildered, we were met with a small crowd amassed around our snowy tableau, phones out, snapping pictures and whispering giddily among themselves about who could have done this—a local artist? A tourist committee? My brothers nudged each other and said nothing. On the shuttle, we were shaking with laughter. Dad was oblivious. Mom eyed Joel.

"Relax," he whispered. "This wasn't my swan song or anything."

"Looks like last time. Should I call Doctor—"

"Don't ruin vacation, Denise. It was dumb fun. If I tried again—"

"It was my idea," Micah quickly added, covering for Joel. "I just needed to move after driving for so long, and Lucy wanted to build a snowman."

Mom nodded, assuaged. The family rule: If Micah was present, everything would turn out okay. All our crashouts happened away from Micah. Joel away in college. Later for me, in Los Angeles. Whenever Micah took off on a backpacking trip, we knew something bad would happen. But we didn't ask him to stay. We never wanted to hold him back.

The shuttle parked, and as I started to follow Mom and Dad to the lodge, Joel grabbed my puffy sleeve.

"Come on," he said, aglow from his installment's reception. "We're doing a black diamond."

This had been my life's dream up to this point, I should add, being included with my brothers. But while I do share a lot of Mom's and Joel's willful traits, those came out later. Back then I was a gooey shell of myself, and I saw danger at every turn.

"I can't."

"Of course you can."

"I can't."

"Lucy." He pushed back his goggles, squatted down to my level. "I've seen you dance in competitions in front of thousands of people. I know you're brave." Impossible to argue with Joel. Thousands, though! What utter fiction. Not in my eleven-year-old wildest dreams.

With a glance up, he added, "Besides, Micah will be there, too."

Like he was summoned, Micah appeared at my side. He smiled at Joel, and I wondered if he'd coerced Joel into asking me. Joel and I used to be close, but when he returned from college something was off. Like he had been avoiding me.

I latched my boots onto my pink skis and glided after them to the lift. We lined up for the chair together—my two brothers and me.

"Ready?" Micah said.

"Sure," I gritted. The chair, swooping toward us. I steeled myself. But it was fine. We were off, lifted into the air, and squeezed together. Suddenly, we were levitating, and then rising. The boys spoke easily, despite our legs dangling in the high wind.

They noted how blue the sky looked, hoping to get in as many runs as possible before lunch. By the time the lift had glided halfway up the mountain, my fear had dissipated. Even when we were deposited at the mountain's peak and we splintered down the slope like breathless animals, I could feel Micah there, whizzing close by, keeping an eye on Joel and me as we sped to the bottom.

Celia

As soon as we landed back in Boston after the win in Anaheim, I began rewatching all the previous Dance Award winners' solos. They were all choreographed by famous choreographers or well-known studio owners. It was clear if I wanted to win the Dance Awards, I needed a new solo. An improvised solo like "Cosmic Love," no matter how startling and deeply felt, wouldn't land me in the top twenty. I needed a solo choreographed specifically for me by someone like Travis Wall or Kirstin Russell. Those kinds of solos cost a thousand dollars. I already knew what Mom would say. So, I went to Joel.

Since Joel had been kicked out of art school, he had worked several middling jobs—after baggage bitch came barista bitch, Amazon driver bitch. All of which ended the same way: suddenly, leaving Joel holed up in his room, Mom banging on the door, demanding to know his next move. Yet, wayward as he was, he managed to purchase a beat-up olive Subaru, which I waited for each night while I practiced my pliés and relevés in the dark of the driveway.

"Prodigal sister!" he boomed as he swung, too fast, into the garage. "What's happening?"

"I need money," I said.

Joel got out of the car and came toward me, still on my tiptoes, trying to make gains on my balance. He smelled like hand sanitizer and basement. "Sure," he said. "You going to the mall with Kim or something?"

"No," I said, extending my left leg, my bad leg, testing my balance and flexibility. He waited. Finally, I blurted, "I need a thousand dollars for choreography on my nationals solo."

He laughed. "Okay. Sure."

I lost my balance. "Really?"

"No," he said flatly. I realized, too late, he was in a mood. Usually I could tell from the way his car swung into the driveway: slow for a sour mood, fast for something else. Last time he drove in fast like this, he came bearing two grocery bags full of loose pigs' feet, having suddenly gotten the giddy urge to make ramen broth from scratch. The dishes stayed in the sink for months; no one in my family cleaned, and we especially didn't clean up after each other. Well, maybe Micah did.

"Please," I begged, trying not to sound like a kid, failing. "Please, it's the only way."

"You don't need a thousand dollars to win a competition. Then it's not really winning, is it? It's who has the most money." Joel turned back to his car and opened the trunk, spilling out a ton of loose mariachi hats. He had been dumpster diving at Party City again.

"It's for my career," I insisted.

"You're a kid. Go be a kid." He slammed the trunk and breezed past me. I stayed out in the driveway for a long time, waiting until he went to bed.

For the next few days, he was gone for long stretches, slapping the fridge shut, his silences heavy and red, and I could not approach him. But time was running out—the Dance Awards were in a month—so I finally cracked and snuck into his and

Micah's room, rifling through Joel's side, looking for dirt to blackmail him.

Don't judge me. This was sibling stuff.

I found nothing, though. Stacks of art theory books. Dead flashlights. A journal with the pages ripped out. An ounce of weed—child's play, that wouldn't be enough. Finally, I procured a practice sketch for a bigger piece, depicting a nude man in the middle of the dark woods. Small scenes were embedded between the lines of trees, a family multiplying then slowly splitting one by one. The title small in the corner—Follow You into the Dark, Don't Be Mad When I—this might be something. Maybe . . .

"Lucy!"

I thought I was going to die. Joel in the threshold of his bedroom door, all dust and leather and menace. He snatched the sketch pad from my hands, flipped through it, and to my great relief, whistled softly. Now, he was in a good mood. Joel announced, "I made it at school. I thought it was going to blow up."

"Did it?"

"No, but I did."

I paused, unsure of what to say.

"Joking!" Joel laughed.

"It's amazing," I insisted. "Really."

He wagged the sketch pad at me. "Let's burn it. C'mon."

And so we went a little ways into the conservation woods, where the boys had cobbled together a crude firepit with slabs of concrete. The spring peepers chirped. Joel slapped the sketchbook in the pit, doused it with lighter fluid, lit a match, and let it drop. We watched the lines of the family wiggle and lift and become bright embers in the blue air.

When Joel started talking, I wasn't sure he was really talking to me or to himself. "All for nothing, huh?"

"It's not over," I jabbed—it's what Mom would say. To my surprise, Joel smiled and rubbed the back of his neck.

"Yeah," he sighed. "That's what they say."

"You can't care about what other people think," I offered, as I assumed his spectacular freakout at college had to do with the constant judgment of his artwork, which he showed no one anymore, except for me, I guess. Sometimes, he'd pass me a doodle—usually of our crappy neighbor. They always made me laugh. I thought the world of Joel. I don't know if I could have even spelled his drug of choice at this point.

"You have to care about what people think," Joel said, looking at me squarely. "If you want to go professional. You need the judges to like you. You're going to get swallowed in the crowd. If no one notices you—will you still want to do this? Would you still love it?"

"I would die if I couldn't dance," I whispered, watching a woman glow and then shrink and then become nothing but black soot.

He slapped a wad of cash in my hands. "Then you better dance."

The Dance Awards Orlando was held in a massive resort hotel on the beach. Mom justified the whole thing as a family vacation to Florida. She hoped the change of scenery would reboot my father, who had recently been dismissed from his longtime position as a middle school science teacher. Gone were the days of ski trips and stability. Here was the era of double shifts at the hospital, a new side gig at the hospice. In many ways, this trip felt like our last hurrah.

Joel said he was excited to get zooted and go on It's a Small World. Micah planned to hitchhike down to Key West afterward to start another attempt at the Eastern Continental Trail—last year, he had been forced to call it quits after a bear decimated his tent. It was right around when Joel moved back home, too. Micah told the bear story often, as if he couldn't quite believe it. I listened giddily each time. Though it lasted only a few short months, home without my brothers had been eerie. I remember being ecstatic to have them both back so soon and unexpectedly, but for unknown reasons, I was the only one celebrating.

When we finally pulled up to the Hyatt Regency, a hotel so fancy that the pool was girded by a faux-stone waterfall, I had never felt so out of place crossing the gilded tile among my bespectacled father, my quirky brothers, my wide and domineering mother. We weren't even staying here. We had a perfectly good camper van, which Joel had spotted *4 Free* on the bad side of Fitchburg, which Mom had refurbished last summer with Micah, who had used some app to find out how to camp on the beach behind the hotel. While every other dancer was getting ready in a lush hotel room, I found myself cowboy camping on the beach, hoping the roar of the waves would drown out Mom's snores and the clinks of whiskey bottles that my brothers gingerly tried to haul down the beach so they could party with some locals.

Let it not be a surprise that our first morning in Florida, I took it upon myself to go to registration alone, wanting to walk in like the senior dancers. Mom accepted this only because it meant she could keep grilling Joel, who had mysteriously crept back to camp with a black eye. By six in the morning, the hallways were swarming with caffeinated parents, pacing dancers in bedazzled costumes, and toe-tapping teachers. The nervous energy was palpable, and I was a sponge. After finding the correct registration booth, receiving my schedule, and pinning my number to my leotard, I realized I was lost. Some ballrooms were empty, some were a swirl of dancers already in class, some had minis, some had teens, where were the juniors?

"Cosmic Love!" A girl was waving me into a ballroom. "Hey!"

She ran up. "You're Lucy, right? You did the Anaheim 'Cosmic Love' solo—do you know it's going viral? Was it really improv? I heard it was improv. I can't believe you're finally doing TDA! Do you want a cupcake?"

"Sure," I said. "Am I in the right place?"

"Of course you are!" She laughed, warmly. She had a good laugh. It was her thirteenth birthday, and she was giving out cupcakes, which I would quickly discover was very Celia. I knew about Celia Walsh, a Black dancer from a very famous company in Arizona, because I had been religiously following TDA since I could type in the search bar on YouTube. You think, *dance like no one's watching*, and you think, *Celia Walsh*. Last year, she had been first runner-up Junior Best Dancer, and the year before that, she had been first runner-up Mini Best Dancer. Yet she only spoke about me, how insane I was and how much she fell into a rabbit hole searching my dances on YouTube and Tumblr. She led me over to a group of stretching dancers, all friendly, all talking a mile a minute. I was thankful—I hadn't realized, until she had called me over, that an iron ball had been clattering around my rib cage. The girls were like all the girls I met during competition and convention, sweet and sinewy and gossipy. Of course, everyone said Celia would be in the top three, how she had to win this time. As the instructor rolled in and started us on across the floors, Celia was still shaking her head.

"You never know," she whispered, her smile almost a grimace.

At the time, I wondered—hoped—she was talking about me. If she was marking me as the one to watch. But even without knowing Celia, I would have known she was the one from the moment I saw her take first position.

I will never again encounter a dancer like Celia. I watched her all class. It was and was not jealousy. I wanted nothing else but to see her move up close.

At the end of class, my wish was granted. The instructor lined us up together as the final group to go out—just the five out of the hundred juniors in the class. As I took first position beside her, as we both steadied our breath, she winked at me, whispered: "You've got the bug, too, Cosmic Love?"

And then the gong hit, and we moved together through the first eight count: push, push, up, spin, ha!, haha!, hit, HA!

I felt, but could not see, Celia beside me, all breath and motion. We were flying together; we were one. And I could feel her watching me too, sizing me up.

After class, while all the girls were toweling off and joking and grabbing snacks, I lingered behind, friendless. Celia fell back and invited me to her birthday party. In a flash, I was in her hotel room, squeezed against the patio slider, watching Celia hold court with what seemed like the entire junior best dancer finalists. It was clear they all coordinated their convention schedule around seeing one another. Briefly, I missed Kimberly. Then I felt bad and needed to be alone, pacing the empty hotel halls by myself. Just as I was leaving to slip around the hotel and back to my family's campsite, the girls crowded into the elevator with me: They were going to check out the pool, and did I want to come?

The hotel pool was unlike any pool I had seen: a teal squiggle carved into stone. The party quickly dissolved into chaos, girls leaping into the glowing water, chasing one another, and of course, making note of the senior male dancers in the hot tub. I lingered around the rim of the pool, drawn to the giant waterfall.

"It's crazy, right?" Celia said behind me. "I thought it was real my first year."

"I've never been anywhere this nice," I admitted.

"Here," she whispered, grabbing my arm. "You can actually hide behind it."

She led me behind the waterfall, where we could sit on a stone ridge unseen by the rest of the girls and talk, our voices slightly raised to overcome the splashing. We stayed until it was so late we barely got any sleep, and for the rest of the next day, Celia would catch my eye and mouth, *I'm dead.* Mostly, we talked about dance, something I hadn't realized I had craved discussing with another dancer, a dancer who wanted what I wanted: to always, always dance. We compared our future plans and found them pleasingly similar. Celia was hoping for Juilliard instead of Tisch, and after that she was less sure, but hopefully a contemporary company out in Los Angeles or New York. Almost immediately, we were fantasizing about NYC coffee dates between rehearsals, an apartment when we were seniors and then poor graduates, going from audition to audition. Celia thought like me, dreamed like me. But unlike me, she remembered what drew her to dance in the first place.

"I'm afraid of death," she said so plainly I almost laughed.

"Sure, yeah," I managed. "Death's, like, wild."

She smiled and didn't seem to notice I was painfully awkward. Instead, she reached out her hand to slice the waterfall, parting it. "It's silly, I know. Our dog died. My family buried her. But I couldn't stop thinking about it, how she was here and then just *so* gone, so not here, and I couldn't stop lying in bed trying to get my head around it, trying to think it through. It became sort of an obsession."

I nodded, scrounging my brain for an equally deep reason. All I came up with was how my dad got fired because a baby raccoon died.

"Is he a wildlife person?" Celia asked. I shook my head. Dad is one of those weird biology guys who can easily articulate the biochemical process allowing an eastern red-backed salamander to breathe through its skin, but has uttered the phrase *I love you* exactly twice in his life, at both his courthouse weddings. When Mom told me about the small-town politicking that got Dad fired, I was miffed they didn't fight it more. Basically: Dad rescued this injured baby raccoon. He had his seventh-grade class try to nurse it back to health. When the little guy perished, he conducted a lesson on the scientific and philosophical process of death, but it backfired: The kids went home existentially terrified, parents called a town meeting, and he was fired the next week. I wanted to take this injustice to a local news channel—at least Reddit. But Mom just said, "Honey, just look at him," and gestured to Dad by the vernal pool just beyond our property, notebook in his jeaned lap, peering patiently into the glassy, temporary surface. That last part I didn't tell Celia. Instead, I ended my story lamely: "To my dad, death is like a scientific process. I don't think he even considered it would be scary."

For a long moment, Celia didn't respond. We both watched the waterfall. When Celia finally spoke, her voice was thoughtful, almost searching. "When I dance, I don't think about death. That's when it all goes away. It's just about that song, stretching my feet, my movement quality, like it's just down to my body. The moment. So with dance, I don't know, dance keeps me from myself."

I confessed to Celia that I didn't have a big reason. "I just . . . really like it."

"Like it?" Celia laughed softly, nudging me. "I can tell you love it, like more than me, maybe. It's almost scary, watching you dance."

Once, my father dreamed of becoming a scientist wading deep into the mossy ass crack of the Amazon to discover some unsung creature, and when that became unattainable, a good teacher, and without that, he became obsessed with salamanders in our backyard. He regaled us over dinner about their mating rituals and personality traits. He spent a fortune at Staples, designing a spiral-bound book detailing his findings, wonderings, some children's book ideas. When the summer heat dried the last inch of water, Dad would retreat into the den, watching without watching television. I told Celia I didn't want to be like that. I didn't want to settle.

Like me, Celia didn't come from a dance family. She knew the sort of sacrifices needed to be a dancer, like, a real dancer, and so she flung herself into this pursuit, cleaning the studio to pay for extra classes, choreographing minis to pay for her own choreography, living in her studio owner's spare bedroom far from her own brothers and sisters. Essentially, living on her own, and only thirteen. "It's not bad," she said, reaching her hand up to slice the waterfall again. "Just different."

"But it will be worth it," I assured her. "It'll amount to something."

She cast me a sideways smile, sort of sad, a very un-Celia look. "I hope so."

I did not see Celia's Best Dancer solo. However, people were abuzz all day after she went up, whispering in clusters that it was out of this world, unlike anything else, and, man, was she coming for the judges' throats.

The next time I saw Celia, we were warming up before the audition combos. I would have stayed away from her during the auditions, knowing she would outdo me, but she waved me frantically over while we were grouping up, wanting to know if I'd seen her solo.

"No," I said. "Figured I'd catch it during the recompete and then during your victory lap."

Her face fell slightly, but she laughed. "You never know," she said. "I always come into nationals just hoping to do my best."

But I knew her well by then, having danced next to her, having listened to her controlled, tight breaths. She wanted this so badly. After auditions, I had only thirty minutes before my solo, just enough time to disassociate in a bathroom stall, not that I had the word for it back then, but still—

"Hey." Celia tapped my shoulder. "Let's get you warmed up."

We found an empty ballroom close to the junior competition room and Celia helped me stretch, pushing down my back, holding my hand as I swung out my hips. She held my dance bag as I changed into my costume, a burgundy leotard with a scarlet overdress. She watched as I applied my stage makeup, taking over when my hands were shaking too badly to apply the cat-eyes. And then she even helped me run through my solo, offering corrections, and as she walked me out to the hall and into the wings of the stage, she gave me a pep talk, telling me I'd do fine as long as I trusted my soul and my body, and that she couldn't wait to watch me, that the "Cosmic Love" solo had set her heart ablaze and she knew finally she'd found someone who felt the same fire.

As I was about to go on, I asked her: "Why are you helping me?"

She pushed me up the stairs to the bright, red-curtained stage.

"Next up," the announcer boomed. "Number 2631, Lucy Gardiner, with . . ."

Below me, in the shadows of the wings, Celia whispered, "It's not winning unless you beat the best, right?"

Then I was on.

When I came off the TDA stage, my family was waiting for me in the wings.

"Good job," Mom said. "You did good."

Joel was beside himself. "*Good?* Are you kidding?"

But I knew Mom was blown away by the fact that she'd said "good" twice. My father wiped his eyes—big softie.

That night, after we made a bonfire and sparred with burning marshmallows until Mom made us quit, I tagged along with my brothers for a walk up and down the beach. They made easy conversation, passing a joint back and forth, though of course I never got my turn. The world pitch black, we strode out to the edge of the ocean. "Oblivion," Joel whispered.

"Wait," Micah coughed. "You said the strain is called—"

"Deep," I chided, thinking about Celia's fear of dying.

After a bit longer, Micah turned back. He wanted to get on a strict sleep schedule before the ECT. Joel stayed behind with me, gazing into the dark nothing.

"Glad I got to play a part in this," Joel said. "The choreography was crazy."

"Yeah," I said. "You saved my butt."

I squinted into the horizon, making out bright points of light. Boats, probably. I asked Joel if he was drawing anything, if he was making anything new.

"Here and there."

I asked all sorts of questions: When can I see, does it involve the mariachi hats, is it a fuck-you to RISD, will it make you famous? And he kept shaking his head.

"I don't know," Joel said finally. "Maybe it'll be something."

I assured him it would, and Joel nodded absentmindedly, staring out at the crashing dark. Like me, he assumed that some point, he would be somebody who made something. A complete, capital Something. Something real that would take him far away and, God, he wanted to go far. But then he would see the work in a new light, and it no longer felt real. And if it couldn't be real, he wasn't sure he wanted to, either. What was the point?

But he didn't tell me all that yet. Instead Joel shook his head, whistled. "That dance, though. You really are something, you know that?"

I nodded and copied him looking into the ocean, feeling that familiar steel burn inside. God, I wanted dance to make me something. "We're gonna do great things," I said dramatically.

"Great things," Joel murmured. "Great things. I hope. The both of us."

When we returned, Mom was waiting up for us. Her eyes stayed glued to Joel. You had to really know her to read the relief dancing across her tight expression, but I recognized it whenever the door opened and there was Joel, alive and well.

I was not surprised when my name flashed on the projector for the top twenty junior female dancers; I was relieved when I was called to join the top ten moving on to the improv round. My body had no time to process what was happening as I ascended the steps, glimpsed the bright, red-curtained stage. The announcer called our names one by one: "Emily! Billy! Theresa! Dok Phi Sua! Lucy! Brooke! Georgia! Andy! Kendra! Celia!"

The lights were brighter, strobes on the red curtain. But the biggest difference was the size of the crowd—an entire ballroom of people packed so tightly it was standing room only, an enormous presence I sensed but could not parse. I focused on stilling my rampant lungs—ah, to be a salamander and inhale just through the skin!—and didn't hear the announcer until he was screaming: "Emily, you're first!" and off Emily flew.

The first song was "Cherry Wine" by Hozier. Cognizant of the camera—they live streamed the Dance Awards—I kept my face neutral as I watched Emily attitude turn to the floor. Nice. Fuck. Was it worse when the dancers nailed their turns, or should I feel happy for them? I knew Celia would be glad. Sneaking a peek at her, I saw her clapping when Billy perfected a butterfly leap right in front of the judges. *I shouldn't be thinking about other people. I should be thinking about what I'll do. I'll start with à la seconde turns, then I'll sink, mournfully, to the floor.* But Emily already had, so I didn't want to copy her, and it would look bad if I executed the same move worse, but then—

"LUCY!" bellowed the announcer and my bones unhinged. The music was soft and slow, so I strode center stage on the knuckles of my feet. With a sudden guitar strum, I backbent to the floor, looking ugly, the audience on the ceiling, the dusty lights swarmed my eyes. Floorwork, sweeping my legs up and spinning until I was standing, facing stage right. My mind traveled—as I traveled back to center stage—to Celia. Knowing her movement quality, she would probably throw in some contemporary wiggles. And then a good leg extension . . . and then she would shake her foot, like that, artistically. I found my balance shifting and so I bent low into a layout. Without trying to, my eyes searched for Celia. There. Her head was tilted, and she was smiling, so softly. For the dance-off—I've rewatched it a million times—she was wearing a black turtleneck leotard and white ballet tights. Her hair was pulled back tight into a single low braid, but strands had already escaped, illuminated in the stage lights. And then her lips slightly parted—was she saying something? Finally, I heard, again, the announcer: "Thank you, Lucy! Here's Brooke!"

I detangled myself and crawled back to my space in line, unable to shake dance off my bones. It was easier on the other side of waiting. The girls went one by one, turning and extending and ponderously rolling on the floor like I had. When it was Celia's turn, everyone leaned forward. She traveled the most, running and leaping and kicking. What was so strikingly different were her facials. While the rest of us were vaguely sad, Celia's face snarled in fear and desperation. And this shook down through her whole body, her flexed feet, the weird twists of her legs and torso, the staticky energy when she threw herself across the stage. Unlike all of us, Celia had been listening to the lyrics. She was the only one to heed the bitterness, to alchemize anger into movement. Celia was the only one actually dancing.

When the announcer called, "Everyone!" and the line of girls jumped forward to join Celia, I hesitated. I hated myself. How had I forgotten to listen to the music? I knew, then, for sure, I lacked something fundamental, something only Celia had. Finally, we were called back to order to get ready for the up-tempo song. Up-tempo improv was so much more binary, so much easier. "River Deep, Mountain High" by Celine Dion. Lots of drums, so lots of hip, lots of fan kicks. When it was my turn, I calypso leapt, busted out neat, quick à la seconde turns. Too soon, the announcer was calling us back to the line, and finally we were standing there, the ten of us, panting and sweating and coming back to ourselves as the crowd cheered. I could see the shadowy figures down by the judges' panel, taking notes. The announcer saying something—I felt a girl, maybe Brooke, push into me—we had to get off stage, it was over, too quickly. We marched off the stage as abruptly as we'd come on.

After watching the teen and senior dance-offs, we were called back on stage to hear the top three; I focused on the dust motes swarming in the beams of light. It seemed odd, you know, that dust would be lurking in a place so hallowed, so important, so full of important people. The announcer got right down to business. "I have a top three . . ."

And I just looked down at my feet and tried to think about what I would do next, after my name was not called—I would convince my mom to go to Olive Garden. And then I would die. No. But I would definitely cry in the bathroom. I would definitely cry in an Olive Garden bathroom after this.

"Celia Walsh!"

She stepped forward, people cheered. This was expected.

"Dok Phi Sua Buathong!"

Beside me, Dok Phi Sua raced forward to embrace Celia. My body went even colder. I would let myself feel bad for this one moment, and then, I told myself, I would get over it. A good try. I was in the bottom of the age category, anyway. Next year . . .

"Lucy Gardiner!"

My hands went to my mouth, I went to Celia and Dok Phi Sua, and we jumped up and down. In the YouTube version, you can see the other top ten behind us, clapping happily, mildly. *Next year*, they're thinking. *Next year*.

As soon as we got off stage Celia and Dok Phi Sua changed into their costumes and went into running their solos for the recompete, so I followed suit. Headphones blasting, I found a corner and ran through the choreo, the spins and splits and little details. Right. I knew this. I had this. My body was a battered kite in a thunderstorm, struck, charged, and teeming. But then I saw Celia being ushered to the stage. Though I should have been stretching or something, I couldn't help it. Clinging to the rails of the stage, I watched from the wings.

Lately, I've been looking up "Celia Walsh" repeatedly, as if today is the day I'll find out what happened to her. There is no trace of Celia Walsh. That's an old, vague name in the competitive dance community, elsewhere completely unknown. She would be twenty-four now. Perhaps she really went to Juilliard, perhaps she is still dancing, just in the dark, still waiting for her moment. She has to still be dancing. She has to. Please let her still be dancing, wherever she is. If she's not dancing, and if I played a part, no matter how small, in Celia giving this up, it would be my greatest sin, more than anything else.

And then she was coming off the stage, and she blew right past me. Dok Phi Sua was on right after—they were announcing her, she was climbing onto the stage—and her solo was also breathtaking, a contemporary piece set to discordant static that showcased her musicality and her sharp technique. I liked her solo the next year better, the one that won her Best Dancer, a jazz funk solo to a Robyn song, which I watched on my laptop in a hotel room in Los Angeles, bitter I could not go, but Bruise wanted me close while she wrote her next song.

The static from Dok Phi Sua ended, and she was getting to her feet and walking off the stage. Applause. My name was being called. On stilted legs, I made my way to center stage and found my start position, lying stock-still on my back. As soon as "Ribs" began my legs and arms slowly lifted, like I was being sucked into an alien ship, but my mind was not with my body. As I ran through the choreography, I was simply going over, again and again, what I had just seen: Celia's dance.

Ribs. The song was about growing older and looking back on being young. I got that much. When the lyrics began, I stumble-ran, arm outstretched, legs kicking like someone was pulling me back. I rewatch this recompete version on YouTube sometimes, especially when I start wondering if I can dance again, more and

Nothing. Silence, wind, then wind chimes, then a Buddhist philosopher talks about what it means to exist: *By being, you have to have been nothing.* Celia danced like her body was underwater. As chimes fluttered, her movements picked up speed, but only in the slight details—her neck, her fingers, the height

more lately. This dance was my technical peak. I was eleven. I was perfect. All downhill from there. The choreographer told me this piece was about fighting to get back to your former self. "Like you can never go back," she told me. "It's hard to understand because you are your former self right now." At the very end, I was back-bent but trudging forward—arms reaching backward as I left the stage so the last thing you saw were my fingers. I don't think my spine could even go half as far, now.

of her slow leg extensions. *But*, the philosopher intoned, *you have been nothing before. The fundamental reality is nothing.* Despite this, Celia smiled through her floorwork. As the drums grew louder, more discordant, Celia's movements sharpened, quickened. Her dancing became so large you barely noticed when the drumming ebbed—replaced by clapping. Celia was clapping. The audience shifted, not joining in, not sure if the dance had ended.

The dances were a prophecy. Everything happened quickly after I left the stage. Just like that, I was all alone, I was panting and dazed in the dark wings. My lungs aflame—even after the hours of class and the improv and the recompete, I was not done. Coming off the stage, I only thought about when I would dance next. I just wish dance was the thing that lasted, instead of the award.

At the end of the week, after the gala was over, after I won, after taking pictures and shaking all the judges' hands, after dodging all my family and my fellow dancers and everyone saying congrats, I found Celia by herself behind the waterfall. Like me, she was still in her gala dress, mine a wine-red, hers a sharp yellow. She was slicing her hand through the waterfall and didn't look up when I crawled toward her. But as I neared, she wiped her eyes and said, "I'm really happy for you, I am. I'm disappointed at myself, that's all. I really put myself on the line and here and . . . I haven't . . . and I've missed . . . and for what?"

"You should have won," I said. "You are the better dancer."

"Yeah," she said, meeting my gaze. "But I lost."

It wasn't like she was asking me to rescind the title. She had come so much further, had risked so much, had given up so much more. Yet it meant nothing. So it no longer meant anything to me.

Mom

Leaving Florida, I couldn't even look at the Best Dancer plaque. I felt like I had cheated, worse than cheated, I had cheated without knowing. I spent the drive back in a sullen daze, peeking at my Instagram account, watching my followers climb and feeling gross.

Only Joel noticed. We stopped at a motel on the border of New York. Mom and Dad were in the lobby haggling the price down. We had already dropped Micah off at a bus heading toward the southernmost tip of the continental states, where he would then turn back to begin the long northern trek up to Mount Katahdin. When he hugged me goodbye, he'd whispered, "I'm sorry, kid" in my ear, and I laughed appeasingly, thinking it had something to do with my win.

"Despite your unimaginable victory, you don't seem happy," Joel declared.

"You saw the other girls in the top three," I said. "Do you think I was better than them?"

"C'mon, Lucy." He rolled his eyes. I kept my stubborn gaze. "I don't know. I'm not a dancer. You were all good. You all were emotional and flexible. Like a sad alien."

"What about the other girl?"

"Which one?"

"The one who went first."

"The Black girl?"

"Well, yeah. Her."

"Yeah," Joel said, slowly. "Yeah. She stuck out. I thought she was really good."

I did not yet have the words for *Did I win because I'm white?* Maybe I still don't have the words. Maybe it was just about dance. Maybe it was because that was Celia's first self-choreographed solo, and it was too wild, inventive, and raw. Maybe we weren't ready for that. Maybe race had nothing to do with it, and it was just about dance, plain and simple. If it were the reverse, would I wonder why I had lost?

Mom and Dad were coming back now. I could see in Mom's face that they had not gotten the deal they wanted.

"Celia was amazing," I said. "I honestly don't know why I beat her."

"Look," Joel sighed. "Dance is art at the end of the day. It's subjective. On another day, yeah, she could've won. But you did this time. Next time, dance so you both know you deserved it, too." He jabbed me in the shoulder. "Because, you know, you do deserve it."

"Thanks," I cheesed. I didn't deserve it.

The car door opened and Mom huffed in. "We're sleeping in the camper here," she announced. "We've already spent an arm and a leg; I'm not paying another limb for a motel."

With that she got to work tucking towels into the windows, and my father was already tilting the passenger's seat back. Joel just shrugged, pulled his hat over his eyes.

"No," I protested, fighting back tears. I would not cry the night I won Best Dancer. "Mom," I insisted. "This is so stupid. You can pay for a stupid motel. We're not that poor."

"No," Mom agreed. "But we're smart."

She closed her eyes and that was that. For an hour the car was quiet, until Joel eased out of his seat, paraphernalia clattering in his sweatshirt. When we made eye contact, he shrugged. *Going to wander,* he mouthed. *Don't tell.*

If Micah had been there, he would have told, but Joel and I understood each other. He knew I wouldn't betray him. He stalked away, his big figure mingling well with the contrast of bright motel and the dark parking lot. I spent the night wide awake, watching cars pull in and out, tracking shady characters skulk into the motel lobby. First I thought up idle stories for each person—she was a sex worker, he was an ex-cop turned drug dealer—and then I began imagining myself as one of them, free to check into a motel in the middle of the night. I would cross the lobby in leotard and sweatpants, coming from one performance to the next—I would slip my own credit card across the counter—and I would be with Celia, we would happen to have the same gigs. In our motel room, we would split a pizza and watch bad movies. Toward the end of the night, we would get to reminiscing and I would confess how after the Dance Awards, I slept in a parking lot with my family. *I didn't know you were that poor,* Celia would say. I would just shrug, like Joel. *Well,* I would say. *I got out of it. I danced out of it.* By the time the sky bruised magenta and Joel reappeared among the hedges, hands blackened with spray paint, I had plotted a full and vibrant life for myself when I grew up, unbeholden to Mom's strange and stubborn ways.

It would not be long before that "full and vibrant life" found its way to me. That summer, things were normal. Mom worked at the hospital. I danced in the garage. Dad watched the vernal pool. Miach hiked. Joel vanished for days and returned with red eyes and videotapes detailing his explorations into abandoned buildings and dark woods, where he was now trying to capture paranormal evidence of his dead (?) mother, trying to suss out if he was going crazy like she went crazy (?), something he would say was an art project if anyone asked, but no one did.

In the fall, I started touring with DanceOne as the Junior Best Dancer, which meant being paid to fly to different cities and demonstrate combos and performing in closing shows. Mom accompanied me on these weekends, and once we left Leominster and it was just us two, she was my favorite version of Mom: letting me channel surf the hotel TV before settling on the Hallmark Channel, which we loved to snark on together. And God, maybe we could have kept on snarking, but in the spring, a casting agent approached Mom with an opportunity to audition for the reality show *Dance Til You Drop, Juniors!!* He had seen me at the Dance Awards, and he'd traveled to watch me perform at a DanceOne closing show. A business card in Mom's hand, an official email in her inbox.

"Just think about it," he said. "Your daughter was put on this Earth to dance."

Once he was gone, Mom stared at the card. My eyes were big, but I stayed silent, steeling myself for a fight. But she surprised me. When we were back in the convention hotel room, sitting on our separate beds, she just asked, "Do you think it's true? You were put on this Earth to dance?"

"Yes," I said automatically.

"Funny, when you were born, I didn't look at you and think: *dancer*. My first thought was, *Wow! Here you are, on this Earth.*"

Without taking my eyes off the TV screen, I scoffed: "What does that even mean?"

She pushed a lock of hair behind my ear. Mom never touched me, so this was unnerving. "It means I'll support you no matter what. Even if you aren't dancing."

"I will never, ever stop dancing," I said, somehow annoyed. "Ever."

"Okay," Mom said softly. "That's okay, too."

Mom has two stories about how she caught the acting bug. The first she tells most people, though technically it's not true. She claims she auditioned for the community theater production of *Oliver Twist* only because she was madly in love with the boy playing Oliver. Her physique and charisma won her the role of the Artful Dodger, so she spent countless rehearsals close to Oliver Twist, slapping his back and cajoling him to steal. "Oh, it was so silly," Mom would laugh, detailing the nights she spent analyzing his moves, trying to decipher what was acting and what could be construed as genuine feeling. All this culminated in Mom's confession the moment before they went on stage opening night. Oliver Twist rejected her outright.

"You're a fat girl pretending to be a boy," Twist sneered before brushing past her to belt "Food, Glorious Food" to an adoring crowd of grandparents. Standing in the dressing room, Mom had two options: flee or carry on with the show. And the moment she stepped onto that bright stage, she realized she had never loved the boy at all, but the rush of acting itself.

The second story I found out only recently. Less funny and sadder, but true. Her parents owned a failing and faintly white supremacist tattoo parlor in Raleigh, which kept them out of the apartment day and night. Mom, an only child, was left with the television as a babysitter. She wasn't sure when her abiding love of TV turned into a love of acting—maybe it was always there. But she spent her childhood rapt in dramas, fascinated and comforted by how it was all pretend. When my grandparents' bitter chaos invaded the apartment, Mom flung herself into high school theater. The long rehearsals and endless theater kid drama was a convenient way to keep herself out and occupied, at least that's my take now. And even in her retelling, theater provides an alternative story to the more sinister reality. Instead of telling how her father used to cover the living room in Confederate flags, how her mother would accost women in hijabs at Walmart, Mom told the tale of missing pilgrims hats the opening night of *The Crucible*. I suspect, as well, there are more nefarious stories about my grandparents, like stories that explain why Mom doesn't hug people, why when she got the news that my grandmother died, Mom refused to claim the body and spent the weekend on a fifteen-hundred-piece jigsaw of an arctic seascape. Instead of stories explaining that, Mom recounted her high school's production of *A Midsummer Night's Dream* or that one act where she accidentally stabbed her husband. And then it was like the *Oliver Twist* story: What was initially an escape turned into her true love.

She majored in theater arts at a state school, full ride. She had gotten another full ride to Occidental College in California, a longtime dream, but by then her father had been jailed for fifteen years for aggravated assault (a bar fight, the other guy ended up a paraplegic) and her mother had filled the apartment with unneutered cats and someone needed to stick around to change the litter boxes. Even still, Mom dreamed of making a life out of acting. In state school, she excelled, leading in four different plays, directing two, writing one, living in a shithole apartment with four friends. It lulled her into a false sense of security, and she thought it might really be possible. But ten, fifteen, twenty long years in New York City said no. When acting didn't work out she found a new love in writing, but her weird plays kept getting rejected. There was one play—*August 8*, a kaleidoscopic take on the end of the world—that she always thought would be her break. Everyone who read it, all her friends, even a few agents, swore it would end up on Broadway, but it always landed back in her drawer. She found herself drifting into her thirties, late thirties, forties. Compounding this, she had taken a job years ago as an EMT to keep her day hours open for auditions. Here she found a new passion: keeping people alive. Nothing more satisfying, she told me, than massaging a person's wet beating heart after getting rejected from an MFA student's unpaid film project. So she said, "Fuck it," started taking night classes, and then worked her way through nursing school. And yet here was another regret: She wished she had gone fully through to medical school, residency, the whole nine yards. But she thought she was too late for more ambition. She settled, instead, for becoming a death doula, traveling to private facilities and houses, wherever her clients decided to die. She was highly sought after, though she charged basically nothing, which was why she often had to take shifts as a trauma nurse in the ER to pay the dance bills.

All to say, having seen her own dreams perish slowly and agonizingly, she was determined not to let that happen to her own children.

The audition for *Dance Till You Drop, Juniors!!* was held in an office park in New Jersey. Mom was glad this was not the whole weekend, like most of our convention weekends. She said more than twice, on the drive down, how she was looking forward to her first free Sunday in months. "Maybe," she teased, "I'll even cook."

"Please don't," I lamented.

"Fine," she said. "Chinese and *X Files* with the whole fam?"

"Deal." My family, when we could, liked to watch bad-good-old TV. Joel and Mom riffed on the dialogue, Micah picked out plot holes, and my father cried if an animal died.

So when we strode into the waiting room, mentally we were already back on the northbound ramp. The place had the air of a doctor's office, except the children were in leotards with numbers pinned to their chests, and the mothers wore heels and paced the perimeter, saying to other nervous mothers that they were the most nervous. I asked Mom in a low tone who she thought seemed more nervous, her hospice patients or these moms?

"That's so insensitive," Mom hissed back. Then: "These moms."

I was proud of us, being above it. One mother was curling her shrieking daughter's hair. Another was loudly running a script with her kid.

"Hey." I poked Mom. "How would you have me prepare?"

"You could listen to my podcast," Mom said, handing me her right earbud cord. She was always trying to get me to listen to this podcaster interview terminally ill patients about *dying . . . well.* Some episodes, like this one, were about a weird thing about death. For example, why are we comforted by oceans? This story, narrated by an Ira Glass–type, followed a terminally ill patient's legal battle to die on a public beach.

"Really puts things into perspective," Mom said.

A producer poked his head in and asked for a Lindsay. The girl and the mother left, and then the rest of the mother-daughter duos renewed their preparation with a frenzy.

"The ocean is infinite," the terminally ill patient said in my ear. "You break onto the shore, and then you go back out to . . . the infinite ocean . . . or something . . . equally infinite."

"Like a circle," the Ira Glass–type suggested.

"No, no," the terminally ill man said. "More like . . . a sphere."

"Mm," Mom murmured in agreement.

Bored, I picked up *Cosmopolitan* and started the quiz "Your Sex Life According to Your Favorite Snack."

"Mom," I whispered. "Doritos or Twix?"

"Twix," she said.

"Mom. Chocolate Pudding or Cheez-Its?"

"Cheez-Its."

"Okay. Last one. Almonds or pistachios?"

"Oh! Both. With a little sea salt."

"You have to choose."

"Why?"

"Never mind," I said, picking pistachios.

The terminally ill man went on, "And I guess I feel better knowing I'm going somewhere . . . doesn't have to be paradise but as long as it's, like, still part of this world."

The Ira Glass–type: "Would you still want to be you?"

"Of course I would but I don't think that's probable. I guess I just want my atoms . . . going somewhere."

"Have you considered that your atoms aren't you? Have you considered your atoms are the atoms of dead people long before?"

When the producer called my name, I turned to Mom and announced, "Your sex life is sweet and salty. You have a big appetite, but luckily there are more than enough fish in the sea willing to taste your bounty."

"Thanks," Mom said coolly. "Will you be good alone? Technically, I'm on call this weekend." When she was called, she would drop everything to listen to a patient's ailments and suggest a course of action. When she took a leave of absence while we were filming, it meant abandoning a lot of dying people mid-death. Their loved ones sent Mom many grief-stained, angry emails, which she didn't mention to me until much later.

"'Course," I said, secretly relieved—I hoped going in alone would make me stand out, seem more independent.

"Sorry," the producer said. "We need Mom there, too. Policy."

"Fine," Mom sighed, following us but keeping her headphones in place, where I knew *dying . . . well* continued, albeit at a lower volume.

The audition was held in the lobby: think glass ceilings and potted ferns, a folding table and four white men each with their own carafe of water. Mom stood far off to the side while I made a beeline for the producers, clutching my headshots and my resume. Joel had taken the headshots, and they were kind of a joke. We had too much fun one spring morning, going out into the woods and me posing like, to quote Joel, "a lost forest child."

Without looking up at me, the producers asked what I would be sharing with them today.

Handing my headshots over, I announced in my most articulate adult voice that I had prepared a contemporary piece titled "Maybe We'll See."

If I thought they would be impressed, they didn't show it. Instead, the music began unceremoniously. I found the thread and picked up the choreography, a solo I had been doing for DanceOne closing shows. Soon the lobby melted and I found my body thinking about the ocean and the terminally ill man, breaking on the shore, giving away, but I felt like I would fight it, like Celia, I would—

"Stop," one producer announced, holding up a hand.

"So," another producer said. "That was weird."

"Thanks." I grinned.

The producer at the end of the table shook his head. "We're not sure our viewers will get 'weird' you know? A little weird but not . . . weird."

"But you have a good look," the blondest producer (they were all blond) said. He looked at his other producer friends. "She has a good look," he said again. "Next-door neighbor."

"She's cute," the end-of-table producer said.

"Eh," the oldest producer said. "A little too Lolita."

"I'm going to play a pop song," the blondest producer said. "Let's see what you can do with that, okay, Lucy?"

Before I could say okay, the pop song rang out. I recognized it as something on the radio all the time that year. Bruise was singing about running with wild horses, except there were no more wild horses. *Where are the wild horses?* belted the chorus. *There are no more wild horses.* It was a banger. Every time it came on, Joel would scoff, "It's the same damn line." But. Her voice got to me—like one of those whale calls, but human. So I danced, jazzy and poppy enough but—thinking of Celia—I kept my movements a tad wild, a tad mournful. *There are no more wild horses,* Bruise repeated, and I fell into a handstand, kicking my legs.

When the song ended, I glanced back at the producers.

"Wow," said the oldest producer. "You can sure move."

"She's not human," said the blondest producer.

"There was emotion," said another. "Our viewers like emotion."

"She could be a fan favorite," said the least blond producer. "If she isn't the brat."

"She's not a brat," the blondest producer said. "She's too cute."

"Thanks," I cheesed. I watched them write things down and drink from their water carafes. Then, they started asking me questions: When did you start dancing? What do you love about it? What do you think about your competitors? Would you call yourself a sore loser? Do you have any trauma? Tell us about your family.

That one began all the trouble. Once I got on my brothers, I couldn't stop. I told them about Micah hiking all over, extending his ECT trip farther into Canada, and of course, Joel and his art, the sketches, the mixed-media projects, the exploring abandoned buildings. The more I talked, the more I wanted the producers to like Joel. "It's not like he dropped out of college because he's stupid. He's going to be a famous artist, you know, and all the famous people drop out early. Right now he's making a piece dedicated to his dead mom, or understanding his dead mom. So he's breaking into abandoned psychiatric wards looking for ghosts. He told me that he's going to make a whole installation of him asking questions and the gurgle white noise, and he knows the white noise means nothing, but people will try to make meaning out of it because that's what we do and it's, like, it's a statement on going insane like how his mom went insane . . . well, it's better when he explains it."

I was met with startling silence.

"Your mom's dead?" one of the blond producers asked.

"But your mom is here," the blondest producer said gently. Mom had come up right behind me, headphones off. I couldn't quite read the expression on her face. It wasn't anger, but it wasn't happiness either.

"Oh," I said, and then started the whole story about the hike and their Mom vanishing and . . . The producers were quiet. They wrote nothing. But they leaned in, looking hungry. I felt like I was doing something right.

"I'm worried we're not going to beat weekend traffic," Mom said suddenly. I gave her a sharp look.

"Wait," the blondest producer said. "We have a few questions for you, Mom."

Lucky Girl • 59

"Fine," she said. I didn't get why she had to sound so bitchy about it. But then came the firing squad: How do you handle a stepson like Joel? How old was he when your husband's first wife died? Do you think he resents your daughter's talent?

Mom batted away each question. The producers' mouths all set into a tight line. "Look," one of them said. "You have to give us something, or no matter the talent, we can't justify . . ."

A long beat. "Well," Mom said, chewing her words. "This isn't my first audition. Before Lucy, I probably went to a thousand of these things . . ."

The producers sat up straighter. "Right," the oldest producer said, very casually. "Haven't we all tried. How long did you pursue acting? When did you give up? Do you believe Lucy's dreams will come true?"

Mom glanced down at me. I grinned. In each recollection, I conjure something different in her face—pride, worry, excitement, trepidation, remorse.

Mom said, "Of course I want her dreams to come true."

We were back home in time for a sudden cold front. As we pulled off Route 2, snow freckled the windshield and Mom sped up the car, swearing. When we'd left for the audition, my father had been furiously researching ways to protect the vernal pool from the chill, including jerry-rigging a greenhouse over the small gully. While we were auditioning, Dad had been quilting together the pelts of milk jugs and Poland Spring bottles to insulate the pool before the snow arrived. It was blustering by the time we pulled into the driveway. Tucked into the blizzard, our house—small, yellow, slanted—looked quaint. But I knew the mess behind the door, the clutter of plates in the sink and the constant lull of the TV and the drawn curtains, and I felt for the first time a certain shame imagining how the producers would spin my home life. As I walked through the door, the familiar musk hit me. Each time dance took me away and I returned, it was like remembering all over again. Ah. Yes. We lived in filth. I began to count down the days until the weekend, when I could leave again and smell only the sterility of hotel lobbies and the fresh bleach of hotel sheets.

Mom tossed our bags on the landing and barked into the living room. "Cody? Joel?" No response but the TV. Mom and I picked our way to the living room, doing careful circles around Micah's ski poles and Joel's rock collection. We found Dad slouched in the living room, *The X Files* playing low on the TV. Dirty plates were stacked on the coffee table before him—I could see what they'd had for breakfast, lunch, and dinner.

"Cody," she barked, louder. "We're home. Where's Joel?"

"The pond froze over," my father said thickly. "They're all dead."

"You don't know that," Mom responded. "It's not over."

She was in the habit of saying this line with a certain, deadly persuasion. When I came in second, when Micah failed to summit, when Joel lost another job, when the environment threatened my father's Jenga-fragile psyche. Somehow, the line seemed both a threat and a plea.

Mom swept a stack of unopened mail off the couch and sank by my father.

"It's not over," she repeated. "Keep trying."

My father nodded, or he could have been craning his head to get a better look at the TV.

I felt so bad for her.

My ears drummed so loud I couldn't hear the rest of their conversation. Peeling off into the kitchen, I was met with more mess: cups lining the counter, bowls in the sink so ancient the milk had crusted and bloomed lilac. Without Micah, the house had gotten much worse. Each time Mom and I got home from a dance weekend, it seemed to have slid further inward. I hadn't noticed how much Micah was holding down the fort until his absence. Again it felt like my eyes were cameras, panning over the wreckage of a home, my thoughts the voice-over for the reality show: *Lucy Gardiner might have clean lines on the dance floor, but at home she burrows in fucking shit. How long until this piglet turns into a fucking fat pig like the rest of her family?* My throat closed up. I scrubbed the crusty bowls with an old sponge.

"Lucy," Mom called from the living room. "Are you hungry?"

Already I knew she was going to order Chinese, already I knew the take-out bag would occupy the counter for months and months, until we needed a poop bag when the dog left a necklace of turds on the carpet.

"No," I choked out. "I'm not hungry."

In the garage I found Joel angling heating lamps toward a bucket of water. It was always a happy shock to see Joel at home, alert and engrossed in something. Just the sight of him took me out of my black mood.

"Stupid," he was muttering. "They're just hibernating."

Inside the bucket swirled the stiff bodies of salamanders and frogs in gunky pond water. Joel, as it turned out, had been aiding my father all day in trying to save the vernal pool from the freeze. And once Joel got on something, he had a hard time letting it go. So here he was.

He boomed, "How was the audition, prodigal sister?"

"Good," I said, slipping my hands into the bucket and grabbing the walnut of a frog. I raised the little guy to my eye level, trying to guess if he really was dead or just hibernating.

Joel pressed, "Good as in you got it?"

"Good as in at least I tried."

Laughing, he stalked out to the backyard and through the woods to the vernal pool, which was covered by a plastic tarp. I followed him out—the snow hadn't stopped, and the night was muffled. It felt like February, not the middle of April.

Joel went around the edges, checking to see if the tarp was secure.

"So much work," he panted. "We should have let nature take its course."

I glanced back at the house through the dark trees, where the windows fluttered blue with the TV. "Was it always like this?" I asked before I knew what I was asking.

"It's not really nature, though, is it?" Joel said. "Nothing natural about this weather."

"Was it like this before me?"

Without saying a word, Joel suddenly stalked deeper into the woods. Like an idiot, I stood by the pond, unsure what to do, until he called back, "Are you coming or what?"

A scarlet skull was festooned on his sweatshirt between his shoulder blades and that was what I followed through the dense thicket. I had never been this deep in the woods, ribbed with old stone walls that the pilgrims had made, or so Dad claimed. Joel seemed to know exactly where he was going, pitching left at some mossy gully, making a sharp turn around a grove of yellow birches, until we finally arrived at the largest boulder my kid eyes had seen. It was sliced down the middle—some glacial happening that predated our understanding—and through the middle Joel slipped and disappeared.

"Hey, wait—"

"Take a gander." His voice reverberated from the boulder. It sounded sad and tired.

I slid down the middle, back scrapping against the lichen. It seemed impossible that Joel would fit, but he must have, so I kept on sidling. Finally, the boulder opened into a little room. The walls were these neatly packed branches and twine. A ramshackled fort.

Lucky Girl • 63

Joel was hunched over by a paper sign. It read "Gardiner Boyz Fort: Keep Out!!"

"Don't know why we put 'keep out' on the inside," Joel remarked.

"This is awesome." I meant it.

"She made it with us," Joel said and I knew he didn't mean my mom.

"It's really awesome," I repeated stupidly. But he didn't seem to notice. He was taking out his phone.

"Any ghosts here?" Joel intoned. "Spirits, can you hear me?"

He held the phone out for a few heartbeats. Then, he played it back.

The snarl of air. If you tried to listen, maybe you could make out words. But really, nothing.

We were silent after that, listening to the storm rattle the branch door like bones. Eventually, there was a metal clicking—Joel was lighting a cigarette, cupping his hand against the wind.

"What now?" I asked.

Joel exhaled smoke. "Well," he said in his big, wistful Joel way. "I guess that's it."

My hand gestured for the cigarette. He raised an eyebrow but let me pinch it from him. The bud was warm and saggy, a burning caterpillar. I flicked it to the floor and ground my heel into the soil, snuffing the embers out.

"Smoking's bad for you," I announced.

He laughed then, so hard I could see tears sprouting in the corners of his eyes. "Oh, Lucy, I forget you're eight."

"I'm twelve," I huffed, though I knew he was being hyperbolic.

When we didn't hear back from *Dance Till You Drop, Juniors!!* I felt a vague okay-ness. Fine. At least I'd tried. Back to normal. Back to the barre.

But then I got the call. Or Mom got the call. It was a Wednesday, and she picked me up from the studio late. "Well," she said. "They want you on set May 12th."

It was May 10. They'd given us no time and no warning. Like cult leaders, reality show producers disorient the willing.

I don't remember too much of my last days at home. It was a lot of packing and a lot of Mom finagling a sabbatical from the hospital. The night before we were set to leave, Joel was nowhere to be found. "Disappointing," Mom said, and then pulled Dad into the kitchen, where she quietly and furiously lectured him about keeping better tabs on Joel—"Yes, I know he's twenty-one, but still, if you let him disappear like that . . . Cody, I would if I was here but this is Lucy's dream and I have to be there . . . production wants me, and you know, they wanted all of us, but we can't afford to—"

Micah FaceTimed me out of the blue, wishing me congrats again. He had hitchhiked all the way into town to get service. "Don't worry," he said when I expressed dismay over him riding with randos. "I'm in Canada."

I asked him when he was coming home, and he couldn't give me a straight answer.

"Aren't you tired of, like . . . walking?" I asked. He had been hiking since July of the previous year, making an appearance for a week over the holidays, but he'd mostly slept, showered, before returning to the trail. If Joel was still searching for their mom spiritually, looking back, I would venture Micah took her disappearance much more literally.

"Where's Joel? How's he doing?"

"Fine. He's doing a cool project." I knew he wasn't fine. But if I said it, it felt more true.

"I'll be home for the finale," Micah promised. "I can't wait to see you live."

Everyone had gone to bed when the ceiling of my basement bedroom flushed with a car's headlight. I scrambled to the living room and looked out the window. A silver Honda dropping off Joel. He got out and so did a girl I had never seen before. They were arguing in a low but urgent tone, throwing their arms up and turning away from each other, then looking back. Finally, he said something that made her get back into the Honda and drive off, revealing a cluster of bumper stickers: *Obama 2008*; *Coexist*; a chicken with a gun, the caption: "Peace was never an option." Joel stayed out for a while longer, rubbing his face and staring at the top of the driveway. I was waiting for him at the top of the porch stairs.

"Hey, prodigal sister," he said sadly.

"Who was that?"

"No one."

"No one's a bad driver."

Joel scratched the back of his neck. "Yeah, well . . ."

"I'm leaving tomorrow," I said.

"Right," he said. "Good luck. Shoot, score, win." He passed me to the living room.

"Would you want to come?" I asked suddenly. "You can just, like, hang out around set. I'm sure it'll be nuts. You fight a judge or something. Get on TV."

I was begging. If Joel had come, none of what was to come would happen. He would have talked me out of it the first night. Away from the girlfriend, maybe he wouldn't . . .

Joel settled in our dad's recliner, turned the TV on low. "Nah. I have something to take care of. But look, when you get back and it airs, we'll have a giant watch party and I'll make fun of the whole thing then."

"Okay," I said, relieved. "That will be my beacon."

Never will I see a single episode of my season of *Dance Till You Drop, Juniors!!*

You might be trying to remember how *Dance Till You Drop!* and *Dance Till You Drop, Juniors!!* could be distinguished from many other talent competition reality shows. Let me refresh your memory with the logline: "Dancers compete in battle-royale-style dance challenges for a million-dollar prize. The twist? To stave off elimination, dancers must brave the Pit."

The pit was a bottomless pit where the judges sent you at the end of the episode. As you plunged down into the pit, you had to dance, midair, until the judges saved you. If not, you died. As in, cut from competition. The rest of *DTYD, Juniors!!* was pretty regular: An episode was typically divided into five segments. Routines were given out, rehearsals had some sort of personal drama, followed by a Pique Challenge, and then dancers competed before a live audience and judges. Then, the Pit. My family and I used to watch the non-junior version of *DTYD!!*, my brothers with half interest and me like it was Jesus unboxing the latest Bible, every Thursday night before *Modern Family*.

When Mom and I landed in NYC, we were sent straight to set to film an intro package. Two producers met us in the marbled lobby, led us to the elevator, and pressed 8B. "That's deep," I remarked. No one said anything. The door dinged, opened, and we stepped out into a normal-looking office. The producers showed me a changing room where I could get into my dancewear. I looked at Mom.

"Pick out something orange," she said dryly. "Show off your electric personality."

I changed, and when I came out, Mom was gone and there was another new blond producer. He said my mom was in hair and makeup, and that he would show me where the set was because they were about to start. I was taken to the main set, a vast cave with red strobe lights and exposed wires on the ceiling. The walls and floors were smooth and obsidian like TV screens.

During performances, they projected a slideshow of images depending on the dance: a sky if it was a lyrical ballad, a fire if it was a redemption-type thing, and so on. I was made to stand on the circular stage with the rest of the contestants, mostly girls and one boy, who kept staring straight ahead as I joined them in line. The girl I was set next to was much shorter than me. She had curly red hair like Shirley Temple, and she kept her arms and feet in first position the whole time. This was Alice. "Hey," I whispered. "Are we being filmed yet?"

She gave me the side-eye but smiled. "Look serious," she whispered back. "That's what they told me." Before I could ask who "they" were, I heard a thunderclap. That's when I realized that shrouded in a low haze beneath the circular stage, there was a clapping audience, maybe thousands of people, clapping and jeering as if on cue. The TV floor beneath us played a light show. Finally, a spotlight beamed and there came the host—I think his name was two first names, like Ein Jacob—shouting into his mic, "Are you ready to dance . . ."

"Till you drop!" shouted back the audience.

Then Ein Jacob waited for an awkward amount of time. It got quiet. Someone coughed. They would edit this part out.

"Juniors!" Finally someone got it. "Juniors!!!" the crowd shouted back, relieved. "JUNIORS!"

"Yes," Ein Jacob hissed, barely concealing his disappointment with the crowd. "*Dance Till You Drop, Juniors!!* Let's give it up for our juniors!"

The spotlight veered to us, hot and obliterating. The crowd flipped out. I snuck a peek at my row of contestants. Like Alice, they were all tiny dance soldiers, staring unblinkingly ahead.

"And!" Ein Jacob boomed. "Let's meet our judges—first, the hip-hop icon Big Duck!"

Big Duck was a white rapper known for being a white rapper. His name used to be Big Dick, but when he became a father, he wanted to be someone his daughters looked up to, so he renamed himself Big Duck. On the opposing end of the set, an impossibly large slider door opened and he appeared amid technicolor smoke in a long red shirt, waving. Everyone cheered for Big Duck.

"Next," Ein Jacob shouted, already going hoarse. "Our dance legend, Ursula!"

Out came Ursula, an aging contemporary dancer who'd made their mark on the drag scene; the show used Ursula to lend credibility to the dance critiques. Ursula glided across the bridge onto the stage, showing impeccable grace for their fifty years, which at the time to me seemed incredibly old.

"And lastly," Ein Jacob whispered now, his voice completely shot, but it worked to build dramatic tension. "Our final judge, who needs no further introduction: Bruise!"

I had never seen a celebrity of Bruise's caliber in person, but her entrance certainly lived up to expectations: the cavernous and glittering setting, the unfurling smoke, the way she strutted across the bridge while the crowd seemed to hold its breath. That day, she wore a tulle dress puffed out from her neck so she looked like a feathery egg. Her hair was lilac. It would be some time before I could count the acne scars on her temple or the crow's-feet that bunched up when she smiled. I would be able to discern her moods from an intake of breath, I would know her deepest and darkest and most ordinary desires, I would plot my words by the palpitations of her heart, but in that moment, she appeared only as a visage beyond my reach. One eyebrow comma'd up, and she asked America:

"Shall we dance?"

Marcel

There is reality TV, and then there is the reality behind the reality TV, and that's why people watch, poised for the moment the visage slips. Reality tastes better after diet reality. Viewers were always surprised to hear we kids were friends. In the eight weeks of filming, we all stayed in a New Jersey luxury apartment complex. All the units looked down to an outdoor courtyard, which had a playground, and this was where we hung out after filming. It felt like a weird summer camp, except millions of Americans were peering through the cracks, commenting on Subreddits, theorizing the meaning of a sigh, an eye roll, a held-back cough.

There were thirteen contestants, including me. It was and was not a diverse cast. There was one boy, Marcel, and he was the oldest, thirteen. He was adopted, and that was his storyline. Wonder was half Chinese, and that was her storyline, and then Alice, Alix, Trixee, Julia Rosary, Lakynn, Piper, Taylör, Bella, Blakely, and I were all white. When I came out onto the playground soon as I was done unpacking, everyone was bunched together watching Alice attempt a 360 rotation on the swings. She was going so high by the time I made it to the group that you could hear the metal stakes in the swing set groan and tremble.

"She says she's done it before," claimed Wonder.

"Maybe because she's so tiny," Marcel offered.

"She's almost there," chirped Lakynn.

"I'll believe it when I see it," I laughed. At that Alice almost flipped completely, the seat floating midair over her butt, and then she came back down. We all groaned.

"Next run," Trixee said, crossing her fingers.

"I can't look," said Bella and Blakely at the same time. They were twins, and their storyline was about being twins.

"Should we stop her?" Julia Rosary whispered. But just then Alice made her final pass; we watched her again float midair at the precipice, we held our breath, and then she fell down the other end, making a complete 360 pass on the swing.

"Would you look at that," Taylör mused.

As she skidded to a stop, we all cheered. Alice bowed, once, twice. "Phew," she chirped. "I feel like a newborn baby!"

At ten years old, Alice was the youngest of our cohort. I would run into Alice many times in my Hollywood life, but especially at rock bottom. We would microdose and then walk around the Broad, spending hours lying in Yayoi Kusama's Infinity Mirrored Room, pressing our shoulders together and feeling like we were dissolving into speckles of light. "This is the only real thing," fifteen-year-old Alice would whisper. "I honestly think this is the only real thing in the world."

EPISODE 1: *V* STANDS FOR VICTORY

Diet Reality

The contestants, their mothers behind them in gaudy pantsuits, gathered in the rehearsal space. Ein Jacob announced the dance challenge: a group dance set to Bruise's #1 hit song that summer: "Mine Is Victory."

Ursula choreographed all our dances. When they appeared, we all freaked out, jumping up and down.

Confession Booth
ANNA | LOS ANGELES, CA
Alice's mother:
I feel like I have an obligation to Alice, you know? A girl with that red hair, those blue eyes . . . it's like she has to be a star, you know? I knew she'd be bigger than me. When I was a teenager, I starred in a show—actually, executives made *Weather or Not* just for me. But it got cancelled. Well, because of Alice, getting pregnant with Alice. But because of Alice, I found my purpose.

Reality

As we gathered, the mothers chatted idly about the amenities of the luxury apartment complex, how there was a spin class just a block down the road. The producers made us clap when Ursula entered. Ursula seemed to instantly know our strengths and weaknesses. They set Marcel and Taylör, the two tallest, as the leaders of the group. I was a bit jealous. A bit.

Diet Reality

Montage of the kids learning the dance, looking exhausted and focused. Lots of me stepping on Marcel's back. Lots of Alice looking lost and crying.

The mothers, in their observation deck, had philosophical differences on the meaning of "victory."

Confession Booth

BELINDA | ORANGE, CA
Bella and Blakely's mother:
The twins are very competitive. Because they're twins.

LEX | NEW YORK, NY
Lakynn's mother:
I was not impressed by Lucy. She supposedly won the Dance Awards, but she didn't really wow me. She's normal.

DENISE | BOSTON, MA
Lucy's mother:
Victory is something you define yourself.

Reality

I liked Marcel. He was quick to tell us his greatest ambition was to own a wingsuit and leap off the Grand Canyon and glide to the bottom. During any breaks, he was always watching GoPro videos of paraglides and wingsuits. But he was afraid of heights. He told me that was why he was doing the show: to get out of his fear zone.

Diet Reality

The first Piqué Challenge was always the same. Each contestant did piqué turns across the floor while explaining their backstory. If the judges

Confession Booth

JACKSON | AUSTIN, TX
Julia Rosary's father:
Look. Look. I don't want to come off as insensitive, but if we're playing the sadness

liked your backstory the best, they hit a buzzer for a spotlight to shine on you. They met us on stage in all their opulence: Ursula in a black dress, Big Duck in sweats, Bruise in a pantsuit, "YOU MATTER" written over and over on her left side, "DON'T GIVE UP" on her right side. Ein Jacob explained the terms and then we were off. Taylör's piqué won: She talked about her dad almost dying in 9/11. They played his voice message to his wife and to Taylör's older sister, who was only a baby. As he ran down the staircase, he recounted their wedding vows and sang a lullaby to Taylör's older sister, until it cut off suddenly. Static. Everyone, including Big Duck, wept.

pissing contest, Julia Rosary's mother actually passed away.

ANNA | LOS ANGELES, CA
Alice's mother:
Alice was premature. Like, premature. She came into this world at twenty-eight weeks. Her skin was literally translucent, you could see her little heart and her stomach and her blue lungs . . .

(Anna wipes a single tear. Reality? Diet reality?)

I knew she'd live. I knew she'd do big things.

Reality

The sudden cutoff and static, I later learned, was added by production. Behind the scenes, Alice was a strange child, stranger than her mother would care to admit. When we weren't filming, Alice would disappear for long swaths of time. Even the mothers began to notice, and began to talk of search parties, but Alice's mom dismissed the idea, saying that Alice needed space.

Diet Reality

Finally, we got to perform our dance before the judges on that circular TV stage we were on the first night. The audience was there again, thousands, buzzing, faceless. The judges sat on their judging thrones. The Group Dance, to "Mine Is Victory," went fine. It was the first time, so we were not used to being a group. Alice ran in circles blinking her big blue eyes. She was not a particularly stunning dancer. Marcel and Taylör were classically trained, definitely the strongest. In the dance, we died one by one until Alice was the last one standing.

The judges' critique: Big Duck said we danced big. Ursula praised our technique. Bruise praised our soul.

Eliminations. The stage opened up and we all plunged into the abyss. We danced. Piper fell forever and was never seen again.

Confession Booth

MELINDA | ORANGE, CA
Bella and Blakely's mother:
I tried. I tried to put them in different activities: Bella in dance, Blakely in singing, but they kept switching on me. *No,* they'd say, *I'm Bella, I'm Blakely.* To the point where . . . I don't know which is which. I'm afraid it got lost along the way.

PAMI | CLEVELAND, OH
Piper's mother:
Everything happens for a reason. I've always lived by those words. So I think—we learned so much this past week, made so many lifelong friends . . . didn't we, honey? Didn't we? I'll remember everyone. I won't forget this. This mattered, right?

Reality

So basically, eliminations. I found out when the stage "opened" up it was just the TV stage pretending to be a rushing chasm. We had to pretend to fall.

After filming, when we got back to the apartment complex, the kids started playing hide and seek in the courtyard and the playground. This was fun in the beginning, when there were a lot of kids to play with. As our numbers began to dwindle over the weeks, our little games became more tedious. Then we started making silly little videos. Looking back, they were all awful: Wonder and I swinging hand in hand, mouthing "Hotline Bling." Marcel moonwalking to Michael Jackson. The twins mirroring each other like sad twin mimes. Wonder pretending to be a Starbucks barista who hates her customers. Just kid stuff. The only ones to survive were the worst. The ones where I pretend to "speak Chinese" to Wonder. Where I pretend Alice is my baby and I'm a teen mother. Here's one video: I lean against the slide, pretending to smoke and rubbing my pretend baby bump. My mouth tears open. I bark: "La'Keisha. La'Keisha! Where you at?" The camera pans and finds Alice scrambling up a slide.

When it came up again, much later, I had forgotten making it. The videos weren't meant to last. It's not an excuse, but the producers dissected Marcel's adoption story into these exact parcels. I was just trying to make sense of what I was seeing. This is not an excuse.

We posted those videos to our YouTube channels and Instagrams. I always imagined my humble thousand-plus followers to be like me: a kid, a fan of dance. Mom also had access to the account, though she lapsed checking the content I was posting. She trusted me. The account was private, and Mom vetted followers. I was counting down the days until my thirteenth birthday, when I would be allowed to un-private, an agreement we'd made long ago. Marcel was thirteen, with a public Instagram, and he had the most followers.

I'll admit, I was jealous. Marcel seemed poised for a similar career in dance, but he was vastly ahead, both in sheer technical ability and followers. He was less well-known in contemporary circles, but absolutely famous in hardcore ballet, like, he had won Youth American Grand Prix, and the previous year he had medaled internationally at both Prix de Lausanne and Varna International Ballet Competition. Those competitions, held from Sweden to Russia, far exceeded the weight of my Best Dancer title. Yet Marcel seemed utterly indifferent. Never did I see him practicing like the others when we weren't filming. On stage, his face wore dully as he danced, and he never spun tales of his love of the art form like Celia had. Even his backstory, with his long-lost biomother, didn't seem to elicit any strong emotion. The only thing on his mind was the Aura 2 Wingman engineered and manufactured by Squirrel, the suit that he claimed had the best aerodynamic design, not to mention the light blue trim and the perfect arch from wrist to feet to ensure both safety and speed. Between filming segments, he would be researching wind currents while Wonder and I filmed each other improving. He often spoke about sneaking to the rooftop if he was eliminated. In the New Jersey apartments, he finagled his way to the roof through a fire escape hatch, and when we weren't goofing around he would be there, sitting on the edge, testing his limits. After episode 3 wrapped, I followed him up there. We were both still in our costumes, faux-ivy wrapped around our crotches and chests, the group dance having been some sort of Garden of Eden motif. "Hey," I said.

"Lucy," he said without looking back at me. "How strong is your finger grip?"

I flexed my fingers. "Fine, I guess?"

"Would you hold my hand so I can lean over the edge?"

I plopped beside him. "Absolutely not. I'm not being responsible for your death. What would be the theme of the next episode? *Lucy killed for the competition?* No!"

He laughed. His voice was deep and rich and I sort of loved it. "Fine. Be that way."

"How dare I not enable your death wish?"

He shook his head. "Death wish? Far from it. I'm trying to live."

His voice was so suddenly wistful I did not know how to respond and so we were silent, sitting there together on the roof's edge. We could see the bigger city on the dark horizon, a cluster of teeming lights. The wind battered us and the plastic leaves rustled and batted my bare skin. But I wanted the moment to linger.

Maybe I liked him. But like all my other crushes, like Celia too, this one was tangled with dance and art and winning so my art could be known as art.

"Why do you want to do all that?" I finally asked. "The flying squirrel stuff, I mean."

"It's almost like flying," he answered.

"But dancing is like flying, too," I countered. "Plus, you don't die."

Marcel said, "No, but I want to really fly. Like . . . I want it to be as close to really flying as possible. Not just the feeling. I want it to be real."

He turned his face toward me. I wondered, then, how similar he might look like his biological parents: the hooded eyes, the apple cheeks, the hair falling in sprigs across his forehead.

EPISODE 4: PROBLEMATIC PROP

Diet Reality

This week's solo challenge: props. They were given to us based on our backstory. For example, Marcel got an empty gold-plated picture frame. For Taylör, a torn American flag, for Wonder, a Buddha, for the twins, a creepy ragdoll. For Alice, the DVD box set of her mother's cancelled TV show from when Anna Bell was young and famous. Digging through the pile, I found a mirror. I looked at the many-headed beast behind the camera crew. *What does this mean?*

Confession Booth

DENISE | BOSTON, MA
Lucy's mother:
Once, when I was in *The Crucible* we lost these hats opening night . . .

NORA | ALEXANDRIA, VA
Marcel's mother:
Marcel was a sweet baby. Never cried. When I held him in my arms, I whispered, *Where did you come from?* . . . Of course, when he's older, or even now . . . if he ever wanted to find his biological parents. It would be a beautiful thing, wouldn't it?

Reality

Out of all the contestants, Marcel was the angriest about the props. I found him on the roof and we talked all night. I told him about my family, the hoarding, about Joel. He told me about what it was like being adopted, which he didn't think about, and it made him guilty. "I know the producers want me to feel like it's a huge part of me. But it's really . . . I want them to focus on the air suit stuff, the skydiving stuff. That's me."

EPISODE 5: BADDA MAMMA DRAMMA

Diet Reality

A fight broke out, disrupting rehearsal. The moms wanted to know if Lucy wanted to act, too, since Denise was once an actor. "No," Denise insisted. "Lucy only wants to dance." "But you must want her to act," the moms insisted. Things escalated, Denise storming into the women's bathroom, pushing a camera guy out of the way. The mothers were incensed! Without Denise present, they gossiped about how she refused to lose weight, how skinny Lucy was, wondering if Denise was harsh on Lucy's diet so she wouldn't end up like her.

Confession Booth

ANNA | LOS ANGELES, CA
Alice's mother:
Alice has always been the driver. She has set these big goals: number one pop star, number one actress, number one dancer, and I'm just there to drive her to practice. Her favorite place is the stage. Everything I do is because Alice wants it. Even when she's sick, I still see that hunger in her eyes—she wants this. If she didn't want this, would we be here? No—she wants this. I know she does.

Reality

After filming DTYD, *Juniors!!* Mom never talked about its incredible, awful fame. There were Reddit threads analyzing Mom's confessionals, her likeness used often in memes and voice-overs now bite-sized TikTok fodder. Neither of us knew how explosive the show would be, more popular and long-lasting than its adult predecessor. The season aired after "Escape" had topped the charts. That was part of the reason everyone tuned in, to see Bruise and me. But what they got was my mom.

EPISODE 6: LUCY HAS A SECRET

Diet Reality

Lucy performed a solo unexpectedly. The mothers were outraged—who told her to go out on the stage and dance right before the big group performance? Obviously, Denise was trying to shove her daughter in the judges' faces. The moms argued with Denise about loyalty. Denise agreed she was not loyal to the team—what team were they? She was just here for her kid.

Confession Booth

GINA | NEWARK, NJ
Taylör's mother:
Lucy has had everything handed to her. Natural flexibility. A million dance awards, she already came into this competition with a silver spoon. So I don't see why she needs to stab everyone in the back, again and again and again. But Tay and I learned a long time ago that good people never have it the easy way. But it makes us stronger. It makes us wiser, nicer, better. In the end, justice will prevail. I believe that, I really do.

Reality

The producers told me I had a special solo. Dancing, I was grinning, breathless—the choreography by Ursula was challenging, something they told me they would normally set on adult professional dancers, and I was so proud I had nailed it. But as soon as I peeled off the stage, the mothers really did go at me. I really did cry. That night, Mom tried to convince me to leave. "We can't," I insisted. "What would it look like if we gave up now?"

EPISODE 8: TAKE A STAND

Diet Reality

The mothers got more political. It was early summer 2016, after all, and the news was all Trump, Trump, Trump. The mothers discussed political figures, and things got heated. The dance, similarly, was presidential. Much fuss was made of who should portray Hillary, Trump, and the coveted role of the indomitable American Spirit. Wonder—who secured the role of AOC—was eliminated that week.

Confession Booth
ANNA | LOS ANGELES, CA
Alice's mother:
Look, I don't like everything Trump says, but at the end of the day, he's tough. And we need someone tough if we want change. And something's gotta change.

Reality

The kids did not talk politics, so enraptured by the pool, the playground, our videos. When Wonder was eliminated, she only cried on the shuttle heading back to the New Jersey apartments. In the back seat, Wonder pulled me into a tight hug. "I'll miss you," she insisted. "I really wish we could have made it to the end together." I cried too, saying the same things back, but even then I wondered how much of her tears were Diet Reality. If my own were.

EPISODE 9: SOLO WEEK!

Diet Reality

Everyone received a chance to dance a solo on stage. Lots of footage of the kids practicing with Ursula and Bruise, who choreographed the dance and created the music, respectively.

The performances were fine. Alice gyrated to a pop song, and I was given a song about the moral bankruptcy of dolphins. The trouble started when Marcel got on stage. He danced to a song about missing home. He finished facing away from the judges' table. Before he could turn around, a fourth chair was suddenly added. A Black woman: his birth mom. The producers had found her after a tireless search, convinced her to go on the show so we could witness the reunion. But Marcel? When he saw his birth mom, he walked away. Face completely neutral. The

Confession Booth
DENISE | BOSTON, MA
Lucy's mother:
And what about Lucy? Lucy wants this. And—Lucy's like me. She's better than me. My daughter is the best person I know. Really, that's what I care about. She could be *beep* at dancing and it wouldn't matter to me. But it won't always be this easy. Does that make sense? Then why am I here? Because I think she needs to exorcise this out. She's the kind of kid who needs to try her hardest, to know she gave it her all. What I mean to say is, she'll always wonder. *What if, what if, what if.* I know I do . . . Like, for me. I wanted to be an actor. Or a writer. I wrote this one play I really thought would make it, but nothing came of it. Life's like that sometimes. But I'll always wonder what if,

Lucky Girl

birth mother was left there, smile slipping from her face.

Bruise sang an impromptu song, her oldest song about heartbreak, while they escorted the mother away.

what if, what if I'd had a mom who supported me from the start? So I don't know, I guess I'm here because I'm trying to be the mom I wanted.

Reality

I found him where we usually hung out on the roof of the apartment complex. We were still in our silly solo costumes.

"Hey," I said.

"I don't care," he said.

"I know you don't care," I repeated, sitting next to him. It took a lot of courage; we were high up.

"But I wanted . . . " Marcel began, faded out. I waited for him to talk, watching the colors swarm on the skyline.

Finally, Marcel whispered, "I thought . . . my mom and I knew they might use it as a storyline. At first, I even thought I wanted it. But once she was there . . . with the cameras . . . it suddenly didn't feel real?"

EPISODE 10: BROKEN HEARTS AND DUETS

Diet Reality

We were assigned duets: Marcel and I paired together. The choreography involved a kiss.

Much was made of the drama with Marcel the previous episode: how he ran from his birth mother, how he didn't handle it right, how it was understandable, but sad, but hopefully he could channel this into the duet.

The moms turned to rumors. How Marcel and I were getting close. Too close. How we were always whispering together, laughing, looking at his phone. How we were both getting distracted. The mothers argued about our chemistry. *Lucy seems a bit . . . mature*, they ventured to Mom. They asked if I dated a lot back home. Mom scoffed. "Lucy's

Confession Booth

LUCY | BOSTON, MA | 12
Kissing a boy is . . . blergh! This is not how I imagined my first kiss.

MARCEL | ALEXANDRIA, VA | 13
I'm not answering your questions.

LUCY | BOSTON, MA | 12
Anyway, I'm not here for boys. Dance is my true love.

MARCEL | ALEXANDRIA, VA | 13
I won't answer that question.

LUCY | BOSTON, MA | 12
When I dance, I just feel . . . I don't know. I can't explain it. I'm just doing what I'm supposed to be doing. I have to dance.

MARCEL | ALEXANDRIA, VA | 13
(Unresponsive)

LUCY | BOSTON, MA | 12
I have to dance.

MARCEL | ALEXANDRIA, VA | 13
(Unresponsive)

only interested in dance." Behind Mom's back, the other mothers wondered if I snuck around behind her back. Texted boys. It seemed I kept a lot of things from Mom.

When the performance arrived, I came alive with Bruise's song, dancing by myself while Marcel refused to dance. The crowd went wild. I was praised for my resilience, while Marcel was eliminated.

Reality

Marcel wanted revenge on the producers. He wanted us to pretend to rehearse: "Play nice. Then, at the final taping, refuse to dance. Refuse to play by their terms. Our moms will be mad. The producers. The judges. But we'll make the statement: We will not be puppets. Let's see how they spin that."

Throughout the week, I was cool with this plan. I daydreamed about how I'd tell the real story to people back home, how much Joel would be into this. Each night, Marcel and I sat on the rooftop, hyping each other up. We knew we'd probably be eliminated. Thank God, we told each other. About time. In the real world, we made plans to see each other. Hang out. He lived in DC and promised to take me to all the museums. *Like a date?* I never had the courage to ask.

It didn't matter because as we marched up to the stage, my resolve waned. As soon as Bruise's voice invaded the stage, I let my body take over. I danced. When this aired, the camera lingered mostly on Bruise's reaction. Of course, Bruise said this was the moment she fell in love with me. Diet Reality—Reality? I'm still not sure.

I found him where he said he would go after elimination, the highest point in the skyscraper. We had been in the basement this whole time, but the network went up eighty-nine floors. The actual door to the roof was locked, but Marcel managed to sneak into the executive office, furniture-less save for a large glass desk and a translucent egg-shaped chair. The office was rimmed by the clear windows. Marcel was pressed against the glass. It wasn't quite night, and below us the sun was setting. We were so high up I thought I could see the Earth curve.

"I'm sorry," I said, approaching Marcel and feeling dizzy at the height. The wind seeped through the glass.

Marcel didn't look at me. "You're still in the show. It's your loss."

"Probably not for long." I lingered by the glass desk, picking up and putting down the stupid desk trinkets—a Golden Globe, those swingy metal balls that clack into each other, an Emmy, a tiny black obelisk.

He laughed to himself. "C'mon. You love it."

"No," I said softly, pleading. "I just want to dance."

"And I just wanted to test my mettle." Marcel tapped on the glass. I almost took a step back.

"Me too." We both were above the stupid show. Literally. I added, "I only went on this show to get better. Braver." As to prove my point, I sidled up next to him, pressed my body against the cold glass, the only material keeping me from falling into the cityscape.

He finally turned his head toward me, smirked. "Lucy—"

I went in for a kiss.

But he pulled back. He wasn't smiling.

"See?" Marcel whispered. "It's all for show." Before I could retort, he was walking away. I stayed stupid and frozen, mouth open. By the time I had an idea of a reply, he was already gone, down the elevator and back to Earth.

For a while longer, I stayed on the top floor. A dollhouse of a city. The height so dizzying I could feel the sandbag weight of my insides. And yet I stayed, pressed to the window, tilted over the edge. I waited until the fear left my body, until it became normal, and then boring.

And then the elevator dinged. I kept my gaze locked on the ground below, thinking Marcel was coming back.

But angry, adult voices reverberated into the office as the elevator opened. I scanned for a place to hide, and my eyes finally rested on the egg-shaped chair.

"—I never said that you—"

"—and fuck me, right?"

A man's voice, deep and curdling. A woman answering him, that voice I instantly recognized as Bruise. Her voice was lower than I anticipated, more gravelly. In interviews and on camera, she pitched her voice silken, barely tangible.

"I'm sad," Bruise was saying. "That's all, I'm just sad."

The man: "So let me just put everything on pause, all my projects, my dreams, so you can build little nests out of your sadness, your mythos of misery."

"Nice phrasing," Bruise retorted. "What great writing. You going for the Golden Globe?"

She walked over to the desk. Neither adult had come far enough to see me in the egg chair. I saw a hand—Bruise's, feminine, slender—come into view. She was reaching for the Golden Globe. As she bent forward to pick it up, our eyes met.

She saw me—she smiled, then winked.

I flashed a sweaty smile back.

Then she was gone out of my view, facing the man again with the trophy.

She asked, "So that's it? You're leaving again? Because I said I'm suicidal."

The man: "You said judging a reality show would make you suicidal. I told you not to, but you did, and I'm sorry, honey, I really am, but I'm tired of feeling . . . responsible! All the time! I can't write, I haven't written anything real since *Dead Heart* and—"

Bruise: "And that's more important than us, you writing the next Best Picture?"

The man: "You're sinking, and I'm sinking with you."

"Then grab a fucking oar!"

"How about you?"

Silence. Then, footsteps—someone walking away.

Bruise, calling after him: "Kons, if you walk out that door, I'll really—"

"Cry wolf one more time!"

"Fuck you," Bruise called back. "Fuck you, fuck you!"

And then she was sobbing, in that quiet, shuddery way you know is real crying. We stayed like that for a long time, or it seemed like a long time. When she spoke, her voice was chipper, bright, like nothing happened:

"And, scene!"

There she was. In her black dress. Grinning down at me. Nice teeth.

"Did you like the show, Lucy girl?"

"Hi," I said, stunned.

She tilted her head. "Running from the producers?"

When I didn't reply right away, she strode alongside the desk, running her hand along the edge. "It's a good view, right?"

"Yeah."

She brought the cool metal of the Golden Globe to her lips. Then, before I realized what was happening, she was widening up for a pitch.

"Wait—" I started, just as the Globe clacked against the window-wall of the office.

"You want a turn? Come on, Lucy, throw something. You can scream as loud as you want—they won't hear a thing."

She seized the tiny black obelisk, chucked it. This left a dink in the window-wall, and I began to get scared.

"We're high up," I ventured.

Bruise grabbed the Emmy. "He was nobody when we first met."

Then she hurled it toward the window-wall with newfound vigor. As soon as it made contact, the glass broke into a thousand silver prisms. The sound was pretty and high, not unlike Bruise's singing. Like melting ice, the shards dripped into the windy abyss.

"Um," I said.

"I get it, though," Bruise sighed. "It's not like I don't get it. I haven't written anything . . . anything real in a long time."

She drew close to the edge of the room, heels crinkling on the shattered glass.

"Um." The air swirled around us, making her dress lift and sway as if it were alive.

Bruise plucked a shard from the side of the broken window and examined it before flicking it off the side of the building.

"End of the line," Bruise whispered. "I gave everything I had."

"I get that," I said without thinking, anything to get her to turn back to me. "When I dance, I give it my all. Always."

She finally faced me. A beat. It felt like she was looking through my clothes, my skin, sizing up my organs. "You're a good dancer."

"Thanks," I whispered back.

"Would you dance for me?"

"Here?"

"No, not for the show." Her eyes widened, an idea. "Just for me."

She would confess to me months later, as we lay in the dark of her wide, cool room in California, that each time she sat at the judges' table, she was making a plan in her head: a final binge, a car, the right playlist, a seaside cliff. Her thing with Kons was over. Her latest album had barely made ripples. But really, the kicker was that she was bored. Nothing excited her anymore: not the prospect of music, which had become an exhausting chore. The many parties she hosted faded to a buzz in her ears. Even her breakup with Kons felt rehearsed. And didn't it seem like fate when I appeared in this random executive office, stopping her from . . . And then everything, the whole screaming world came rushing back. And in typical Bruise fashion, she thought of a song.

In the executive office on the top floor, she knelt to my level and kissed the crown of my head. "Lucy, Lucy, Lucy girl. I'll write a song for you. Just for you."

Then she was leaving, her dress sweeping behind her. I stayed, thoughts flatlined, feeling the faint cold and wet of her lips. The window wind battered my stupid body. Without thinking, I knelt and began gathering the dirty window shards in my palm.

"Leave it," she called, a pillowy, disembodied voice down the hallway.

"What?" I called back.

"Honey, leave it. Maintenance will take care of that mess."

Alice

It is easy to forget about Alice. She had the looks of a child star but the presence of a frightened third grader, which she was. Her Bambi-round eyes signified placid and thoughtless goodness. She had learned early to keep her thoughts to herself, to cover her tracks.

Fame ran in Alice's family. Her mother, Anna, had been a child star as well, appearing in brief snatches across the nineties whenever a flashback called for a feisty, red-haired child version of the main character. As Alice's mother's acting career gained traction, her family made the leap from Virginia—according to Anna's memoir, leaving behind a Victorian home with a many-branched oak—to a squat, colorless ranch just outside of LA. The downsize was worth it when Anna landed her first main character gig in a sitcom about a tween who controlled the weather. But the show was cancelled after just one season, despite impressive viewership: Anna, just fourteen, was pregnant. And it's one thing to hide a bump, entirely another to overlook nascent promiscuity in a network catering to Bible-belted housewives. Anna's sex-capades got traction also; trash magazines speculated on the father, paparazzi tracked the young mother to clinic visits. Anna learned her first Hollywood lesson: Fame is fame. Alice's raw baby face plastered in magazines across America, the kind you see waiting in checkout lines at the grocery. The prematurity, the transparent skin, the pin-sized hole in her purple, rubbery heart, the weeks in the NICU, all a flare of drama that Anna believed promising for Alice's career.

But Alice was weird. It is easier to tell in the TLC docuseries, *ChildMother*, in which she was super young, how weird she was. For one thing, she had to be naked. Many teaser trailers depicted a blurred Alice tearing through the house buck wild, Anna rolling her eyes and going back to her flip phone, a cautionary tale of teen motherhood. The late 2000s was the Wild West of reality TV, and still I'm shocked with how much they put up for the world to see: shots of Alice's diaper blowouts, a whole subplot of Alice pretending to be the family cat, down to using the litter box before she was even toilet-trained. As Anna got older, she wised up, got her act together, and by the time Alice appeared on *Dance Til You Drop, Juniors!!* they were only visible through the discerning eye of social media, whitened and brightened through the Papyrus filter, a sanitized version of mother and daughter. You would not know that Alice had grown crooked, as she would put it, sensitive to the invisible drumbeat that ran this world, a magical sense that later colored scientific; in other words, she was always the sort of girl with ants zippering her arms and legs, who knew when the family cat's limp signified life-ending pain, who could watch turtles' slow copulation among a thatch of weeds, and it took her a long time to realize that this thrum in her ears was unheard by most people, that their lives were dictated by another drum.

And so it was not surprising that when I searched for Alice to say goodbye, she was alone in her apartment kitchen, down on her belly, whispering to the sink pipes. Only when I crouched and touched her back, did I see the possum's bright yellow eyes in the dark.

"Shit!" I swore, leaping back.

"She's sick," Alice said. "She's been sick."

"Why don't you have your mom call animal control?" I asked.

"Animals shouldn't be controlled," Alice said simply. She reached for the possum, and a low hissing emanated from the bowels of the sink cabinet. Alice drew back her hand, murmuring, "All right, all right."

I cleared my throat. "Anyway. I'm leaving the show."

That got her to spin around, her cerulean eyes bright. "Leaving?" she hissed. "But you're supposed to win!"

"I got a better opportunity," I said. "So I'm going."

"But we still have to finish our video series," Alice protested, her voice getting squeaky. "And you were going to teach me to dance. With you gone, I have no friends."

"Well . . ." I started, gesturing haplessly to the sink. Then I saw something pink and squirming. Alice, following my squinted gaze, gave a soft coo.

"Babies," she marveled.

Indeed, if you squinted, if you shined your iPhone's light into the sink cabinet, you'd illuminate the wet and rosy tangle near the mother's hind: I counted at least nine baby possums, still shimmering from their recent expulsion into the world.

"Holy shit," I gaped.

For a beat, we stayed looking at the possums, their blind mewls, the mother's low and urgent hiss.

"I have to stay," Alice said. "I need to look after them, you know? I'm sorry, Lucy."

She apologized as if her coming with me was a matter we had been discussing. I laughed. My heart had a warm spot for Alice, her strange and mysterious antics.

I hugged Alice tightly. "You better win, all right?"

She would win *DTYD, Juniors!!* and if you freeze the clip when her victory is announced and confetti rains down and Ein Jacob and Big Duck and Ursula and Bruise, who returned for the final filming, are swarming little Alice, the camera pulls in and you can see a weird bulge near her sternum. Viewers mistook this for a nipple, the clip blighted from the web upon public noticing, but Alice later confirmed to me it was just a baby possum, the smallest, most shriveled one the mother had abandoned in the bottom of the sink cabinet. During final rehearsal, Alice was more preoccupied with saving the possum's life than remembering choreography, keeping it close to her skin like a mother possum would, wetting her fingers in milk from the cafeteria, all while avoiding her own mother's worried gaze. In the end, her efforts were fruitless; the baby possum died in the green room before she went on stage for the final time, or at least, that's when she felt it go cold and rigid against her chest. Alice danced with a dead possum in her leotard the whole finale. You wouldn't know—it was the best she ever danced, such frantic sorrow chillingly incongruent to Bruise's track "Lick It All Over," yet so startling she snatched the win right out from under Taylör's nose. The notoriety would launch Alice's career only somewhat; she would appear in a few music videos for minor stars. Once those opportunities petered out, Alice and her mother would retreat to Instagram, volleying from destination to destination, living primarily out of hotels, her grid becoming so oversaturated with bright linen I stopped paying attention to Alice until she reemerged, years later, in the Calabasas-based TikTok hub called the Hoopla House.

But back in the kitchen with the sounds of the baby possums in our ears, Alice gripped the back of my shirt so persistently I thought it would tear. "I want to go home," she muttered. Her voice took on an adult bitterness that would later mark her speech. "I want to go home."

"Then you win either way," I whispered, detangling from Alice. "You win if you lose and you win if you win. Right?"

"Okay," Alice said softly. "Right."

How wrong I was.

In the diet reality of the show, my sudden departure is attributed to Mom's jealousy. The other mothers accuse her of being jealous of my success, of sabotaging my opportunities with her apathy. In the observation deck, watching me rehearse with Ursula, Alice's and Taylör's mothers' squawking builds—"You never cheer Lucy on, you don't want her to win, you never made it, you're living through your daughter, I would never . . ."

Mom ignores them at first. But the jabs at her failed acting career mount, she gets emotional—the camera pulls into the wet corner of her eye, deeply uncharacteristic of the unshakable Denise—and then she wallops Anna with her handbag. This is replayed several times in the teaser trailers for this season. The handbag makes a satisfying sound as it collides with Anna's head. Security is called, emergency personnel, followed by several frantic shots of the dancing children crying. Denise Ward is escorted off the set by security, and so am I, never to be seen again. It's all very dramatic and sad.

In reality, the morning after I encountered Bruise in the executive office, Mom received an email from Bruise's people. She wanted me, needed me, to star in a conceptual music video for her new song. The email showered me with praise, talked about how taken Bruise was with me each new episode, until she couldn't stand it anymore—she had to have me. "And you know Bruise," her new manager wrote, "when she's actually inspired, we have to move fast."

Like, tomorrow-fast. Already Bruise had fled New York for Los Angeles, the mysterious song written in that hazy flight. Somewhere between Ohio and Colorado, Bruise penned "Escape," the song that would bind us permanently, the song that broke records and platinum deals, the song that even to this day I listen to all the way through, because despite how twisted and ruined my life would become after this song, it's still my favorite song. It's everyone's favorite song. The song of college parties, first loves, long car rides. Mostly, it is a parting song. It's played at a lot of funerals because it is the kind of song that makes even grief beautiful.

"Writing it was like old times," Bruise would later tell me. "I just grabbed a napkin and the lines fell out. Like they had been there all that time."

I did not tell Mom about how I'd run into Bruise up in the office, how she broke the window and kissed my forehead. Mom assumed that Bruise was simply struck by my talent. It was close enough to the truth that I didn't correct her. Bruise's team requested I drop out of DTYD, *Juniors!!* as the timelines did not line up. Very well. In reality, our departure was staged. Mom came away from her final scene still fake-handcuffed, grinning ear to ear.

"Did you see me?" she asked as we got into our NYC taxi, arranged by Bruise's team. We were going into the city so I could learn choreography before heading to Los Angeles the next day.

"Yeah," I replied cheekily. "You were great."

"The acting bug never goes away," she giggled. Mom! Giggling!

"The single tear was a touch," I added. "And such violence!"

"Only half acting. I really wanted to hit that woman."

"So it was all worth it," I stated, hopefully. "The show was . . . dumb, but worth it."

Mom was silent for a while, weighing her response. Finally: "You reeled in a big one."

"*Bruise*," I emphasized.

Mom's phone buzzed, and she began thumbing away. "It's your father. Joel's . . . well . . . he'll be okay. He can make it one more week."

It was my turn to be silent. We had been away so long—two and a half months, minus a few quick visits on weekends—that I had begun to think of Mom and me as a single unit, and my brothers' chaos and that musty house as something entirely separate, something not our problem, certainly not mine.

The taxi was coasting through Greenwich Village, brownstone after brownstone. I stared hard at the leafy and crowded blocks, trying to envision my adult self walking up one of those stoops.

"Did you live here?" I asked Mom. "When you were trying to be an actor?"

She threw her head back, laughed. "No, God no. I was too poor. I lived across all my friends' apartments. Maybe one time, I think, I got to sleep in Greenwich Village—my friend's rich uncle needed a cat sitter. That cat was crazy. Orange and always screaming and then—" Mom palmed her face, remembering.

"Right," she said. "I opened the window and the cat jumped right out. The rich uncle was so mad. Kicked me out a few weeks early. I slept in my car, too embarrassed to tell anyone. Spent the days putting up flyers and walking around alleyways with bags of shredded cheese. God, I felt so bad."

"You were homeless," I said, scandalized.

She did a weird nod-shrug. "No. I was just too embarrassed to tell my friends. They would have let me stay with them."

"You were homeless," I said, louder.

The taxi slowed, arriving at the hotel Bruise's people were putting us up in for the night. A green-coated man rushed out to unload our suitcases.

"The cat came back, by the way," Mom mused. "It had its little adventure and was on the guy's doorstep months later, screaming to get back home."

The next morning, before our flight, we took the train to the off-Broadway studio. In that crowded train, in my leotard and tights and thick Uggs, I was happy again, primed to be dancing again, truly dancing, not recycling the same eight count. Mom was happy to be back reading her thick death-doula books in the corner of the rehearsal space, finally a true stage mom again, ignored, perfunctory. The choreographer was European and each time we worked together, his V-neck got deeper and deeper.

"So you're the precocious Lucy," he declared when we first met.

"I don't know," I replied, meaning that I didn't know that word or if I was what it suggested.

He squinted at me. "I told Bruise not to work with children. Her material—the material she wants to get out—it's not for children, you see. But then she called me, all fired up, saying you're different."

"Oh," I said weakly. "Well—"

He tossed me a mannequin. "And this is your dancing partner. Bruise said it's essential you feel this mannequin like . . . a partner."

"Oh—" I said louder. The mannequin was heavy, all limp-boned and rough to the touch. By the time I met it again in the Los Angeles warehouse, its arms and legs would be detached, and the artist would paint sleeping eyes on its chest. Magenta, many-lashed.

The choreographer was still muttering: "And I was thinking it would be just another sexy dance for sexy children. But then I hear the song. And I realize, you must be special, if you made Bruise write like the old Bruise."

He was opening his MacBook and pulling up the audio file. He pressed *play*. And her voice—her real voice—filled the studio.

I don't know this Bruise, I thought to myself after the choreographing session ended and Mom and I were heading back to the hotel in a packed train. During the filming of DTYD, *Juniors!!* I hadn't thought much of her, besides as the disengaged and eccentrically dressed judge. I was more fixed on Ursula, the former dancer, as the celebrity to bolster my career. Bruise was a popular singer, yes, but she had been popular for so long I felt almost numb to her stardom. But now I began to wonder, with a sense of urgency, as I stood pressed against Mom during rush hour, looking up at the vacant faces of New Yorkers, how many other people I had overlooked.

Before we caught our red-eye, Mom took me around her New York City. First she showed me a diner that used to be another diner where she used to beg for leftover coffee and fries while working on her plays in some corner booth. At this new diner, we read off glossy menus and ate specialty burgers. We had gotten into a really nice groove, Mom and me. Separated from our regular lives, we had become a real team, busting out of the reality show early, relishing our freedom by spending decadent nights lying on hotel bedsheets, eating room service, and watching crappy TV. Neither of us mentioned that, soon, we would be on the other end of that equation. No—instead, Mom gave me a tour of her life pre-me. We snuck into a Broadway play for just fifteen minutes to say we caught a play. Mom still knew all the secret tricks. We walked block after block after block, Mom pointing out an Old Navy that used to be the playhouse her friend started, an apartment complex where an old boyfriend lived, the street corner where she almost got murdered. The first hospital she worked at. The coffee shop—now another Old Navy—where she first got her idea for *August 8*. It was the nineties and the early aughts and Mom and her friends were trying to make it as art people, by day hacking away at day jobs and by night gathering to trade audition war stories and pitches.

In the background of all this hummed Bruise, the new star, the one who had just made it. To Mom, Bruise's earliest music was summer nights in Brooklyn, a dirt-patch courtyard and the starless sky, and your friends all close, saying, *someday, someday.* Back then, Bruise was real: a seventeen-year-old girl with mousy hair, sequined jeans, and yellow teeth. Her first album was all about how ugly love could be—the grotesque lyrics coupled with her pretty voice was delightfully off-putting. In those early nineties' afternoons, you could not go two blocks without hearing the album being blasted, without seeing Bruise's baby face on magazines and television ads. Not much was known about where she came from. It is like she was just suddenly there on every billboard, commercial, and kids' choice awards. Tabloids speculated—sex, blackmail, more sex.

Mom and her friends didn't mind how she'd come by fame. For them, Bruise embodied what it was to be an artist in the real world, someone who bottled lightning and doled it out spark by spark. In time it became clear Bruise's success was exactly as rare as being struck by lightning, and one by one Mom's cohort scattered for safer shores, until she was one of the last ones still peddling her plays, still riding in the back of an ambulance, still auditioning and pitching, and still only getting called back for roles like "Fat Mean Babysitter." It was also Bruise's songs playing in the coffee shop when Mom and Dad first met. Bruise's mournful voice hovering about my parents' heads while they stirred milk into their coffee and discussed salamanders, dead wives named Lacy and motherless sons, abusive parents and apocalypse plays that never get made, broken dreams and characters named Lucy.

"You know," Mom said, voice tinged with humor. "Bruise's songs actually inspired my final scene for *August 8*. I was listening to her when I finished the final, final draft."

Imagine: finishing your magnum opus on a Tuesday afternoon a few months after your courthouse wedding. Mom still wrote in brief snatches during the day, while the boys were at school. She wrote "the end" for the final time, and then the screen door clattered—Joel, ten, his fingers blackened with charcoal and crayon, asking if she wanted to see the latest sketch he'd crafted to spook the poor grief therapist. Then I arrived. Unexpected—she was forty-seven and didn't think it was possible. Life still had some surprises left. So one final shot: She mailed *August 8* off to playhouses and publications near and far and wide, heard nothing back. Unsurprising. Well. Life goes on.

"Get out," I said. "But your stuff is serious." Not that I'd read any.

We were walking down some liminal New York street, flinting between dark residentials and flashing bodegas. Mom's face was jigsawed in light.

"Her stuff was serious," Mom said. "Sad, funny, serious. Weird."

"Like your stuff," I added.

"Hardly. My stuff . . . well, I don't know if I'd even call it stuff at this point."

We were waiting at a stoplight. I was beginning to get impatient—I wanted to go back to the hotel so we could get ready to make our flight.

"Who's Kons?" I asked suddenly.

"Oh," Mom laughed. "Patrick Kons. He wrote that movie *Dead Heart* fifteen, twenty years ago? The horror one that's a cult classic. He kind of dropped off the map after that. People laugh at it. Your brothers especially."

"Hmm," I said.

Mom was back to musing about Bruise: "It was a bummer that she sold out so quickly. After that first album, she just did pop junk for years and years. But seems like she's trying to go back to what made her famous in the first place."

"A return to form," I added, a phrase Mom often used. The light changed, we crossed into some square park, all mulch and playground. A couple was on the swings, talking loudly about something. It was hard to tell if they were fighting or laughing. Mom sighed her heavy sigh and pulled out her phone.

"Can I read your play when we get back home?" I asked. "The *August* one?"

Mom squinted into the bright square of her phone. "I think we missed a turn."

On July 28, 2016, we landed in Los Angeles, where I would spend the majority of my dwindling childhood. A driver met us curbside at LAX's arrivals, ushered us into a tinted black SUV. I pressed my face against the dark window, my eyes sucking in all that was still alien: palm trees, stucco walls, flat desert. By the time Bruise's motor gate was opening, the sky was dark. I didn't perceive the scope of her estate until the following morning. The mansion itself was built into the craggy hill below, so when we walked across the driveway, we saw only the top third: white walls, a flat roof, and a tall glass doorway. My mom rang the doorbell.

"Mom!" I chastised.

"What?" she sighed. "Celebrities don't use doorbells?"

But the doorway parted and there was Bruise, clad only in a T-shirt dress depicting the autopsy report of Kurt Cobain. Her earlobes hung low with chunks of amethyst. Fuzzy no-slip socks. A casual look.

"Welcome," she said in her breathy voice. "Welcome, welcome."

The mansion inside was large and empty and clean and grand, betraying its tiny front-facing appearance. Such was the way of all wealthy housing in Los Angeles, I would learn. The door opened into a loft-lounge area the size of my old house. Most of it was nothing but smooth white floor, save for a cluster of modernist armchairs by a black railing, where a chandelier—a stalagmite of dripping light—presided over the actual mansion below. We followed Bruise down the coiling staircase to the open-concept second floor. Her current lover reclined in an oversized leather armchair, examining his own hand. Without looking at us, he drawled: "The talent has arrived."

"Oh," Mom said. "You're Matt Callus."

"I'm Matt Callus," Matt Callus said. He was a young screenwriter Mom had followed ever since she watched his debut film, *Neptune, Neptune*, at the Coolidge Corner Theatre with Dad. The black-and-white flick was about a priest who tried to have sex with the ocean.

"I loved it," Mom gushed to Matt. "The way the movie balanced historical accuracy with . . ."

"The ocean fu— copulation," Matt Callus said, with a glance down at me.

"This house is nice," I said awkwardly.

"You're telling me," Matt Callus said. "When I came to LA, I lived in a studio that had no kitchen."

"All in time," Bruise said dreamily. She gave us the tour of her mansion. The floor we'd met Matt Callus on was framed entirely by a glass slider opening to the deck, so there was, as Bruise put it, "a seamless indoor-outdoor experience." Mostly it was a white-on-white experience: white tables and white chairs and white leather couches, separated by such a great distance that my kid brain imagined that rollerblading was the only conceivable reason you'd have this much empty white space. The next floor was the kitchen, a massive marble island with golden faucets and three ovens and a servants' pantry all four of us could walk into. Bruise proudly claimed she had no servants and no assistants, hiring help only when she hosted parties— and even then she only hired up-and-coming screenwriters and actors to wait on her industry friends, just in case all they needed was that connection.

"That's how we met," Matt Callus said, and Mom and I waited to see if he would elaborate on their relationship. In the pantry, I noticed Bruise had three boxes of Cheez-Its and I thought that was funny, like, huh, celebrities like Cheez-Its, too.

After a weird pause, Matt Callus touched Bruise's elbow. "We must show them the basement."

"Yes," Bruise said. And so the four of us sauntered down to the basement, composed of low lights and dark mahogany beams, giving it the feeling of an endless labyrinth. They showed us various saunas and movie theaters and wine rooms and treadmills that lurked in smooth concrete rooms, and even the black pod that Matt Callus said was a sensory deprivation tank. Bruise said it helped with creativity. Matt Callus claimed he'd thought up the plot of his latest script in there. Mom tried to explain why it made your brain hallucinate. "Mm," Bruise said every time Mom finished a sentence. We all stared down at the fat kidney bean, where I would lose my virginity in a year and a half's time.

Finally Bruise and Matt Callus brought us to his writing room, a dark oaky office with pages of scripts hanging clothesline style all around. I felt Mom light up.

She inspected a hanging page. "Can I?"

"Of course," Matt Callus said proudly. "Read away."

Bruise squeezed my shoulders. "Let me show you the outside," she whispered in my ear.

So I left Mom with Matt Callus and his logline and followed Bruise outside. Here would be my favorite place in the world, for a time: Bruise's backyard. As Bruise slid open another massive glass slider, I inhaled sharply. A stucco patio shaded by olive trees and a lattice tangled with vines and flowers. A broad swath of turf before a glass infinity pool, lit by alternating rainbow lights. Just beyond the infinity pool was the entirety of Los Angeles, a shimmering, horizonless ocean of stars, like the universe had flipped and I was peering down into the cosmos.

"Heaven," I said, and Bruise chuckled.

"That's not even all of it."

A metal-cage enclosure was hidden on the left side of her yard. Bruise undid the latch and I waited for her to emerge with a chicken. Instead, she came out clutching an infant sloth in a purple onesie.

"Ah!" I squealed. "Cute!"

Wordlessly, she transferred the mewling sloth to my chest. His long furry arms reached up, a hard claw touched my jawline, another wrapped around the back of my neck.

"It's so little," I mused.

"I just got these brothers yesterday." Bruise reached into the enclosure and pulled out another baby sloth in a yellow onesie. He was even smaller, mewling like crazy.

"Here," Bruise said. "We can feed them while enjoying the view."

Cradling the sloth, I followed Bruise to the edge of the cliff. We lapsed into silence, feeding the sloths until they unlatched and yawned in unison.

"Where you'd get them?" I finally asked.

Bruise explained they'd been orphaned because of deforestation in Nicaragua. Companies burned the rainforests there—a thousand acres a day. These guys were badly burned when the protection agency found them. Their mother either died or abandoned them.

She rocked her sloth back and forth. The baby's eyes, black and wet, began to droop.

"But I saved them," Bruise whispered. "I saved them."

Joel

I'd left Joel in the living room of the Leominster house, and I more or less expected him to be there when I returned. Maybe he'd break into another abandoned house. Maybe he'd sketch, crumple it up, sketch again. Maybe a few parties in the woods. Maybe he'd drive around the reservation with his girlfriend, and they'd talk about trauma or make out or argue or get high together in her shitty Honda. Maybe all the above. But those parts of him I didn't see clearly yet.

Later, I would try to retrace his steps those last few days before everything changed. How quiet the house would have been without me or Mom or Micah. Dad probably just watching *The X Files*. Joel painting in the garage. More likely: Joel, high, scrubbing through social media. Another person announcing gallery representation. A former classmate's cartoon pitch had sold to the highest bidder. His girlfriend's text eclipsed his feed, asking if he wanted to come over, she had something new. Inevitably, my mind paired these conjectures with my own steps that early morning. Bruise softly knocked on the guest room door. Mom, sleeping beside me, didn't stir.

"Big day," Bruise whispered when I opened the door. "I wanted to show you something."

She took me into her bedroom, the floor plan the size of our house back in Leominster. But totally empty, no Matt Callus in sight. White walls and carpet, a white bed, a white nightstand, which Bruise rummaged through until she found what she was looking for.

"This is me when I was a little older than you." She handed me a waxy, yellowed Polaroid. I stared at it, still bleary from sleep and unsure what to say. The girl in the Polaroid was unsmiling, leaning against a red convertible and squinting into the sun.

"We were testing album covers," Bruise continued. "My manager at the time—also my boyfriend—had me lean against this random car. I was sixteen and so embarrassed, afraid the owner would come out and yell at me. I knew I had something special, but I felt like a poseur. Still. I would have done anything to make it big. I had to escape. Like the song title."

I nodded, following. She wanted me to understand her so I could convey it properly in dance. She was testing me. Later I would wonder if it mattered if I understood "Escape" or not, if she would have assumed my genius no matter how I danced. At the time, it felt like it truly mattered, that it all came down to this one music video, my dream life on the other side. I had amputated so many parts of myself—student, friend, teammate, crush—all to become this kind of dancer. So I asked, "What were you escaping?"

Bruise smiled sadly, looking down at her past-self. "A very small and dark place."

When I returned to the guest room, Mom was already dressed. Call time was 6:00 AM. "Big day!" I said, throwing up my hands.

"Are you nervous?"

"No," I lied.

"We should call your brothers for good luck," she said, getting out her phone.

"But it's LA time," I said. "Which means it's like 2:00 AM their time." I had gotten the time zones reversed—Leominster was three hours ahead, around eight in the morning.

Mom nodded. "We'll have to call after, then. Ah! We should have brought them here!"

"Even Joel?" I asked, half joking.

"'Course," Mom said. "Maybe he'd like California. I always thought he'd end up somewhere bright and artsy."

On the drive to the studio, I stared out at all the brightness LA offered and imagined my brother here, too—concurrently wondering what he was doing right now.

5:51, Los Angeles.
He would like it, I think. The sun butters the highway. Meanwhile, I'm breathing through a panic attack. Mom's making pleasant conversation with Bruise about the election. She's trying to convince Bruise to at least post on her socials for Hillary. Bruise is saying it's uncomfortable to have that much sway in what people think.

5:58, Los Angeles.
"Lucy girl, before we go inside, I want to say—when I watch you dance, it's like

8:51, Leominster.
Joel, alone, sits on the edge of his girlfriend's bed. He counts out pills and stares into his palm, a diver peering over the precipice, into the pool. On the other side of the wall: TV blares, his girlfriend dozes. He knocks back the stuff, closes his eyes, eager for that dark, thoughtless place his mind crawls toward.

8:58, Leominster.
"Joel?"
  "How many did you take, Joel?"

Lucky Girl · 109

falling in love. You woke me up. You saved my life. And now—I'm going to change yours."

"Joel, why . . ."
"Joel, say something."

"Cue music!" the set director yelled, and there was a pause before it really began.

My body was a struck chord. Humming, ready. Discreetly, I pulled the red thong out of my butt crack. Think pieces would think much about the red panties and the red bra, how disturbing and awkward the dichotomy between child body and sexy clothes, but many argued that disturbance was necessary so we could see the pain young Bruise went through. For days after, my butt crack and rib cage itched.

The music video set was a dollhouse: three walls, chinaware, coffee tables. Get well cards on the coffee table, a dirty casserole dish in the sink. Faceless mannequins dressed to the nines: cabled sweaters, pearl necklaces, sleek wigs. My starting position straddled a headless mannequin, lying stiff on a hospital cot. All the other mannequins faced away from us, grief personified on their backs. But beyond the dollhouse, all eyes were on me. Everyone on set—PAs unspooling wires, Bruise in her big coat—counted on my dancing. My eyes searched for Mom. I needed to see her one last time. Make it like before a competition dance, like it was just the two of us ahead of everyone. She would nod at me once, sternly, communicating, *Get it done, Lucy*. But when I finally spotted Mom, she wasn't even watching me. She was on her phone, talking urgently, and I—

Bruise's bottled voice rang out: *Love is a prison cell but we're the jailer . . .*

Me

There was the song and there I went. The music was not Bruise's regular pop. Gut-punched, full-throated. The notes almost got away from Bruise, high and higher and even higher. I bared my teeth, I leapt and I landed so hard I felt my kneecaps shift, my skin tear. When I twirled, I let myself spin out. If I collided with a mannequin, so be it. As Bruise's voice reached crescendo, everything melted: the set, the cameras, and my worry. My body chased the choreography: reach, reach, kick, illusion to the floor, crawl to the mannequin, place a hand on its smooth chest, shake it, plead, dance-plead, cartwheel and take the torso along for the ride, waltz with the mannequin, spin with the mannequin, until my eyes watered, and here was the big finishing move, but then—

Mom

"Joel, this better be—"
"Who is this?"
"Honey, calm down."
"Yes, I'm the stepmom."
"Blue skin? His lips—"
"How long—"
"Do you have Narcan?"
"Hang up and call 911."
. . .
"Cody, pick up—"
. . .
"Cody! Joel's—"

I collided into Mom's stomach, falling backward. The mannequin clattered to the floor. For a beat, my brain couldn't process what had happened. She had stepped onto set before the take was over. She had ruined the take. The camera was still recording, Bruise's song still playing. No one reacted, not even me, not even Bruise or any of the set people. Mom grabbed my hand.

"We need to go," she said, quietly to me, then louder, addressing the entire crowd. "There's a family emergency, and we need to go."

I wiggled out of her grasp. "I haven't even done one take yet."

"Lucy, we have to go."

"Why? What's happened?"

She opened her mouth, but before she could explain, Bruise stepped onto set, weaving between mannequins. "A family emergency?"

"I'm sorry," Mom said to Bruise. I had never seen her like this, desperate. "We need to leave right away. I'm so sorry."

Bruise was clutching her chest. "What happened?"

Mom looked down at her phone, a blank screen. "My son . . ."

Oh. I relaxed. Micah probably twisted his ankle on the trail or Joel got caught by the police again sneaking into some ghostly warehouse. "We can't leave," I repeated. "This is a job, I can't walk off."

She gave me a withering look. Like she hated me. "This is serious," Mom said. "Joel . . ."

I stared up at her, waiting. But she couldn't say it.

"I need to make another call," Mom said absently, ire dissolved. Again I relaxed, my focus returning to the dance, on the next take, I'd—but then, Mom grabbed my arm.

"Let's go outside. I'll tell you there."

"No," I hissed. "Mom, you're making a scene."

The production people. The cameras. Bruise. Even the faceless mannequins. My heart, a kicking rabbit in my chest. Mom's grip tightened. Her voice was strangely thin.

Mom said, "Lucy, I need you."

And I said, "But I have to dance."

Her phone vibrated and Mom released me, made her way outside, as I later learned, to triangulate Joel's status, charter flights back home, and speak medical lingo at the emergency doctors poised to receive Joel at the hospital.

Bruise rested a hand on my shoulder. "Your mom is dramatic."

More to myself, I said, "I hope it isn't really bad."

"My mom once called seventy times right before my first show. I ignored each one. Turned out, my father had died. Lung cancer. Long time coming."

"Oh," I said. "I'm sorry."

"But what I put on stage that night, I've never re-created. It was . . . it really was." Bruise was holding my shoulder, and she squeezed harder as she remembered whatever it was. "Use this, Lucy girl. That's how we'll make something real."

I flashed a smile and thanked her. Resumed the starting position while the little dollhouse became a beehive of activity as production reset the mannequins, dusted my bruised knees, rewound the record, trained the camera to my face, completely neutral as I brought myself back to a body waiting for its signal. Five minutes later, I danced the most watched music video of all time, perfect in one take. On the other side of this take, Mom would be herself again, composed, controlled. But across those five minutes, something broke between us.

Seven hours later, my body was thrown across the country and landed in a hospital waiting room, the scratchy lingerie set still beneath my jeans. When "Escape" dropped, everything changed. But everything changed anyway, because from then on I knew Joel was an addict.

The hospital felt empty except for Dad, sleeping, head tilted up, every few seconds punctured by a great snore. Micah tapping his foot beside me. Mom was at the nurses' station—of course, she knew the nurses—talking in low conspiratorial tones. Somewhere past midnight, Micah nudged me to get air, and we found ourselves in an echoey parking garage.

"I should have been home," Micah whispered. "Fuck."

Lucky Girl • 113

"It's not your fault," I said, more to myself.

"I knew he was spiraling."

"It's not your fault," I said again.

"Fuck!" Micah spat, kicking a concrete post. In answer, a car chirped. Someone using their keys to wake their vehicle. Then and there I decided God did not exist. We went back to the waiting room.

When I came off the set after the real take, Bruise was crying. She took me into her arms, thanked me again and again. "You brought it back, Lucy girl," she whispered into my hair. "You recaptured the magic I lost."

He woke, and it was a miracle. When the doctor told us, my family sprinted to his room. Except me. For the first time, my body betrayed me. I couldn't will myself over the threshold and join them. Joel's head was bowed, he was crying, and Mom was standing over him crying, and Dad was crying and Micah, too. Then Joel must have made a joke, because Mom cuffed him on the head. Micah was reenacting "borrowing" a car to get home in time. Dad, still crying. It was like a scene from a TV show, something I had watched so many times that when it arrived in real life, it felt almost like a performance.

If I had gone inside, if I had willed my body, Joel would have spotted me behind Micah. He would have said something ridiculous to offset the tension. I would have laughed, would have said something ridiculous back. Then cried—I would have let myself go. I would have stayed home, would have watched Patrick Kons's stupid movies and listened to Bruise's new music. I would have been there to welcome Joel home from rehab. I would have been there when he first read *August 8* and thought, *This could be a video game.* Maybe I would have seen Joel finally drawing again, late into the night, his mind cleared and purposeful like it hadn't been in a long time, his hands retracing plots Mom had written many years ago. Maybe I would have helped or maybe I would have rolled my eyes, lost in some arcane teen drama. But I would have been there.

Instead, I stayed frozen outside his door. Pulling out my phone, I refreshed and refreshed Bruise's YouTube, waiting for the music video to drop—for my guilt to dissipate, for my life to change, for my name to be everywhere, for Bruise to whisk me back to Los Angeles. Already, I knew my vaulting ambition would drown Mom and she would sign off on Bruise as my guardian on set because she needed to take care of Joel, to supervise his every waking hour so this never happened again. Fine. Bruise would be there for me when I got off the plane, her smile bright and wide, her arms outstretched. She would squeeze me in a tight embrace, she would sway and hold me a little too long, she would whisper in my ear—

"All right, Lucy girl. Let's make magic."

Act II: Fame

The Alix DeJesus Show

The talk show host asked Bruise about our relationship. All segment long, they had been dancing around the subject, raving about the success of "Escape," how it gave so many people hope after the 2016 election—then they pontificated about the meaning of hope, how Bruise needed hope when she was a little girl, how all little girls needed hope in the wake of Trump's presidency. Bruise told the story of the night after the election, how we drove to the deepest stretch of desert to scream our female rage into the starry abyss—though if I had been on that couch, I would have reminded her that we only joked about doing that but never really did—and finally Alix DeJesus leaned in, narrowed her eyes, and asked, "So, what is your relationship with Lucy?"

A picture from our performance at the Music Awards last week flashed up on the overhead television. Bruise sang behind a curtain, and I capered around stage. In the picture, my face is snarling, unrecognizable in hyper-felt agony and joy. That had been a good night; I danced in front of the largest audience ever in my career. Celebrity after celebrity gushed about my dancing, but what I remember most is the second before we went on stage, Bruise whispering in my ear: "Wake them up, Lucy girl. Wake them all up."

Bruise's gaze found me, in the wings, itching beneath the red mesh of my bra. After they were done talking, we would perform "Escape." I had danced the choreography on so many live shows that each move was ingrained in my body, which was growing rapidly, but I stretched religiously and ate sensibly no matter where I was, which was increasingly one of the many guest rooms of Bruise's mansion. Staying there between gigs just made more and more sense. It was hard to be home, too, the place from which everyone else had fled: Joel to rehab, Dad to depression, Micah to the Pacific Northwest, and Mom to double shifts in the hospice.

Bruise said, "As soon as I met Lucy, I felt like I was home."

Teen Girl Photoshoot

Mom texted right before I went into hair and makeup. I was behind in online school. She was getting emails: I had a geometry test overdue and a narrative essay due on the eighth.

K, I shot back. All our texts were now like that, dwindling in length and frequency by the second.

"Chin up," Bruise's stylist ordered me. Her name was Charley, and she was cool, like, in-her-twenties cool. She often hung out with us, lugging her palette kit so we could have impromptu photoshoots on the beach or by the pool. She was the first person to shape my eyebrows. Charley was best at Instagram captions that didn't seem like you were trying. Bruise's January 18, 2017, Instagram of her face: half drag makeup and the other half nude, captioned *im tired.* All Charley.

"What's with the mug?" she asked. "You look worried."

I told her I had forgotten an important geometry test.

"Stop, don't tell me you're in middle school," she said, her voice tinged almost in disgust. "Where do you find the time?"

"Clearly, I don't." I tried not to flinch as the brush tickled my cheek. "I'm super behind."

"Honey, we can help!" Bruise yelled across the room. She was in a bathrobe, her breast out, eating a banana.

"Your boob's out." Charley rolled her eyes. "Lucy is a minor."

Bruise tossed the peel in the trash, declared: "Lucy is a dancer. She's not afraid of the human body."

I nodded, trying to play it cool. Bruise often went topless at home, warming tortillas and cheese in the microwave and yelping when nacho shrapnel landed on her collarbone. She liked to start each day drinking coffee at the edge of her backyard, where all of LA could feasibly get a view of her bare chest if they just looked up. At first, it did unnerve me. But then it became normal. As with most things in California, I was shocked at how quickly I got used to it.

Charley finished my face and patted the top of my head. "All done."

"Okay," I said, pulling up the geometry test on my shitty Chromebook and narrowing my eyes at the first problem: "So let ABCD be a rectangle inscribed in a circle with a radius X. The length of BC is equal to b and the length of AD is equal to a."

"Huh." Bruise put her fragrant head on my shoulder and squinted at my Chromebook. "Where are the numbers?"

Charley rounded on Bruise, asking, "What did the *Vogue* people want on you?"

I told Bruise, "My brother always said the higher you go in math, the less the numbers matter. Then it's all about concepts."

"Is he hot?" Charley asked lightly, angling Bruise's cheek and applying highlighter, freaky sharp like usual.

"Girl!" Bruise said.

"I'm lonely," Charley whined.

"He's . . ." I started, but my thoughts loosened. My brain always clouded when I tried to bring up my family because the right words no longer came. Plus, Bruise's face always tripped me up when I talked about my family. It wasn't unkind, but smoother than usual, tense without seeming tense.

Then Bruise went, "Hey, we're going to the Women's March after this, right?"

"Yeah dude," Charley said. "I've got our picket signs all designed."

Election night was when I'd first met Charley. I had been living—for lack of a better word—on and off with Bruise for a few months when she hosted a little election watch party with all her friends, which somehow ballooned to two hundred people. Of course, they were all liberal Hollywood types, so the night quickly descended into drunk, weepy chaos. Matt Callus sweated through his blue suit in the sauna, reciting *King Lear* as if it were prophecy. Bruise just kept her eyes glued on the television screen as red blotted the country, trying to convince anyone in earshot that this was not the end, that if we got Arizona and Michigan . . . Mostly, people drank and wept in clusters by stairwells, the infinity pool, the patios. I snuck away to be alone in a guest room, to watch *Calamity Kitchen* in peace. Everyone was acting like the world was ending, so I needed my comfort show, where chefs were forced to cook through absurd situations. Contestants were whisking quail eggs in an absurdly large bowl when Charley randomly burst in, furiously scrolling on her phone.

"Jesus fuck!" she shouted when she nearly walked right into me. "You're that girl. The dancing girl."

"People are going crazy," I explained, almost apologetic. The only thing I felt about Trump being elected was enormous guilt for not feeling enough. Probably it would have registered more if I had been with my old family, my old friends, my old studio. If I had seen my teachers and parents reacting, I would have had something to mark this event by. But in this world, everything seemed dialed to eleven.

"It's always been crazy," Charley sighed. "White people are just catching on."

I laughed, as if I was not a white person also just catching on.

She plopped down next to me, asking what show we were watching. Then we were watching *Calamity Kitchen* and chatting like we were old friends, and just like that, everything seemed to realign. Of course, now I know Charley was just as bewildered as I was, almost as young, nineteen to my thirteen. Like me, she was new to Bruise's orbit, plucked to be her stylist after Bruise happened upon her popular YouTube series where she did literary-themed looks: Ophelia from *Hamlet*, Camilla from *The Secret History*, Lauren from *Parable of the Sower*. She was studying theater design at Emerson College when Bruise suddenly dropped into her DMs with the offer of a lifetime, alluring enough for her to drop out and not look back; well, not look back too much. Now what I know about Charley suggests that probably seconds prior to meeting me, she had retched in the second-floor bathroom, dialed and redialed her old college friends' numbers without pressing send, before stumbling into a random room and finding me, tiny and thirteen and shell-shocked. And Charley did what she will always do: She put on a show to make others happy.

This photoshoot was the first of many in my career. It was for *TeenGirl*, accompanied by a review of "Escape" and an interview with Bruise, where she gushed about how my dancing had inspired her to finally create something real again. I was not interviewed, merely included in the photo spread as an accessory to Bruise. She and I wore matching lavender dresses, fluttery and sheer. Against a white backdrop, we embraced each other, our faces nearly touching, mouths agape as if we were both mid-yawn.

"God, I'm hungry," Bruise whispered to me between shots. "Let's grab something before the march."

After stopping for lunch, we met Bruise's manager or publicist or agent—I was never sure—Lena, in downtown Los Angeles for the Women's March.

"There's a guy in a bear suit," she told us as we got out of the car. "He has a sign that says, 'Eat the Rich.' Get it? Because he's a bear."

"Damn," Charley said. "I just have 'Love Trumps Hate.'"

We followed Lena into the throng of people in pink dimpled hats. As soon as we were moving within the chanting crowd, I realized I hated crowds. The electric crackle zipping between bodies set me on edge. Instead, I tried to fix my brain on the geometry problem, tracking an invisible triangle with points ABCD and circle X . . . but the image was impossible to hold as each screaming face enveloped my vision. Bruise screamed the most, Charley some, and Lena not at all. I liked reading the signs—"Pussy Grabs Back" and MLK quotes and "Not My President" and "I'm With Her." Bruise pointed to one, "Our Children Are Watching," and commented, "That's you, Lucy girl."

"Please," Lena remarked. "They mean six-year-olds that don't know what's going on. Lucy is fully aware and participating."

At the time, I assumed Lena was in her forties, but more likely she was in her mid-to-late thirties. Bruise had just hired her, saying that with the sudden fame of "Escape" she needed someone fresh and new to take us to fresh and new directions. To me, Lena didn't seem fresh or new: She always wore the exact same black turtleneck and black skinny jeans. Her hair was a pixie cut perpetually styled with the same model-y flatness. Prior to being scouted by Bruise, she'd helped tween singer-songwriter Jay Corpus make the leap from Disney star to real star when she got him onto a slew of indie films, one of which snagged an Oscar. Lena was always three steps ahead, booking the talk shows and the photoshoots, keeping things moving. And she had to keep moving—Bruise had told me that she was in the middle of a sudden and bitter divorce, that her wife had taken their dog. She was throwing herself into work, which was nice for us, because Lena was good at work.

"Get on the steps and hold up your signs," she told us, angling her phone sideways.

Charley, Bruise, and I got into a formation on the steps of some government building, while the march bottlenecked farther down. We held up our signs and pouted our faces. This was not a smiling matter. Everyone except for me was wearing sunglasses, so we looked cool and serious. In my head, I was calculating and recalculating the area of a circle with its radius . . . or was it the triangle?

"Good, good," Lena kept saying, taking shot after shot.

"The caption should be 'girls just want fundamental rights,'" Charley said.

"Should we keep going?" I asked, watching the writhing snake of people.

"I think we've done enough," Bruise said, scrolling through the pictures.

"Now what?" I asked.

Bruise said, "My friend just opened a restaurant in La Brea. We should support him—he is an immigrant, after all."

When we got home, it was late. Matt Callus was in his writer's room, writing, for he felt his presence was unwelcome at the Women's

March. Bruise took me outside to talk. Bruise loved a deep talk, which meant talking about Patrick Kons. Since "Escape," he had been texting again. "What about Matt?" I asked. "Why keep him around?" And Bruise laughed and said, "Lucy, you're a riot." It was late by the time I climbed up to the guest room. The place was still plain, like a hotel, the sheets crisp and cold, always reset whenever I returned. Despite her claims about having no servants, Bruise had cleaners, though we were always out early and in late those days and I never saw them. I labored over the geometry problem and the narrative essay, scribbling an illiterate piece about the Women's March. By 3:00 AM, I was finished. The room was dark and empty and for the first time that day, I felt like I'd accomplished something.

Done, I texted my mom, who didn't respond.

Charity Work

Every other night, it seemed, Bruise hosted a party. Someone she knew had released a music video. A TV pilot. A movie. Or there was a birthday. A charity event. Bruise was a slut for a good charity event, especially for animals. Save the Dolphins. Save the Elephants. Save the Tamarins. Save the Wild Horses. The orangutans with their pensive eyes. But regardless of charity or entertainment, the parties always devolved the same. Always it started with just the four of us: Charley and Lena and Bruise and me, lounging around the inside-outside family room, talking about random shit, passing the Bechdel test. Then, the first actor would arrive. Then, a director, a writer, a gaggle of suited men. Tiny cubes of cheese appeared, crackers slathered in rich marmalade. A buzzy chitchat, drinks sloshed together, glasses clinking, inevitably shattering. A litter of puppies in champagne flutes, Bruise tenderly kissing each one, pledging to adopt them all. In the morning, she rose early and took them diligently outside to potty, fed them scraps of tenderloin and little pails of whole milk. But a month later, Bruise would vanish, another song on the tip of her tongue, and the puppies were left to roam the mansion, wild, until Lena quietly found them suitable homes.

Ring-tailed lemurs, their soft leathery fingers hooked around my thumb.

Lizards and snails and snakes blinking as if life itself was agonizingly boring. They made me think of Dad, so I stayed away from them.

The crickets for the lizards got loose, and the hallways chirped like the announcement of a plague for days after.

Those nights at Bruise's all blurred together, dissolved into murky shreds of moments, where in between I would return home to Leominster and wonder if they'd ever happened. Home was quiet. Since Joel's overdose, home swelled like a beached, half-rotten whale. Unused seed packets, hobby magazines, grimy snow globes, rusted gardening shears—things my father refused to throw out. Dad parked in the living room, the television a flickering candle. Micah working a new job at Lowe's. Mom on a double shift. Joel stuffed away in rehab. I was a ghost there. Dancing in the garage. Scrubbing brown filaments off the sink and mold off the shower. Ignoring the pictures of us before the fame on the mantel, all together and smiling and squinting at the camera.

Bruise once rescued a little Chihuahua named Moxie. He died eight months later; he had cancer, and she knew he had cancer, and she had adopted him anyway. The limited timeline actually worked to their benefit. She was diligent with Moxie, as she always was with her babies in the first months, administering medicine and feeding him hunks of boiled steak. When it was time, she remained with him even when I went into the next room, scared to see the end. She sang as he fell asleep in her arms. When she came out, I was surprised to see her face so unemotional, almost bored.

She told me, "There's no pop song for dead dogs, Lucy girl. And it's a shame."

Only much later did I think I could have asked why she didn't write one.

Bruise filled her basement with water in solidarity with Flint, Michigan. We all gathered outside and watched workers pump it full of tap water while Bruise talked to the press about awareness. The bottom windows, which you could see from the backyard, became waxy and distorted. Bruise had flown in some children from Flint for the charity event. They were my age and younger, and they all wore the same bright red T-shirt, which read "We Need Clean Water." All the kids wanted was to swim in her basement, but Bruise couldn't let them for insurance reasons. So instead, we built pyramids of plastic water bottles and made a game out of hurling water balloons at them.

"This is lame as heck," one of the Flint kids muttered under his breath.

Once, when I was home in Leominster, I offered Mom money. I knew I had a lot. Since "Escape," Lena had set up my Coogan account, even called Mom and walked her through the finances in the world's most terse Zoom call. So Mom also knew how much money I had, knew she had access to 15 percent of my net worth: eight hundred thousand dollars.

"You guys could buy a new house," I suggested. "Or a second one, in LA."

"It's your money," she shot back without looking at me. "When you're eighteen."

She was driving me back to the airport. Bruise needed me that week. "You know I don't care about money," I added. "I just want to dance."

"Well," Mom said. "You are."

She brought me to the gate. Bruise would meet me at LAX, insisting on driving herself so we could gab about everything I had missed. When the week was over, Mom would be waiting for me in a beat-up Honda. The ride to Leominster would be static electricity. I would be filled with these crazy LA stories I longed to tell Mom, while she spoke only about how Joel was doing, which would make me frozen with guilt. As soon as she dropped me off, she would turn back to hospice, administering morphine to withered veins, opening blinds and hanging bird feeders outside the windows, informing loved ones in her brutal way that it would happen soon. An hour, a day, maybe a week. Make every second count.

Bruise probably watched *The Lake House* about two hundred and eighty times. You've seen the movie? Probably not. It is a 2006 Keanu Reeves and Sandra Bullock flick about a man and a woman who fall in love through a time-traveling mailbox. Charley, Lena, and I always wanted to make fun of it because the whole thing was so tantalizingly make-fun-able, but Bruise viciously swore us to seriousness each time she turned it on, which was all the time. After rehearsals, before rehearsals, chilling out before parties and especially after parties. Once, she told me that as a kid, her celebrity crush was Keanu Reeves. They say you stop mentally aging the day you turn famous, so I am forever twelve and Bruise is forever seventeen, watching *Bill & Ted's Excellent Adventure* in a wood-paneled basement.

Someone tried to fly a car off the hills. To be fair, it was a flying car, the brainchild of whiz man-kid entrepreneur Eres Mårtensson. We all gathered as the car took off into the hazy horizon. It made little sound as it sped off the cliff face. It was too far away for us to hear the collision as it dropped into an apartment complex in the Valley, putting dozens of families out of a home. They all sued Eres Mårtensson, but the court drama only served to increase Eres's infamy, the same currency as fame. Later, he would become very important to Bruise and, by osmosis, me. But then and now I regard him as he appeared that evening: a toady man desperate to be seen. But Bruise didn't see him yet—she was still looking for Patrick Kons.

Once, twice, Patrick Kons would appear in the frenzy of models, writers, actors, athletes. It was always Charley's or Lena's job to report the sighting to Bruise. He first showed up at the fundraiser that Bruise threw for the victims of the flying car accident. The first time, he orbited around Bruise's place without crashing into her, making small talk with directors and producers. The second time, at a party Bruise threw the next night to get over the fact that he had sullied her party, Kons gave her the briefest, curtest nod. That was the first night I saw Bruise do cocaine, a quick sniff when we were in the master bathroom debriefing Kons's nod.

The frantic drumming of a squirrel's heart, its liquid-soft body clutched in my palm. These critters Bruise had rescued from an episode of a television show about hoarders. They escaped the next day, and every so often, I'd see a cereal box delicately shredded.

Back in Leominster, off-brand cereal still sat in our pantry, the same rust stains in our bathtub. You'd never know Mom used all the money my Hollywood exploits afforded her—100 percent of her 15 percent, stretched down to the last cent. It went to Joel's fancy rehab, and then the mortgage, then to the mountain of credit card debt Mom had taken out for dance classes and convention fees but never told me about, plus the loan for the roof repairs years back, plus all the fines for having the cat colony because our shitty neighbor kept calling animal control like it was our cat colony, plus loans for Joel's unfinished college degree, better psychiatric help for Dad, and, finally, groceries. Without "Escape," we probably would have foreclosed. All this I learned later. Mom didn't want me to feel responsible, and she was ashamed and hurt and couldn't look at me, and I couldn't look at her.

In the after-spell of a music video or a party, there would be a moment when I would glimpse Bruise the person. When she would be in repose, her face haloed in the glow of her phone, and we would be alone, and I would know the veneer had fallen, and only I—not Lena, not Charley, not even Patrick Kons—was seeing Bruise the person. The real Bruise. But even as I try to render her, I have failed to do her justice, and looking back, she still seems more character than human.

"Base Instinct"

I danced with wolves. They were flown in from a sanctuary in Vancouver directly to set. The set was an abyss: a white backdrop, the floor flooded with an inch of water. Digitally, it would look like me and the wolves danced in this infinite, watery oblivion. In reality, the same crew—backward-capped men, famed director, the chaos of cables and rigged cameras—watched me from just beyond the backdrop. I was garbed in the same threadbare red lingerie set. Again near-naked and shivering, nerves primed for Bruise's voice.

Bruise had kept the song secret until we were on set and the cameras were rolling. This time, there was no planned choreography. Everyone trusted me to just dance. I was confident I could dance the same as before, perhaps even better. Seven months since Joel's overdose, six since "Escape" premiered, three since the election. All I had to do was give my body over to Bruise's strange wails.

The thing was the wolves. Four beasts—brown, gray, white, gold—surrounded me, poised and panting, larger than any dog I knew. Black tongues lolling, eight bright eyes fixed on me, they tensed when I tensed. Their shaggy tails wagged, nervous, curious. My body anticipated their lethal, kinetic energy. Sure, there was a trainer on the set, a whistle on her wide Canadian chest, but what good was that? The wolves paced around me, noses working furiously. They sensed—as I sensed—the atmospheric pressure of this place.

"Lucy?" called the director. "Are you ready?"

My body set into a runner's lunge, eyes fixed with the white wolf. She kept her big head low, locked onto my every move.

"Let's get this over with," I whispered to her. "Then we can both go home, okay?"

Home. I envisioned my anonymous room in Bruise's mansion, working on homework late into the buzzing night.

The white wolf lowered her head farther. The director was counting down now. Everyone was holding their breath. Then—

I was not surprised Bruise insisted the wolves be included in the release party. They were a part of the creation, she argued with Lena, and they deserved to be recognized. And so, tastefully muzzled, they were allowed to mingle with the guests while "Base Instinct" played from a massive projector onto the biggest wall, so you could watch me scream at the wolves and calypso leap away from nearly every point of Bruise's house, from the third-floor balcony down to the landing. Lena had invited a whole cast of characters, producers and actors and music people, singers and heart throbbers. It was the biggest party I had ever been to. Charley styled me, darkening my eye shadow and fitting me in a blue blazer with a plunging neckline that reached all the way to my belly button. "Lack of boobs opens up a whole world of fashion," she teased. By the time we emerged from preening in my guest room, the party was ablaze. Writers pitched stories back and forth across the marble island, singers clustered by the infinity pool, and producers gathered in the backyard, watching Eres Mårtensson pilot a drone. The wolves were chasing the drone, and their pretend hunt drew the most attention, eclipsing the actual music video blaring from the side of the mansion. People crave reality, Bruise was constantly telling me.

"Damn," Charley said. "This is like your debut ball or something."

"It's a release party for Bruise's song," I countered. "This is Bruise's debut."

Charley shrugged. "It's your face."

We watched the full video for "Base Instinct," or at least, I did, critiquing my technique, which suffered for the sake of a raw performance. I was not sure how this dance would do in a comp like the Dance Awards. Not well, I suspected, but I guessed that wasn't the point anymore. It kind of made me sad. I wondered what a dancer like Celia would think of this performance. I wondered if she had seen "Escape." Probably. Why didn't she reach out to me? When the loop restarted, Charley pulled me down the spiral stairs to check out the food. Bruise had staffed the kitchen with hungry writers and actors, whisking deviled eggs and plating bacon-wrapped scallops. Charley joined in, de-shelling eggs and talking up an actor who told her that he had just moved to Los Angeles. His first gig was happening tomorrow, a PSA for meth abuse.

"I'm the before," he said. "The face before the meth."

Charley asked, "Who's doing the after part?"

The before-meth actor shrugged, then he noticed me, reaching for a third fistful of pita. "Hey, that's you!" He pointed to the music video playing on the broad white wall.

"That's me," I said, biting into a plain pita.

"She's incredible," Charley gushed. "I did her look. I'm Bruise's stylist."

He sized her up with more interest. "She looks good," he said.

We watched him pipe the deviled eggs, Charley eating them one by one. The music video began a new loop, and the before-meth actor asked, "So, what is it about?"

I told him what Bruise had told me in late-night, after-party confessionals. If "Escape" detailed her escaping her old life, then "Base Instinct" was the second part to that story: After her album took off, people turned into wolves hunting her down for their big break. She couldn't even break up with her first manager without it being a headline. Her body was suddenly a commodity: Paparazzi hunted her on private beaches, her mother sold baby photos to *People* magazine. She just wanted to sing, just wanted it to be about her voice. "It's why she's no longer appearing in her music videos or doing live shows," I said. "And instead, having me dance."

It took the before-meth actor a long beat to reply. "Then why put you up there?" he asked finally, nodding at the music video, the wolves crouched low as I arched back, scratching at my eyes. "It's like throwing you to the wolves."

"No," I laughed. "I want this. I've always wanted this."

He looked like he wanted to push the issue in that boyish devil's advocate way I would later come to abhor, but Charley, always my hero, came to my rescue.

"Do I have a before- or after-meth face?" she asked innocently.

"Definitely before," he said, focusing intense blue eyes onto her. "It's sad, the faces after meth."

I felt awkward, so I left the kitchen and wandered onto the patio. There I found Lena, a goblet full of wine in one hand, looking down on the backyard, where the wolves were sprinting and barking after the drone, producers goading them on.

"What kind of look do I have?" I asked Lena.

She and Bruise and Charley would often comment on people we saw on the street or at parties: a haggard look, a romance look, a Marvel look, a CW look.

She gave me a once-over. "I don't know," she finally said. "You're very Lucy."

We watched the wolves sprint the length of the backyard and back, the men laughing and cheering. The wolves' pink tongues lolled as they plunged into the infinity pool to cool off. The drone banked just above, taunting them. I noticed the white wolf's ears flatten, her gaze steady, almost calculating. She looked even more menacing with the muzzle on, a comic book villain.

Charley came up, eggless and manless. "That guy was hot but, like, too dumb," she declared. Then she glanced at me. "I did a good job with your face. You look seventeen."

I asked, "When I'm seventeen, will I look thirty?"

Sudden commotion below. The white wolf had brought down the drone, pinning it with her muzzled jaw. She systematically destroyed it. The other wolves joined in, pecking at the propellers and snarling at one another. The producers and Eres Mårtensson encircled the chaos a good distance away, murmuring helplessly. Finally, the wolf trainer got to them, whistling. "Harlow! Harlow! Enough!"

"Ah," Charley commented lazily. "The boys lost both their cool toys."

We watched the wolf trainer escort the wolves to the once-sloth enclosure. The enclosure had been empty since Bruise last tried to have goats. The wolf trainer unleashed and unmuzzled them one by one. She seemed to be lecturing them on property damage, and the wolves seemed to be listening intently, maybe sheepishly. They only listened to the wolf trainer. She had dried chicken liver in her pockets.

"Where is Bruise?" I asked.

"Dunno," Lena said, draining her goblet.

We split up after that: Charley back to the aspiring actors, Lena to her contemplation, and me to seek out Bruise. The party intensified. Inside, singers talked even louder, writers pitched even harder. House music pumped through the walls, people began to dance along the balcony, the landing. I could not find Bruise anywhere. Later, she would tell me that she was kissing Patrick Kons. In the high of this new release—of being back, baby, really back, she finally let him back in.

Unfortunately, she forgot about Matt Callus.

In other words, they slipped into the mahogany writer's room to make love, not knowing he was there, typing away on his waterlogged typewriter. She didn't even acknowledge him. The writing was proverbially on the wall—his fifteen minutes was up. With Bruise, with Hollywood. People saw him storm outside. He was seen in line at the outdoor bar, his face stone.

I didn't know any of this, because I had gone outside, too. I wanted to see the wolves.

They regarded me on the other side of the enclosure with even, gray eyes. I sat a foot away from the cage and regarded them back. Beyond, the party was beginning to migrate to the motor gate. Eventually the wolves resumed pacing the cage, except the white female, Harlow, who remained unblinkingly focused on me.

I wanted to pet her. During the shoot, I had been too afraid to touch them, and that gave the video what Bruise called texture, this push and pull, this certain raw energy. While dancing, I had felt their breath quicken when I shrank back, I felt I could read them, but I had not yet shown them kindness or gratitude. After the shoot, Brusie had gone to the wolves first, petting their great big heads without trepidation. They had licked her cheeks, even the white one. "They don't do that with everyone," the wolf trainer told Bruise.

Slowly, I extended a hand through the cage's metal bars. Harlow regarded my outstretched fingers, long whiskers twitching. I hesitated, and then she tilted her neck forward, so my fingertips would reach her chest. Her golden-white coat prickly to the touch. It wasn't like any dog I had petted—certainly not as soft. But still, my hand stroked along the groove of her fur, my drumming heart easing with each second. It was a good moment. Harlow leaned against the wire cage, offering her whole body for me to pet. She closed her eyes. Beyond the hair, I felt hard, ropy muscles along her legs.

"This isn't what you expected," I whispered to Harlow, whose restless gaze scanned the dark cliffs.

Suddenly, a low thrum vibrated deep in Harlow's chest.

A voice behind us boomed, "There's the costars!"

I turned. It was Matt Callus. Since I had entangled my life and career with Bruise, he had made himself scarce when I was around. I just thought he was busy, like Hollywood-guy busy. Bruise said she liked having young, potential lovers so they had material to write about later. These soft boys would allegorize her, metamorphize her, enshrine her in art. Matt Callus's dress shirt was open and flapped in the night wind. He had two drinks in his hands, both clear, which I stupidly thought were water. When he offered one to me, I sipped it without hesitation. Of course, it was alcohol. My nose burned, but I swallowed and frowned.

"Chilling with the wolves," he announced. "You're something else."

"Where's Bruise?"

"I don't give a flying fuck."

It was so unexpected, I laughed. He plopped down beside me, but not crazy close, like a foot away. "This was a big deal," Matt Callus said after taking a long sip from his drink. "You're a big deal."

"God," I said sheepishly, still petting Harlow.

"What's next for you, though? You're not going to be Bruise's back-up dancer forever."

"I'm not a back-up dancer."

Matt Callus polished off his drink with a dramatic flourish and threw his cup into the dark. "I could make you more than a dancer."

I laughed politely. "That's all I want to be."

But Matt Callus kept insisting, sidling closer until we were shoulder to shoulder. "Why are you a good dancer? You're an *actress*, that's what makes you special. You've got these big eyes and this big face that says something, this mouth that . . ."

He was speaking into my neck, and his breath was sweet and hot. Vaguely, I felt Harlow move under my hand. I could hear her shake off. The other wolves were watching, pacing back and forth, whining softly under their breath. But I was stuck. It was like being in the hospital again, looking into Joel's room: My body failed me. I could lock my knees, point my toes, jump twice my height in the air. And yet I could not shrug him off, could not sidle away, could not even mumble, "Excuse me, I have to go."

"I've got a story," he was whispering quickly. A hand was on my knee, moving up. "In my next script, I'll write it just for you, Lucy, Lucy girl . . ."

His touch burning my skin. I heard the cage door rattle, and the wolves were panting.

I started to whisper, "Hey—"

Before his hand got any farther, physical pressure was replaced with sound. Screams, he was screaming. The door to the enclosure had opened, and the white wolf was upon Matt Callus. She had his right arm, and she was shaking her head back and forth, like his arm was a dog toy, but now I saw the real function of that shake, which was to tear—red. There was a lot of red. Then the other wolves were slinking out of the cage, and they ran past me and the shrieking Matt Callus, leaping down into the dark cliffside, into the starry map of the city. I would have watched, dumbly, forever, except arms were pulling me up, pulling me away and into safety. Bruise. She was breathing hard. She pulled me behind her, fingers tight on my shoulder.

Shouts from above. "Wolves! Wolves!" The lingering partygoers had noticed the commotion below. From far off, I heard the wolf trainer whistling. "Harlow! Stop!"

The white wolf registered the trainer's calls. She released Matt's arm. Her chest and mouth were scarlet. The ends of her hairs had become drawn and pointed and dripped blood. Then she looked at me. Evenly, calmly.

She bolted to the dark cliffside, joining the other wolves in escape.

"Help," Matt Callus spat and sputtered. "Help me!"

"You don't touch her," Bruise said, her voice ragged. "You don't look at her."

He didn't reply—his vacant gaze had found the pulp that was his right arm. And then the crowd was upon him, people calling for an ambulance, the trainer calling hoarsely for her wolves.

But they vanished into the Hollywood Hills and went undetected, save for a trail of mangled house cats. Soon they became a distant Los Angeles legend: the wolves of the Hollywood Hills. Matt Callus would vanish, too, into the Illinois suburb from whence he came, unable to write solely from the lack of a right arm—Matt Callus always handwrote his first drafts, and once that magic was gone, so was the magic of writing altogether.

As for me, I could feel the trauma sinking into my body as I settled in that night. In my clean, white guest room, I could not shake his shrieks from my head or the feel of his since-swallowed hand on my knee. I knocked on Bruise's door. She answered in the same outfit of the party: a full-length faux-mink gown. When I hugged her, it scratched like Harlow's wiry fur.

"Do you want to watch TV or something?"

"Lucy girl, of course."

We slipped into her bed and she turned on *The Lake House*. She wrapped her arms around me and for the first time that night, I felt my body relax. *The Lake House* was always the same. Keanu Reeves was gentle and loving. We got twenty minutes in before I asked what she thought would happen to the wolves.

"They'll stay out there," Bruise said. "Or they'll get found. Eventually, they'll die."

"I didn't . . . I mean, Matt and I didn't . . . "

"You need to fight back," Bruise said sharply.

"I know," I whispered. For a long time, I would ask myself why I didn't.

"You can't just sit there and take it."

"I know."

"But I'll watch over you until you can," she said. "Until you can fight back, I'll be there."

And she was true to her word.

First Farlock Brothers Cameo

My first acting gig was not without dance. Lena got me a guest appearance on the Disney show *The Farlock Brothers* as a dancer who "breaks a leg" after Jimmy Farlock accidentally pushes my character into oncoming traffic. Guilty, the brothers spend twenty-two minutes trying to delay my big show so the bitchy understudy can't steal my chance at glory. In typical *Farlock Brothers* fashion, they end up accidentally breaking the legs of all the company dancers in a misguided attempt to demolish the stage.

"It's a start," Lena said when I looked up from the script, my face an open book of cringe. "Everyone starts somewhere."

"Could be good experience," Bruise said thoughtfully. "And no one watches this garbage, anyway."

"Do it," Charley piped up. "I hear Chance Rodriguez is a real hottie."

I took the gig, if only to meet the Rodriquez brothers. Contrary to Bruise's claims, I had watched and secretly enjoyed *The Farlock Brothers* in my former life. The Farlock brothers were seventeenth-century chimney-sweep brothers who got a second chance at life when a high school science teacher accidentally reanimated their corpses. By day they lived as your average high school duo, by night they raided graves to keep their decomposing bodies in working order. But the brothers were really hot. Girls in my old dance studio had posters. Before going to set, I read their Wikipedia page and learned that their father was a famous pet psychic and their mother had died, though not before she'd starred in several slasher flicks in the eighties.

The set was a skeleton of what I'd imagined. As I followed Lena, I glimpsed the high school classroom where Jimmy Farlock had his first kiss, where Jack Farlock misplaced his ear. For some reason, the stacked desks and green chalkboard seemed fake in real life. But it was in this room I first glimpsed Ronan acting.

Ronan whisper-yelled, "I forgot my tap shoes!"

Chance whisper-yelled back, "I doubt your decomposing legs could handle a ball change, brother!"

Their sassy friend who did not know their secret yelled, "What's that smell?"

The director yelled, "Pause for laugh track!"

And then all three actors and the extras remained still, blinking, in an eerie silence.

Despite the eeriness, I was excited to act. I was enraptured by what Bruise called "the high of creation" and I wanted to see how the sausage was made beyond our work together. Plus, I was excited to take gigs outside of music videos, to extend myself as a working dancer.

So I arrived early with Lena by my side as my manager (agent?). We watched the scenes before mine, the Farlock brothers fumbling to their Broadway field trip, losing fingers and making snide remarks about how New York used to look back when they were alive. And finally, it was my time. The first scene was easy.

I just danced. Mostly they just had me turning. Attitudes, back attitudes, leg hovers, à la secondes, so many à la secondes, until my spot burned into my optical nerve. The room warmed to me. "Good," the director chanted. "Good, good."

But then came actual acting. When Jack, played by Ronan, accidentally pushed me and I "broke" my leg.

"Ow," I cried. "My leg!"

"You were fine," Lena assured me before my next scene.

"Really?" I said again. "I felt like I . . . wasn't believable?"

"It's for kids! What, are you expecting an Oscar?"

"No, definitely not."

We were quiet for a bit. I wished Bruise was there. She would say something that would make it click—would make me magical.

"I just didn't expect to be so bad," I finally said.

During state-required breaks, the kid actors would hang out between the set and the trailers. Mostly, they played HORSE and around the world in the parking lot. There I found that the Farlock brothers were as different from their Disney personas as could be, Chance especially. Flinging the basketball for trick shots, he spit out words like *cunt* and *raw dog it* before retiring to the sidelines, drinking heartily from a wilted plastic water bottle that only now in recollection do I realize probably did not contain water.

An air ball. I threw my head back and groaned. Ronan bounced the ball back to me. Everyone else had gone inside Chance's trailer.

"More power," he said. "You need more juice. And in acting, you need less juice."

"I feel like no one's trying," I said, taking a shot with more juice.

It barely scraped the top net. Ronan caught the ball. "It's a Disney show. Relax."

"I am relaxed," I grunted, heaving the ball with all my might.

The ball careened against the backboard, and Ronan had to leap to nab it. Instead of tossing it back, he walked it over to me. "I get it," he said. "I want to be taken seriously, too."

He handed me the ball without taking his hand off it. "In basketball and acting, you have to combine power with technique."

"What do you mean?"

"Here—"

Then, leaning over my body, he guided my hands into position over the basketball, puppeting me until I got the right flick of the wrist, the right arch of the basketball in the air. We practiced a few times. *Ronan Rodriguez is teaching me to play basketball*, I thought to myself, drafting a text to old dance friends I wouldn't send. His breath smelled like Coca-Cola and salad dressing.

"Okay," I said. "I got it."

Then I dribbled a few times, getting in the right mindset. Breathe, breathe. My hands seized the ball at the right places, took aim, gathered power, and flicked into a perfect arch. The ball swished into the net with stupid ease.

"Hey!" I cheered, spinning around to Ronan. My arms were up, and he mistook it for a signal to hug. He was small back then, basically my height. Still, he was strong—lifting me up, spinning.

"Stop," I laughed-breathed. "Stop!"

Just then, the bell rang. The director used the high school bell from the show to signal that it was time for the next scene. Ronan set me down, our faces dangerously close.

"I didn't make it around the world," I said.

"Well," he countered, "you made it to China."

Lunan

Ronan kissed me twice before we officially began dating: first upon a Mulholland Drive vista in the dead of night, and the second time in the pet cemetery bordering his family's Studio City mansion. It was during his sixteenth-birthday pool party. Girlish laughter beyond the hedges. While we kissed, I read the names on the tombstones: Fluffy, Peanut, George, Sir Farts.

"Hey," I whispered. "We should get back."

He stopped kissing me but kept his mouth on mine, thinking. I inhaled his hot breath. *Wow*, I thought. *I've never been this close to someone before. Never someone this famous.*

"Okay," he finally said. "Let's go."

It's unclear when Bruise and Patrick Kons became official again. Officially in love, officially together. Charley claimed it was the night of the music video party, the night of the wolves, the night Matt Callus— For Lena, it was when they were paparazzi'd together shopping for a new car. But for me, I think something changed the day Patrick Kons gifted her the parrot. We were in the basement, Bruise and I. She was having workers rip up Matt Callus's old writer's room to put in a dance studio. It was the end of the first day of construction, and the whole room was gutted, exposing the concrete and the wooden exoskeleton. Big slates of mirrors were propped up against the orange plywood walls. Bruise had laid three different sample squares of dance floors for me to try some turns on.

"It's too much," I repeated. A whole professional dance room, just for me.

Bruise shook her head. "All you want to do is dance. And all I want is to make you happy. So try it out."

I prepped a turn on the first one: starting in fourth position and centering my weight. And then I was off, spotting the same mark.

Then there was a figure slipping between the beams. With each spin, the figure grew larger until I could discern tortoiseshell glasses, salt-and-pepper hair, Birkenstock sandals.

"Patrick!" Bruise exclaimed, and I toppled over.

"Hope I'm not interrupting anything," Patrick Kons said. I recognized his voice. The executive-office male voice. This was the first time I was really seeing him, the object of so much ire and passion for Bruise. I was kind of disappointed. He looked like an older Matt Callus. But he was Patrick Kons, and he spelled a new era of my tenure in Bruise's orbit.

"Nothing at all," Bruise said, her voice pitched higher than ever. "Not interrupting anything."

Patrick Kons extended his hand, on which perched an African grey parrot.

"I just came to give you this guy."

"Oh my God," Bruise gasped. "It isn't . . ."

"It is," Patrick Kons grinned. "It's Mercury Blues."

Bruise petted the bird's delicate head. "How'd you . . ."

Kons explained he was consulting on the bird's final project. When the funding got pulled, when the crew was talking about roasting the bird, frustrated by its lack of performance, which led to the stopped funding, he knew he had to act fast. And he knew the perfect home.

"Of course," Bruise sighed. "It would be an honor to house Mercury Blues for his retirement."

Gingerly, Patrick Kons handed the bird to Bruise. Briefly, their fingers touched.

Fan accounts called Ronan and me "Lunan." They coveted rare photos of us, called "rares," and role-played pregnancy scares. At the time I was barely aware of the depths of this niche Internet community, so enraptured was I with Ronan, with dating Ronan, with being a girl who dates. The idea I was still thirteen—still a kid—never crossed my mind. Certainly that was alluring to my fan accounts, owned by girls who went to middle school with a tiger as the mascot, and only dreamed of dating, of working on their own. Today I'll see TikToks of these former fans, having grown up, confessing they were once a superfan, revealing and reacting to a carousel of clips from their old fan accounts, now ancient relics of a bygone era. How I envy them. To close a fan account and retreat to your anonymous life, to have gone to a school with a tiger mascot—ah! But I did inhale the hot breath of Ronan Rodriguez.

Not only was the parrot, Mercury Blues, famous, but he held special symbolism to their relationship. Bruise and Kons first met in Cannes. She was seventeen, newly famous, newly dadless, newly hailed as a prodigy singer and songwriter, her weird sad voice ringing across the globe. It had all happened so suddenly—she recorded her first album on the floor of her bedroom, had her boyfriend pretend to be her manager and send it to a studio, and it seemed like an hour later, she was in Cannes in a thin blue dress that threatened to reveal her nipples, being asked to sing for people she had only known on movie screens. Kons was similarly stupid and young, similarly bewildered—his plucky student film *Dead Heart* suddenly an overnight sensation. You can imagine the trauma bond as the two of them found themselves sitting together watching the premiere of *Blue Echoes*, the film that launched Mercury Blues's career—the film Bruise and Kons bonded over, laughing themselves silly at the after-party, her hand over her mouth, giggling, and she only giggled like that when she was a kid, not famous but like any girl, giggling with her soccer team, as if they were all one girl, slick and ponytailed and orange-peel smiles. It seemed to Bruise that Kons was the only real person there—the only person laughing at the absolute absurdity of the movie and this party the way people back home would. They stole crab cakes and a bottle of expensive wine and vanished into the French night, wandering the cobblestoned streets and the crashing beaches, talking about their lives before their big breaks, and what they hoped would come after. The rising sun found them picking their way through a rock scramble, waves sweeping over bare feet, their presence setting up a flock of seagulls, silhouetted black against the burnt red of morning.

"Bet Mercury Blues wishes for nothing but this," Kons remarked, and Bruise realized she would always love him.

Ronan and I posted on Instagram many times before it was official, leaving breadcrumbs of rares for these accounts: Ronan's distinct wavy hair in the corner of a frame, my pointed foot in the corner of Ronan's mirror selfie. It was fun to watch people speculate. Sometimes we'd post individual pictures from the same place: Melrose trading post, Venice Beach, even a cabin in Big Bear, which we rented with Bruise, Kons, Charley, Lena, some of Ronan's friends, and his brother. That was the weekend, I believe, Charley and Chance Rodriguez first slept together. Ronan and I went stargazing and came back to find Charley on the balcony wrapped in a big quilt, smiling mysteriously.

The peak of Mercury Blues's career, ten years later, found Bruise and Kons cresting over their own apex. While the parrot was starring in black-and-white dramas about repressed homoerotic pirates, Bruise's fourth album was met with middling reviews and Kons's latest attempt to recapture the magic of *Dead Heart* (another coming-of-age movie about a sad writer who met a sad singer) was shown in only a few art houses. While Mercury Blues married a delicate she-parrot and fathered a roost of grubby, shivering parrot babies, Bruise and Kons were plastered across the tabloids for their on-again-off-again shenanigans. They watched Mercury Blues proverbially walk the red carpet for his first Oscar nomination on the floor of Bruise's Hollywood Hills mansion the week she closed. *That is it*, Bruise thought. *They had won, hadn't they?* A big house on a hill and each other? Watching the Oscars together, on the floor of her first big house?

"God," she giggled to Kons. "Look at poor Mercury Blues—not a thought behind those sweet eyes."

The camera had pulled in close to the parrot after showing a clip of Mercury Blues's nominated role. His pale eyes dilated wide, feathers ruffled up as people clapped, beak agape.

But this time, Kons wasn't laughing. "It's not fair," he muttered. "A fucking bird nominated and not me? It's not fair. Are they blind?"

"C'mon," Bruise said, softly. "It doesn't mean anything."

Yet it did, it did for him, and they had their first real fight. It began about Mercury Blues being nominated for an Oscar and ended with Kons declaring that the relationship was stunting him. That fight, Bruise would later tell me, was the beginning of the end—when it all started to matter. Sure, it had started to matter beforehand—it started to matter after that first concert in Cannes, after that second live interview, after she got that award and after she signed that autograph. But at the end of the day, what mattered was that she got to sing and yeah, but it wasn't the same, not like before she was famous, when she sang on the bus home after away games and the national anthem before football matches and promised to sing at all her friends' weddings. But back then, it really wasn't real, not like now.

But it was, beyond being two semi-famous people, like a first relationship. Ronan and I texted at all hours. We made out in our respective bedrooms. We cuddled while watching TV, lying on Bruise's double-wide couch. Ronan was nearly as short as me, despite being sixteen. He had the sort of body that felt the way it looked: knobby, two-dimensional. His stomach was absurdly flat, and I remember being more jealous than attracted. It was his face that won him roles. Ronan's encyclopedic knowledge of film extended far beyond "living in Hollywood." He knew old Hollywood, like black-and-white movies and black-and-white actors.

"This was when movies were movies," he always said. "Back when it was a real craft."

"It still is," I always protested. "Like, *Stars Wars* is art."

Something Joel would say.

Ronan rolled his gorgeous eyes. "I want to make real movies," he whispered fiercely, wrapping me in his little arms.

Mercury Blues's career exploded—quite literally. A stunt gone wrong, a spooked horse kicked over a lantern, a prop barn caught fire, and all the pyrotechnics burst into a colorful, peppery nothingness. The parrot unfortunately was caught in the fireball, suffered burns and hearing loss. Psychologically, the scars seemed to run even deeper. Before the accident, Mercury

Blues often brought up his sensory issues during Actor's Craft interviews. "Loud hurts Blue-Blue," he croaked, perched on the very edge of the director's chair. James Lipton nodded seriously. "Light and sudden scare Blue-Blue. Bad dreams all time. Blue-Blue scare, all time."

Widely, fans understood Mercury Blues drew from a vast and complex darkness to truly embody his increasingly dark and complex characters—a bird that goaded his owners to kill themselves, a bird that cuckolded another bird, a bird who partnered with the Zodiac Killer.

All those dark roles disappeared after the accident. Mercury Blues refused to utter a single word after that. A few psychologists tried to heal him, but he was locked in, unreachable. Occasionally, he got picked up by a writer or producer with gumption, believing they had a role juicy enough to get Mercury Blues to speak again. That was how Kons got ahold of him. By then, Kons mostly fell in with Bruise between relationships, their magic extinguished just like their art. Their last real fight the night I first met her rang with a new finality. But she had gone and launched herself over all their heads, had finally recaptured that magic not once but twice, and by God, he would find out how she did it after all these years, even if it meant standing in the shadow cast by her new light for a bit. She probably knew he was curious about me, more me than her, about my capacity to rekindle, reignite, renew, *re—re—re—re*—the sounds of cicadas in the heavy summer air, the sound of soccer camp and first loves, when everything still seems new and possible.

We fell asleep in each other's arms after watching his favorite movie, *Casablanca*. That was another first. I woke in the middle of the night, my neck pinched, Ronan's beautiful smooth face deep in sleep. I left him there. Antsy. I went looking for Bruise.

She was singing; I could hear discordant notes throughout the open floor plan and finally I found her on the third floor in a room where she kept all the pianos. Bruise looked the same, scarlet underwear and a tank reading GLOBAL WARMING IS REAL. I had changed, grown five inches, highlighted my hair blond, tweezed my eyebrows. All good, productive things.

Bruise was staring hard into an open notebook, her mouth bent on stray lyrics. Mercury Blues was perched on her shoulder, eyes closed, swaying in time to the melody.

"Be careful," she warned dully, snapping her notebook shut. "Love like that—it can make you dull."

"I'm not in love," I said quickly, because I knew I wasn't.

"Good," Bruise said. "We still have work to do."

Rose Bowl Concert

While I was kissing Ronan Rodriguez and performing at the Rose Bowl with Bruise, Joel was sitting in his childhood bedroom for the first time in a year, bewildered at how much worse things seemed. Like me, he noted the uptick in hoarding, the way the house had become an ant tunnel of newspapers and magazines, cardboard husks of long-ago purchases, Micah buzzing around trying to organize the mess into donate, trash, or keep piles, Dad sleeping on the recliner, Mom somehow nowhere and everywhere and certainly never sleeping. She made sure he was never unsupervised, that he got to his therapy sessions, and even connected him with a job from an old NYC theater friend, doing odd gigs for a puppetry show in Groton. Every other evening, Joel collected tickets from bright, peppy moms, cleaned out toddler-obliviated bathrooms, hauled set designs and props between acts. Of all the odd jobs Joel had worked, it wasn't the worst, almost funny, perpendicular to enjoyable, and he even thought to thank Mom and tell her all these stories that he knew she would have some quick word about; in fact, he found himself missing that quick word, because she never seemed *there*. Often she was out, either at work or at mysterious appointments. It seemed Mom lacked substance suddenly, sapped of spirit and presence. Like me, Joel came to the natural conclusion that it was all his fault. And perhaps like me, he would have fled first chance he got, but instead Mom slipped up.

One day, Joel later recounted to me, it was time for his appointment and Mom never showed up to drive him. She had one of two family cars; they'd sold his beloved Subaru after the overdose, and Micah was using the other to take Dad on a hike, patiently trying to entice the will to live back into him. Joel waited, anger and annoyance cooling into confusion. Mom had never been late. By the time she finally pulled into the driveway that evening, he had been checking the news reports for some terrible crash on 495. The screen door clattering noisily. Typical Mom—a huff wherever she went. We used to joke she was echolocating. But for once, she didn't seem aware of her surroundings, of Joel, tucked in the living room behind one of Micah's "donate" piles. He watched her place a used, withered grocery bag on the kitchen table, unload orange pill bottles one by one. At first he assumed it was all for him, but this notion was quickly dispatched watching Mom unsecure the caps, tilt a single pill into her palm, lift her palm to her lips. Later he would find the pill bottles squirreled away inside her nightside table, the labels equal-parts damning and terrifying: cyclophosphamide, paclitaxel, Celexa, and other capsules increasing in dosage and syllables. A quick Google search confirmed what Joel began to fear that day: Mom was sick (breast cancer, we would later learn) and very sad and she was hiding her sickness and sadness because there was no one to take care of her. Dad, equally depressed; me, making out with Ronan Rodriguez; Joel, recovering addict teetering on oblivion and/or an ancillary job in puppetry; Micah desperately trying to dig us out. The skin of her face seemed wafer-thin, the sheen of wax dolls and funeral-home corpses. She was sixty and she never got to be a writer, a doctor, an actor. But she was just as good as

Bruise. Actually, far more interesting and deep as a person. And yet. For every Bruise, there is a Denise Ward, someone who could have been but wasn't and so she's just your mom.

When Joel swung through the kitchen, making his presence known by complaining about what the pissy toddlers did to the puppet show bathroom today, she was making a good show of cleaning out the fridge. The plastic bag of cancer and depression meds still crinkling from her touch on the kitchen table—she wasn't trying to hide it so much as ignore it.

"Where have you been?" she asked without looking at her stepson. Rather, she was squinting at a murky jar of olives.

He said his typical line, the meaning taking on new gravity: "I'm here now, aren't I?"

Interlude

Charley loved a good gossip. Always she was playing with palettes and our faces and regaling us with stories from her Indiana high school, which had a rich lore. A girl lost her finger in dissection class. One fall, people dressed up as clowns haunted the woods bordering the school. All her friends loved the same guy, a triangle-chested track star named Chester Sheets. "We all spent sleepovers drooling over this guy," she told me. "Sleepovers comparing texts from this white guy." Chester Sheets enjoyed the attention and ran through Charley's friend group like he was on *The Bachelor*, but he never made it to Charley, because during their junior year her father randomly died and Chester Sheets graciously informed her that he didn't want to make things more complicated for her. "That was probably the worst part," Charley always laughed. "All I wanted was stupid Chester Sheets, if I just banged Chester Sheets I would be *okay*, and I patiently waited my turn, and then he used my dead dad as an excuse to skip over me, the only Black girl. That's the real reason." At "*okay*," she jammed my eye with an eyeliner pencil.

I should have known Charley wasn't okay, was never okay, but she was so cool. If Bruise vanished in a song, I filled my days with Charley. Ostensibly she didn't live in the mansion, but a studio in Belair. It was fun to spend a few weekends at Charley's, to play the part of a twentysomething artist in Los Angeles. Charley's apartment was filled with light and lemons and ferns. I would hang out with her and her LA friends while they pregamed some hidden speakeasy, and then I would chill alone in her apartment while they were out. Sometimes, I admit, I'd snoop, flipping through Charley's books, which she lugged around even though she'd dropped out of college, just like Joel. Before Bruise DM'd her niche makeup channel, she majored in theater design because she loved the drama of opening nights, of seeing all the actors make reality of a world she'd nailed and glued and painted together. But that ended when her phone twanged and she was staring at Bruise's Instagram handle. Her old life vanished the second she replied, *sure, love to come trial for you!*, all the Emerson friends and whatever asinine Emerson set drama she was pissed about. The only habit she kept from her old life was that she read voraciously—Charley was the only reader I knew, besides my mom. She loved everything: romance, pulpy sci-fi, Pulitzer stuff, but especially mysteries. Her bookmark was a yellowed photograph of a man sitting in a camping chair, laughing. This was, I guessed, her dead dad. Late into the night, Charley would return, always alone. She'd drunkenly order McDonald's for us and pull up a history documentary about how the pyramids were built, how it might have been aliens. "Unreal," Charley would whisper. "Fucking unreal." Always in the mornings, she would rap on my door and crawl into bed and debrief the night. Somehow it would always come back to how Chester Sheets was now some lame investment banker and her dad was still dead, but she was in Hollywood styling a celebrity, had her pick of any burgeoning, handsome actor.

"This is the life," Charley would say, more to herself than me. "I am living the life."

Cinders Audition

"Daddy," I recited. "Don't leave us!"

"More feeling," Ronan insisted.

I slapped the script on the kitchen counter. "My voice can't go any higher."

Ronan shook his head. "You're just reciting lines, though. It's not about volume or pitch. I don't feel like you, Phoebe Mayweather, have just lost your papa."

I smirked. Ronan's passion for acting sometimes made me uncomfortable.

"You want to get better at acting," Ronan said. "So I don't get why you're not trying."

I flipped through the script and huffed. "I am trying."

"Babe," Ronan sighed, pulling me into his arms. "Babe, this isn't dancing. You have to convince without leaps and turns. No body—just your voice."

He was touching my face.

"But that's all I know," I whispered. Ronan kissed my neck. He had been extra handsy lately. We had been dating four months, so I supposed that tracked. While we made out on the sectional—Bruise out with Kons again, leaving me to make out with a Disney star—I kept mentally reviewing the script. *Cinders* was an indie drama about a broken family with a pyromaniac son. The pyromaniac son was being played by Jay Corpus, Lena's other famous former-kid client, the one she'd helped leverage into an acting career. The single mother was being played by an actress who had won an Oscar. Really, my acting opportunity was made possible by Patrick Kons—he had written the script. He had told the director about me. Kons wanted me for the innocent sister.

Ronan got a boob—I had boobs now—and he was kneading it. I didn't feel so innocent. Maybe that was the problem.

I read my lines to Bruise a few days later, when we were driving down the coast. She wanted to get away for a few days, and so she drove up to Big Sur. Her songwriting for our next big project inspired by her life was on hold—she had to cook up the soundtrack for *Cinders*. She thought it might be helpful if we camped, watched some stuff burn. We both missed trees. In whatever A-frame cabin she rented, we planned to sit on the porch, inhaling the clear and piney air. She also hoped that nature would cure Mercury Blues, still bleakly, forever quiet on her shoulder. But this escape was cut short due to traffic, bumper to bumper. Without looking at me, Bruise said, "So, you're seriously into acting?"

"I'm not good at it. Besides, I'm a dancer."

"You're not good at it, and yet you want to keep at it." Bruise kept her eyes glued to the road. "That means you love it."

I was quiet, wondering if I liked acting. No. I was just bothered that I was bad at it. Bothered Mom would see me act and know I was bad at it, that all this was for—

"Ask Mercury Blues," Bruise added suddenly.

The parrot remained on her shoulder, even in the car. He was always there, silent and dazed. She fed him crackers when she remembered. Sometimes he would bob up and down if she sang, and she always thought she was perpetually on a breakthrough with him, that he answered to her and her only.

"Uh," I started.

"*Ask me,*" Bruise said out of the corner of her mouth. "*I'm a real famous actor, after all.*"

Mercury Blues blinked, wearily.

Buying into the joke, I asked, "Blues, what's the secret to acting?"

"*What do you want, little girl?*"

"You mean what my character wants?"

"*Sure, whatever. What does your character want?*"

"For her daddy to not leave."

"*Okay, what does she want behind that?*"

"Behind what?"

"*There's always something behind the first want. A real want behind the fake want.*"

I stood before the casting people in a small, windowless room. A few women, and a man, the director. Before each of them, an unopened bottle of water. "Take it away, Lucy."

I didn't need to look at the script. I tensed my body and focused my energy on a vague spot in the room, somewhere above their bland heads. I pictured my house as I once remembered it. The den full of rowdy boys, my brothers' friends playing video games. My father in the garden. Micah in the front yard, setting up his new tent. Mom opening wet food for the cat colony we're not supposed to feed, complaining about something. Joel in the garage, spray-painting something unholy.

"Daddy! Don't leave us!"

Farlock Brothers: The Movie: The After-party

On the limo ride home from Ronan's first movie premiere, he kept loosening his tie and repeating, "This won't be my last film. This can't be my last."

Except it was. The only film Ronan Rodriguez would ever star in was the direct-to-TV *Farlock Brothers: The Movie* special. No one hated that movie more than Ronan. When the *Farlock Brothers* show was cancelled the next year, he would go on to make a few cameos on other TV shows, but the gas eventually petered out until he reappeared, years later, on the podcast *Ribbing It with Ronan*, inviting celebrities to discuss their roles, their divorces, their political or spiritual beliefs, or their opinion on mayochup. Too often the topic lands on sex. And I have to hear his weird laugh in my AirPods while grocery shopping or stuck in traffic, waiting for Ronan to tell the public about his first time. To see if he'll talk about me. And then, finally, on episode 291,

"Pickles and Rickles," Ronan made a vague reference: "Yeah, yeah. Everyone's firsts are going to be. . . not ideal."

That's as close as we'll get. Not ideal. Well.

The movie's after-party was back at Bruise's mansion, big and secluded and in the Hollywood Hills. I had gotten better at being at parties. With Ronan, I didn't have to vocally participate, I could just concave my spine into his chest, disassociate, nod occasionally. And there was plenty to nod at—pitched ideas, fun gossip, sad gossip, weird gossip. In the beginning, the party had some fun moments: Chance surfing down the spiral staircase, Charley face painting randos, the infinity pool filling with almost a hundred people, their legs warped in the lit glass below.

Things went sideways when Chance hopped on the marble island in the kitchen and slurred some speech about how we were celebrating the best movie in the world, how they were the best duo in the world, how they would always, always act together, a package deal.

Beside me, Ronan stiffened. But he was supposed to love this movie, love the show that gave him fame, love his brother, whose proclivity to self-destruction constantly threatened the solo future he whispered so often just to me.

Just then, my phone vibrated. For some stupid reason, I picked up. "Joel?"

"Come up here, brother," Chance yelled, extending a meaty hand to Ronan. "It would not be possible without you."

Joel's voice crackled in my ear, "Did you know Mom has cancer?"

"What?"

I didn't see Ronan seethe beside Chance as he gave his speech, because I was ducking into the narrow hallway meant for servers. Still, the noise pervaded the white walls. One of my ears

Lucky Girl • 165

tried to follow the party, the other trying but not quite heeding Joel's words.

"Mom has cancer," Joel repeated. "Did you know?"

"What's going on?" Since his overdose, I had talked to Joel maybe once or twice.

He explained his discovery of her medication. There were toddlers giggling in the background. Knowing what I do now about his time, I can easily imagine him behind a velvet curtain, hands ensnared in puppet strings, phone pinched between ear and shoulder. "Micah told me it's breast cancer. He had to drive her back from a procedure. She was drugged, out of it, and I guess she finally told him. Breast cancer."

"But why didn't she tell me?" I asked stupidly. Exiting the hallway, I paced around the party, trying not to cry. People's eyes snagged over me, questioning expressions. I was searching for Bruise—if I could just make contact with Bruise, she could set this right. Put this in context. Tell me that it didn't matter. But the faces whirled together—I couldn't find Bruise, and I wouldn't find her—she and Kons were fighting on the rooftop. She had heard rumors: The producers of *Cinders* had tapped her for the soundtrack only as a way to get to me. Kons assured her it was the other way around, and she cried with relief, and he pulled Bruise close and they had sex up there, the parrot watching them unflinchingly from his perch on the satellite dish. All this I know because Bruise told me the next day, elated I had sex the same night she did. For Bruise, it meant we were still connected in some bigger way. It meant we could talk sex now, too, and finally Bruise could tell someone else about the specific things Patrick Kons did, and how did it compare to—

Over the phone, Joel was asking, "Did you get the part? The movie part?"

"Yeah," I said miserably. "We start filming in a week."

"Mom says she's coming out to be your guardian," Joel said. "She's bringing all your presents. Birthday included." It was a little after Christmas, the first I had missed—Bruise and I had filmed a holiday concert special for NBC, then the *Farlock* premier, then filming for a clothing brand I was launching, and 2018 would kick off with me filming my first movie. I had just turned fourteen.

"Do you think she'll tell me then?" I asked Joel. "Is it serious?"

"Well, it's cancer. But they caught it early, Micah says."

"But why didn't she tell—"

Sudden shouts rang out in the other room. The brothers—Chance and Ronan—were entangled, roaring and sparring like bears. Ronan had his little body wrapped around Chance, barreling him into people and countertops and glass figurines. I hung up on Joel and started screaming at Ronan to stop. They fell to the floor, writhing on top of each other. A few guys got ahold of Chance and pulled him off Ronan, who sprang up and ran off, swallowed by the crowd, and then Chance was standing there, hair disheveled, lip cut and bleeding. People just stared. Everyone was waiting for him to set the tone.

He boomed, "That won't make it into the director's cut." A few actors laughed. And the party continued. I left, found Ronan in the basement plucking at the grand piano.

"The movie sucks," he said without looking up. "It's not the peak of our careers."

I sat on the piano bench next to him. "It's not."

Ronan's cheek was already bruising. He kept playing the piano, discordant notes that didn't make any sense. "But if it is, what will we do?"

I smashed the keyboard, making him jump. "It's not."

He kissed me, and this kiss felt weird. So much softer and longer. "Lucy, I love . . . how you're still new to this."

Relieved, I brought my hand to his temple. His eyes were brown, almost black. "You're cut," I whispered.

He grabbed my hand and pressed it against his forehead, squeezing his eyes shut. I'm not sure what he was thinking. For my part, my mind wandered back to Mom not telling me she had cancer. Probably she didn't want me to worry, didn't think I could handle it. But look at me now, consoling my lover. *I have a lover! I* . . . that's when my gaze fell on the sensory deprivation tank, unused since Matt Callus's sudden and bloody departure. I had always wanted to go into it, to try it out, but I had been too afraid to go alone. And no one would see us, even if they came down for more wine.

I said, "Hey—"

After. I couldn't sleep, even after the party had died down and Ronan and I had gone up to my bed, after his breaths deepened and his grip slackened. My whole body felt abuzz. I pulled out my phone, let the light drill holes into my rods and cones. My favorite *Attack on Titan* fan fiction writer had finally updated a chapter. I still kept up-to-date with the story, and I now checked occasionally out of habit. Reading, I felt calmer than I had all night. It felt like the day had never happened, because I was doing the same thing I did most nights. It made me feel like everything was normal, like I could still text Kimberly. I still had her number. If we were still friends, I would text her after something this monumental. I would ask her what it meant that I felt nothing; that in fact, I didn't think I liked it. She would say something thoughtful, that maybe I was too in my head or maybe it just wasn't the right person. But I didn't text Kim. Instead, I left a comment on the fanfic and wondered if she'd see and know it was me.

Cinders: First Scene

My movie brother didn't want to hurt me. I mean, the actor, playing my character's brother. Jay Corpus was famous in Hollywood not only for his fame but also for his gentle nature. Like Ronan, he was small and fragile and beautiful like a waifish Victorian child. Unlike Ronan, he was old: thirty-two. *Cinders* was his coronation after making the unthinkable transition from tween Disney music sensation to a serious A24 actor. In this movie, he plays Peter, a pyromaniac fourteen-year-old boy who doesn't care what he burns, even bugs, even cats, even his sister, played by me. In reality, Jay Corpus seemed apprehensive about even poking me with the prop.

"I don't want to scare you," he said.

"It's fake," I assured him. "I'll know it's fake." The prop looked super fake. It was a green rectangle. All the fire in *Cinders* is CGI, rendered in postproduction. We were sitting in the first scene, when Peter first burns himself at a campfire. The script, by Patrick Kons: laughably intense. But even so, I was unprepared for the intensity of Jay's acting, of what real acting looked like close-up.

Script	Acting
Peter and Phoebe sit by the campfire, each holding a twig burning down to the nub. There are many sticks jutting from the fire; they've been at this game for a while.	As soon as ACTION hit, Jay became Peter. His back hunched, his eyes clouded. Even his voice changed, from husky to wet paper.

Peter
First one to drop it is a pussy.

Phoebe cocks her head. It's adorable and innocent.

I must confess: I hated Phoebe. She was dumb and annoying and one-note.

Phoebe
What's a pussy?

This sound bite would become a TikTok meme years later.

Peter
I don't know, Father called Mother a pussy when he was drunk last night. Another fight about joining Ladder 58.

The father, who looked like Dennis Quaid, was a firefighter driven to madness chasing fires.

Peter's eyes narrow as he watches the flame eat up the stick, getting closer and closer to his dirty fingernails. Then . . .

The way he looked at that stupid green rectangle. Like it wasn't a green rectangle. Like it was alluring, frightening, like a real flame.

PETER
Ow!

He drops the stick; the flame flickers out.

PHOEBE
Haha! Pussy!

She is still holding her stick, the flames licking her fingers, but she's holding on.

PETER
Whatever. Guess you don't feel pain.

He grabs another stick. But instead of holding it out like normal, he points it at his sister. She has long blond hair. Dry and combustible. He extends the burning stick, considering for a second, then . . .

A sharp, guttural yelp. Jay's Peter was, indeed, a pussy who could not handle pain. The flickering fire: a green rectangle.

I made my voice go high, Phoebe tasting the word *pussy*.

The director wanted me to wince like it was painful, but my acting wasn't convincing enough. So we went with a Phoebe that felt no pain, some nerve damage. It was for the better, given her ultimate fate.

I wasn't acting. Jay was so fucking scary. The way he was holding it. The way he was breathing. My hair, heavy extensions, lifted in the slight wind . . .

I kept flinching. His acting felt real. It took a million takes, and it was like that for every scene. My Phoebe was halting, flat, flinching every time Peter flicked a match. "Cut!" the director shouted. "Cut, cut, cut." Bruise was never there—writing a new song about Patrick Kons and love again—and so I was left with the man himself, his disappointed gaze each time I butchered his precious lines. I began dreading set, knowing everyone steeled themselves when it came time for Phoebe. Normally, I trusted my body to get it right, but acting was different. I wasn't naturally good, but I couldn't stop thinking about how I wanted to be good, how I should be good. Acting was in my genes.

As if I needed reminding, Mom came to California for a couple of days, one of the few times she was my guardian on a job and not Lena or Bruise. Whenever Mom was in LA, she insisted we stay in the hotel production assigned, as if Bruise's mansion were not my real home. As if she and I were still hopping from dance convention to convention, as if nothing had changed. Like there wasn't her cancer diagnosis between us, something she hadn't mentioned, something I hadn't brought up. Maybe I also wanted everything to be normal. But instead of stretching on the thin carpet and watching hotel cable, I slapped a copy of the *Cinders* script into her hands. "Practice lines with me?"

"Oh, honey, I haven't run lines since . . . oh my God, 2003? 2004?"

"And now you can say you picked it back up in 2018."

Mom opened the script, flipped through the pages. I sat on the bed across from her, showed her the correct scene. The TV played on mute, like in Leominster. It made me think of Dad, and I wondered if she had it playing out of habit or because she missed him. But once Mom said her first line, my thoughts were only: Fuck. She's good. Better than Corpus. Better than the Oscar winner playing the real Mom character. Better than me. Better than anyone.

Phoebe and Mom are in the master bedroom, folding laundry. The TV is playing on low, but they aren't watching. Instead, Mom focuses on the scorched stain on Phoebe's dress.

Mom
Where did that come from?

Phoebe
What?

Mom
The burn on your dress.

Phoebe
Oh, nothing. I don't know.

Mom
Did Peter—

Phoebe
It was an accident.

Mom *(after a long, stunned stare)*
Something's wrong with that boy.

Phoebe
He loves me, I swear! He wouldn't hurt me!

Mom

Tomorrow, I'm taking you to your aunt's. He's escalating, and he targets you especially. It's not—I'm not a good mom if I just do nothing.

Phoebe

No! I can't be away from family! And Peter isn't like that, you don't get it, he . . . *(long pause)* line?

Mom

. . . he just likes fire!

Phoebe

He just likes fire!

Mom

God, this script is dumb.

Lucy

Mom! I'm in the movie!

Mom

Sorry, I mean, it can be dumb and do well. Did Patrick Kons really write this?

Lucy

Yeah. He did. And he especially wanted me for it. Like, they are just having Bruise make the soundtrack just so I would agree. He told me secretly.

Mom opens her mouth, closes it. An awkward beat.

Mom

Have you thought about going back to school next year? You're starting high school in the fall. It might be cool, being a normal teenager. Friends your age. If you don't start this year—

Lucy

Do you think I'm good? Good at acting. Am I good?

Mom

Well, you're a beginner. Oh! There's an acting game we could try to get into character—

Lucy

I don't want to play a game. Do you think I'm really a beginner? Like, dancing, I feel like, added a lot of sideways experience. And I wouldn't have gotten this role if I was a beginner.

Mom

I just mean this is your first real acting role, honey. In high school, you could try out for plays, get even more experience without the stakes of . . . you know, this.

Lucy

I'm tired. Do you want to order food?

Mom

Thai? Same place?

Lucy

Sure.

A simmering pause. Lucy watches the mute TV. Mom pulls out her laptop, orders online. A year ago, this was routine, but nothing's right, nothing's the same. She had sex for the first time and didn't tell Mom. She doesn't know how to talk to her anymore. And it's never going back—

Mom
Pad see ew and iced tea for the both of us?

Lucy
Actually, I'm just gonna call a Lyft. I don't want takeout. I want to go to Bruise's. I'll feel more comfortable, and maybe not act like a beginner tomorrow.

Mom
What? We—you can't just drop in, she's not—

Lucy
She's like family. She says it's fine.

Mom
But I'm here.

Lucy
And you didn't tell me you have cancer. It's so weird you didn't tell me.

Mom closes her eyes. Lucy can hear her own heart beating, anticipating the worst.

Mom
It's in remission. I'm fine now.

But how can Lucy believe her? She didn't say anything when she wasn't fine.

Lucy
Oh. That's good. Thank God. Oh my God. You're fine?

Mom
It was minor, not even stage . . . and I didn't want to distract you while so much was going on. So what do you want from the Thai place? Something new?

Later, Mom will be honest with Lucy. About how it wasn't the cancer that scared her but the people surrounding her, trying to buoy her with love and goodwill. Death—the final spotlight. How she didn't want Lucy to come back to take care of her, like she had for her mother. But in this moment, she doesn't say any of that. She asks what's for dinner and Lucy thinks, This is it, this is what my relationship is with Mom now.

Lucy
Then I should stay at Bruise's, because it's really distracting going back and forth. And I have a lot going on here, I'm not going to backtrack to a random high school!

Mom
You're right. I should have told you. I just—I didn't want anyone acting— It was so wrong. I'm sorry.

Lucy *(still angry and can't put it away)*
Okay.

Mom
But I am better, and I—look, I'll set up post here, if that's what you really, really want.

They exchange a searching look. Mom is standing, Lucy still on the bed. Then—

Lucy
No.

Mom
What?

Lucy
You can't just quit your job. Your death-doula practice is important. And Dad. Micah. And Jo—Joel. I'm fine here. And you don't have to be here all the time. You have a life.

Mom
Lucy, you're my life.

A half beat. You can't hear it, but something glass inside Lucy shatters.

Lucy
But that's like . . . really sad.

Mom
Honey—

Lucy
Watching me act when you never . . . That's really sad.

Mom *(colder, like the mom she knows, not this sweet stranger)*
Don't feel bad for me.

Lucy
But I do. You just gave up. And you could have—if you just tried to lose weight, if you actually took those casting calls for fat women, who knows where you'd be! Not a shitty hoarder house in Leominster, that's for sure!

Mom *(Lucy has said the quiet part out loud, and she's shocked)*
Lucy!

Lucy *(cont'd)*
Like, it's unsuitable for habitation, and you expect me to *want* to go back? The smell alone—you don't try! Dad gave up, you gave up, you're mad at me for still trying, like it's bad I'm ashamed.

Mom
Stop it. You have NO idea—

Lucy
Exactly! I have no idea! When you were sick, when Joel was—was—

Mom
Come on. You knew. You knew, and I will *never* forget how you chose that music video when we got the call he OD'd—didn't know if he was going to die or live and you still danced!

Lucy
I didn't know how bad it was!

Mom *(simultaneously)*
Even then you chose to go back, made such a big deal out of that talk show, another music video, now this movie, it's never ending—always "me me me me" like everything revolves around you, when you're just—

Lucy *(simultaneously)*
I had no idea he was—and I couldn't just turn every job down—well, it's not always about Joel—he probably needs the distraction, like maybe it was you pressuring him and yelling at him all the time that made him—

Mom
I don't recognize you. I never raised you to be so selfish, so egotistical, so self-obsessed.

Lucy *(seething)*
I hate you. Like I really, really hate you. You never got to be who you wanted to be, fine. But I will never be you. I'll take care of my body. I'll have a clean house. I'll be happy and surrounded by people who make me feel worthwhile, because my whole life you've always made me feel like this awful, doomed, worthless person, but I'm not—I'm not like you!

Mom gets her purse, starts for the hotel door.

Lucy *(cont'd)*
Just leave me, great!

Mom *(turns back, and she's crying, and Lucy has never seen her cry, ever, ever, oh my God)*
I'm not leaving you. I'm just going for a walk because I need a second. You have hurt me beyond—you have really hurt me.

She leaves, shutting the door loudly. Right away, Lucy gets on her phone, dials a number.

Lucy
Bruise? Can you pick me up? Like right now?

Cinders: Last Scene

After we got home, Bruise called Mom to let her know where I was. When she came back into her bedroom, she was smiling.

"I'll be your adult on set tomorrow. Your mom's going home early." She knew about the cancer, about Joel, she knew everything about my life by this point. She didn't ask any other questions.

"Are you sure?" I asked. "I don't want to interrupt your process. Or ruin your day."

I was near crying again—my voice doing that awful hitching thing. I kept running through the script of our fight, every word hurled at Mom. The last shot of her ruined face. Then my brain played the next scene: Mom alone in the hotel room, Mom digging through her suitcase, unearthing my old stuffie, a pink elephant I used to squeeze for good luck before a competition, a surprise she'd planned to reveal tomorrow on set. Maybe I really was crying then because Bruise wrapped me in her arms, assured me it was no problem; in fact, she was excited to see me act. Then she turned on *The Lake House*. A good distraction. And we settled into her big Alaskan king bed and spent the rest of the night talking about how good *Cinders* was, how much this meant to Patrick, how impressed he was by my acting, how this project was going to change both of our careers. From his perch on the bedpost, Mercury Blues watched us.

On set, Bruise sat behind the camera, bantering with the director and Kons, laughing loudly to let me know everything was all right. Left to my devices, I knocked on Jay Corpus's trailer before our last scene together. The door cracked open, and I swear to God, cartoonish vapors of lavender trailed out. "Come in."

It took a long time to find him—the trailer a thatch of purple haze. He was standing in front of the sink, watching the tap run. Later, he would talk about his ritual in *Vanity Fair* and I would turn to a girlfriend at the time and say, *I saw him do that.*

"I need help acting," I said.

"You need a lot of help," he murmured.

"Any advice?"

Jay turned the tap off, and the trailer went eerily quiet. "To be her, you must let go," he whispered. "I don't know if you can let go of Lucy."

I looked away, trying to find the words. Finally: "This is my last scene, and I want it to count." After this, Peter would burn his childhood house, killing Phoebe and his mother. The rest of the movie is a weird physiological game of cat and mouse between the estranged firefighter dad and Peter.

Jay's expression softened. "Okay. Look. Who is Phoebe?"

"Phoebe's a little sister who wants her brother to love her." She is so one-dimensionally good she doesn't notice her brother burning cats in the background. In every scene, he's one inconvenience away from burning her alive and she's always like, *Brother, play with me!* Stupid.

Jay seemed to understand what I was thinking because he leaned in and said, "But what if she wasn't that stupid? Wouldn't that be more interesting?"

"But it's not in the script."

"No," he said, with a touch of a smile. "It's not."

An hour later on set, Peter cupped his hands around my neck and looked deeply into my eyes. "I wouldn't hurt you. I swear. I wouldn't ever hurt you or Mother. I wouldn't hurt a fly!"

Behind Jay, the camera and the people and the whole set blurred. There was only Peter. I let myself go and became Phoebe. This Phoebe had been holding back. She had been trying to kill him with kindness, but Peter won. But before she went down, I wanted to give Peter something to think about for the rest of his days. She put her hands over his and smiled her sweetest smile. A challenge. "I know," Phoebe said. "I know you wouldn't ever hurt me. Well. I know how much you try. You are trying, right?"

The Lucy Collection

Charley was tired. She had been up all night with this boy-band boy, driving up Mulholland, gazing upon vistas, sharing spit and childhood traumas. To the boy-band boy's brush with skin cancer, Charley divulged how her father died suddenly in the lawn-care aisle of Home Depot—*Heart attack*, such a Dad way to go—she would remark so often, as if one day she would finally find it funny. All to say, she kept yawning as we flipped through mock-ups of the Lucy Collection, dancewear I had designed.

I hadn't. Promotional video for the Lucy Collection highlighted me touring a garment factory, plucking a square of patterned cloth off a rack, and holding it up to the camera.

"This is for kids, isn't it?" Charley yawned again. "Shouldn't it be bright and peppy?"

Little girl, where did you . . .

Bruise was still fishing for lyrics for her third single, the one that would complete the trio of "Escape" and "Base Instinct." But it wasn't going well. The next song, which she'd titled "Are You, You?" was about meeting me, and she really wanted to capture that initial magic.

We have each other to stop from XOXOX *ourselves.*

Charley flipped another page. "Don't hate me," she whispered. "But I'm not sure if I like this one."

Home. Another short stay. Despite my protests, Lena insisted it would "look better on the books" if I had a break. Normally, Lena planned for me to visit home once or twice a month between gigs. But suddenly there was a tsunami of gigs. After that, she had me booked for a string of auditions and press and filming Bruise's music video, and then the *Cinders* premiere. I wouldn't be home again for a long time. If retrospective-me could shout warnings across the sands of time, I wouldn't be itching to head back west, but I was, especially after my fight with Mom. I was already counting down outside the airport pickup, shivering even though it was fifty degrees and the snow had melted. But things had changed, Micah told me, picking me up from Logan. "Changed for the good," he claimed. They had rented a dumpster and went to work. "You can even see the floor in the basement!"

"Glory hallelujah," I said flatly, watching the fog lift off Route 2. April 2018 and everything east seemed brittle: the trees, the yellowed grass, the biting air as we stepped out onto the driveway. From the outside, home seemed unchanged: canary clapboards, thinning hedges, the rusty basketball hoop. But true to Micah's word, as we opened the door it was like stepping into a new house. Gone were the heaps, the empty aquariums, the frog wind chimes. Cabinets and countertops were battered, and the familiar musk of Pine-Sol and boy lingered, but still. The place looked nice. Except the place was vacant—not even Dad parked in front of the TV.

"He's at work," Micah explained.

Work!

Yes indeed, my father had a part-time gig heading science expeditions at the Boys and Girls Club in Leominster. Afternoons, rain or shine, he led a troupe of children into the Doyle conservation land to measure soil quality, examine the egg sacks of a mother frog, split apart coyote scat with a stick, marvel at the logarithmic spirals of tadpoles and baby crayfish in an oily pond, explaining that only one out of a thousand would make it to adulthood, kind of like child stars.

"We're all busy now," Micah explained, and to prove this point, he immediately headed back out, for once not hiking but working at a rock-climbing gym. When was the last time I had been home alone—truly home alone? I couldn't remember. In the old days, this was a joyous treat. Eleven-year-old Lucy would commandeer the garage, blast her improv music as loud as it could go, and dance without brothers bursting in and roughhousing or hiding from some pissed-off girl. Without thinking, I headed there now.

But the garage was already commandeered. Every inch was nuked in color: whiteboards packed with black and red handwriting, sketches like birds' nests in the corners, maps and landscapes taped to the walls, the same sunny color scheme. Life-sized iterations of the same girl fluttered on a clothesline.

And there was Joel.

He came in for a hug when he spotted me. "I didn't know you were going to be home!"

"Just for a week or so," I said, still eyeing his new work. "Joel, this is—"

Amazing. Different. Not Joel. Pre-rehab, his work was hyperrealistic and tessellated and gritty and horrifying and itched my brain long after I was done looking. This artwork was cartoonish, bright, chaotic. The colors fuzzed together, yellows and purples and greens. I wasn't sure I liked it.

"I'm working on something new," Joel explained. "Actually . . ."

He pitched *August 8* to me, then and there.

"Wait," I said. "Didn't Mom write something like this?"

"No," Joel corrected. "This *is* it. Her play. I'm just revamping it as a video game."

I looked again at his concept art. At the girl, who Joel explained was the main character, also named Lucy in both Mom's play and Joel's game. Lucy Wiesermen. In some iterations character-Lucy was spunky and sneering and short-haired; in others she was soft and sad and flower-crowned. Ultimately, she would land somewhere in-between, smart-mouthed and sad-eyed.

I raised my eyebrows. "She's okay with it?"

"More than okay," Joel insisted. "When I read *August 8* for the first time, I wanted it to be seen. I wanted it to be real so much, but then I was like, I could make it real. Anyway, it's keeping my nose clean and I'm not thinking about what a loser I've been, so. Yeah."

His eyes were bright, and he was talking fast. I wasn't sure what to make of this Joel—if this was recovery or relapse. By the end of my weeklong stay, it wasn't any clearer. Like the old Joel, he worked long, furious hours, though now he remained in full sight, listening to David Bowie as he tweaked character design and tinkered with loglines. And unlike the brother I remembered, he constantly sought Mom for her opinion. Dinnertime talks were long and involved, interrogating Mom on character motives or tonal shifts between acts I and II. Mom seemed invigorated by their discussions, uncharacteristically happy. She only steeled herself for me. The whole week, Mom never so much as glanced my way, and I never said a word to her. Luckily Joel talked through the silence. It made me weirdly mad. He was so earnest and confident that this game was going to be made, whereas all his other stuff—the gritty, more technical stuff that I'd once praised—he'd never spoke about with such assuredness. I didn't get why.

On the last night of my visit, there was a knock on my bedroom door. "What?" I said flatly, expecting and hoping it would be Mom, ready to break the steely silence and initiate a reconciliation talk. But instead, there was Joel.

"Want to go for a little walk?"

We went to the old fort deep in the woods, past the salamander pool, past the gully where new unneutered toms kept spawning no matter how many times Mom castrated them. We leaned against the lichen-roughened side, blundering through a circular conversation about the weather and the feral cats and Dad's salamanders, Joel updating me on the Shakespearean drama the amphibians seemed to cultivate, dames cuckolding males, sons overthrowing brothers, moms eating daughters, herons wiping out whole dynasties.

"I think Dad just makes all that stuff up," I finally said.

"Maybe," Joel shrugged. "Hey, check this out. It's my skull." He scurried into the boulder, came out with this human skull.

"How is this your skull?" I asked, turning the hard cast over in my hands. Joel explained his experience weaning off drugs. The sun-drenched Arizona rehab that Mom was siphoning my bank account to pay off? Really worth its salt, turned out. Well. In terms of extrapolating face topography to skullage—we got our money's worth. We still have Joel's replica skull on the mantel, the mold mustarding with age for perfect authenticity. The rehab's therapeutic concept was to confront your ultimate fate if you keep abusing. Well. If you think about it, everyone's fate. Morning and night the director had everyone—patients, doctors, nurses, cafeteria workers, you name it—hold up their own personal skull and recite the same monologue. *Poor Yorick, I . . .* Joel brought his skull everywhere. Group therapy, single therapy, morning yoga, art therapy—no. He never attended a single painting session, knew ambition was the real habit he should kick. Mostly he drank fancy rehab coffee, played pickup volleyball, and counted down the days until he could be released. *Alas, poor Yorick, I knew him. . . .*

When he finally got punted into fancy outpatient therapy in Boston (Mom driving him there under threat of death; *If only*, he'd think, a sick half joke to himself), the Yorick-skull trend continued. Every time he thought about using, he came out to the fort and looked at the skull. It was the first time he had acknowledged to me what happened.

"Can you do it now?" I asked.

He held out the skull, readied himself, and recited the whole thing, stumbling a few times, fudging some lines. *Alas, poor Yorick, I knew him well . . .*

"Dang," I said when he finished. "Impressive."

He turned to me, suddenly all serious. "Would you want to voice Lucy?"

"What?"

"Sorry," he said, flustered. "I mean, for the game. The main character—you could act the main character. You would be great, really. I mean, you are Lucy."

"It's not getting made yet, is it?"

"We could get it made," he said. "Lucy, come on. You're kind of a big deal."

"I'm just a dancer." The words rang hollow.

"If you vouched for this, if you got Bruise on board or one of Bruise's people, you could make it happen. And then . . ."

It felt strange to hear Joel say Bruise's name. "Then what?"

"We would work together. Make it happen."

"A video game?"

"It could be fun," Joel said, scuffing his shoe against the boulder. He was picking at his nails. I wondered if he wanted to use right then. Probably.

"Yeah," I said slowly. "It would be fun."

Really, I had meant it. The more I thought about it, the more my chest warmed. This awful guilty feeling I'd carried since his overdose drained. On the walk back, at home sitting in Joel's bedroom as he showed me once again the sketches, the plotlines, the characters, this warmth expanded into something else, like being dipped in gold. Even touching down in LAX, I still felt it. I wasn't going to work on something muted and beige like dancewear or silly movies. No—my brother and I were going to make something. It would be fun.

August 8

August 8 is about the last day on Earth. An asteroid is about to hit, and there's nothing to be done about it. This is the end. The play follows people as they make meaning out of their last day—some try to dig a bunker, scrambling to cheat death. Others call their exes or estranged mothers or lost friends, trying to make final amends, while others get married to strangers. But most of the play follows Lucy Wiesermen's last day. Lucy Wiesermen is—or was—determined to live her day like it is any other August 8. She never tells anyone why, even when her family pleads with her to return home to perish together, when her friends call saying they've secured a bunker, or when her ex cleaves to her, begging for one more time. Instead, Lucy drinks two mugs of coffee and reads the next chapter of her book—does not bother to finish it or even read the end. She chats with her feeble and half-insane upstairs neighbor while she lets her dog out to tinkle. She works, copyediting for an online magazine no one will read anymore, at her favorite coffee shop, while around her people are looting and sobbing and begging God. In the afternoon, she goes on a third date with a guy. The whole play, Lucy's talking about not being late for this date, and the whole time you're thinking of course he's not going to be there, the world's ending. But lo and behold, the guy's just as crazy as Lucy and there he is, like nothing's going on. They tour an art museum and as they're gazing at the paintings, workers tear them off the walls, hauling precious artworks away to safety. "Like they'll still mean something without humans," Lucy jokes to her date, Alex. Some people are literally fucking or strangling each other in random exhibits. Then, Lucy and Alex have dinner, microwaved ramen back at her apartment because everywhere else is closed. For a moment, they consider sex—but it's too soon. Still not wanting the date to end, they walk around the city, talking about random things until the conversation veers into the deep and poignant and fragile and vulnerable and hopeful and you forget the world's ending until mid-sentence everything just goes black and the curtain falls.

In Joel's video game pitch for *August 8*, you control Lucy. You decide how you spend your last day. Any choice you make— reading to the end of Lucy's book, trying to catch a cab out to your family's home on the edge of the city—closes off other choices you could have made. If you're not in the area to meet Alex, he'll just shrug and continue with his last day. Whole dramas get played out whether you're there or not to experience them: A family dies by suicide in the park across the street, and if you're not there to talk them off the ledge (an hour and a half), then you might stumble over their corpses later on. In other words, there is probably an infinity of gameplay within those twenty-four hours, an infinity of people and stories and little moments.

"Is there a true ending?" I asked him.

"The Alex-date ending is the only happy one," he replied.

"It's not really happy. I mean, they still die."

"Everyone dies no matter what."
"Still . . ."
"Well, would you write it differently?"
"I don't know."
I still don't.

Are You, You?

I am fourteen, scrutinizing my near-naked body in a giant shard of mirror. Behind me, the desert landscape unfolds pin-straight against the red bluffs, its ruggedness marred by the small crowd of filmmakers in rapt discussion of my ass.

The costume is the same red lingerie set I wore for "Escape," except this time I'm not twelve, so it looks like a porn shoot, especially the panties riding up my butt crack. There was talk of having me dance naked and then blurring out my breasts and ass. Charley—my savior—kept insisting on a virginal white dress, and it would look beautiful and flow with the movements, and she was doing set design, why was no one listening to her? Bruise, increasingly annoyed at Charley for butting in, increasingly peppered the discussion with the word "vision." The only part of her vision I liked was Mercury Blues on my shoulder. At the last second, Bruise transferred him over. I asked what he represented, thinking how the wolves symbolized her coattail riders, the mannequin from "Escape" symbolized her past life. Bruise regarded Mercury Blues, who regarded her silently, steadily back.

"The unattainable," she said, before retreating behind the camera.

The mirror slabs were hurting my eyes, so bright and full of me. This was Bruise's third original song since our fateful meeting. To keep with the narrative consistency, it was crucial that I wear the same red lingerie set, ass crack be damned. This, unbelievably, was the shoot I managed to get Joel to visit.

You'll see how I dance, I'd texted him. *Like the Dance Awards.*

It was a long shot. Joel had moved to LA less than a week before and he didn't have a car. Over the phone—he called nearly every day since I'd agreed to voice character-Lucy, though he said he just wanted to check in with me—he'd assured me his new place was like some kind of royal palace, that it even had a pool. He'd found the sublet on some sober-living Facebook group. I looked up the address and stared through Google Maps at the bleak concrete block wedged between an Armenian grocery store and a Rite Aid and thought, *Holy shit. He's definitely going to relapse.* It scared me, that he'd suddenly flung himself at the feet of LA with nothing but his half-made pitch bible, a tendency to implode, and me, selfish me, his only support out here.

Sure, if they let me in, he wrote back. Then: *Will there be free food?*

There was free food, trays of finger sandwiches collecting flies atop folding tables. There was also the set to behold, giant mirrored slabs indented into the ground, gingerly placed by cranes and now peppered with the bloody kisses of several unfortunate desert birds. Mercury Blues's gaze lingered on the imprints, before flicking to me. Seven shards in total, in various angular shapes. All seemed precarious, like they could fall at any moment, though I was assured they would not. As Bruise sang, I danced within the giant slabs, searching for her. Only at the very end would I find her, and we would have a moment. The problem was I could see myself in these mirrored slabs, and seeing myself made it hard to dance like no one was watching.

"ACTION!" the director called. Bruise, somewhere, drew out her first wavering line: *Little girl, dancing by yourself, where did you come from? / Put on Earth to show me how to run back the clock.* And I was run-dancing toward the first slab, trying to find a way around, but my vision kept catching on my thighs, soft and heavy, plunging from the skimpy red thong. Spinning from the mirrored wall, I faced the camera, and all those people watching me, and beyond them, Joel, watching me, and how different I looked from all those years ago, hair straw-stiff, boobs heaving out of this stupid costume. The echo of Mom in my nose and eyes and the framing of my jaw, the body in the mirror soft and wide like Mom's body. And now Mercury Blues's eyes snagged on mine, I swear I saw an infinitesimal shake of his parrot head, like he knew I was slipping. Bruise's voice a lost needle in the great desert expanse, and I couldn't think of how to move because I was thinking about the last time Joel watched me dance, how it was for the Dance Awards, and how light everything had felt, dancing something sure and easy. I used to search the crowd for his and Mom's faces; they used to meet me in the wings, and now my face looked like Mom's in the mirror and each time I spun to the next mirror I'd wish I could look different, a trick of light and angles.

"You're not yourself," Bruise declared. We were taking five. My throat was hot and there was nowhere I could look without glimpsing my body. This set was the biggest orchestration she had ever done, all to showcase my performance, how far we had come—and I was floundering. At every turn lately, it seemed I was boring Bruise, that our magical relationship waned the more things heated up with Patrick Kons. Last night, she hadn't come to my bedroom like she normally did to muse about the day—she had fallen asleep with Kons and forgotten. And I found myself—I don't know—missing her?

"I can do it," I assured Bruise, my voice cracking. "I just need one more take."

"Honey, honey." She took me and Mercury Blues into her arms. "It's just like how we found each other, remember? In that office. We found each other."

"My brother's here." I pointed. There he was, awkwardly off to the side, arms laden with Tupperware of stolen set food. He gave us a sheepish thumbs-up. I'd told him today wasn't the day for us to pitch the game—soon, I promised. For now, just be visible.

Bruise regarded my brother with an even face. I remember being disappointed. I wanted her to like Joel, especially Joel.

"The one who overdosed?"

"He's recovered," I pressed. "He just moved to Los Angeles."

"Be careful. When you're famous . . . people tend to want things from you."

"Not Joel," I said proudly. "He's anti-capitalist."

She smiled and shook her head, lost in some memory. "Even without fame, people always want something from you. Every relationship is just that, wants butting against wants. Fame just brings everything to the surface."

I searched her face for the lie. Bruise squeezed my shoulder once more.

"Dance, Lucy girl. Dance like yourself again."

I returned to the starting mark, arms stretched toward my mirrored self. As the director counted down, I tried to grasp that old struck-chord feeling before a performance. On my shoulder, Mercury Blues's breath quickened. I followed his gaze. Behind, in the flat blue sky, a dark V of geese retreated or approached.

Cinders Premiere

Once we made it into the theater, I saved a seat for Joel. He kept texting and calling, asking when would I come by his apartment, when would I read the script, practice some lines for character-Lucy? *We could grab some pizza and I'll give you the whole spiel*, Joel often texted. *I know a good pizza place now!*

Sure, I texted back. *I love pizza! Soon!*

Bruise always said there was no good pizza in LA. Her words lingered in my brain: *When you're famous, people want . . .* I knew she would take Joel's pitch the wrong way, that it would go badly and Joel would use again and die and then it really would be my fault. So I texted back platitudes until he sent a screenshot of *Cinders'* Instagram account, circling the premiere date, asking if wayward brothers of the star were allowed. How could I say no?

But when it came time for the limo to leave, Joel still hadn't shown up. We left without him. "How ominous," Bruise said, her eyebrows raised in a show of worry. He texted me just as the limo pulled up to the red carpet, apologizing and claiming he would meet us at the theater. But there was no sign of him even as the movie began playing full blast. Jay Corpus flicked on a match, snuffed it out, lit another, his sweaty T-zone highlighted.

Meanwhile, I couldn't concentrate on my acting debut, my girlish voice ringing through the Chinese Theatre, because my brain looped on the image of Joel nodding off somewhere. I kept checking and rechecking my phone, wondering if I should call Mom even if we hadn't spoken more than five words since our fight, sparse logistical things over text. No. I didn't want to think of either of them, so I watched Phoebe-Lucy cup my fake brother's face and whisper, almost bitingly, that it wasn't his fault, he was trying. Joel would have rolled his eyes at a few plot twists: The firefighter father was a hallucination the whole time.

Heading out, you could tell from the questions the press asked how the reviews would trend. Even the most scathing still revered Jay Corpus's acting, which all the critics agreed was too good for this bad of a movie. A few reviews lobbed compliments my way. But they torched the rest of the movie, especially the plot. Not good for Patrick Kons, who wrote the "cursed" script, or Bruise, whose soundtrack for the movie would be described as "passably benign noise."

On the ride to the after-party at Bruise's place, the mood was dark. There, Joel was waiting. He had been pulled into the tide of the party. The backyard was filled with abused circus animals, braying and huffing. Right. I'd forgotten about them. Two weeks ago, a huge *Vulture* article exposed this particularly famous circus for horrific animal abuse, and Bruise purchased the whole stock to save them. I was riding out this phase at Charley's place, waiting for Lena to quietly rehome the last pony. As we entered, Joel ran up bearing a bundle of roses he'd clearly gotten from Ralphs, claiming his roommate's car's engine gave out so he had to take a Lyft. He had gotten to the Chinese Theatre late and they wouldn't let him in. So he snuck by the ushers and watched from the theater's aisle, just in time to see me die.

"You were good," Joel managed. "You died really well. Dramatic."

"Thanks," I said, trying to laugh. He didn't seem high, but what did I know. His eyes were wide, bright, and I could tell he was nervous. In the clean light of Bruise's mansion, my brother looked dusty: to our premiere outfits, he wore what I knew to be his nicest flannel shirt, the one he'd worn to his high school graduation, the one Mom bought off the sale rack at Nordstrom.

"My brother made it," I announced, but my found family was already pushing past us, Charley darkly swearing that she needed to hide from Chance, since she'd heard cops saw some stuff on his phone, and she wasn't going to get involved with that. Lena went off to greet Jay Corpus, Patrick Kons headed to a lounge chair, where he would refresh his phone for reviews, Bruise after Patrick Kons. Only Ronan stayed back, his hand protectively on the small of my back.

"This is my boyfriend," I told Joel.

"Oh," Joel said lightly, not hiding his shock. At home, I didn't really mention Ronan, and it was clear no one in my family was googling my name. "You're—"

"Rodriguez," Ronan said.

"Farlock Brothers," Joel said. "Wow, that's—I've seen some episodes."

"I know," Ronan said, his tone darker. "Shall we enter the fray?"

The backyard was a swirling galaxy of famous people and battered circus animals. Celebrities—actors, directors, writers, all people I could tell Joel recognized—marveled at the emancipated elephants, skittish camels, teary-eyed seals, oohing and aahing. They provided a welcome topic of conversation, rather than *Cinders*, which baffled even the quirky A24 writers. Eventually we crashed back into Charley, who gushed about how a producer had hinted that her favorite fantasy book was being made into an HBO series and it was a secret so don't tell anyone. "Oh," Joel laughed awkwardly. "Lips are sealed."

We were next to the circus seal pit. "Ha," Charley said before launching more into the HBO show and how she was going to spend all night stalking the producer until she got word she could be something on set—design coordinator would be ideal, but she'd take anything.

"Good luck," Joel offered as Charley slipped off with a wink. Then, to me: "Should we do the same for *August*—" Before he could finish, we were pulled into a circle of other vague celebrities yakking congrats at me, how good I was at being Phoebe, how they'd cried when I stopped, dropped, and rolled into an early death. By the time we detangled from the crowd, I already wanted it to be over. We were in the corner of the yard, watching Hollywood elites chatter among themselves, the elephant's swaying head just visible. Splashes and shrieks and the din of glassware. The decorations were fire-themed: fire gowns, fire tinsel littered across the lawn, red and black curtains. Against the back of the mansion, a giant projector ran the trailer of the movie, mostly of Jay Corpus, a five-second clip of me playing with a marshmallow on fire, looking like a little kid, snaggle-toothed and doomed.

"Be honest," I said. "Was I that good? At acting?"

"You were good."

"Be honest. No one's honest here."

Joel chose his words carefully. "I don't think you were given a lot to work with."

"But Mom—"

"I don't think anyone here knows how awesome you are," Joel said. "Not even Bruise."

"How?"

He fought for the words. "You love what you do—that's what always comes through."

"No," I protested, but inside, I was glowing.

"And look," Joel continued, "when we make *August 8*, then they'll really know what you're capable of in terms of being part of something that's really . . . I don't know, good. I hope good. It's good, right?"

The glowing-inside feeling fizzled. Back to my low-grade fever of guilt. "Right."

"We just need someone to throw money and their names at us. Bruise, any of these suits, her boyfriend—Kons? We can approach them tonight, pitch it."

"Soon. Maybe not tonight, though."

"What do we have to lose? This is your party. No one here will say no to you."

"Is it ready? Like, do you seriously think it's ready?"

"You believe in this, don't you?"

The worst part was I did believe in *August 8*, from the moment he'd read the logline in the garage of our shitty house. At least, I believed in the possibility of the story. It was Joel I didn't believe in, his shaking hands and simplified art. He looked at me like I held his lifeline in my hands. He was late.

I announced I had to pee and gunned it inside, not looking back to see if he was following. My destination wasn't the guest bathroom but the "water room," which was just a closet with a toilet inside it, within the bathroom. So I could lock the bathroom and then lock myself inside the toilet room, sit inside the dark coolness and count down the seconds until it would be weird if I stayed any longer.

When I finally emerged into the glittering backyard, I couldn't find any familiar faces in the throng of beautiful people and huffing camels. Almost by accident, I stumbled on Jay Corpus smoking and stroking the back of a miniature pony, statuesque except for its labored breathing, the crescent wet whites of its eyes expanding with each breath.

"So," he said. "Looks like we made it out."

"I guess," I said, reaching out to stroke the pony's back. The ponies were all interchangeable. They were all named Marigold, since the abusive circus did not care about its ponies.

"You don't seem happy," Jay Corpus declared.

"I don't think I like parties."

"You'll need to like parties if you want to be an actor."

"I'm not an actor. I'm a dancer."

"But you're talented." Jay crouched next to me. Marigold shook her little head. "Look. Once I had a girlfriend who wanted to be a sheep herder. She read all these books about sheep herders being closer to God or something. So I say, sure, anything for you, *babe*, and I got her a bunch of sheep and a bunch of herding dogs to keep the sheep. But do you know what I learned about herding dogs? It's not a trick that can be taught. It's all instinct. Either they can herd or they can't, and if they can't, they never will."

"What happened to the sheep?"

"It's like that with acting," Jay Corpus continued, chewing on his cigarette. "They say it can be taught, but it's just . . . you either have it or you don't. That's the dirty secret. And you, Lucy Gardiner, you have it. You know what happened to the sheep? My dogs couldn't herd, so the sheep ran away and got torn apart by coyotes and my girlfriend left me."

"Because of the sheep?"

"No," he sighed. "I cheated on her."

"Mm," I said, rising. "I better find my brother."

He lit another cigarette, lifted it to his eyeline so he could watch the smoke pull off the orange nub. "I'll be watching your career with interest, my dear."

I let the party swallow me back up, away from Marigold and Jay Corpus. Before I could find Joel, Ronan wheeled me to the snack bar on the patio, asking if I'd mentioned him to Jay. "No," I said, and then he wanted to know what we were talking about. "Sheep."

"Bullshit. What did he say to you?"

"He told me I had it. He's watching my career with interest." Ronan snorted.

"What?" I said, though I should have dropped it. I knew what he was going to say, but I wanted to hear it. What everyone I knew was thinking, but not saying.

"We just watched the same movie. Do you think . . . I mean come on, you're a great dancer. But you know you weren't . . . acting, you're not good."

He said that final line apologetically, as if he had been waiting a long time to tell me.

"Like you're better," I laughed.

It was the cruelest thing I could have said, knowing how much the craft of acting meant to Ronan, the one real thing that insulated him from his spiraling brother, a childhood knowing you were already cresting past the point of no return. In that regard, we might have understood each other, but it was too late. We exchanged more barbs, voices rising. By the end of it I knew magazines and gossip blogs would be declaring time of death.

He was storming away, and maybe I would have gone to him or maybe to find Joel, but Charley touched my shoulder, whispering that she had gotten a promise from the HBO producer that she would have a job on the fantasy series, the one that was also her dad's favorite—had she ever told me that?

"No," I said, still reeling from Ronan—less the breakup, more that my acting was subpar, I knew it, I knew it, a black hole of shame and frustration yawning inside me while Charley gushed about this series, a fantasy with people of color and dragons and robots, and well, it had everything, it was written in the late eighties, and her dad had read it to her as a young girl and, finally, here was a project she could really see herself doing, like something she was meant to do, here was the reason Bruise had whisked her to Hollywood in the first place, why she'd left everything behind and why she didn't feel like the same person anymore— "But that's good, right, it's good that I'm not the same angry girl from three years ago, I'm better, right? I'm . . ."

I asked her where Bruise was, but she just shrugged, said another fight with Kons, and then I came out with it that Ronan had broken up with me. Charley clicked her tongue sympathetically. "But you wanted him to, right?"

It was then, staring into the crowd, feeling sorry for myself, I saw Joel. God, he looked so awkward. Clutching a platter of olives and artichokes arranged in roses—they must have mistaken him for a waiter. His head was craning this way, that way—looking for me.

I left Charley, threading my way through the crowd, the camels chewing and the elephant slow-blinking in agony. The air was beginning to cool, but all the human conversation seemed to make everything heavy and impenetrable.

A hand snagged me before I could reach Joel. I smelled her before I saw her. Bruise.

"Lucy girl," she whisper-yelled in my ear. "Lucy girl, I need you."

She was squirreled away on the very edge of her property, where the rugged scrub met the manicured lawn. Below, the great expanse of the Valley. At her feet, bottles of tequila, glasses, whole limes and lemons. A paper plate of red sauce, exoskeletons of many shrimp.

"Kons left again," she said, voice fighting to be casual. The reviews had started coming out—the film had bombed. He started a fight, they exchanged words, each more loaded and painful than the last, but of course, the lines meant more than the lines, the want behind the want. He wanted everything to be the same, like when they walked the French beachside and they were young and brilliant and beloved. She wanted the same. But the universe didn't want that, the ceaseless march of time didn't want that, and rather than fight the ceaseless march of time, they fought each other. Of course, that's how Bruise conveyed their final breakup. If I could talk to Bruise now, I would tell her: You're actually both boring people incapable of sustaining deep, evolving relationships. And my worst fear is you've made me the same. Instead, I said: "Ronan's left, too."

We giggled, and then we couldn't stop giggling, giddy, heartbroken giggles. Without saying it, we both knew they'd left for the same reason. The movie flopped, the music video flopped. Our spark was dying out, and there was nothing left for them to peck over. We kept on laughing, dizzy with a strange, familiar relief—we still had each other.

"I think it's time you had a drink," Bruise said finally.

She uncorked a bottle of tequila, took a swig, full-body shuddered. Handed it to me.

"Just don't think, Lucy girl. You have to let go."

Somehow, I knew she wasn't asking me for one sip—she was asking me to get drunk.

Just like dancing, I thought, bringing the bottle to my lips. *Just like acting.*

We took swig after swig, commiserating. This was the Bruise I liked best: raw, vulnerable, and only for me. She told me about how the first time Kons left, when she was twenty, he had cheated on her with a model. It felt like the world was ending. She drank a whole bottle of vodka by herself in a Paris hotel room, woke up the next morning with a shaved head and her first scandal, half sex with a British royal. "What's half sex?" I asked, and Bruise said you don't want to know, and we both laughed like we did.

"Regardless," Bruise said. "If I learned anything, it's that there's always something next. Even if the world's ending."

By this point, the lights in the Valley were winking at me, and my mouth tasted sweet and I felt like everyone at the party liked me. I wasn't even thinking about Joel. Mercury Blues, perched again on Bruise's shoulder, seemed to be nodding in approval. *You did good, bitch*, he seemed to be saying. *You got that herding-acting instinct, just like me.*

My back against the cool grass, feeling like I was undulating.

"Lucy girl," Bruise whispered beside me. "What should we do next?"

The sky was starless, and it made me sad. I had never been to Paris, or even met a British person.

So I whispered back, "See the world, I guess."

"Mm," Bruise said. Then, with more gusto. "*Mm!!*" She sat up. "A world tour. I'll take us on a world tour."

"A world tour?"

She grabbed my hands, pulled me up. "First, Lucy girl. People! We need more eyes on this, more eyes and ears and wallets."

We made a beeline for Lena, surrounded by suits. Producers, directors, art people, money people, their faces lighting up as Bruise and I pierced their circle. Immediately, Bruise poured into her world tour concept, a vision far exceeding any other tour or movie, something that would break status quo, would change lives because what she was missing lately was the moment, the intimacy, the—

And then I saw Joel making his way toward us.

"No," I whispered. Shook my head slightly.

"Lucy!" Joel called, elbowing his way toward us. "There you are!"

Bruise stopped mid-sentence about the world tour unifying the world through a common musical language. The producers and directors and art people and money people began murmuring, benign things about the circus elephant and Mercury Blues, who was staring intently at Joel, as if to say—*Go on. Let's hear it.*

"My brother," I said weakly. "Joel. He just moved here."

"How lovely," Bruise's voice skated on ice. "How lovely of him to finally make it."

One of the money people asked why he'd moved here.

"Lucy's big premiere," Joel responded. Then he smiled, as if to himself.

Don't say it, I said telepathically. *Wait, wait, wait.*

"And we might be working on something together."

"Oh?" Bruise cocked her head, annoyance giving way to smug confidence. I didn't need eye contact to feel it radiating off her. "Oh? What are you working on?"

Without inhaling, Joel launched into his elevator pitch for *August 8*. First shakily, haltingly, and then he gained his footing, and the arcs and slopes of the story took shape. He began with a question: If you knew the world would end, how would you spend your time? The pause was barely perceptible before he rushed into the explanation of New York City at the end of times. "Time," Joel said, his voice wavering, "is really important to this story." But before he explained how time worked in his game, he talked about how different time felt after his overdose. How each second since had seemed more delicious. Like, all of a sudden, you realize what's worth your time, who should get your time. He talked about Denise, his stepmother, who wrote *August 8* across three decades—half her life in New York City, trying to get this play made. How she met our father and packed up her life, spent all her time on him and his children. Before his overdose, Joel thought she'd wasted time trying to get just one thing made, all that time for nothing, but then one day, helping his stepmother clean out her desk—she was weak from chemo, needed help—"And I was trying to be better—actually listened to her, learned about what she went through . . . anyway, I read *August 8*. And. I just got it. Got her. Why she spent so much time trying to get it made, why she put it down. But it's just—it was the story I needed. Even now, I can't get it out of my head. It's the story people need more than ever. And I thought I could spend some time trying to pick up where she left off."

When he finished his pitch, my eyes were misting, thinking about how far *August 8* had come to reach Hollywood, how much of Mom's heartbreak and his heartbreak and mine had gone into making this moment possible. All of us, the important art people, Lena, Bruise, me, were staring at him, our mouths agape.

"Oh my God," one of the important people exhaled. "Is Jay Corpus fucking that pony?"

An exclamation of voices, the bray of a horse. As it would turn out, Jay Corpus was not fucking a pony, but elbow-deep in its rectum, as the pony had been in labor this whole time. People just thought it was a cute fat pony. Without context, it was just Jay Corpus elbow-deep in a pony's rectum, and so everyone whizzed over to get a good look. Everyone, except me and Joel.

"Hey . . ." I started.

But he was storming away.

My body froze yet again. I let a swell of minutes pass, staring at without seeing at the buzzing crowd, hearing without hearing the labored neighs and wet squelches of the foal hitting the plastic turf and the snap of the cameras. And then, I heard a whistle and glanced up.

Mercury Blues. Perched on the wrought-iron fence that held Bruise's menagerie. So captivated by Joel's pitch, I hadn't noticed the bird slipping off Bruise's shoulder and onto the post. Lately, he had been inching away from her, and she took it personally.

"Well," I said. "Did you like it, at least?"

He blinked. Without thinking, I extended my hand, feeling again his sharp animal talons dig into my skin.

I found Joel in the quiet motor gate, staring down at his phone, calling a Lyft.

"Hey," I repeated. "Are you okay?"

"I really thought it would happen this time."

"It's not like they rejected it."

"But they didn't care. It's just like Denise said, but I thought with enough moxie, enough . . . humanness . . . God, after everything, I'm still really stupid, aren't I?"

He looked up from his phone, saw my face. "I'm sorry, Lucy. That was a shitty position to put you in. It was your night, and I ruined it. Again."

"S'okay," I said.

He checked his phone. The Lyft must be rounding the corner.

"You want to come?" Joel asked. "We could go back to my apartment, get pizza or sushi, cry about my failed pitch, your stunning debut. I have an air mattress."

Automatically my head swiveled to the mansion—in the backyard, an elephant was trumpeting, people were laughing, a newborn foal was crying.

"Maybe . . ." I murmured.

I heard, without seeing, the crunch of the Lyft's tires. Still, Joel didn't move.

"Come back with me," Joel repeated. "Hell, you don't even have to go back to Mass. We could get a two bedroom here, and I could work on the game and you could do online school. I'm sure there's killer dance studios out here."

"I don't have dance practice anymore," I said softly.

"Lucy," Joel said, taking on force. "I don't like leaving you here."

"I don't like you here either. In LA."

"Why?"

I closed my eyes tight. I hated how flaky my voice sounded. "You were late, Joel. Like an hour late getting to my premiere. Probably you missed the whole thing."

"My friend's car—"

"I'll never know for sure," I said, finally facing him, even if my eyes were hot with stupid tears. Joel was standing at the Lyft, his eyes red. But still, I continued: "I never know anything, no one lets me know. You, Mom—I never get to know . . . So that's why I'm here—doing my own thing."

"Please," Joel said. "I won't force you. But please—get in the car. Let's . . . you don't even have to help me with *August 8*, just let me . . ."

"They just didn't like it, Joel. I'm sorry."

It was only when I was back in that grandiose lobby that I remembered Mercury Blues was perched on my shoulder, silently observing the whole thing. His orange parrot eyes melancholic or judgmental, I couldn't tell.

Objects in the Mirror Are Closer than They Appear

I was fifteen when I headed to high school for the first and only time. Not real high school. A television set of a high school. While Lena was organizing travel itineraries, while Charley doodled costume designs, while Bruise arranged the music, and down in the Valley Joel pitched his game, I was cast in a teenage science fiction show called *Objects in the Mirror Are Closer than They Appear*. Pitched as *Death Note* meets *Stranger Things* meets *Back to the Future*, the show revolved around a group of friends who realize they can time travel by adjusting the rearview mirror of the main character's car. Obviously, they decide to use their powers for good, killing famous villains from history, but a botched attempt on Genghis Khan's life sets off a chain reaction our heroes must undo before the world's timeline unravels.

It was the only project I liked in the thousands Lena had lobbed my way since *Cinders*; plus, it seemed like the sort of role a real actor would take.

Fuck you, Ronan Rodriguez.

Bruise and I mourned the ends of our relationships both together and apart. Together, we watched *The Lake House*, weeping real tears when young Keanu Reeves booked a reservation at a fancy restaurant three years out. (He waited for her!) We drank red wine and ate whole boxes of Cheez-Its, proclaiming we would never date men again, at least not for a long time. Rather, it would all be about the world tour, about setting the world ablaze with music and art and us doing the music and art. Separately, Bruise threw herself into writing angry breakup songs in the basement, assuming that I was down in the studio, angrily practicing the choreography. Instead, I sounded out my lines for the first soft shoot. The director of *Objects in the Mirror Are Closer than They Appear*, a bohemian madman-type artist, wanted to see the cast "in the wild" before he finished writing the season. During preproduction meetings, he only ever referred to us by our characters' names: Savannah, Ian, Dina. For the soft shoot, he shoved the cast in a random high school in LA—to this day, I'm not sure he got permission—and instructed us to spend a regular day in character. I was determined to do just that, to spend a day shedding the version of me who listened to Bruise cry herself to sleep, the version of me assuring Charley she should call the producer of the fantasy series, the version of me ignoring texts from Joel and Mom, the version of me all my other versions agreed was the worst. No, I would be Dina, plucky sidekick and eternal best friend to the main character. Here, I met Reyna.

She was playing the main character, Savannah. I had glimpsed her headshot in passing before we first met for the screen test, and I remember being jealous that she was cast for the main part, jealous she arrived to promotional shoots with her entire family in tow, jealous she was prettier than me, black hair that rippled as she cracked her neck, some sort of acting warm-up. When we started filming, the stylist chopped her hair pixie short—Savannah was a tomboy. The way her hands kept running through phantom locks, I knew before I knew her that she hated how she looked, but I always thought short hair suited her. That had been my first thought, seeing Reyna alone on the highest row of bleachers, squinting down at the football players running drills: *main character shit.*

I clambered up. Dina and Savannah had been best friends since childhood. I tried to convey this in my greeting: "Thought I'd find you here, Sav."

Without looking at me, Reyna groaned. "Urgh. Mr. Smith was on my case, so I went hiding. He's so annoying, right?"

"Yeah," I said, not knowing what she was talking about. She was riffing. Finding her character, like the director had instructed us. Reyna was a professional.

"Geology," Reyna said. "Who gives an *F* about geology? Like, the Earth is flat, isn't it?"

I paused—Savannah was a straight-A student, so I wasn't sure where she was going with this. Reyna covered her mouth like she was trying not to laugh.

"Yeah," I said slowly, thinking about what Dina would say. She was boy crazy, so I pointed down at the football field and commented, "Just like those football players. I mean, their asses. So flat."

That was when Reyna turned to me, her face twisted into a sort of smile. For all her talent, Reyna was never good at keeping character around me. But she persevered. "Yeah, did you see Derick's ass in Spanish today? It was so . . . flat."

"Why are boys' asses so flat?" I mused, perhaps with too much weight. Rey, as I could come to know her, choked. Then we were breaking down, giggling. It took us a long time to recover. I sat down next to her and apologized. I worried I had broken the scene.

But Rey seemed happy to break protocol. She asked me if I had ever been to high school. "Is that how girls talk?"

Neither of us had been to a normal school past sixth grade, we discovered. Rey had only a few memories of a fourth-grade classroom. She recalled a school project where they had to build dioramas of the Alamo; she had been pissed her partner went so heavy on the glue that the whole thing wilted. But that was before she made it big on television, starring as a child victim in the TV remake of a famous child murder in a series called *Child Murder*. The crazy thing was, she told me, she thought it was make-believe, like it didn't really happen to a kid like her. Still, the remake made her into an actor, and she found marginal success as a creepy, ethnically ambiguous little girl on paranormal and crime shows. It was enough to move her family to a house on a hill in Torrance. And though she couldn't imagine not acting, she couldn't help but feel jealous seeing her younger sisters getting ready for school, or doing homework on the countertop before dinner, just regular stuff—she missed that.

"I know." I told her about how jealous I got seeing my brothers and their friends in the driveway, playing basketball and talking about random teachers.

"You have brothers!" Rey exclaimed, lightly pushing me. "I didn't know you have brothers. How many? Where are they now?"

She seemed like she genuinely wanted to know. So I told her everything I could about my two brothers, but mostly things about Micah gathered from texts and scant calls. Rey's eyes and smile grew wider as I talked, noting the similarities: She had a sister that liked the outdoors, too. And there was another she didn't mention to me: an older sister who nearly drowned when Rey was five and now was so significantly brain damaged that she couldn't speak or eat, but her parents were convinced she was still in there, somewhere. I'm sure the sister was on Rey's mind, but she didn't tell me then, not yet, just like I didn't elaborate on Joel.

We were too lost in conversation to notice the director watching us far below on the football field. "Ladies!" he called, clapping his hands. "Let's get into character."

"How does he know we're not in character from so far away?" I asked.

Rey rolled her eyes. "Dina." Her fingertips interlocked with mine. It was startling how quickly she could get into character, like stepping into one's favorite pair of jeans. I turned and there was Savannah, my best friend, her eyes glowing conspiratorially.

A sudden, far-flung memory: Kimberly in that wood-paneled basement, stifling giggles after we had hidden our goriest comic from her mothers.

"Dina," Rey repeated. "Let's ditch next period and go to Taco Bell."

"What about Mr. Smith? What about geology?" I protested. We had it backward—Savannah was supposed to be the Goody Two-Shoes and Dina was the slacker. But still, in character, Rey pulled me out of North Hollywood High School and across the intersection to the Taco Bell. Even though it was close to three in the afternoon, the place was more packed with high schoolers than the actual school.

"We need to observe regular high schoolers in the wild," Rey breathed, her face pressed close to mine.

We passed the rest of that period in a crowded Taco Bell booth, picking at grande nachos and eavesdropping on teenagers. They entered in packs, bearing sagging backpacks, talking loudly, leaning over tables to get a look at each other's phones. We were in pretty intense hair and makeup, and no one seemed to recognize us. Slowly, my insides uncoiled. There were some couples who couldn't seem to get enough of each other, hands slipping into pockets. For a long time, a group of girls our own age remained at the booth next to us. They were doing algebra homework and alternated between complaining about the teacher, who didn't know how to teach, and gushing over an artist's hyperrealistic rendering of Disney princes in jockstraps, but like, ironically so. These would be Savannah and Dina, I realized, though these girls somehow seemed too young. In the pilot, Savannah and Dina's dialogue was straight to the point: *So, Jimmy Henlocks caught you and Trina. / Wait, don't you need a car to get to the party?* I didn't see how we could fit a whole life between the lines, make them seem as real as the girls cracking up over Disney dicks.

Rey shook the ice in her drink. "I think I'll need some more Baja Blast for the road."

When she came back, she checked the time on her phone. "Damn. We still have an hour left. Want to just walk around?"

With nowhere to go, we read the flyers along the school hallway: mock trial announcements, volleyball tryouts, mathletes, Spanish culture night. I suddenly felt sad. It all seemed so familiar and ordinary, and yet exotic. I would never go to a high school like this. I would never skip last period for Taco Bell. I wouldn't take the SATs, wouldn't aimlessly wander a hallway with my friend between classes.

Rey ripped a flyer off the wall. "Oh my gosh," she said in a fake Valley girl accent. "Dina, look at this. Tryouts for *Twelve Angry Men*. Want to go for it?"

I blinked, almost irritated that Rey wasn't even trying. Savannah was supposed to be shy and reserved and bookish. It would take me a long time to understand that Rey was building her own Savannah, testing things out, experimenting. Acting.

"I always wanted to act," Rey said shyly, looking at the crudely photocopied leaflet of a single angry man. Then she looked at me, and I couldn't tell if it was Rey or Savannah. "If I'm honest, I kind of want to be a famous actor. I mean, we live in Hollywood, after all."

"North Hollywood," I corrected her.

Just then, a voice barked at us. "Hey! Where are you girls supposed to be?"

An older teacher was slumping through the halls, her lanyard making an ugly clank. "Do you have a hall pass? Ladies!"

"Uh . . ." Rey looked at me, her mouth twisted again into a smile. "I think Mr. Smith's class? Geology?"

The teacher's fury only built. "Don't act smart! What are your names?"

"Dina!" I yelled before I could stop myself, then I grabbed Rey's arm and sprinted the opposite way. The teacher yelled for security—schools have that?—and we booked it as fast as we could down the hallway. Rey was laugh-breathing in my ear: "Gogogoogogogo!" Finally, rounding a corner, we ducked into an open door.

"Safe," I exhaled, and we collapsed against the wall, still hiding. It was an empty classroom, with music stands and big suitcase-like coffins. On the walls were posters of men in white wigs bent over pianos. And then—we both saw it at the same time—a couple making out. The noises they made were wet, like stirring macaroni. Though they glanced up, our presence didn't seem to disturb them. Rey saluted them.

"Carry on," she said in a deep voice. "Nothing to see here."

I bent over in giggles, and she did too, clutching my fingers. Even when we ventured back out into the hallway as the final bell rang, the giggles hadn't been extinguished, and all one had to do was to say, "Carry on" before we would dissolve into a fit again.

Rey whistled as we made it back out to the football field. The sun was just setting in a blaze of pink and orange. It was January, balmy. "God," she sighed. "I haven't had a friend my age in a long time."

The Future Tour: Beijing

Until she left us, Charley and I shared a hotel room. Like little kids, we leapt from double bed to double bed, investigated the mini fridge, and ordered a gross amount of room service. I have a memory of Charley from that first city on the tour, standing before the wall-to-wall window in her underwear and T-shirt, eating a two-hundred-dollar cheesecake.

"I can't believe how many people live here," she was saying. "More than Los Angeles."

"How many?"

"Twenty million."

"I simply can't fathom that," I said. "My brain just says no."

Charley didn't respond right away, just licked her fingers and looked down at the streaked, rainbow lights of the city. "I bet there are more dead people than alive people."

"In total?"

She set down the cheesecake; she didn't eat the crust because she was supposed to be gluten-free. "How many people have lived and died since, like, all of human history?"

I looked it up. "Around 117 billion humans have been born, and there's only about 7 billion alive right now. So that's about 110 billion dead people."

"Wow," she said, and then started to say something more, something probably deep, maybe something about her dead dad, but her phone vibrated.

"Is it the producer guy?" I asked. Since the *Cinders* party, she had been hustling to squeeze her way onto the crew of the HBO fantasy series.

"No," Charley muttered, frowning at her phone. "College friends."

"You still talk to them?"

"I get push notifications whenever they post. I mean, I could talk to them, I'm just, you know, crazy busy."

"Yeah," I said, thinking of my family. Charley kept staring down at her phone, a pained expression across her face.

"What are they doing?" I finally asked.

"They all graduated from Emerson today. I would have, too."

In my mind, Charley was so much older than me. It is hard to fathom her as she was, just twenty-two. The age I am now. At the time, she seemed so self-possessed, and I was too self-obsessed to notice she was lonely, second-guessing her choice to drop out of college and work for Bruise. But hey, you only live once, and then you're just part of the 110 billion dead.

To take her mind off it, I let her read the fantasy series out loud. It had been a long time since someone had read to me, and Charley had the best reading voice. The fantasy series followed a young girl who becomes a dragon rider in a cybernetic city. When it finally came out years later, I had nearly forgotten about this night, the stark smell of the Chinese hotel, Charley's steady voice. Despite myself, I binged every episode, scanning the credits even though I knew. When the final scene faded to black,

I wanted so badly to text Charley, *the book was better, anyway.* But no, that's too far ahead. Charley read. We were just getting into the first fight scene—the bad guy curling his long fingernails around the young girl's throat—when my phone lit up.

Can't sleep, Bruise texted. *Lake House with me?*

The Future Tour: Tokyo

Charley's favorite movie, *Lost in Translation*, was filmed here and though we'd planned on watching it in Japan, there was always something that got in the way. The first night, Bruise wanted to do karaoke. The second and third and fourth were filled with grueling rehearsals and sound checks in the morning, and at night, grueling makeup, grueling press, grueling performances. After, Bruise called the core team to sit in her hotel room, *The Lake House* playing in the background, while she poured over the press and articles, trying to see if people got the narrative of the tour.

But on the fifth and final day in Tokyo, there was nothing planned, and Charley pulled us into a famous temple to have her *Lost in Translation* moment. The four of us—Lena, Charley, Bruise, me—walked through the red gates, admired the slanted roofs, the gardens, the concentric pools feeding into bigger pools. Scattered about were buffed stones, inscribed with Japanese symbols; names, someone told us, of people important to someone. They looked like hooded figures watching us walk past. For a long while, we glided one by one, quiet for once, and I let my mind wander ahead to *Objects*—as Rey and I had been privately abbreviating the title—which was starting principal filming in two weeks. It would put the tour on hold.

Bruise never mentioned this delay in her pep talks, but passively made clear it was very much noted. "Two months? You've never gone that long without dance. Do you worry you'll lose your spark?" She asked so often it was clear my project bothered her, like it was sacrilegious to wish for anything but the tour. I tried to stop thinking about it, as if she could read my mind. *Focus on the overlapping pools*, I thought. The fact that I was in freaking Japan.

Charley's phone cried out. Everyone shot her a look, but she was smiling down at the caller ID and took the call by the bamboo fountain—filling with water until it tilted down, striking the rock with a distinct noise. I watched Charley across the pond, golden from the late-afternoon sun. The water was so still it seemed an unbreakable surface. On some dark human impulse, I flecked pebbles into the pond, disturbing the perfect veneer.

"Beautiful, right, Lucy girl?"

Bruise sat down next to me. I nodded.

"How are you liking the tour?"

I nodded again, wanting to relish the silence more. But Bruise was staring at me.

"Good," I said finally. "I like . . . I'm having fun."

"This is all for you, you know."

"For me?"

"I wish I could see the world through your eyes," Bruise said. "You don't know how badly I wish I could do things over again, do things right like how you get to do them."

"I . . ." My mouth struggled to find the words. "Happy."

"Good." Bruise squeezed my shoulder. "I'm glad you're happy."

When Charley returned, she was glowing but wouldn't say what the phone call was about. "Later," she whispered when I asked, eyes jabbing toward Bruise.

When we got in the car, Bruise didn't want to go back to the hotel. She was giddy, too—the rocks with names had given her an idea.

"Lucy girl, I need your hand."

Without saying what for, she had the driver take us deep into the city. Bruise led us into a musty place, the lights low, everything smelling like old wood and chemicals. A tattoo parlor.

"Oh," Charley said, mood still riding high from that phone call. "I could have designed a tattoo for you. We could all get matching ones. A tiny dot, a circle, infinity . . ."

Bruise took my hand and placed it on her sternum. "I want Lucy's handprint. Right over my heart."

No one said anything. Not Lena, not Charley, not me—but one could heed, from the intake of old wood and chemical air, that we were stunned. And yet we all let it happen. My hand pressed into the armored knob of her sternum as Bruise's breaths tightened, eased. Carefully, the tattoo artist traced the outline of my spread fingers, the needle jabbing so close I braced for impact; I could feel without feeling her pain. When she posted the video of us, my hand pressed on her chest, the tattoo artist slowly threading ink around the slope of my thumb, people went nuts, marveling at the heights of our bond, twinned flames still after all these years. Yet for the first time, it all felt so unearned. *Lucy girl*, she captioned it, *how to capture the mark she has made on my heart?*

That night, in Tokyo, I slipped away for a walk by myself. By the second block, I had forgotten about Bruise's tattoo. By the fifth, even my trepidations about *Objects* faded. Each shop or restaurant was full of brightness and people, on each street corner my ears caught a wisp of a conversation. When this was all over, I would get into a debate on Reddit about different versions of the afterlife, defending the spectator concept: a wandering eye among the living, observing without intruding. Many commenters claimed this would be the worst afterlife, citing the anonymity, the eternal alienation. No, I commented. Spectating is the best. To be rid of being perceived and to only perceive—that's the life! (Not many upvotes, but I thought it was funny.) In reality, walking alone in a strange city at night is probably as close as I'll come to heaven. I walked as far as Shibuya, then my spectator body wandered down smaller streets, narrowing and becoming quiet and dark. I especially liked finding open shops in these anonymous streets, knowing they were familiar to someone, just not me. As I was thinking of heading back, an anime storefront caught my eye. It was a tourist trap, full of little *chibi* characters, and I recognized *Attack on Titan* characters. I thought about Kimberly. Instead, I snapped a picture to Reyna.

Stop, she snapped back. *I have always wanted to go to Japan. Are you a weeb?*

A little, I wrote back. *I've only really watched Attack on Titan.*

When you get back, we have a long list ahead of us, she wrote.

God, I wrote. *Only cool stuff, tho. I have a reputation to uphold.*

Of course. Send me more Japan pics! I want to live vicariously thru you.

And then I kept walking, snapping pictures of all the storefronts and ads and alleyways, all the bright signs and even the dark puddles along the curbs, the grates with steam lifting, the flickering banners of messages I couldn't interpret. By the end of my walk, I was FaceTiming Rey, holding out my phone to this side of the world, listening to her *ooh* and *aah* and take it all in.

The Future Tour: Manila

Waves broke against the black cliffs. From our spot on the resort beach, you could watch the surf throw itself again and again into the jagged maw. There was a cave you could walk in, one of the waiters told us, but only during low tide.

It was another rest day, but this time, I was too tired to explore Manila.

"You look tired," Charley commented. We were sunbathing on the beach, on the verge of becoming sun-sick. Beside us, Bruise was sleeping, like fully sleeping, belly up, my handprint reddening on her chest. She'd been up all night, on the phone with Lena, who was in Toronto with Jay Corpus, on his next movie set. It worked out, because Lena could meet me in Vancouver and act as my guardian adult while I filmed *Objects*.

"*You* look tired," I shot back.

"Let's take a swim," Charley suggested. "Check out the cave."

"It's not low tide."

"That's just a liability thing. C'mon, nearly dying on stupid adventures—that's kid stuff. What you should be doing while traveling!"

So we did kid stuff. We swam into deep water, letting the huge waves crest over us, bringing us crashing back onto shore. Eventually, we made it into the cave. "God, God, God," I kept saying, my brain short-circuiting. To swim inside the mouth of a cave, to feel your head press against the damp, cool stalactites? Kid stuff indeed. The water cast everything a wrinkled blue: Charley's face, the drip-castle walls, the tiny pricks of sunlight that made their way through the cave. Like being inside the lungs of the sea, feeling the waves shrink, inflate, shrink, inflate. Sleeping that night in the big hotel bed, my body rose and fell with the waves.

When we finally returned, dusk was spilling over the beach. Bruise sat by herself, all our discarded things spread around her: Charley's weathered copy of *Day Break*, my phone with eighteen unopened Snapchats from Rey.

"Where were you?"

Charley said, "Just swimming."

"The waves are high. It's dangerous."

"We just dipped our toes in," Charley panted. "Right, Lucy?"

"Right," I added, giggles bubbling up. I looked away from the heat of Bruise's gaze. For the rest of the night, dinner and then gossip in the hotel room, *The Lake House* playing on double-speed, she never stopped looking at Charley, her expression tight.

The Future Tour: Sydney

It was all over the news before I even touched down in Sydney. At least, all over my newsfeed.

How is she? I texted Charley, hurtling from terminal to terminal, my suitcase—the same one I had had since I was twelve—rattling across the tile. I had just come from shooting *Objects*.

Idk. Measured? Charley responded.

At tech rehearsal, Bruise was quiet. She said hi and didn't talk for the rest of hair and makeup. Oddly, I enjoyed her like this, not gushing about how much she'd missed me while I was gone.

Only when we were alone did she crack. We always clung to each other right before showtime, perched on a platform that rose up onto the stage. This part I dreaded the most: hearing the sleeping dragon of the crowd, the metallic clink of the rig. Bruise's hot breath mingling with mine, our nerves primed for performance.

"Did you see the news, Lucy girl?"

"No," I lied.

"Patrick Kons is dating Nina Englewood."

Nina Englewood was a nineteen-year-old actress with striking dark eyes and soft blond curls and a Marvel role. She was a big Gen Z deal. It was dumb luck she'd agreed to Kons's new film, a stoner comedy about a cryptocurrency start-up.

"Whatever," I scoffed. "He's sucked you dry enough."

"This is different," Bruise said.

"Or a new beginning?"

The platform began to rise, always excruciatingly slow. I barely heard Bruise through the mechanical shriek: "And this world tour is just . . . God, it's just like everything else. Nothing I make is good anymore. Nothing feels real anymore."

Weakly, I protested. "But it is real?"

Bruise's tone rose: "It's okay, Lucy girl. I'll be dead soon. That's what you want, right? For me to die? Then you can film your show and hang out with Charley without me."

"No, Bruise, I—"

We were rotating up, so my vision was segmented: half the underside of the stage, all dark wires and metal beams, the other half, ten thousand Australian faces in a stadium, waiting for us. We took our starting poses: back-to-back, heads down.

"It's okay, Lucy girl," Bruise whispered right as the sound guy deep in the wings was counting us down. "I'll be out of the picture soon enough."

And then the mic guy was flashing the sign that our mic was on, and Bruise was turning to the screaming crowd, her voice a shimmery, echoey spray across the stadium.

"Hallo, Sydney! How lovely it is to be down under!"

The Future Tour: London

For the next three weeks, Bruise did not text me that she couldn't sleep, that she needed me—instead, for the first time since Patrick Kons left, I went to bed in my own bed. We rehearsed, we interviewed, and it was all the same: On camera, Bruise was sticky sweet, and I was charming right back. Amazing, how good I was getting at acting. Off camera, she slammed her hotel door so violently I felt it before I heard it. We slept apart fitfully, the dread only loosening from my chest when Bruise appeared for breakfast or call time, her expression unreadable behind sunglasses.

The only bright spot: Charley was officially offered a position on the HBO project. She was brought on as a design assistant, a massive step down from what she was doing with Bruise, styling and costuming all people and sets, but whatever. To celebrate, she and I got room service and watched *Planet Earth.* She loved heckling the predators, cheering on the prey, laughing at the goofy seals, except when David Attenborough would talk about the melting icebergs and the warming globe; then, we both went stone silent.

"I have to tell Bruise," Charley finally said. She would have to leave the tour early, months before the last scheduled date. I guessed they would have to limp through with Lena hiring randos at every city, something Bruise would hate. She liked having a close-knit team.

"She'll be cool with it," I said, uncertain.

"Are you?" Charley asked.

"Of course! It's your dream!" My performance of the line was shaky.

"I feel bad leaving you."

"What do you mean?"

Charley gave me a knowing look. "The tour's a mess. Bruise is . . . maybe she's always been, but Bruise is kind of a bitch."

"The thing with Patrick Kons tripped her up."

Charley shook her head. "I don't think she's loved him for a long time."

"How do you know?"

"It never felt real, watching them. Not like my parents. You know, once you see what real love is, you can see when someone's pretending."

"Hmm." I tried not to wonder about my parents. It was real. I already knew. Even when they were quiet and just in the room together.

"But yeah, I feel weird leaving you with her."

"It'll be fine," I insisted. "She's nicer to me."

"I hope," Charley said, her gaze still glued on the TV, where a drone sped over a graveyard of shrinking icebergs, a lingering shot of a polar bear perched on the tip, mournful black eyes meeting the camera. "It'll be fine."

The Future Tour: Dublin

Bruise sat scrolling through Nina Engelwood's Instagram, as we waited in another random dressing room, killing time before the show.

"She's nothing special," Bruise drawled.

"Mm," Charley said, distressing my hair, teasing it up and clouding it with hairspray.

"What would they even talk about?"

"Stuff," Lena intoned.

"Things," I said, trying to match her laissez-faire energy.

"Maybe she likes it up the ass," Bruise said breezily. "Kons always—"

"Jesus." Charley recoiled. "Lucy is right here."

"I don't mind," I added quickly. Very much, I minded.

Bruise ignored Charley. "I would be embarrassed dating someone that old—Nina is basically a child. Basically Lucy's age. It'd be like Lucy fucking Kons. I mean, Lucy basically did with Matt Callus. These men, they all want children, like, literal children."

In the vanity, my eyes met Charley's. We often talked about that night Matt Callus touched my leg. "Do you think about it?" Charley once asked. "No," I lied, but by then Charley knew me well, and all she needed was to hold her gaze on mine for another beat for me to break. "I think about it too much," I confessed to her. "It's stupid—it's not anything. Not like what other people go through." By then I was crying, and Charley was holding me and whispering, "It's okay, it's okay, it was fucked up, big or small it still stays with you, maybe always."

I never asked Charley what stays with her.

"Hey," Charley said to Bruise. "Can I be honest?"

"Of course," Bruise said, in a tone that suggested anything but.

"Don't you think this Patrick Kons stuff . . . it's, like, run its course? You've been back and forth, back and forth, for years? He's just one guy, you know?"

It seemed like every molecule stopped vibrating the moment Charley spoke. I could almost see the little quarks and strings and particles hovering there, watching to see how Bruise would respond.

"One guy," Bruise said coolly.

"I mean, you're Bruise!" Charley said, talking fast, trying to play it off as a joke, a typical Charley thing. "You're a musical goddess and we're traveling the whole world! Just . . . your life is bigger than one guy! Right? Also, he isn't interesting. Like, really. If I'm being honest."

"You're overstepping." She was smiling, but it was meant as a warning.

Charley shrugged, trying to be cheeky. "Just trying to help."

"Well—don't. You're my stylist, not my friend."

Charley dropped her head. "Right—sorry."

A mic guy came in and mic'd Bruise up, and then Lena talked us through corrections as we hustled down the hall. On the rigged platform beneath the stage, Bruise and I clung to each other and didn't talk.

The Future Tour: Paris

Charley showed me around the cathedrals. Not Notre-Dame—it was burnt—but Sainte-Chapelle and Saint-Eustache and we ended at the church where a thousand kings and queens were buried in the catacombs beneath the pews. Charley prattled on about gothic detail and history this and history that in the same rapt tone that she used for gossip about her love life. She knew a lot. I liked the change of pace, the dusty silence of a church. The heights of the stained glass made my stomach swoop. You got why people believed so fervently in God if all they had were these palaces of soft light and domed ceilings. We ended the tour staring at the tombs of kings—pupilless statues of sleeping men, their big stone hands cupped in prayer. Charley stared at them for a long time, while I got bored and snuck glances at her, awed by how candlelight danced on her jawline.

"She's going to blacklist me," Charley muttered. "When I tell her."

"She wouldn't," I pressed gently. "You're her sister. So you fight like sisters."

"Everything's fucked," Charley said. A few tourists glanced up, but Charley didn't seem to notice. She was staring hard at the dead kings, her eyes bright and glistening.

I turned sixteen in Paris. Never in my wildest dreams did I think I would turn sixteen in Paris. I would've guessed that I'd have a big party like my brothers, full of school friends and sheet cake and Mom ceremoniously handing me the van's keys before snatching them back, a joke she perfected every year. Joel turned sixteen when I was six, and it truly seemed like he became an adult after that birthday, suddenly coming and going whenever he wanted, having a full life outside of that suffocating house.

But in Paris, instead of a party, Bruise and I drank too much wine at a fancy restaurant, and then she took me to a secret society party.

"Do you think they recognize us?" Bruise whispered as we waited in line.

The secret society was hidden in an alleyway beside an old storefront selling cheese wheels. Everyone in line was bunched in groups, rapt conversations flurried in the cold air. They were young, slight, bohemian. They spoke different languages, knew about secret societies, and probably read first thing in the morning. These were not the same people attending her concerts. Briefly I felt a twang, something like pity. "I don't know."

The society people were opening the door, and we moved with the crowd. Bruise grabbed me and murmured, "No one recognizes you, Lucy girl. You're grown up, and you look like a real woman, and they only think of you as that twelve-year-old dancing for me."

Inside it was like a normal club: people dancing, people drinking, people yelling over other people. Bruise got us right onto the dance floor, a checkered board with sexy rooks and knights and

Lucky Girl • 237

queens. The place was popping with music so loud I could feel it in my throat. Elbows clipped my sides. So this was club dancing, not dancing dancing. Bodies jumped up and down and swayed their arms. I couldn't let go. Lately, I had a bad habit of seeing myself outside myself.

But Bruise helped. She shimmied with a knight, pretended to caress his stone jawline. *It's a joke*, she seemed to be insinuating. *This whole stupid thing is a joke, the tour, this club, this night. So let loose.* I did some faux ballroom footwork, like a bird doing a mating dance on a dummy. It all was hilarious, and we were a little drunk. Bruise pulled me close, and we spun around like little girls. Only Bruise remained unblurred, her gaze sweeping from me to the blurring rush of people around us. She was waiting, I realized, for something to happen. Waiting for a man, any man, to approach her, to take her mind off Kons, whom she did love, a love that scared her so because it was movie love, book love, lost love, the kind of love everyone experiences, but she wasn't supposed to be everyone. My eyes scanned the club for something to distract Bruise, something to make her happy again. I spotted broomsticks, neon owls, and winged golden balls before it clicked.

"Hey," I shouted into Bruise's face, blitzed with light. "This is a Harry Potter club!"

"You're my best friend," she shouted. "My best friend, Lucy girl!"

At that exact moment, pressure on my tailbone. A man was behind me, big hands on my hips, pushing my butt into his front. I tried to wiggle away, but he kept insisting. He wasn't a bad-looking man, but he was closer to Bruise's age. Helplessly, I looked to Bruise.

And she wasn't dancing. She was standing completely still in the middle of the club, looking at me like she'd looked at Charley, her mouth pursed in disappointment.

Help me, I mouthed, laughing because I didn't want to cry.

"So popular, Lucy girl," Bruise shouted. She laughed along with me and squeezed my hand, so tight it was almost painful. "So popular," she repeated and jerked me away. And then we were dancing like nothing had happened, spinning away from the man, my hand still clasped in hers. My organs were a bag of stones. I forget what happened next. Then I was in the bathroom stall, music a distant thud in my skull. Pressing my forehead against the cool metal stall and counting inhales, exhales. Nothing worked. I took to my phone, messaged Rey.

Have you ever been drunk?

Nice, she said. *Yeah, once. I threw up in a toilet. It sucked. Embarrassing. It was a wrap party with just adults. I was just bored. I think I told everyone I had food poisoning, and my old director tried to sue the catering company.*

I haven't thrown up yet.

Wait, it's your birthday, right? Happy—

But I didn't have time to read the rest of her message, because just the thought of throwing up made my throat ripple. Clutching the dirty rim of the secret society Harry Potter toilet, I threw up everything I had consumed from Paris—the snails, the wine, and the shots and the steep cathedral walls and the endless domes and the soft, dancing candlelight and Charley's distant face and Bruise's cold expression and the man's hips against mine and the feeling that everything was held together by a fraying string.

The Future Tour: Buenos Aires

We were in—you'll never guess it—another dressing room when Charley's phone went crazy.

"What do you mean?" she repeated into the phone, first quietly, then loudly, then super loudly. "But honestly—what do you mean?"

I was keeping busy, head down on my *Objects* script for the next episode, except I was so tuned into Charley's conversation, I just kept reading and rereading the same scene, circling the same line.

Bruise, meanwhile, was thumbing away on her phone. She was trying to interact with fans more on Twitter and Instagram, which meant lots of behind-the-scenes stories and pictures and video. She was probably adding stickers to a selfie when Charley came right up to her.

REALITY	THE SCRIPT
Bruise What?	*The kids share a look across the swirling portal.*
Charley I got cut from *Day Break*.	**Dina** But what if the time loop doesn't close?
Bruise *(looking back down to the phone)* You were going to work on *Day Break*? I didn't know that. That's the fantasy project everyone's geeking out about? The one that starts production in two weeks, even though the tour won't be over until August?	**Savannah** What choice do we have? **Ian** *(bravely)* I'll go first. *The kids share a look across the swirling portal.*
Charley I'm the design assistant. And yeah, I was about to tell you I'm leaving. But you said something to the director.	**Dina** But what if the time loop doesn't close? **Savannah** What choice do we have? **Ian** *(bravely)* I'll go first.
Bruise *(sweetly)* Antoni? I didn't say anything to Antoni. When could I have spoken to Antoni? Honest, I didn't speak to Antoni.	*The kids share a look across the swirling portal.*

Lucky Girl • 241

Charley *(voice rising)*
I know you did. You said I was drama, that I have unstable relationships, that it gets in the way of my work. You told him that.

Bruise *(infuriately calm)*
Ask Lena. Isn't Corpus on the project? She'd hear if I—but I would never, right, Lena?

They both look to Lena, tapping away on her computer. She gives a vague shrug, a barely perceptible nod. This means different things to the women.

Bruise
I'm sorry, honey.

Charley
Don't be sorry. Fix it.

Bruise
Maybe it's this Corona thing. People are panicking. Lots of projects falling apart.

Dina
But what if the time loop doesn't close?

Savannah
What choice do we have?

Ian *(bravely)*
I'll go first.

The kids share a look across the swirling portal.

Dina
But what if the time loop doesn't close?

Savannah
What choice do we have?

Ian *(bravely)*
I'll go first.

Dina
But what if the time loop doesn't close?

Savannah
What choice do we have?

Ian *(bravely)*
I'll go first.

Charley
No. They would postpone, but I wouldn't get dropped. You know how much this meant. My dad loved the series and . . . four years working for you, and it wasn't easy, Bruise, but if it led to this show—

Bruise
But you do come with drama, don't you? Chance— he was a lot of drama. He got in a knockout brawl at my house. Broke a glass table. And leaving in the middle of a job? That's just unprofessional. Not to mention talking about my personal life—

Charley
Is it because I told you to chill with Patrick Kons?

Bruise
You need to calm down.

Charley *(getting close to Bruise, getting in her face)*
I followed you everywhere,

Dina
But what if the time loop doesn't close?

Savannah
What choice do we have?

Ian *(bravely)*
I'll go first.

Dina
But what if the time loop doesn't close?

Dina
But what if the time loop doesn't close?

Dina
But what if the time loop doesn't close?

Dina
But what if the time loop doesn't close?

Dina
But what if the time loop doesn't close?

I dropped everything for you. You said you had to have me. Didn't you message that to me, *You're just what I need*—four years later and you fucked me, Bruise. You totally fucked me.

Bruise *(dialing her phone)*
I'm calling security. Lena? Security?

Charley
No—you need to call Antoni. Call him now. Tell him you didn't mean it—please, you can't just—it's my dream!

Bruise
I wasn't enough, huh? This wasn't enough?

The door clanks open: security. Two men in white dress shirts and thick knuckles and shiny wristwatches. Wordlessly, they flank Charley, tiny in an oversized Bowie T-shirt.

Dina
But what if the time loop doesn't close?

Dina
But what if the time loop doesn't close?

Dina
But what if the time loop doesn't close?

Dina
But what if the time loop doesn't close?

Dina
But what if the time loop doesn't close?

Charley
Hey—wow. You're not serious, Bruise?

Bruise
Why don't you leave?

Charley *(half a laugh)*
You're kidding me.

Bruise
Don't make a scene. Security?

A beat, and then Charley closes her eyes, inhales deeply, and leaves. On her way out, her eyes meet Lucy, sixteen, a failure who disappoints everyone. Lucy manages a smile. She should have mouthed that they'll catch up soon, in their hotel room, like she thinks they will. She doesn't know, can't foresee the next scene, where she ENTERS *the hotel room and Charley's luggage and books and white noise machine she carried across the entire globe, Charley's smell and Charley herself are all gone, like they* never were. Lucy opens her phone, pulls up Charley's contact information. Will she call her? Text? But a text from Bruise disrupts her—*Lucy girl. I can't sleep.*

The Future Tour: New Jersey

In the week and five concerts since Charley had left, Bruise made us go out every night to after-parties. I started throwing up in a lot of toilets, at every club and hotel room and even before performances, somehow always nauseous. She hadn't texted me yet. Was she angry at me, too? I should have messaged her that first night. The more time passed, the more frozen I became, like all the other times. I was even freezing up on stage; posts on social media bashed my shitty tour dancing. I wanted my old body back, the skinny straight thing. That body did things right. It would have texted Charley.

The Future Tour: New Orleans

"How are we doing, New Orleans?" Bruise called out in her breathy voice.

No response. The stadium was so bare that I could see the empty rows in the mezzanine, a lone custodian sweeping napkins and wrappers into his bin.

Though we had many months and many American cities left, the tour ended abruptly the next day: March 15, 2020. Lena forced Bruise to cancel, even though Bruise didn't quite understand the scope of the pandemic yet. Who could? She blamed Lena, blamed her fans, thought it was another sign that her career was over. It was, like many things, the beginning of the end. At the time, I saw it as a blessing. I wanted nothing more than to go home.

Quarantine Live

Home. The mansion was clean and white-walled and smelled like oranges. It seemed like another hotel. On the landing, we were greeted by a half-dead parrot. When Bruise started planning the world tour, Mercury Blues was regulated to a cage in the living room with hamster shavings and colorful ropes. She must have forgotten to tell Lena or someone to arrange care. To this day, I don't know how Mercury Blues survived all those months. Before we left on the tour, Bruise had thought he was on the precipice of speaking. Now he was in a state worse than after the accident that robbed him of speech. He had plucked nearly all his feathers in distress, revealing pinkish skin stretched tight over bird bones. "Oh my God," Bruise cried, collapsing to her knees. She lifted the skeletal bird to her chest, wept. "I'm sorry, I'm sorry."

For a time, Bruise's attention zeroed in on nurturing the bird. Forgetting the tour, Charley, or new music, she thought Mercury Blues's highlight reel might bring him back to life. Early quarantine nights were spent in the movie room, forcing Mercury Blues to watch his younger and chipper self, my favorite being his role in the 1988 rom-com *Shimmer Me Timbers*, wherein he plays the titular parrot, Shimmer, who plots to bring a pirate and his feisty captive together. In the cold open, we see Mercury Blues flying high in the cobalt sky, breaching clouds before diving down, down, down at mind-numbing speed.

"Tharrrr she blows, well I hope she did!" Shimmer squawks, making a crude remark after the love interests emerge from the cave after a cold, shipwrecked night.

"See," Bruise whispered to the old Mercury Blues. "See, look what you could do."

He cast her a cold, yellow side-eye. In between movies, I fed Mercury Blues sugar water through a pipette, and in a few weeks, he was growing feathers again. Soon after, we ran out of Blues films. Bruise started watching her old music videos on loop. She watched herself fake-play the guitar, toss her mermaid-long hair back and forth, bite the lip of a Wolverine-looking guy.

"Great guy," murmured Bruise. "I remember being nervous to talk to him between takes."

She started writing—not songs, claiming to be over music—but trying her hand at a movie script. For long hours, she would be on the patio, drinking sunset-colored spritzes and typing furiously. She was convinced Covid would save her. Things pre-Covid were a nosedive, but with Covid, time stopped. She could remake herself again. "You'll play me," she told me. Bruise told me the plot was about a washed-up singer who goes back in time to show her dying father how successful she became after he died. The few early scenes read, to me, like a knockoff of *Objects*. In the end, she called it *Mothership*, and it would ruin my life.

For a few furious weeks, Bruise wrote obsessively. It was like being roommates with a ghost, gleaning presence by the things left behind: pill bottles floating on our duvet cover, cereal bowls stacked in the sink, wine-stained glasses, clothes heaped in corners. A pipe burst and stayed burst. Grocery and food delivery left by the gate, forgotten. When I found Mercury Blues perched on the concrete banister, blinking at me with those hurt lemony eyes, I knew Bruise had again tired of him.

"It's okay, bud," I murmured, stretching out my hand. "I'm still here."

In April, Bruise started going live on Instagram. I think it was for the company. Even though we were alone and there was no end in sight, she could hold 10,216 people in the palm of her hand. That was the peak number of accounts watching her live, a stat she often recounted.

"Hey, beautiful people," she'd drawl. "How are you hanging in there?"

It got to the point where she would pace the length of the mansion, singing herself hoarse to 10,216 people. Old songs, new songs, mostly nonsense lullabies. She took requests.

"We need this," Bruise whispered to her phone. "We need this togetherness."

I hated when Bruise went live. My heart began to violently pound every time I needed to venture from the guest room. At any moment, 10,216 people could be flung in my face.

"Lucy girl," Bruise sang. "Lucy girl, Lucy girl, dance for me. Ready—"

"No," I laughed, shook my head. "I'm not feeling . . ."

Bruise cocked her head like a puppy. "Lucy girl," she sang in a high falsetto. "In these times, we need your dancing more than ever."

Bruise's live voice had this sweet, stupid, earnest tinge. She smiled hard, angling the phone at me. No, I didn't want to dance. But 10,216 people were watching Bruise sweetly ask. "Sure," I chirped and Bruise sang and I rolled around like I was lithe and twelve again, and later, on YouTube, I watched it back, and each comment confirmed my worst fears.

Looking at myself in mirrors, I wished I could wring myself out like a sponge. Instead, ab workouts on YouTube, fifteen minute repeats repeated and repeated until Bruise knocked on my bedroom door. Whenever she did, Mercury Blues would, with great comedic timing, look me dead in the eye and open his beak, like he was mocking her, saying:

"Hey, where'd you go?"

Objects:
Season 1 Finale

My savior from quarantine, from Bruise, came in the form of capitalist gravity: *Objects* was almost done filming, but not yet wrapped. Too much money had already been sunk into the project to postpone the Netflix debut next summer. Postproduction and marketing were already in full swing, and we just had to film the last episode. The penultimate episode had ended on a cliff-hanger: Savannah and Dina and the teenage gang were stranded on a remote volcanic beach sometime in the dinosaur era, the rearview mirror shattered. In late April, the new plan was laid out: an aggressive Covid protocol, a deliciously long filming schedule. Cast and crew would live in studio apartments, quarantining between each shoot. All in all, I would be away from Bruise for most of the summer. She took the news fine, enraptured still with going on live and writing her script. I said, "Cool" and stole Mercury Blues, knowing for sure he would die if I left him behind again.

When the final script was sent out, Rey and I got together to read. We met at the Hollywood Forever Cemetery. I had just gotten my license that week, bypassing driving hours thanks to the pandemic and Mom's e-signature on some documents. Mom, who said she was fine when I called, but you know, what did that mean anymore? The drive took forever, and my skin buzzed, seeing Rey in person. She waited outside the gates in a *Naruto* T-shirt and a sunflower-patterned mask. "Damn," she said when I got out of Bruise's old car. "It's weird seeing you drive."

"It's weird seeing you," I said after we air-hugged.

"Everything's weird, period," she replied. "What's with the parrot?"

Briefly, I explained Mercury Blues, leaving out Bruise's part in his mistreatment. She remembered, vaguely, something about a parrot that almost won an Oscar. Carefully, I transferred the bird over. She stroked his head gingerly and Mercury Blues seemed to melt into her. During filming, she would help me build a space in our dressing room for him, making sure that the crew didn't discover it. Together, we fussed over him in our studio apartment, buying special birdseed and oils to help his feathers grow back. Long hours were spent in our little kitchen, coaxing him to fly from one hand to the other. Once we really started living together, our texts morphed into just pictures of Blues that we sent back and forth, as if he somehow became the living symbol of our friendship, our—

"Do you always read your scripts here?" I asked, after we had expelled enough chatter about the advent of the bird. I was following her through the cemetery. It was so LA: sunny and feverish. There was a peacock, infinity pools, a movie projector, reflective tombstones.

"It's one of the few Hollywood places I like because it's not . . . it makes death more casual. Almost cool."

We stopped at her favorite grave, a weeping woman before a stucco white grave marker: F. W. Blanchard.

"So casual," I remarked.

Rey spread out her blanket on the grass in front of the grave. "I don't know. Like, I like thinking someone will still be sad over me a hundred years from now."

"You think you'll be buried here?" I said, and then immediately regretted it. What a stupid and dark thing to say.

But Rey was Rey, and she said, "I've been reading about these eco suits that turn your body into mushrooms. They put your corpse in it and leave you in a forest. Supposed to be more environmentally friendly."

The image of Rey's decaying body made me weirdly nervous.

"Anyway!" With flourish, I opened the script. We dug in. I was particularly fond of a scene where Rey's character and her love interest, teenaged Leo Tolstoy, stroll along the prehistoric shoreline before sharing an almost kiss, interrupted by the arrival of time-traveling ancient Roman soldiers, out for our time-traveling blood.

"I don't know." Rey squinted at the pages. "Ian just died. Would Savannah move on so quickly? Besides, there's so much going on. I don't think she'd just drop everything to . . ."

"You can play it more subtle," I said.

Rey titled her head. "Like how?"

"Like maybe Savannah is holding the conversation without really paying attention to what's happening." I thought of how I felt lately interacting with Bruise. "She's probably thinking, oh, God, when we get back to the library of Alexandria, I've got to find that golden time book, yadda yadda, not even noticing that Leo is having this other romantic moment."

She grinned. "Let's try it."

SCRIPT
Leo Tolstoy and Savannah walk along the beach, clipping hips.

Leo Tolstoy
I never thought I'd see the world like this.

Savannah
Like what?

Leo Tolstoy
No people anywhere. Just empty land. It's sad.

Savannah
That's how it's been, longer than there's been people. For most of time, it's just empty space. Trust me, I've seen it all.

A pregnant pause.

HOLLYWOOD FOREVER AND THEN REAL SET
In the graveyard, I played Leo Tolstoy. He was a poet-type, sensitive, always connecting the dots. He loved Rey, and that was easy. My actual character, Dina, was busy piecing together the magical, shattered rearview mirror and couldn't be bothered. When this was actually filmed on set, I hung to the sidelines, watching Rey act.

In the graveyard, when I said, "empty," it was easy to imagine a landscape barren and peopleless.

Later, on set, when Rey said her line about the world being empty space, her gaze swept over the green screen backdrop and the crew. While she was talking, the Leo actor was breathing heavily, his chest rising and falling out of his tunic. I wondered if he liked Rey in

Leo Tolstoy
But we're here now.

Savannah
We're here now.

They almost kiss. They hover for a long time, afraid to make the leap.

Leo Tolstoy
Savannah, I've waited my whole life for a girl like you. To think you were hundreds of years ahead—

Savannah
But, we're here now.

She goes for it, but just before their lips touch, Roman voices pierce the romantic scene—

real life. In between takes he mostly read *War and Peace*.

In the graveyard, we practiced "We're here now" over and over. We disagreed about the want behind the want. I thought Savannah was thinking about Ian, our best friend who'd just died—Rey thought Savannah would be worried about Dina, who blamed herself for Ian's death.

In the graveyard, we both looked up when we got to "kiss." Laughed awkwardly. "From the top?" I suggested, fighting both relief and something else when Rey said, "Yeah, from the top."

On set, even as their lips barely touched, it was clear Rey was elsewhere. She was looking past the actor, past the crew and the director, past the tangle of set pieces. She was looking straight at me.

"But, we're here now," she said.

Hoopla House

The peak of my career coincided with the peak of my friendship with Rey. Mostly, I only cared about the latter. Though the production set us up in two identical apartments, we just lived together. Most of our hours were spent with horror video games: *Outlast* and *Little Shop of Horrors* and *Amnesia* and *The Last of Us*. We played so late and often we'd still be gripping controllers by the time we had to leave for our 4:00 am call time. To me, early summer nights in 2020 was screaming, "Go! go! go!" while Rey got overwhelmed by zombies, or hiding our faces in blankets during chase scenes around psychiatric hospitals or the ruined Boston statehouse. After, we were too wired to sleep, so we talked. I ended up telling her about the Leominster hoarding house I came from, how I barely talked to Mom. Rey finally told me about her special-needs sister, how she knew how to switch an ostomy bag in under thirty seconds, the reason why even a major role in a major TV show didn't make her feel like the main character. Still, it paid the salary for full-time home health aides, a big help to her parents. Without saying it, we both knew loving someone didn't always feel like love.

I didn't tell her about Charley. It was like Charley never existed in my dwindling sphere, except late at night, when I'd sneak a look at her socials. Nothing new since Brazil. Sometimes I started typing a message—*Hey, how are you, wow the world really ended after you and Bruise had that fight!*—but never sent anything. *She's fine*, I told myself. Probably not even thinking about me. Charley was bright, brilliant: twenty-two and recently fired and college-degree-less and alone in a luxury apartment during a once-in-a-lifetime pandemic after having her dreams explode in her face. *Of course she'll be fine!* I was an awful friend and an awful person.

Eventually, it got to the point where Rey and I didn't have to talk—we could just lie on her bed and scroll through the endless tide of TikToks, which I needed to promote *Objects*. But also, scrolling was addictive, endless, pacifying. It was where I went to work up the nerve to reach out to Charley. Accordingly, the algorithm quickly flooded my brain with dance videos. And it wasn't long before Alice came across my For You page:

@aliceinwonderland
click link in my bio to see if @smilegang
is right for you #smilepartner #ad
🎧 She Gon Go @Trill Ryan

I sat up. "Holy shit."

"What?" Rey leaned over to see my phone.

"That's Alice," I said, tapping my phone, freezing her mid-twerk. "I know Alice."

She looked like an adult woman. When I'd left her in that New Jersey apartment block funded by DTYD JUNIORS!!, she was big-eyed and red-haired and quirky. I gazed into the moving museum of 2020 Alice: She had turned big-breasted and slim-waisted. She owned her own business, the business of herself. Alice lived at the Hoopla House, and that was all the excuse we needed to see it for ourselves. The Hoopla House was the first of its kind that popped up all over Los Angeles that summer: gaudy mansions filled with beautiful teens dancing, pranking, vlogging, generating ad revenue.

Leaving Mercury Blues in our cloistered apartment, Rey and I promised each other we wouldn't spend more than an hour visiting, tops. If we kept our distance, we could mingle with some guys, enjoy our youth before the pandemic gobbled it all up, right?

"It's a stealth mission," Rey joked as we pulled into the car-filled driveway. Already, we heard boyish laughs and girlish shrieks and Dua Lipa. Otherwise, it was just like any Hollywood party: a weirdly shaped pool, neon lights, slick bodies gyrating before a camera. Bruise's parties, in comparison, at least had horses or wolves. Alice recognized me right away. She was entwined in the beefcake arms of Tommy Krew, the official head of the Hoopla House. Eighteen and already a homeowner: it was like he'd materialized with the TikTok app, and prior to the summer of 2020, he had been incubating in a quivering egg sac along with every other influencer here, and now they were all squirming around like mucus-slick pupae.

"Lucy?" Alice gasped, prying herself from Tommy Krew. "Lucy the dancer?"

"Lucy the barely dancer," I managed.

She hugged me before I could protest about staying six feet apart. "Dude, you were so good. I remember looking up to you like crazy."

"That was so long ago. So long ago."

"I was a baby." Alice nodded. Her tank top could have been from the baby section. She wasn't supposed to live in the Hoopla House, being just fourteen, but everyone knew she basically did, and that maybe she was not just friends with eighteen-year-old Tommy Krew. But Alice was no longer the strange, possum-loving girl I had known. We played adults then, introducing Rey to Alice, Tommy to me. Then Alice and I reminisced about the reality show, how cringe it all was, showing Rey and Tommy some highlights on YouTube that we all laughed about. People started to set up an inflatable slide on the Hoopla House roof. Tommy Krew shoved off to oversee the prank. Finally, Alice asked if I still danced.

"Not a lot," I said quickly. "I'm acting now."

"Stop," she screamed, pushing me. "You'd kill TikTok."

But I insisted no. "I'm focusing on—"

"I kind of want to see you dance," Rey teased. "Like, in real life."

Alice blasted Doja Cat. She was a fine teacher, though she taught the moves through the lyrics and not the counts. ("At 'notice,'" she said, "you pretend to knock your head. At 'focus,' you make a square with your hands and pull in. Then body roll, body roll.") TikTok dancing, to me, wasn't real dancing, but it was fun, like Alice said. After maybe twenty minutes—accounting for Rey, who'd never danced—we had nailed the "choreography" and posted it to Alice's account.

Even when Alice floated away to the inflatable slide on the Hoopla roof, Rey and I kept running the "choreography." I had forgotten dance could feel like this—kinetic, bubbly, fun. I even threw in some Charleston shuffle, which elated Rey.

"You are good!" she declared. "Why don't you dance anymore?"

Bodies were slipping off the slide and into the pool with a hard, wet slap. For a while, we watched the scene. There went Alice, shrieking with laughter as she parabola-ed in the dark desert air. Slap. So incompatible with her past self. I wondered if she had finally figured out how to camouflage, to slip through the cracks like her possums. I wondered if she thought the same of me.

"The pandemic," I answered finally. But it wasn't quite right—I couldn't pin when, but I had stopped caring about dance a long time ago. "Or maybe—"

Rey must have picked up on something in my face, because she interrupted. "I've seen them all—your old videos."

"Like . . ."

"The Dance Awards solo to Lorde? That was the first one that came up."

My cheeks burned. "How'd you find that?"

"I wanted to see your dancing before Bruise," Rey confessed. "So I did some digging."

I rolled my eyes to hide the riot of feelings. "Okay, stalker."

"It's not weird. Anyway, could you dance for real? Right now."

My answer came automatically: "No way."

"Please," she asked again. "No one's looking."

"Like, it's been—"

"I bet you're still—"

Clairo was playing on the loudspeakers, the kind of song twelve-year-old me would have loved. So I took a few steps back onto the soft lawn and danced. I tried not to look at Rey's face, instead pretending I was eleven and back in my garage, blasting the music until Mom poked her head in to say I had homework, or dinner was ready. Here and there, I relied on old combos, but they felt heavy in my new body, my joints cobwebbed. When I tried a set of turns, I fell out almost immediately, but Rey still gasped like it was real dancing. I wanted to tell her no, this wasn't my real dancing, but what could I show her? Other old videos? This was how I danced now. I fell into jerky contemporary wiggles, desperate to find something that still felt right. Without thinking, my hand took hers.

"Hey!"

"Partner work," I panted and dipped her low, so low her hair brushed fake grass. "It's improv," I said. I brought her up and spun her, and then brought her into a ballroom waltz. The music had changed to Megan Thee Stallion. We waltzed back and forth, shyly, dramatically. The guys and Alice had gone inside. I was nervous, so I kept talking, telling her the rules of improv. "You don't know what you're going to do next, but you just go with the flow."

Rey said, "Like this?"

She dipped me low. Upside down, the mansion looked like a haunted house. I thought to tell her this, but I didn't know how to work it into the moment.

I retorted, "Like this."

And I swear I meant to do something else, but instead I kissed her.

My brain was empty—I was letting my body carve out the space. That's what my dance teachers would have said.

After, we took a few steps back.

"Okay," I said, my voice shaking. "That was improv."

She laughed her big Rey laugh. "Oh man," she said. "I've never seen you flustered."

"I'm just—"

We kissed again. This time, she led.

"Going with the flow," Rey whispered in my ear.

Bruise's Black Friend

My Instagram was filled with black squares. June 2020. I tried not to look away, tried to see not just the video, but the person, learn everything I could about them, tried to read all the things I should have been reading. What had I been doing, all this time? Everything felt like it wasn't enough, and it wasn't enough. Rey and Alice and I painted signs, took to the streets, chanted, and it wasn't enough. I was a half-baked influencer, couldn't I influence? But every time I opened my notes app or Instagram, the words always came out melodramatic, empty, circular, more self-serving.

Of course, I thought about Charley. A memory: a guest room, November 2016, a nineteen-year-old girl comforting me with shitty Food Network TV, claiming white people had just figured out how bad the world was.

I wondered what she thought of all this.

So I pulled up her Instagram and there was a new post, her first since Bruise kicked her out of the dressing room. The title of a *New Yorker* article, the text in bold, blocky letters sitting atop each other:

BRUISE'S BLACK FRIEND.

It took me halfway into the article, reading without reading, to realize Charley was the author. My mind whizzed to Bruise in the Hollywood Hills, pacing the empty halls, humming an empty tune, the pill bottles on her bed, her cabinet . . .

"Fuck," I said out loud. "She might really—"

"What?" Rey said. We were sitting at opposite ends of the living room, Rey thumbing around on a controller, me lying feet up on the couch, tooling through my phone. Since the Hoopla House party, we had not kissed. We didn't talk about it, and I couldn't tell if it was a we're-so-chill-about-this kind of thing or something else.

I announced that I had to go check on Bruise. "There's this article and she's being cancelled and if she's alone she might—"

I rose, collected my things. Car keys, book bag, a change of clothes in case I needed to stay over. Mercury Blues clung to his rope swings. One of his classic slow blinks: *Don't get ahead of yourself, girlie.*

"Whoa, whoa," Rey said, putting down the controller. "Slow down. You're leaving?"

I slowed down just enough to explain some scant details: Charley and Bruise's fight in Brazil, Bruise's growing instability, the things she would threaten during dark nights ever since.

"But she must have someone else," Rey protested, standing as I rummaged through the apartment for more of my belongings. "Friends she can rely on. A PR team, at least."

She didn't get it. Once, I had told Rey that Bruise was like Mom, and she had laughed and said, "I thought Bruise said sisters or best friend. Now it's *mother?*"

"No," I insisted, zipping my backpack with finality. "There's only me."

In her essay, Charley described what it was like living so close to a celebrity, how at first it was like living on the surface of the sun, how the brightness and heat blighted out color and shape and sound, so you couldn't see the red flags, couldn't hear the alarm bells.

Throughout the drive across LA, I steeled myself for the scene waiting for me in the Hollywood Hills: Best case, Bruise is on her fifth glass of wine and wants to watch *The Lake House* while we don't talk about the article; the shares ticking into the thousands on Twitter each time I check. Comments range from shock to outrage to disbelief. In the article, Charley recounts every microaggression, things I vaguely remember across four years, but everything seemed benign at the time. She had even laughed when Bruise said some of this stuff. I remember her laughing. And now HuffPost is picking it up, an article about Charley's article: *Black employee accuses singer-songwriter Bruise of . . .* Worst case, Bruise is . . .

When I arrived at the motor gate and flung myself through the door, Bruise seemed fine. Better than fine. Sitting on the second-floor patio, bubbly spritz in hand. When she turned and saw me, her face glowed in an open-mouthed smile.

"Lucy girl! Breaking quarantine for a visit?"

She must not know, I thought.

But then I saw the orange pill bottle by the table. Near empty. My heart, lungs, everything seized.

Bruise wants you to think she's in on the joke. That the smoke and mirrors are, through self-awareness, a work of a genius, that anything she touches is genius, that within her brain resides lyrics that deeply change a person; but I want you to know, from someone who's been on the surface of that particular sun, that particular star, that she's no one special.

"You need to throw up, Bruise."

"Why? I'm fine."

"I don't know how many you took, and . . ."
"I'm really fine, Lucy girl."
"Just throw up. For me? Please?"

Bruise is the girl you went to college with who slept with one guy, and for the rest of your four years, wouldn't shut up about him, him, him. Of course, her love must be more profound, more special, more intense than yours. To be Bruise's makeup artist is also to be her friend, to console her through her own prophetic journey. To keep this job, I had to compartmentalize. And Bruise is deceptively good at breaking you down into compartments—the sexy / feisty / Black / messy / youthful / artist. I'm still trying to put myself back together.

Things escalated. One minute we were on her second-floor patio, next the bathroom, Bruise retching in the toilet, next a club, a suspended lounge area looking over a dance floor, and my tongue was dry. Between sips of champagne, we talked about light things. Bruise claimed she was seeing someone new. It wasn't Patrick Kons, who was still dating Nina Englewood, and what's more, they'd announced a pregnancy! "Can you believe that," Bruise kept saying, tilting more oblong pills into her palm despite our previous bathroom drama. "A full-ass Kons baby. Never wanted one with me—well, I never wanted one. No one asked, but I never wanted kids."

I was quiet, thinking about how my mom hadn't wanted kids, how I was a surprise.

On the wall across from us: a ginormous modernist painting of a woman with three boobs or eyes, I couldn't tell. I kept staring at it.

"It was never about race," Bruise muttered.

"I guess," I said, fighting for the right words. "Charley . . ."

"Did she really think she could use me to get ahead? God. Now she's just using what's happening, the news, and it's awful, it's really disgusting to use another person's tragedy to get ahead."

Bruise rubbed her face. She looked old.

"Never mind. It's over, though. I'm done being the bad guy. I'm done being anything."

A ringing finality. Her eyes took on a hazy, unfocused zeal.

To take her mind off Kons and Charley and babies, I told Bruise everything. About the Hoopla House and running into Alice. About kissing Rey. She listened with a neutral, almost bored expression.

"So are you guys dating?" Bruise asked.

"No," I said quickly, defensively. "I don't know."

"So you're a . . ."

She let the sentence go, waiting for me to fill in the blank. A lesbian, a bisexual, a pansexual, a dancer. An actor. But I didn't want to vocalize anything, because to speak it was to make it real, especially to Bruise. She would take it and run with it, make it something I hated about myself.

Finally, I said, "I don't know what I am."

Her relationships are symbiotic in a purely Hollywood sense: The men use her for a muse, the employees she uses for friends, the manager she uses for a confidant. But the strangest and most concerning relationship is with her dancer, her little muse, Lucy, whom she claims as both sister and daughter, best friend and collaborator, whom Bruise declares to have saved but other points will tell you that Lucy saved her. But I worry—who will save Lucy from Bruise?

My last memory from that night is clipped, fragrant with panic. Bruise and me back on her patio. Night, the lights below dizzying, the city galactic and cold, a long drop down. Bruise's legs straddling the glass guardrail.

"It will seem like I was drunk and tried to jump into the pool," she claimed.

My lips moved slowly. "Wait—"

She sighed. "Would it be better from the roof? I think I could actually make it, though. And what good would that do?"

"Don't—"

Bruise looked back at me. "In my obituary will I be Bruise? It's funny—Bruise was my cover, so I could keep my real identity safe from fans. But now even I think of myself as Bruise. I'm going to die as Bruise: the monster they made me into. But when I die, can I go back to being . . ." She faced the open night, steeling herself to—

"But you still have to make that movie?" I said suddenly. "*Mothership*?"

"*Mothership*," Bruise repeated. Her leg came back to the right side of the glass rail. "That's it—I could use *Mothership* to respond. To show Charley, all of them, that I'm not this racist monster, that in fact, I'm . . ."

"Right," I said, relieved, ready to return to her big Alaskan bed. "You're not!"

"Lucy girl," Bruise whispered into my ear that night. "How many times will you save me?"

Interlude

How many times have I looked up Charley? Enough to know she's an art teacher in her hometown, that she runs the fall play and the spring show every year. That she's married. Her wedding website was cute. If I messaged her, that's what I would start with: *Cute husband!*

Thanks, imaginary-Charley might say. Or: *Fuck you. Why didn't you call?*

What? I would say. Or: *God, I'm so sorry.*

When the article dropped, imaginary-Charley would say. *You could have gone to Bruise, or to me. There I was, riding out this viral shitstorm all alone and you—only you knew what we went through. Fuck, I needed you.*

I'm sorry, I would say. Or: *I'm really, really sorry.*

Why? imaginary-Charley asks. *Why Bruise and not me?*

I could say a lot of things—while Bruise was threatening self-harm, Charley always seemed fine, on top of it.

Bullshit, imaginary-Charley says.

Or that I assumed she had other friends. Better friends.

Come on, imaginary-Charley insists. *Just say it.*

But really, Bruise was easier to save. And it was easier to see myself the way I wanted to be with Bruise, but with Charley—

So that's it, imaginary-Charley whispers. *It's about you, then.*

When I imagine her wedding, I see an empty chair with her father's picture. When I imagine her life, Charley and her husband watch the new episode of *Day Break* every Sunday and say to each other that the book was better. She is every student's favorite teacher, the one who consoles and pushes, the one they thank in their graduation speeches. In all my imaginings, she does not think of me.

UrFace Mask Sponsorship

Did I fathom the script as a living possibility? Could I have predicted the movie, in all its potent, career-ending colors? Bruise called often that summer of 2020, wanting to pick my brain like she once did with Kons. Vague scraps of plot reached me, stuff about a plantation side plot—but you've got to understand. When Bruise talked, things tasted different.

To answer the question: No. I didn't really think anything of the script. Rather, I was occupied with my own life, with falling in love and keeping it quiet, with filming the end of *Objects* and searching for my next project. Quickly, Alice and I went from estranged costars to friends to dance partners. We were both sponsored by UrFace Mask, and it made sense to film together. UrFace Mask was a start-up company that sold hyperrealistic masks of the client's face. All we had to do was dance in random places around Los Angeles in these masks. We were strategic: Shoot a bunch of dance videos one hot Thursday afternoon, post them across a month or two. What sells better than sapphic, rhythmic teens?

Rhythmic, yes. I was still dancing. Dancing with Alice was plain fun. Her movements sharp, her joy tangible, her energy infectious. At first, it was hard to reconcile the strange ten-year-old I knew on DTYD, *Juniors!!* with this version four years later. Where Alice once fed a dirty possum with her bare hands, this new Alice had a seven-step skin-care routine, which she dutifully filmed each night because each step was sponsored. Everything Alice did was filmed: Her mother had vlogged first steps, first period, first stalker, first kiss, and first diaper explosion—not in that order. Now Alice held the selfie stick. People regarded teen Alice as a sweet, if vapid, sexy girl. Alice seemed to encourage this understanding of herself, and often appeared in "pop culture moments I can't stop watching," reels of her misjudging the size of the sun, mispronouncing *Harajuku*, misremembering quotes from the Declaration of Independence as from *Hamilton*. Those closest to her—perhaps only Rey and me—knew this was an act. Alice was more calculated than she let on, and talking to her was like running on a treadmill. The leaps her synapses took—you could go from the traffic on the 405 to wildfires to the several ways climate change could play out to colonialization on Mars to "If the universe is expanding, what is it expanding into?" in the span of a thirty-minute conversation. Let it be known: I didn't introduce drugs to Alice; she introduced drugs to me.

My TikTok account was blooming and I was addicted to the dances. A ring light, my upper body, music—Curtis Waters, Doja Cat, "WAP"—body roll, hip thrust, pinwheeling arms, peace sign. Easy enough. No one commented on how much flexibility I had lost, how far I had let myself go. Instead, the comments assured me that I was hot, sexy-hot, that people wanted me. Well, they wanted my body, but wasn't that all I was?

Of course, Alice went crazy over Mercury Blues. From the moment the PTSD-ridden parrot was presented before her in all his gruff glory, the old Alice materialized.

"Oh my God," she cooed. "So cute, he's so cute!"

Mercury Blues and I exchanged a look. His feathers had grown back sporadically, leaving his head disproportionally bulbous. The rest of his skin was knotted with scars from where he clawed himself from feral anxiety. He was not cute.

We were in her bedroom, which was Tommy Krew's bedroom, in the Hoopla House. First, we would shoot some sponsored content, and then we would do some "get ready with me" content for the party tonight, which was just another content farm.

"God, I'm tired of it," Alice said. "The rat race."

"Speaking of rats," I asked coyly. "Do you remember the possums?"

"Jesus," Alice said. "When that baby died, a part of me did, too."

She was plugging in the ring light, which glowed so bright the halo permeated my vision long after we filmed. She fastened her phone and gingerly positioned Mercury Blues on her shoulder. Her phone started counting down as she readied herself for action, the numbers blinking and fading, a sound like a bomb about to go off. Five . . . four . . .

"I can't wait to be irrelevant," Alice bemoaned.

Three . . .

"What'll you do then?" I asked.

Two . . .

Her blue eyes slid toward Mercury Blues. "Fly far away," she said softly, almost not like a joke.

One . . .

"'Stunnin'" by Curtis Waters started up, and Alice fake-strutted toward the light, walking fast but going nowhere.

Van Audition

Out of the blue, Lena—still my agent, though Bruise had long shed her—mailed me a script, a stripped-down indie project called *Van*. It must have been a hot script because every day, she called and asked if I'd read it.

"I'm a little busy right now, but I'll get to it soon," I assured Lena, mouthing, *Hold on* to Mercury Blues, who was bobbing his head and waiting expectantly to continue filming TikToks. Look, say what you will: The bird loved "WAP."

"Busy doing what, making two-second dance videos? Lucy—I have a good eye. Look at Corpus."

"Look at Bruise," I countered before I could think.

Lena was unfazed. "Are you with Bruise still? You really should get your own place."

I told Lena I hadn't seen or talked to Bruise in a few weeks—that I was living near LAX in a one-bedroom apartment, all marble countertops and luxury gym membership and rooftop access where you could tan and watch the planes take off. I neglected to tell her that it was really Rey's apartment, just like I neglected to say that Bruise had emailed me the script for *Mothership*. Without reading it, I'd told Bruise that it was brilliant, that I couldn't wait to act for her, that it would be like old times.

"Good," Lena said. "Once you land *Van*, no one will associate you with Bruise."

"Really?" I asked, shameful of the hope tinged in my voice.

"When you were both my clients, I couldn't speak candidly," Lena remarked. I imagined her then, strutting on a walking pad in a fern-filled downtown office. "I should have pressed harder to detach you and me after 'Escape.' There's a whole world of possibility beyond dancing for Bruise."

"Really?" I repeated, wanting to hear it again. Acting—that I was good. It wasn't just mirrors and smoke up my ass.

"Corpus thinks so," Lena said with curt finality. "Honestly, I only took on Bruise to get to you."

"Really?"

"That's how I'll spin it in your memoir. Get it, kid."

The story of *Van* was simple: Our main character, Rachel, has spent her whole life in a Westboro Baptist Church–like cult, and grows up protesting funerals with the most offensive slurs spray-painted on picket signs. When Rachel is appointed to run the church's Twitter account, her beliefs are quickly challenged by the greater discourse. But discourse alone doesn't cause her to steal the church's van and run away. No—the Good Lord can't fathom the lengths a cult-repressed fifteen-year-old will go. She thinks she's driving into the arms of a Twitter user she's fallen in love with, but quickly finds out she's being catfished as the guy (or girl) sets her off on a wild-goose chase from state to state searching for love until it's just Rachel, alone in the barren West, nothing to her name but a stolen white van with THANK GOD FOR DEAD FAGS scrawled in angry red across both sides. And that's only half the movie—acts II and III follow Rachel driving aimlessly around the United States, desperately searching for a sign from God or anyone to tell her what to do, where to go, who to be.

"Oh my God," I announced, looking up from the script. "This is incredible."

We were on the beach, Rey and Alice and me. And Mercury Blues. Lately, Alice had taken over his care. It was Alice who coaxed music from Mercury Blues. Her goofy singing persuaded a low hum from his bird throat, the first I had ever heard. Alice, who noticed the way Mercury Blues looked at the gulls; Alice, who first thought he might want to fly. He had been trained to free-fly: His IMDB page proudly stated that Mercury Blues never had a stunt double, that he alone performed every action-flying scene in his long career. Not that Alice cared; she just wanted to make him happy. She had been watching YouTube videos on free-flying, practicing the different types of whistles that signal takeoff and recall and loop-de-loop. We often brought him down to the beach, where she believed the wind and social pressure of the gulls would help him take flight. While I read *Van*, Alice held her arm aloft, whispering sweet encouraging nothings into the bird's newly feathered ear.

"Script that good?" Rey asked.

"It's going to be big," I predicted. "God, I have to get this part."

"Guys," Alice called. "Guys, he's doing it."

We could see them down at the shoreline, Mercury Blues's wings outstretching as he prepared for flight. It was shocking, the width and grandeur of his wingspan. All his movies and not one did it justice.

"You'll get it," Rey said. "When's the audition?"

"In two weeks. You'll practice lines with me?"

"'Course," Rey smiled. "Look at you—a real Hollywood actor."

"He's going! Going!" Alice shrieked, sounding like a little kid again. Just like that, Mercury Blues took off, each pump of his wings taking him farther and farther into the expansive horizon until he was just a black dot.

Lucky Girl · 277

"How does she know he'll come back?" Rey asked.

"They always do," I assured her, retelling the story Mom had told me about the lost cat and a fancy Greenwich Village apartment. But I didn't remember all the details, why it was so bad the cat ran away, how it came back. I only remembered wishing Mom would hurry up—we had been walking home, and it was late summer, and the sky was magenta and people were sitting on stoops, and I couldn't stop thinking then about how I was going to live alone in the city one day soon, and I wouldn't have to walk with my mom. Maybe I was remembering it wrong, making it worse than it seemed.

"Except my mom tells it better," I said finally, straining my eyes to keep track of Mercury Blues.

The audition was held over Zoom. I squirreled away in a corner of our bedroom, hauling in a barstool and taping up a white sheet so it seemed like any liminal place. Rey was in the kitchen, trying not to make me nervous. For the past two weeks, we had done nothing but read the same script over, sometimes in different places: in restaurants waiting for our table, at the Hoopla House in the middle of a party, on hikes, and in the early morning and late at night, sometimes even after we'd been kissing or doing stuff—that side of our relationship picking up so organically I don't remember the second time we kissed. I had even tried to enlist Mercury Blues. Like I'd predicted, he always returned to Alice's hand after flying, though each trip to the sky lasted longer and longer. He chased seagulls, darting in and out of their pack, an awkward teen trying to link up with the cool kids. The gulls cawed and broke apart, only rejoining when Mercury Blues retreated. He watched from his perch on Alice's shoulders, his pale eyes whirling in his head, as the gulls fought over an empty

Pringles can. One day, when we were packing up our beach stuff, Mercury Blues finally broke his silence.

"Why?" he croaked. His first human word in nearly a decade.

Rey and I looked at each other, speechless. Alice, of course, knew the right words.

"It takes time to make new friends," she answered softly. "We'll try again soon."

And so we tried, and each time the gulls fluttered away, dispersing until he rejoined our sad human trio. But the effort seemed to enliven Blues, and a chaos of language erupted from his beak, as if, having failed to bird, he was trying to human. "Naked," he declared one morning when I was coming out of the shower. After that, I instructed him to turn around whenever I got changed. When I read my *Van* lines to him, Blues refused to play ball. "Done," he squawked. "All done."

"No," I insisted. "Just practice for me."

"Who?"

"Me, Lucy. Your . . . owner? No—I'm your friend? Lucy . . . friend."

His black talons scratched his ears, and he shook out his new feathers, thinking.

"Okay," Mercury Blues croaked finally.

"Friends?"

"Read script to Blue-Blue."

Faithfully I recited my lines, unsure of how the bird would take it, how he could help. Blues didn't say much, but his pupils swelled until they nearly eclipsed all the yellow in his eyes. When I finished, he only said: "Again. Again. Feel. Again. Remember."

Remember. I wished I could tell Charley about the audition. But if I texted her, I would have to explain why I hadn't reached out to her before. Again, I pulled up her socials. She had moved back home to Indiana, and there were pictures of her and her mom together. I imagined Charley alone driving homebound, Los Angeles shrinking on the horizon.

When I got the part, I also got the van: an old, refurbished Chevy, still reeking of cigarettes and milk. The budget wasn't much, the female directors, a married team, apologized. Before filming, they wanted me to spend some time getting used to being in the van—once shooting got underway, the van would have slurs painted on the sides and it would just be me and a skeleton crew across the country. Until then, I had a fun time pretending to live in the van. The first weekend I had it, Alice and Mercury Blues, Rey and I drove up to Big Sur, went right up onto a public beach, and camped there for a whole week. Most days we acted like feral children, digging massive trenches and building sand castles, letting the huge surfer waves erode them all away. For lunch, we ate blocks of cheese and white bread like medieval orphans on an adventure, Rey liked to joke. The nights were blistering cold, but the sky out there was blitzed with stars, the kind you don't see in LA. Passing a vape back and forth until our heads clouded, we'd talk about our deepest fears. Me: that any call might bear bad news. Rey: snakes. Mercury Blues: fire. Alice: her psycho stalker. First came love letters; the stalker had watched her grow up, consumed every scrap of her that was out there, hooked from the first bath time vlog. Sometimes he still sent love letters, but mostly now he sent death threats. He loved describing how he was going to kill her, though it changed every time, she said with a shrug. Sometimes it started from her toes, other times he went right for the throat.

Rey and I just stared at her, waiting for her to say, "Psych!" But no. It was real.

"You should train Mercury Blues to gouge out eyes," I managed. Blues was flying in great concentric circles above our heads and thus could not vouch for his ability to gouge eyes.

My comment made Alice laugh. Then we talked about whether Mercury Blues understood crime and punishment, if any animal understood morals, talking deep the way only three high teenage girls could. When we were tired of philosophizing, we talked about stars, how we missed them in LA, what constellations we remembered from our scant education, could we make up new ones, breaking our necks looking up so much, our fingers blindly rooting through a shrunken bag of Takis.

"This is nice," Alice said right as we started drifting off to sleep. "You know, we don't have to go back to LA. We could stay out here and just do this—like, chill, forever."

"I have to film *Van*," I countered, just as Rey said she couldn't take off on her family.

"Right," Alice whispered. "I keep forgetting you two have a reason to live."

An awkward space of silence between the three of us—half of my brain scrambling for something to say, the other half thinking about what Rachel would say.

"Joking," Alice laughed, a little too hard. "I'm joking."

Mothership

She called me out of the blue. I was home—I mean, Rey's apartment. *The Last of Us Part II* had dropped over the summer, and we were finally getting to play it, our last big hurrah before I left for principal filming. *Van* would keep me away for months, something Rey and I didn't talk about. Instead: *The Last of Us Part II*. We cleared our schedules, refused any events, planned only to binge the game. When Bruise called, the first bag of chips had just been opened, Rey was clutching the controller, and the loading screen was about to give way to the first cutscene.

"We're ready to shoot *Mothership*," Bruise said. "We've got a director, crew, everyone."

"Great," I said. "Okay."

"We shoot next week," Bruise said. "Very on the down-low. You have time, your schedule's still synced to mine, so I checked."

"Next week?" I repeated, making eyes at Rey.

No, she mouthed back. *No, we've been waiting for this for so long, you can't—*

Last time, I mouthed back to Rey. *This is the last time, and then she'll go away.*

Why? Rey mouthed back. *What makes you think that?*

To that, I had nothing to say. Why? Because I didn't have "no" in my vocabulary when I was talking to Bruise. Because *Mothership* was my idea. Because I owed her for everything. Because I truly thought this would button up our time together. Because it was instinct.

"Great," I murmured back to Bruise. "When and where do you want me?"

Shooting took just a month. Bruise birthed projects like horses birthed foals—fully ready to canter within an hour—and a movie was no exception. It was an indie project like *Van*, just the smallest crew, only her and me as the main players. A few extras were sourced locally from Atlanta. Often I return to this month, October 2020. Did I know? I must have known. I did know. From the moment I read the script on the plane ride to when I stepped onto set, a gorgeous Victorian home deep in the South. Those massive white columns. Pristinely, ruggedly kept cabins dotted the land, hidden within a grove of ancient oaks. A former plantation. I must have known. Even when the cameras started rolling, I could have left. Could have walked off set, could have hailed a Lyft and taken a plane back home, wherever home was, to Rey or even to Leominster. But I didn't. I did what I was told.

We stayed in separate hotel rooms. Bruise never texted me late at night, never draped her arms around me, never squeezed my shoulders. Instead, she presided over a new group of people—new managers, a new stylist, a new lover. Nightly they gathered in her hotel room, sipping hard seltzers and pretending a rich history lay between them. The new managers: a husband-husband duo named Fitz and Conrad. Bruise introduced them to me as her besties. It was Fitz and Conrad who'd helped Bruise cull *Mothership* into a musical drama, procuring all the funding a girl could ask for by promising investors an original Bruise album attached to the project.

Her new stylist was about a year older than me—Mai, a waifish eighteen-year-old that Bruise had plucked from TikTok after liking a series of her "get ready with me" videos. Bruise DM'd her about needing a new stylist, and just like that Bruise had this new whiz kid. Mai didn't say anything—it was part of her bit, something Bruise also thought was so special, and thus we silently beheld each other as I tilted my chin up, bracing for the tickle of a makeup brush, each dab of darkened foundation another nail in my proverbial coffin. Well. But what I most remember is the weird sense of déjà vu watching the new group gather around the proverbial campfire of *The Lake House* after a long day of filming, Conrad and Fitz gushing about how Bruise was in love. Her new great love was Eres Mårtensson, the tech billionaire guy. More than that. "Your husband's calling," Fitz or Conrad said dryly the first night, handing a phone to Bruise, who scurried into the hallway. I didn't react, just watched Sandra Bullock protectively wrap her sweatered arms across her chest and stare out across the lake. But the next morning, before ready, set, action, I asked Bruise, "Husband?"

"A quiet ceremony," Bruise explained. "We didn't invite anyone. I just . . . wanted to be caught up in the moment, you know?" She explained how Eres Mårtensson had started commenting on her Instagram, it escalated into direct-messaging, and after a vacation in Tibet they fell in love and had to act quickly. Eres Mårtensson was the kind of space billionaire who said things in an overly articulate way that some people mistook for intelligence. He believed, quite fervently, that the world was ending, and that made it acceptable for him to act like an evil space billionaire. It didn't explain, at least to me, why he had so many kids. I stared into the peeling white paint of this old house. It was nice, not caring vastly about Bruise anymore. If she had been direct-messaged by Eres a few months ago, I would have been there, barefoot at the beach and holding Bruise's wedding train, already dry-mouthed from booze and queasy at the thought of third-wheeling the after-party.

Bruise told me that after filming wrapped, she would live with Eres, who split his time between New York City, San Francisco, Dubai, and a small island his great-grandfather had colonized. Primarily, they would reside in SF, but she fixated on the island, where, Eres claimed, as a child he'd subsisted solely on mussels dug up from the black-sand beach. She liked the idea of starting over, of being a stranger on a black-sand beach. She would visit Los Angeles, but never again would she be a resident.

"What about your place?" I asked.

"Oh, I'll leave it as is," Bruise said idly.

"Just in case?"

Bruise cast me a look. "No, I won't go back. Besides . . ."

A crew member was making his way toward us. The show was about to start.

"It's a sort of memorial, isn't it, Lucy girl?" Bruise whispered as we shed our robes and took position. The codirector was counting down, one . . . two . . . But even as the camera trained on us, Bruise was still talking: "That place on the hill is a memorial to your childhood. It's where you grew up, wouldn't you say?"

"No," I choked out. "I grew up—"

"Action!"

Mothership changed greatly from its nascent Covid start. If Bruise began the script as an unfinished conversation to her dead father, the project ended as a space opera with frequent stopovers in the antebellum South. Hints of the original version remained: The general plot was still going back in time to correct a mistake, but in this case, it was racism. The movie begins in the future: a washed-up singer performs in galactic clubs. Society is divided between those born on Earth (poor) and those born on Mars (rich), and the washed-up singer (born poor) wishes to make a difference, but poor or rich, Earth or Mars, no one listens to her. Long story short, she steals a time-traveling spaceship and contrives to use the power of song to free enslaved people. In the end, the found family returns to the future and musically convinces society to dissolve class and racial divisions. There are twelve musical numbers interspersed throughout, culminating in a massive dance number. I played both the washed-up singer's daughter and ancestor, whose race is never clarified, but perhaps implied to be somewhere in-between. I don't think I asked. I was so checked out. This is not an excuse. But I was on autopilot. Mentally, I was not there. I was, though. Clearly. My face is on the poster.

My last filmed scene was a solo dance number. The singer sang to coax her ancestor aboard the mothership to save the future, and my character danced goodbye to her plantation home. My character leapt over bannisters, swept her hands across polished silver, made grotesque faces, ended at the doorway, fist raised. The codirector called, "Cut!" Everyone clapped. Bruise wept and made eyes at me, mouthing, *Beautiful, beautiful.* But I felt nothing. I knew I would never dance again. I also knew I was going to cry, but not the artistically fulfilled crying Bruise wanted. The kind of crying felt first in the back of the throat, a lump that is working its way to your eyes. Without looking back at Bruise, I walked swiftly to the tiny plantation bathroom no one was supposed to use. I locked the door and slid down to my knees, breathing hard. I didn't even bother turning on the light, but enough late-afternoon sun knifed through the window, murky with old glass. For a while, I stared at the light, enjoying its sturdiness. Finally, I pulled out my phone and dialed the first number that came to mind.

Her voice was the same. Sharp, annoyed, a little coy. "Hello?"

There were people talking behind her. Older voices. She must have been at work.

"Hi, Mom," I said, my voice sounding surprisingly normal. Acting! "Just checking in."

"Oh. What do you need?"

"Nothing, I—I'm filming a new movie."

Barely a pause. "Good for you."

"And I'm a lesbian. I think." (*I think*. I didn't know how to explain it to Mom, or where to begin.)

"Oh! Well . . . good for you," she repeated.

Quickly, I added: "Your friends are lesbians. Kimberly's moms."

"Yes, they are. Divorced, though."

"Really? When?"

"Recently. Middle of the pandemic. It was very sudden. Thea ran off to Amherst with a coworker. Left in the middle of the night. No warning."

"That's horrible," I said. There was another long pause. Fumbling on Mom's end—she was probably prepping a vein, stripping a sheet, titrating some meds.

"Okay," I said. "I'll call again soon."

"Sounds good," Mom said, and then I hung up.

She sounded old.

Van

Too soon after getting back from filming *Mothership*, I found myself cut off from the outside world, living in a white van. The crackle of walkie-talkies announced my day's beginnings and ends. Each morning brought a different picture from the rearview window: a flat Walmart parking lot, a bright desert plain, the shaggy green of a mountain forest. As filming for *Van* wore on, my chronological understanding of time and self frayed. The wife-and-wife directors wanted me to live as closely to Rachel's life as possible. Sure, a skeleton crew caravanned ahead or behind, and oftentimes my passenger's seat was occupied by the cinematographer training a bulky film camera on my grimy face. But besides radioing about shoot locations and schedules, they kept their distance. For all intents and purposes, I was alone in the van, my home for three months. The cabinets below my mattress were filled with old laundry, and the same hot plate cooked both Rachel's and my meals, the same cheap mac-and-cheese-and-hot-dog combo.

In the name of art, slurs were painted across each van door, though when we weren't shooting, huge magnetic sheets covered them. It was very important, I was warned, to keep them hidden from the public as much as possible. Someone might think it was real, and we didn't want the first press to be a firestorm. Otherwise, the van quickly became my coworker, a familiar beast tamed by miles and miles of cross-country driving.

By the end of the first month, I knew every crusty cupholder like the back of my hand. Any unpredicted mishap—an exploding tire, a herd of buffalo, a flash flood, a tornado—posed an opportunity for me to react as Rachel. Going to the bathroom on the side of the rushing highway, I was Rachel. Hitting a deer in the middle of the night and watching it draw its last, bloody breath, I was Rachel. I was Rachel until I began to think of myself in the third person.

Rachel was expected to keep a journal, first as an exercise to get into her head and then because we both loved writing as a messy, meditative practice. She wrote often about her siblings, all of whom she'd left behind in her hateful church cult. Memories conflated into nostalgia and guilt the more miles she put between herself and them. Some nights she raged against her mother and father, whose choice to follow the hateful church cult led her to this confusing, alienating journey to nowhere. And yet, driving during a terrific rainstorm that obscured visibility, it was her mother's driving lessons that saved her: *Go slow and follow the inside white line until it passes. The storm always passes.* More advice buoyed her: *Fill up on gas whenever you can. If you're feeling sick, eat a banana. Check the tire pressure each morning.* On dark nights, Rachel often toyed with setting her GPS homeward bound. She imagined her brothers' voices when she walked through the door. And yet. She couldn't get enough of the bluffs on the far blue horizons and the feeling of putting real miles beneath her each long day. She knew she deserved this loneliness because it was only here, nowhere, that she began to feel like herself again.

Except: emails, texts, calls from the outside world pricked holes in her world. After each notification, she would have to write in her journal to get the taste of Lucy off her tongue—Bruise raving about the edits of *Mothership*, the director of *Objects* telling her to rest up for the upcoming press cycle.

She rested by becoming someone else, and someone else camped in the deep Idaho mountains, inhaled wood-smoke and morning chill. Someone else showered in clear, cold waterfalls.

The trailer for *Objects* dropped online. She watched it from her phone after a long day of filming. Her heart fluttered, seeing her other character sprint through ancient temples that were once green screens. It wasn't her, but Dina, plucky best friend. *But at the same time*, she wrote in her journal, *it was her*. She was a real actor. She called her best friend and together they gushed about the project, how good it looked, how big it was going to be. Even after they hung up, she watched the trailer again, again, again. And she would have again, but an hour later, Bruise Tweeted and Instagram-ed: *couple of big things. One, I married @eres. Two, @lucygardiner and I made a movie together. Guess which one I'm more excited about?*

She included behind-the-scenes photos of the two of them, grinning like idiots in yellow bathrobes, as well as her private beach ceremony with Eres Mårtensson. Bruise's Tweet broke her silence from the Charley article and her cancellation, and it quickly flooded news outlets. From then on, all her notifications and mentions were inundated with speculation about the Bruise movie, think pieces about Eres Mårtensson—could he truly love another who wasn't Eres Mårtensson? But no matter what the topic, Lucy's name again was sucked into the great hurricane of Bruise.

Why the same night? she wrote in her journal. *Why the same hour? I know she's excited, but she could have waited a few weeks. Or am I being selfish?*

Out of the blue, Joel called to congratulate her on *Mothership*. They hadn't spoken in more than a year, since he left her at a party, but they acted like nothing had happened, and she was surprised at how easy it all was, acting. He said he'd heard about the Bruise movie and that it looked neat from the behind-the-scenes photos. He didn't know about *Objects* until she told him. She sounded angrier than she meant, and Joel's chipper tone faltered. He coughed out, "Anyway, how are you doing?"

How could she answer that? Pulled over on the side of the road, waiting for the crew to scout the next location. Rachel had just shoplifted from a gas station and was feeling paranoid, like every car and God were staring down at her and her stolen energy bar. But she was starving at this point, running out of money fast. Soon, something would give. She told her brother that she was fine, watching the procession of cars along the desert highway without really thinking. Her brother told her he was still living in Los Angeles and—get this—he'd actually sold *August 8*.

"Joel!" she shrieked, sounding like her old self. "That's amazing!"

"I know," he agreed. "It feels really amazing."

They spoke the same circular *amazing, amazing* platitudes, both neglecting to tell the other their real realities. He did not tell her about all the sleepless nights already put into making the game himself, through sheer, stupid will. He didn't tell her how, when the pandemic hit, he completely lost himself in making it, going entire months without doing anything but coding, designing, writing. He did not tell her that he worried if this was somehow worse than his first addiction—at least, why did it feel worse? He did, however, tell her that he had a girlfriend and it was kind of serious.

"Cool," she said.

"So do you, right? Mom said you kind of came out to her."

"Kind of. It's complicated."

"When you get back, let's hang out. Get the complicated girlfriends together."

"Yeah," she laughed. "Yeah, for sure."

Before concrete plans could be made, her radio crackled—the next scene was about to unfold.

Bruise texted and called her often. "Religiously," Rachel would say. She hit REJECT as soon as her phone lit up with Bruise's name. There were feelings, but she couldn't quite separate and name them. In her journal, she chalked it up to staying in character, that Bruise—more than anyone else—made it harder for her to feel like Rachel.

When she returned to Los Angeles, it was early June and she still didn't entirely feel like herself. The months of filming and road-tripping and being alone had morphed her body into more Rachel's body than her own: the callused hands, the cramped legs, the dusty feet and untrimmed eyebrows. The first week, she didn't tell anyone she was back, not Rey or Alice or Joel or Bruise, even though the premiere for *Mothership* was rapidly approaching. It all felt too soon—hadn't she just filmed that movie? True, that was how Bruise worked. Meanwhile, *Objects* was still brewing, though each trailer garnered more and more bubbling hype. She knew that press would happen soon, and she would be swept up into work, and so for a week she let herself linger in Rachel's quiet van, kept the magnetic sheets covering the slurs, showering at Planet Fitness like normal, relishing her anonymous life. When *Mothership* premiered, she faithfully reported for duty. She let Bruise's new stylist strip her eyebrows and powder her nose and squeeze her into another low-cut pantsuit. She smiled for the cameras, held hands with Bruise, watched the movie, but nothing registered—besides, Bruise was whispering the whole time about Eres and how this love was better than Patrick Kons, and "This scene right here, Lucy girl, this scene is what will win you an Oscar." And she smiled and chirped, *Yes!* and ignored how nothing felt real, nothing felt right.

She didn't go to the after-party. She texted Rey that she was back and zipped to their old apartment. The whole time her head was a beehive of worry: It wouldn't be the same, she'd ruined it by leaving, she always left her loved ones and ruined things. But as soon as she climbed the apartment stairs and knocked on the door, Rey flung it open and lifted her up and spun her around and then they were kissing, like the way they always had, the way lovers kiss, and we were back.

"You were gone forever," Rey whispered into my shoulder.

"Not quite forever," I murmured back, breathing into her hair, which had grown long.

We stayed hugging in the doorway for some time, swaying back and forth, and for the first time in a long time, everything stopped, rightened, and I slid into myself.

The next day, we grabbed Alice and went to the beach. Soon, I would have to return the van, but we wanted one more night just the three of us, saying big things gazing out into the oceanic abyss. Sharing a blanket atop the van, we smoked and talked until finally I realized I hadn't seen Mercury Blues in four long months, and he wasn't there. The thought made me panic.

But reaching for her phone, Alice explained Blues enjoyed long, solo sojourns now. She'd strung a GPS anklet around him so she could always know where he was. He checked in every few days or so, suddenly pecking at her window with a new gang of crows—he'd finally made bird friends. Sometimes she worried he would ditch her for them, but he always came back. She observed he roosted at Bruise's mansion. "Wish I could hide out there," Alice said darkly.

We pressed for why, and quickly she caved: Things at the Hoopla House were crumbling. Tommy Krew was picking fights with her in public places and stranding her on the side of the road. Gossip channels loved this. But she couldn't go home, couldn't stomach joining her mother's new vlog channel with her half-siblings. Not that it mattered. Her name was a joke.

By the time we were drifting off to sleep, a plan had been formed—soon, we would move in together, we would move into Bruise's abandoned mansion. It wouldn't be a content hive like the Hoopla House. But it would be normal, like normal friends living together. We would take a break from the rat race after the *Objects* premiere, just chill and regroup and work on our dreams. "Like vet school?" Alice ventured. "Yes," we hyped. "Yes!" Then we started sharing all of our dreams. Rey surprised me, saying she didn't want to act after this. "I'll start live streaming horror games," she said dreamily. "And one day, maybe I can get into voicing them, maybe making them."

"My brother is making a video game," I said without thinking.

Rey pushed me. "Get out of here. In LA? Why didn't you ever say anything?"

"It's complicated." I smiled to myself. "Tomorrow, let's swing by his place."

It was decided. We walked along the beach, professing bigger and bigger things. By the time we burrowed back into the van, dizzy and breathless and giggly, happiness was giving me vertigo. The life I wanted was right there, starting tomorrow.

At two in the morning, Lena called. Three times, four times.

"Answer it," Rey groaned. We were still squirreled together in the van, our heads throbbing with dreams and promises, weed and vodka.

"Answer it," Alice groaned this time.

"Fine," I sighed, sliding over to accept the call. I thought it would be about *Van*, or how she had another audition lined up. Instead, she asked, "Do you have Twitter?"

"No. I mean, yes but I never use it. Why are you calling so late?"

"I can't sleep, and lucky for you. It's all over Twitter."

"What?"

"Bruise's new movie. It's all over Twitter."

Finally I slipped out of the car. The beach was still and silver. The moon seemed to frown at me. "How bad is it?" I asked. "It can't be . . ."

"It's Twitter's new hashtag," Lena said. "It's bad."

"Should I go on Twitter?" I asked dumbly.

Lena let out a dry laugh. "No. Get some sleep. I'll touch base in the morning."

We hung up. I did not sleep.

im sorry

For your average viewer, cancellation proceeds with narrative regularity. Even for the cancelled, there is a comfort in knowing the trajectory. First, the offense is brought to light: a YouTuber's ill-thought 2013 Facebook statuses or a novelist's anti-vax tweets. Other times, in the case of *Mothership*: white artist(s) tell the story of enslaved people in a manner laughably insensitive, melodramatic yet toothless, gaudy without grit. In her defense, Bruise claimed jazz musician Sun Ra as inspiration, that she was following—nay, adding to—a well-trodden tradition, and who can gatekeep the stories we tell and isn't it the job of artists to push the envelope, to pay homage, to respond to the world's pressing matters? But as any good therapist will tell you: It's intent versus impact. She intended to write, direct, and act in a movie that had a great impact: The impact was people watched the movie and found it offensive.

"But I didn't write the movie," I repeated to Lena over the phone a week into the Twitter storm.

"But you acted in it," Lena countered. "You said the—"

"But I hated every second. I didn't like any part of—it was just a job."

People were split into two camps regarding my culpability, with one side insisting I was sixteen when it was shot; sixteen, an innocent baby. Other people said this was exactly why you should take accountability even when doing what you're told. For my part, I read everything online fervently, waiting to see how much I should hate myself. Otherwise, life was quiet and my whole body itched. The wife-and-wife directors had yet to reach out to me after we'd wrapped filming. *Objects*, the premiere just weeks away, had been renewed for a second season, but I hadn't heard anything about a shooting schedule. I worried the press with *Mothership* would make everything vanish, all the things I actually cared about, and then I would have nothing. A van and two friends.

"Should I release an apology?"

"Just let it die," Lena cautioned. "Don't bring attention to yourself, or they'll start digging."

"Digging for what?"

"More things to talk about."

"There's nothing else," I scoffed. "Just—this stupid movie."

"Oh, Lucy," Lena warned before she hung up. "There's always something."

And I would have followed Lena's advice, but I still had to post my sponsored content: UrFace Mask and TeenGirl Lashes and the Lucy Collection Leggings, and I couldn't just post with some basic caption. I had to make my normal content and slip the brands into the corners, like I genuinely used the stuff in my real life. So, to the naked eye, it seemed like I was acting as if nothing had happened—getting ready in the morning, moisturizing and dancing in my kitchen, making HelloFresh like I wasn't integrally part of 2020's version of *Birth of a Nation*.

Since *Mothership*, every comment asked me what I had to say for myself, how could I keep posting, how could I say nothing?

"I have to say something," I told Rey. "Like, it's disingenuous to ignore them."

For her part, Rey had been supportive, agreeing that I had been doing a job, that I didn't know how bad the script was until I got on set. "Yeah," she agreed. "You should say something. Make it clear that you didn't want to be a part of it but felt like you couldn't walk away because . . ."

I nodded, taking out my phone to write. When Rey's pause lingered, I goaded her on. "Because . . ."

"Well, there's a weird element with Bruise and you."

"What weird element?"

"Like, sometimes I feel like you act like you're, I don't know, responsible for her in a weird way?"

"I don't want to mention Bruise at all," I said quickly, firmly.

"Okay," Rey said softly. "Okay."

Together, we crafted an Instagram story. The next chapter in cancellation: the apology. I took the easy way out: a quick handwritten story. Against a black background, I wrote that, essentially, I was deeply ashamed of my role in *Mothership*, that I had a bad feeling the whole time on set but didn't speak up. I should have. But I'm listening and still growing and never again will I put my creative energy toward a project that actively misrepresents and misinterprets such a dark and painful part of history. I promised I would actively unlearn what I had been taught. I would speak up and be a voice of change.

"Good?" I asked Rey before hitting *post*.

"Good," she assured me. "You're good."

I was at the Hoopla House when the first video dropped. It appeared on some Instagram gossip accounts and then spread across all social media, a forest fire in late summer. Lena forwarded the first video to me in an email with no body text, a signal of her fucks left to give. I was filming some TikTok with two guys, twins, I think, micro- and macro-influencers. When they heard the voice, they looked up and floated over to me (we were all in a hot tub).

"Who's that?" they asked.

"I dunno," I said.

"You're gonna get cancelled," they remarked, almost giddily.

"Well, I'm twelve in the video," I added.

They tilted their heads at the same time. "Twelve is old enough to know better. You can have babies when you're twelve. You can kill someone when you're twelve."

"But I didn't kill anyone," I countered.

At first, I didn't recognize the little girl in the grainy video. She was skinny and leggy and there was glitter on her eyes. She blinked too much. She leaned against a yellow slide, pretending to smoke an invisible cigarette.

"La'Keisha!"

The girl's voice was both froggy and kiddy, and I didn't claim it as my own. Only when I spotted Alice—ten, kid-bellied, giggling under the swings—was I able to place the era and the people of this video, was I able to, on some level, acknowledge the girl, whose mouse-brown hair and pale skin were a thing of the deep past, as me.

"La'Keisha! Get your black ass over here!"

The girl's accent was caught between Black vernacular and a Southern accent, clearly something born out of ignorance. Childish ignorance. Something she had seen on TV, something she was copying. She was so young. It wasn't not her fault. But still. Can age really excuse the ugliness in her voice? Would I forgive her, if she wasn't me?

Lucky Girl

The next day, Bruise called without warning, saying she was in town. We met for lunch at a coffee shop famous for its thumb-sized croissants. Cancellation seemed to have no effect on Bruise's evergreen appearance: Her hair was the color of amber leather and bounced in curls around her face, newly freckled. We discussed boring stuff: how LA had changed since she'd left, what married life was like, how Eres Mårtensson had such an interesting mind, nothing like Patrick Kons's; Eres was concerned about reality, not fiction—cars and computers and companies that went to space and space travel and time travel, she said with a nod toward my show, like real-time travel. And then finally we were talking about *Mothership*, and all the hate it got, and Bruise was telling me about how hard she took it, how all those bad feelings came up, how she almost—but then she just started writing a new song. Something so deep and personal. She'd never written a song like this. A new single—"it's never the end (wrong answer)"—all about her struggles with mental health. And then Eres got the idea to film the music video in space, the first real music video in space.

"No," I said before I could stop myself, horrified at the idea of being launched that high. How could they expect me to dance in zero gravity?

Bruise bit another thumb-sized croissant. "Yes!" she chirped, as if I'd reacted with expectant joy. "Yes, it was incredible!"

"It was incredible," I repeated, brain not quite caught up.

And then Bruise was explaining what it was like, being launched into orbit, the rush and rattle of her small compartment, and how she could look through a small port and watch the blue merge with black and she really was not in LA anymore— "And Lucy girl, it was just incredible seeing Earth, like the actual planet, from such a great height, like we really are just floating out in a vast plain of darkness. And then the cameras were trained on me and I was singing—the first person to sing in space— Hey. Are you upset? Why do you look upset?"

"Nothing," I said quickly. "Just—how do they get these croissants so small?"

"Probably a machine. Lucy girl, I'm sorry I didn't reach out sooner. But you know, this project—it just felt personal. Like it should just be me up there, singing."

"But it says hand-baked on the menu."

"Lucy girl," Bruise whispered after a nearly imperceptible pause. "You didn't think we'd be doing this forever, did you? And you're doing your own thing, so why shouldn't I?"

"You're right," I said, eyes burning. "They probably don't really hand-bake them."

That night, I went to the Hoopla House and got too drunk, too fast. Memories fragmented, broke off—the shattering of glass against concrete. The throbbing light of the pool. Clutching the rim of a toilet bowl. Sobbing big stupid baby sobs. Rey asking if I was okay. Alice saying we should get me home. But as they were hauling my weeping laughing ass out to the driveway, we were met with a scene. Hoopla people crowded around my van. The magnetic coverings on the side had been peeled off—to this day, I'm unsure how—revealing the red THANK GOD FOR DEAD FAGS slurs on either side. Angry whispers. Phones were out. I just had to laugh. Snapping to life, commanding the situation, like Bruise would, I told everyone, "Guys, guys, it's not real. It's for my movie. Sure, take pictures. You just can't post them. I'll even pose in a few. Smiling. You can even take video of me jokingly saying, *Death to*— It's okay, I am one, anyway. It's not offensive, once you get the context. I'm starring in the movie. And I am a lesbian? A gay? I don't really know, but it's my movie. Just promise you won't post them."

im really sorry

As soon as I heard there was a script change for *Objects'* season 2, I knew I was dead.

Viewers had been calling for my death—my character's death—for weeks now, ever since the photos and videos surfaced, me grinning next to THANK GOD FOR DEAD—

"Maybe not," Rey said, forever the optimist. "Maybe they're just..."

The sentence drifted off as we read. Outside of Rey's trailer, the set was buzzing with the calls of production people, furiously touching up the Time Council chamber set before the first take. I could barely read. Too hungover, maybe still drunk. I knew my eyes were red—the makeup people had furiously caked foundation on before the director swept in and said it was fine, better even.

"Wait," Rey declared flatly. "You're dead. Like super dead."

What's worse is that Dina doesn't even have a heroic death. At the last second, she has a change of heart and wants to save baby Hitler from the Time Council, so she betrays the whole gang. She ends up getting ripped apart by Time Worms, and Time

Worms are fucking terrifying, slimy, many-teethed beasts. (In reality, guys in morphsuits lunging at me.) They gulp baby Hitler whole, tear Dina open with ease. Her intestines flail around like garden hoses. She screams and screams and begs her old pal Savannah to save her—but no one notices: Hot, young Leo Tolstoy is already holding Savannah's hand as they use the distraction to make their own desperate escape down the Time Hatch, back into 2019, but a 2019 where Hitler and Genghis Khan and Dina Weiss never were.

Sprawled out on the cold metal floor, bathed in my blood, waiting for the final dizzying pan away from my lifeless corpse, I had a lot of time (aha) to run through the five stages of grief. First, I thought, *They'll bring Dina back. This is a time-travel show after all.* But then, no, there was this whole expositional scene where Sigourney Weaver explained that the only way to be permanently taken out of the Time Loop was being devoured by Time Worms. At least I had Rachel—except the directors were ghosting me. No distributor wanted *Van* after such a scandalizing start. Years later, it would indeed appear on the big screen, but basically rewritten and reshot: Rachel dies in an unseen car accident thirty minutes in, the instigating action for her grieving brother, played by Jay fucking Corpus, to go on this soul-searching road trip in another church van to reclaim her sinful body.

After my *Objects* scene was all over, I was back in my trailer's bathroom looking at my face, still plastered with purplish, gory wounds, and I thought, *Yeah, that's about right.*

But I showed my face at the *Objects* premiere a month later. In the back of my head, there was the nagging thought that this might be the last time I got to play dress-up as a famous dancer-actor-model. (Still my Instagram bio from Charley.) So in our studio apartment, Rey and I squeezed ourselves on the bathroom counter, doing our own makeup.

"It's like prom," Rey said sadly, hopefully.

I drove to my own premiere in the van. The rest of the cast was arriving together in a limo, and, I don't know, at this point, I was flaunting the van to get the *Van* directors to at least call me back. I think it even shocked the paparazzi as it came chugging up to the red carpet. Joel would have loved it. Joel. He had called a few times. They all had, even Mom, but I let it all go to voicemail. *I'm fine*, I would say—if I answered—and they would know I was not fine, but I wanted them to think I was fine because it was embarrassing to be not fine. Now I could forgive Mom and Joel for not letting me know when they were not fine, but I wasn't thinking about them, but about how I was not fine.

"Are you okay?" Rey whispered as we climbed the Chinese Theatre steps.

"I'm fine."

Instead of watching the first episode in that big stupid ballroom, I vaped in the bathroom until my brain took on a granular filter. It was a nice Hollywood bathroom, where each stall was its own latticed closet, the toilet gold-rimmed, a bright silver handle. The sinks were those obsidian troughs with flat-headed faucets. Nary a paper towel dispenser was in sight, but those thick, good quality paper towels were in a little wicker basket replete with little bright trinkets, tiny lotions, and perfumes and seashell soaps. At some point, I would have to leave this bathroom and go back outside, where cameras flashed and flashed and my castmates avoided my eyes and the director just gave me a tight smile and there were trays and trays of finger food, but I wasn't eating anymore. I was off solids, except tiny pills that Alice kept me in good supply of, and at some point, hiding in the bathroom, I decided to let them all dissolve on my tongue because why not push my body to the brink once more.

"Time is a funny thing," my character Dina once said. "We like to think it's as simple as point A to B, but really, it's a loaf of bread." All to say, the last continuous thing I remember was tightrope walking back to the stupid theater ballroom to take my seat beside Rey.

Today, I don't follow Rey. I don't follow her on Instagram and I don't follow her TikTok or Facebook, and if any new social media platform comes out, I won't follow her there.

On the big screen, every time Savannah came on screen, everyone cheered. Rey was well-loved, a fan favorite. She was perfect for the role, the likable main character, sweet and sardonic, tough and plucky. Like any main character, she was an everyman. You liked her because she was you.

Today, Rey streams herself playing horror video games. At the height of her fame, she might have garnered more views but today she maxes out at a hundred, two hundred if she's lucky. She always starts her streams with the same big, cheerful greeting: "Hey guys! Reyna here!"

Dina is working furiously on making a rearview mirror out of the sea glass the gang found. Everyone would be left to rot in a desolate strip of beach if it wasn't for Dina. But no one cheers. They will cheer when Dina is ripped apart by Time Worms, just like they will cheer inwardly when the headline splashes across their For You page: Lucy Gardiner found dead in hotel. A park. In her car. Lucy Gardiner, gone. Never to be seen again. Never to think again. Do you feel bad? Do you feel guilty? It doesn't matter because she's gone, so she isn't thinking about being liked. She isn't thinking. A wishful, growing thought.

Savannah and Dina have a moment before they try to escape their time banishment, knowing they might die trying. They confess all sorts of mundane things, like how cringey their photography girl phase was, how someone needs to go back in time and burn all their cheap Polaroids of the same light bulb, the same awkward candids. And then they promise they'll always be friends, no matter what, and how they wish they'd never found that magical rearview mirror, how if that never happened, they would be studying for some midterm right now in some late-night Taco Bell, not trying to save the world.

Suddenly, I was back in the bathroom with Rey. The premiere far off, buzzing, beginning. Maybe just ended. I remember thinking I should ask Rey but I was too dizzy and dry-mouthed, so I just listened to her telling me that my life wasn't over. "There'll be other projects," she kept repeating. The sink was running—she was dabbing my forehead with a wet paper towel because she was Rey and even though she'd spent the premiere—the biggest thing she'd ever star in—babysitting my slobbering mess, she didn't hold it against me.

"No one wants me," I whispered.

"Hey," Rey said. "I want you."

The pills had softened my vision, and I could only see her faintest outline. But that was all I needed. I knew she was quick to laugh and I knew she scanned AskReddit threads before going to bed and she liked gore because it made her feel safe because the worst hasn't happened to her. I knew she wished her life could be normal. I wished that, too.

"That's it," I said, standing too suddenly. "We could go official. Public."

Without thinking I pulled out my phone and ran through the carousel of photos of Rey and me. Most were blurry, jokey selfies: Rey and me sticking our tongues out, making faces with Alice. Lots of just Rey: Rey and the view of the Hollywood sign, Rey mid-tumble in the middle of a NoHo Target, her hoodie drawn tight over her head, Rey on the beach. That was the one I selected, and quickly drafted an Instagram post: captioned it, *btw, im in love with her.* Tagged Rey's handle. Before I hit *post*, I looked up. Rey's gaze was on our reflection in the mirror. I should have waited, but my mind was already spinning out—if I could explain that I wasn't homophobic, that it was a bad inside joke. And if I could love someone this good, maybe I wasn't so bad.

"Here," I said. "Look."

Rey laughed nervously, her lovely dark eyes scanning it briefly.

"That's a goofy picture," she said lightly, breaking away from me to the row of sinks, and started picking through the dumb gift bags at premiere restrooms like this: an iridescent ball sack of mints, tiny character figurines, hand lotions.

"Can I post it?"

Barely audible, still squeezing the gift bags, Rey whispered, "Not like this."

I inched closer to her: "If I'm going to go viral again, it should be about you. About us."

"I'm not ready," she whispered.

"But you love me." A statement and a question.

"Everyone knows so much about me," Rey said, and she might have been crying, the way her voice pitched up. "I thought our friendship—that's something I have to myself."

"Friendship." My hands dropped to my side, Instagram post forgotten, heart pounding inside my ears.

"I don't know," Rey choked out. "If I don't know, I don't want them to know. I just want us to just keep being us without it being anything."

I broke in, "But it could be something! It is something."

"But you were my first real friend," Rey said.

"You're all I have left. If we're not . . . then I'll . . ."

"No! Don't put that on me. I can't be it— Please, can we just go back to—"

"We're not friends," I said, suddenly calm. "We're not just friends. We're either official or we're not anything."

"Please," Rey hiccupped, stepping toward me. "Please, you're my best friend."

"No," I whispered. "It's either we are or we're not."

Say we are, I pleaded internally. *We are, we are, how can we not be?*

She opened her mouth—as a crowd surged into the bathroom. The premiere must have ended. Each woman gave a surprised chirp, spotting Rey in the mirrors. Everyone congratulated her. And Rey really was a great actor. "Thanks, thanks, thanks for coming, see you at the after-party, thanks," she repeated, all smiles. She took my hand, squeezed it once, twice. But it wasn't enough. I wasn't even invited to the after-party. And I would ruin the night more if I crashed it. And I didn't want to ruin anything else for her.

im really, really, really sorry

After the premiere, I went to the Hoopla House and did some questionable things. I spent the night in the van, because I could no longer go back to Rey's apartment. In the morning, I donated all my money to the charities Charley had pinned in her Instagram. Then, I went back inside the Hoopla House and did more questionable things, and after that, time got fuzzy. The last thing I remember is Tommy Krew talking about shooting a vlog at a pop-up carnival happening down in the Valley. I remember thinking I wanted to see a carnival one last time. But when I parked under the 170 and staggered across a North Hollywood park toward the carnival, I was alone. I had one of Alice's pill bottles and a vague plan. "Get ready with me to . . ." I slurred into my phone, noticing the pop-up carnival behind me, bright carousels, janky metallic rides, and fried-dough stands. But it seemed abandoned and no one else seemed to notice it, and for a second, panic surged through my body, like I had already crossed the line, and this was some final psychological step into the afterlife. But no. The carnival just wasn't finished being set up, and it was getting late. Like almost night. The carousel lay scattered in pieces, wooden horses planted face down in the yellow grass. Other rides were half-created, unceremoniously plopped down, the Tilt-a-Whirl in jigsaw bits, the kiddie roller coaster ending in nothing. "Tomorrow," a sign promised, "it will be ready for you."

My body was first drawn toward the infinity swings shifting in the night breeze like a willow tree. But then my eyes landed on the perfect escape: the mirror maze. The glass torched orange as the sun slipped beneath the low horizon. Before anyone could see me trespass, I ducked inside. The maze was constructed out of those cheap, plasticky mirrors, and yet I was still high enough and sleep deprived enough to soon lose myself entirely in its iridescent labyrinth, watching without interest as my body deflated and engorged, my shadowy face stretched and pinched and swallowed one pill, then another. My fingers clawlike, thighs heavy water balloons. Another pill, chemicals blooming in my veins instantly, seeping into the blood-brain barrier, whatever that is. My face shifting in each mirror, my eyes catlike and bulging, my cheekbones an over-pronounced syllable. Like when you repeat a word over and over until it loses meaning, so was I losing myself. I was incredibly high. Three pills down, ten, maybe nine more to go. But now that the plan was in motion, I was in no particular rush. Another pill. Nine, maybe eight more. Then I would curl up and sleep and fade into the mirror maze.

The last time I'd been in a mirror maze, I was just a kid, nine, maybe ten. The Big E was rolling into Rhode Island and my parents decided it was excuse enough to visit Joel. In his first semester at RISD, he had yet to contact Mom and Dad, which was troubling, knowing Joel. Micah, on his first attempt up the ATC, managed to contact home more often, even without cell service. The whole ride, Mom was muttering about how we should never have let him go, scholarship be fucking damned; he shouldn't be left alone, not after the year he'd had.

But when we pulled up to Joel's dorm, he greeted us as if he'd been expecting a visit—in those days, Joel was a genius at hiding his addiction. You'd never know—at least, young me didn't—that he hadn't stepped foot into a single classroom. Certainly, he was making art at art school—his dorm was full of sketches and still lifes and sculptures, but all were made in snatches of lucidity between parties. At night, Joel felt he could bullshit his way into feeling like he belonged at college, that he was going places. But as soon as he started across the quad to those brick towers, his head bursting and his hands already feeling shaky, he knew the professors and all those important people would confirm what he knew was true: his art wasn't anything special and, in fact, not worth the riot in his head, what he had put his family through.

All this led to Joel giving Mom, Dad, and me the fakest tour of random classrooms and quads and diners and museums. Then we all went to the Big E per our cover story, and then Mom was demanding Joel take me through the mirror maze. "Sure," he said, secretly hoping he could lose me for a quick hit the second we got in there. But I was nine and saw danger at every corner, and Joel was my big brother, so I stuck close to his broad back as he sped through the maze, ducking low and avoiding eye contact with a thousand reflections of my watchful face. The faster he went, the closer I stuck with him, until he was full-on sprinting down the narrow halls, so fast his reflection was almost a blur, so fast that when he slammed into a mirror it made a terrific crack. He bounced back, the pills in his fist scattering everywhere like Mario coins.

"Fuck," he spat.

"Your vitamins!" young-Lucy cried and scrambled to help pick them up.

Later, Joel told me: my earnestness made him want to cry, so he laughed. And then I laughed, glad to have said the right thing.

We were still laughing, collecting his pills in the bowels of this mirror maze. But then Joel glanced up and saw the scene: his deep-set eyes and his gaunt, stretched-thin skin. Suddenly his eyes got misty, like right before a movie actor cries.

"I don't know how to get out," Joel finally confessed.

Young-me was so stupid, she thought he meant the mirror maze. So she stood up, arms akimbo, and declared: "It's easy! You just go back the way you came!"

And she took his hand and led him straight out, where their parents were grimly waiting for their return, waiting to deposit Joel back in his dorm, where they knew something was not right. And he got worse before he got better. But he came home. And eventually, without me, he did get better.

It was dark this deep in the maze, and the mirrors gave no reflection. I had a weird sensation of being on a sinking ship. My head swam, and I felt my consciousness freckling away. Eight—seven? six?—more pills left. But instead, my hand was lifting my phone, so absurdly heavy. Clumsily, I dialed, and held the phone to my ear, and waited.

He answered on the first ring.

Act III:
No Tomorrow

Joel

I stared up at the ceiling. Morning light patterned the wall. Joel's booming, distinct laugh came through the closed door. Something sizzled, the belch of a coffee machine. For a wild second, it seemed I was in my bedroom in Leominster, and everything had yet to happen. I was eleven, just a kid sister with a silly ballerina dream and my brothers were cooking breakfast after some party, and my mom was already on shift, but when she got home, she'd lose her shit with all the dirty pots and pans in the sink, and she'd curse Joel out, muttering darkly as she drove me to dance.

Dance. I don't feel up for it. My body—

Right. And then the pain of my body came flooding back, first a stabbing headache that radiated down to my stomach, back to vomity lips, the acid coating in my throat. Closing my eyes again, I focused on breathing. Then, slowly, gingerly, I pressed myself up.

I must've been in Joel's bedroom. It was like his room back home. Sketches on the floor. Dirty laundry. A desk with three monitors. Before I'd called last night, it seemed, he had been scrolling LinkedIn while playing a game called *Frostpunk* and watching select episodes of *The Sopranos*. In other words, a very Joel evening.

"The prodigal sister is up!" There he leaned against the doorway. He had grown a beard since the last time I saw him, but otherwise, the same.

"Hardly," I said, my voice all gravel.

"Are you a coffee person? Tea? Vodka? Maybe that's not the best idea."

"Water," I croaked. When he reappeared with a glass of tap, I gulped it down. After four or five glasses, I felt steady enough to take my body out of bed and limp to the small kitchen. Joel set down a plate: scrambled eggs and bacon and toast. He had made the eggs Gordon Ramsay–style: slow-cooked and buttery and oh, my God, I couldn't remember the last time I'd eaten anything solid, and once I took one bite, I couldn't stop myself.

Joel broke the silence. "So . . . how you been?"

"Fine," I said, keeping my voice light between bites. "You know—fine."

He nodded, poured more coffee. "Fine in the mirror maze. You were fine last night."

"Fine— My van!"

Joel's eyebrows furrowed in confusion.

I explained that I lived in a van, but I'd left it in the underpass by the 170. Just the thought of my stupid van lying vacant, open to the world—all my belongings, that stupid suitcase I'd had since I was eleven, filled with old jeans and phone chargers—just the thought made me dizzy.

"You live in a van," Joel said, no judgment in his tone.

"It was for a movie project," I countered. "And yeah. Things suck. How are you? What about *August 8*—it got bought, right?"

Joel winced. "Actually, the company that bought it wanted to attach a big name to the project, but no one took it. So they're kicking it back to me. But you know. We're taking it like a champ!"

My eyes passed over the rest of the apartment. Mismatched board game cards and twenty-sided dice scattered on the table. Everywhere you looked, there was a seltzer water can, a veritable army of flavors—lemon lime, black cherry, apple peach—lining each conceivable surface.

"I'm pitching it again soon," Joel said. "Anyway, back to you."

"They killed off my character in *Objects*," I offered. "And it felt like I died."

"I quit my job when I thought *August 8* was bought."

"I broke up with my girlfriend and made her cry in a bathroom last night."

"My girlfriend cheated on me with one of my roommates."

"I'm not graduating high school," I cried out, and then clasped my hands over my mouth.

Joel started laughing. He put his coffee cup down, laughing so hard, spilling it everywhere.

"What am I gonna do?" I cried, not laughing at all. It had been in the back of my brain for a long while, a heavy shame that I'd let myself bury. I had lapsed in my online schoolwork since the tour, and in the chaos of the pandemic, my schooling kept on lapsing.

"It's going to be okay," Joel said.

But I was running my knuckles over my forehead, muttering: "I don't even remember my password. I'm like two—oh, my God, two and a half years behind. My computer is in my van, but it's probably stolen unless someone blew up the van—I'm sure you've seen the pictures, the really offensive pictures—but you have to know I am really, really sorry about everything, like I wish I could—"

"Lucy," Joel cut in, somehow both gentle and stern. "It's going to be okay."

"How do you know?"

"Let's get your van. Open your laptop. See if you can do all the late coursework. And then it won't seem as bad. Maybe."

The van had not been blown up overnight, though someone had spray-painted ASSCRACK across one of the sides in McDonald's colors. Luckily, it covered the slur, so, finally a win.

"Nice," Joel said, circling the van, inspecting its dents and scrapes. "Really yours?"

"Kind of," I started, then thought about it. "Not really. But no one's asked for it, so."

Last I'd seen Joel, he had been carless. Lucky for me, he'd recently purchased a ratty, Iowan-plated Honda Civic off a new transplant. Now he was hoping it would last each DoorDash delivery. The Honda would randomly die, so we'd spent a lot of time on the side of busy LA roads, cranking the ignition again and again, Joel bobbing his head to the engine's death rattle as if it was the next big summer hit.

"Step two should be a paint job," Joel suggested. "Or maybe just return it?"

I opted for the paint job, a full afternoon in an abandoned Sears parking lot, working through four or five cans of spray paint. Joel did most of the work, coaxing an autumnal forest and reflective lakes and stars and crescent moons over the ruddy white hood and sliding doors. "I'm missing fall," he explained. "Like, real fall." It was early September, a balmy eighty degrees. The rattle of the cans, the chemical smell of black and red and burnt orange, Joel's concentrated face; I could have been nine again, shivering in another empty parking lot, watching my brother casually instill a work of temporary genius on another temporary surface.

"There," he finally said, stepping off the back.

"It's fantastic," I grinned. There was a pause, and I knew I should monologue an apology. Something articulate and moving, encompassing everything—dancing in a music video while he overdosed, not helping him with *August 8*, not believing in him, not following him after that awful party, leaving him in this city, vulnerable and alone. All I managed was: "Joel, I'm sorry I was a bitch."

His face didn't betray anything. "Let's get back."

We drove it back to his place and there my van remained undriven except to move from one side of the road to the other on street-cleaning days. Otherwise, I never left Joel's apartment, which he shared with two roommates, Pete and Peter. The whole time I stayed with Joel, I rarely saw them. They worked in the industry for long hours and spent most nights playing *Dungeons & Dragons* at another person's apartment—the cheating ex of Joel's I never met.

It was easy to slip into his life, a ghost with no past, present, future. He slept on the couch, and I commandeered his bed. Each morning after Pete and Peter had gone to work, I spread out my worksheets and computer and books on the kitchen table, trying to unravel dangling modifiers, the essential meaning of the Constitution, the value of X, the nature of salt solubility. The last time I had given myself to school, I was trying to prove to Mom I could ace it online. Back then, my mind dashed from point A to point B. Now thinking was like trying to wade through snow, and on the way to point B, I started to worry about how long it would take to arrive at point C. I often leapt away from a problem set, horrified at how much my brain had atrophied. I hated myself for being stupid, and for being stupid even when I was smart, thinking I would always be smart. Joel would come home from DoorDashing and find me white-knuckled by his little kitchen table, blinking away tears like crazy.

"Hi," I'd croak. He didn't look much better. His eyes were purpled and tired, like the old days. Trying to schedule pitches and network, constantly reworking his art and storyline to make it more likely someone would bite again—no one seemed particularly interested. But it was good, the best thing he'd ever made. Why was it taking so long? He had exhausted all studio contacts except one, a pitch in six weeks—his last shot.

"Hi," he'd croak back.

Most times he'd bring cancelled orders for dinner. My favorite food memories from LA aren't from the expensive restaurants with Bruise or producers or executives, but my brother's North Hollywood apartment, slurping glistening pad Thai between sips of orange Thai iced tea. On bad nights, if he got a rejection email or if I failed a test, which was a lot of nights, we'd walk down the block to an outdoor Mexican place, where you could watch them roll and press tortillas by hand, listen to the hiss of the grill and the easy conversation all around. For days my jacket would harbor the smoky, salty tang. We'd eat tacos off paper plates beneath the glow of the parking lot lights.

The liminal space would loosen us up, and we'd talk about memories of home, like when we saw the moose on the way to the ski trip or the time Micah had his first breakup and took a cold shower that lasted a legendary three and a half, almost four hours. To this day, Mom won't shut up about that water bill. It seemed impossible that once I was a falsetto kid who played Jenga with her brothers, who put on concerts for her family, who obsessively drew comics, who threw tantrums when Joel decapitated my Barbies for an art project. "Sorry about that," he grumbled.

"It's okay," I grumbled back. "Sorry about—"

"Nah," Joel shot back, too quickly. "We're fine."

But we weren't. In the silence lay heaviness between us, reminding me that our old magic hadn't yet been regained. But maybe he didn't need a monologue.

While Joel was DoorDashing, I started to flip through his *August 8* pitch bible. Then I was digging through his computer, reading all the scripts and playing through the humble beta chapters he had spent three years making. Three years making—and Mom thirty years writing—and I can't describe what it was like to step into that world, only that it was brilliant and dark and funny and my first thought was that Rey would love it. When the beta chapters ended, I started daydreaming about it, like Joel, like Mom. Soon, I couldn't just daydream.

"Hey," I said casually one night at the taco place. "Have you ever thought about adding a horror section to *August 8*?"

Joel smiled, tilted his head. "Horror? Isn't the end of the world one big horror?"

"In the bunker sections," I said, like I was just thinking of it now. "You could make the concept art more ominous, like your old art. There's a big market with horror gamers now."

When we got back to the apartment, Joel sketched out some ideas. They were exactly what I'd had in my head. "Yes! Also—game-Lucy needs a pet. A cat, maybe."

"Players could choose to release it," Joel added.

"But it comes back to Lucy right before endgame, if you meet conditions."

"Like choosing the Alex date!"

"Otherwise, you find it run over."

"So dark, Lucy!"

An annoyed knock on the wall. We were being too loud for Peter/Pete.

"Sorry," I whispered. And then, really: "Sorry. *August 8* is—I want to be a part of it."

"You like it?"

"Yes. Really. I wish—I should have jumped on when you asked. I'm sorry, Joel."

He grinned, shrugged, but it was a big deal. "Hey. You're here now."

Just like that, I was in the world of *August 8*. And it was fun, like I knew it would be, making things up with my brother. Holed up in his room, spinning in his office chair, Joel would ask me what I thought about a side-quest idea, or if I thought we should go into game-Lucy's backstory? In Mom's original, forever unpublished play, we don't get much about why character-Lucy doesn't take the train to see her family one last time before the world ends. In his current pitch, Joel had designed the family as a bunch of stern boring folks. Cold, unsentimental. If the player chose to waste three game hours getting over to her childhood home full of wooden crosses and fine china, they would be rewarded with a bland reunion, almost a waste. But what if her family was actually loving, zany, a little broken? Or what if her family was like Mom's parents—what if game-Lucy visited there for a cathartic fuck you?

What if... What if... the more Joel prodded and asked, the more I fell into the story, the artwork, the character, the other Lucy. I let myself think that if I could get game-Lucy famous, then it would make up for everything. *Everything happened for a reason*, I deluded myself into thinking. If I could help get *August 8* into shape so Joel could successfully pitch it, then my broken, warped childhood happened for a reason.

"Stop hitting yourself," Joel said. He had come into the kitchen to ask another *August 8* what if, but found me steeped in math modules, hitting my head each time I got an answer wrong. I'd failed trigonometry. Bruise's space song had released to rampant praise—the old Bruise was back.

"I'm stupid," I said. God, I was so tired of crying.

Joel just shrugged. "You know, I need a break. Let's get out of here."

We went to a shitty movie. It was about a French painter who falls in love with a waifish blind girl. She will never see his paintings. Very sad—until she touches the wet paint and sees (ambiguously) his vision. They make love. Then she gets consumption and dies.

"I go to bad movies to find inspiration," Joel said as we were leaving the parking lot, blinking back the sunlight. The air smelled like wood-smoke, which would be pleasant except it meant there was a wildfire. That summer, the wildfires never stopped. One would finally extinguish and another would pop up. All along the mountains, you could see the flashing red-blue-red-blue lights of fire trucks. Last night, Joel and I had driven as far as we could to a parking lot on the edge of the Valley, watching a helicopter douse a pillar of flame.

"Geez," I said. "Why?"

He tilted his head back to the movie theater. "Because if that can get made, so can our stuff."

I didn't open the door, just looked at him across the hood of the car. "You probably thought that with *Cinders*."

He made a face like, *You caught me*. For the drive home, I was quiet, watching the Valley blur and focusing as Joel stopped at each light, thinking about *August 8*. What if game-Lucy was actually a professional dancer? What if game-Lucy could date both men and women? When game-Lucy is walking around the ruined museum with her date, Alex, what if we punched that up? What if she went to the theater and trained . . . what if game-Lucy was a writer? What if in the game, Lucy was writing a book about a child star who lost her way? Or not a writer, that's too cliché, but what if you wanted to still make things? What if you wanted to—do this?

"You're good at this," Joel told me later that night. We were sitting in his room, tweaking the wording of his pitch bible. "Maybe better than me."

"I'm literally a high school dropout."

"No—and I mean this positively—you think like Denise."

"How is she?" I asked lightly. Joel called Mom every day. I'd made him swear not to tell about the magic mirror night.

"You know Mom. She doesn't really let on, but she's torn up about what happened between you two—what happened between you two?"

"Nothing," I said automatically. Then: "Why doesn't she help you more with *August 8*? She's the original author."

"I think a lot of Lucy's—game-Lucy's—backstory is her backstory. It's hard to go back after so much time."

"But game-Lucy's backstory is super dark. The sexual abuse stuff? The stuff with her dad? Her dad's friend?"

Joel's voice was gentle. "That one I know is real. She told me just before I moved out here."

"She never told me."

"You were young."

"Why'd she name me after game-Lucy? Why put that on me?"

"You'd have to ask her. I think you're both ready to start asking questions."

Later that night, lying in Joel's bed, I googled "Denise Ward" for the first time. Plenty of junk from *DTYD JUNIORS!!* came up. But I didn't have to look very hard to find PDFs of her old plays: a space opera, a comedy, a drama. Like me, Mom had a digital footprint one could follow—ancient YouTube archives of college rehearsals, monologues, even a LiveJournal from the nineties and early 2000s, all the way until I was suddenly born. A digital garden of Mom, untended and untrodden. Another metaphor: I was the ghost of futures past, watching her scribe manifestations like

Octavia Butler the night of her college graduation: *I am an actor and playwright. People read my works. People come to see me perform. I am loved.*

A few days before Joel's pitch, I got my last casting call. Producers wanted to film a reunion episode of *Dance Till You Drop, Juniors!!* It had been five years since the inaugural season, plus Big Duck had announced his retirement from the show after becoming a grandfather, wanting to finally spend time at home with his family. The network wanted to capitalize on this news by filming a live reunion. All former judges were going, including Bruise. For her, the timing couldn't be better, so soon after her song and space music video had released.

My call with the producers wasn't even over before Alice was texting me: DTYD *demons call you??? btw, let's hang out idk where you've been???*

Alice was staying at Bruise's abandoned mansion, where we once promised we would live together. But since my fallout, it was just Alice and Mercury Blues and an entire flock of crows seeking harbor there.

"Blue-Blue king now," Mercury Blues greeted me when I pulled into the horseshoe driveway. He was perched on the roof, flanked by a vanguard of crows staring down as I knocked on the door.

"I see that," I shouted up at him, shading my eyes.

"Blue-Blue joke. Crows just rest from scorched earth. Soon they fly again."

"Rehearsing for an audition?"

The parrot blinked slowly at me. "Blue-Blue done. Face fear. Blue-Blue not run."

I found Alice in the backyard, lounging by the infinity pool. She was in a bikini and sunglasses, throwing tufts of bread into the murky water for screaming crows and listening to an Andy

Weir audiobook on speaker. When my shadow stretched over her face, she asked, "Where the fuck have you been?"

"Being cancelled?"

"Rey skipped town too—she's in Canada filming season 2, allegedly."

Plopping down beside Alice, I asked, "The DTYD reunion. Are you going?"

"I won the first season so I have to."

"I'm not," I declared. "I can't face Bruise. She'll want to sing and dance like old times. I don't want it to be old times."

"Maybe I'll bring Mercury Blues," Alice joked grimly. "We've been training on gouging eyes." Then she was quiet. Her galloping mind, zeroing in on an idea. "Wait, what if we . . ."

Alice started on a plan of going rogue: She wanted me to accuse Bruise of grooming me during the live broadcast. It was a word Joel and Rey and Alice often used, trying to get me to say it: *I was groomed.* But I was smarter than that. Wasn't I? Groomed or not groomed, I was angry at Bruise. What if she hadn't picked me for "Escape"? What if she'd let me be after? Why was so much of this about her, and she wasn't even that particularly interesting, that deep, not any more than anybody—and meanwhile, I was just finding out dark things about my mom? *I hate her*, I realized, staring into the burning haze of Los Angeles. Oh, my God, I fucking hated Bruise.

"Okay," I told Alice. "Yeah, let's do it."

Alice grinned. Her eyes glittered. She was angry, too—at her mom, at the producers, at the Hoopla House, her fans and hate watchers, the entire circus sucking her childhood dry and still wanting more. Alice had reasons to be angry, but there was too much to say and only so many fingers to point. "Why did you groom Lucy?" was at least a complete sentence, a place for her to start.

"We should go in," she said, pulling herself up, coughing. "Not safe breathing all this in for more than, like, twenty minutes."

Another uncontrollable wildfire across the Valley, this one was like the final boss. It had swept in from the Angeles Forest and settled along the wild hills surrounding Burbank, growing steadily along the dry ridges wrinkled throughout the city. After our visit, that specific wildfire seemed to pervade everything—fissures of bright red in every window at night, every topic of TikTok I watched, the very air I breathed.

Joel's pitch lasted less than an hour. I knew before he even opened the driver's side door that it was a no. The whole time, I had been sitting in the van, staring at the red gash widening across the hills. We had agreed that attaching my name to the game would sink its chances. The stupid fires, the stupid wind blew the blazes farther into the city. People were being evacuated. Bruise's old neighborhood had been closed off—Alice was forced to return to the Hoopla House.

"Too ambitious," Joel sighed when he got in the car. "They liked the premise, but ultimately it was too ambitious, too scattered. They said players would be overwhelmed."

He started the car without looking at me.

"So when's the next one?"

"Lucy . . ."

"What?"

He met my gaze sideways. "I've been hearing a lot of nos."

"So? You just keep trying. Self-publish?"

"Sure, but we need to regroup." He began drumming his fingers on the dashboard. "Like, maybe we should go back home. To Leominster."

"We can't just give up because of this no."

"I'm out of money," Joel insisted. "Out of a real job, our living situation sucks, and more and more I've been craving—look, I'm fragile and this clearly needs more time."

My eyes were getting hot. "But what if I get famous again?"

"Lucy, enough—"

"There's a reunion for DTYD," I cut in. "And I'm invited, and if I accuse Bruise of grooming, then it'll change the conversation around me! People will feel bad once they know the truth, things will go back to normal, then I can get *August 8* to the right people!"

He looked like I had just thrown up. "I want it to get made because it's good!"

"Joel, we have to be smart about this!"

"I just have to get lucky," Joel snapped. "Like you!"

"Lucky?" I laughed. "I wasn't—lucky?"

He shrugged. "Lucy—come on. You've been very lucky."

The van was peeling off an exit—our exit. When we stopped at a red light, we stayed silent. "No," I said softly. "I've worked hard."

"So have I. And so has Mom. And so has every actor, dancer, writer in this whole— You said it yourself once, remember? You didn't know why you won, and Lucy, I didn't come out and say it, but you were just lucky. Lucky the judges connected with you more, lucky the producers picked you, lucky Bruise noticed you, lucky—"

"That's a lot of lucky," I shot back. "Almost like, too much luck."

"Not really," Joel said. "It just takes once, and then—you're lucky forever."

"Well—now what?"

"Lucy, stop."

He sounded tired. I turned on the radio. And of course, there was Bruise's new song, in the middle of some crackling bridge:

Why does every beginning start with an end?
Semicolons stitch sentences together.
Even stars burn out eventually—
Entropy and all that.
But then why do I keep getting hotter and hotter?
Why am I rising higher and higher
above all your heads?

For a minute, two, we just stayed in the van, listening. When the song finished, the radio people raved about how good it was, how she recorded it—in space! Then they played it again.

"What do you think?" I asked.

"The song fucking sucks," he said, trying to laugh. But it wasn't funny.

Bruise

Mom was my age when she arrived in New York City. It was just a day trip, sure. By nightfall she'd be back on the southbound train home, where—if her life were a play, it would be pitched like a sort of macabre Cinderella. It was the seventies, and Mom wore a black turtleneck and overalls and chunky glasses. Seventeen-year-old Denise was as sixty-four-year-old Denise still imagines herself: brainy, overlooked, on the cusp of something great. She had ditched school to catch the opening night of a dying playwright's last new play. But first, breakfast. A coffee shop, a muffin and a latte and her open notebook. Some homework, maybe. People would think she was a New Yorker playwright. A college student at the very least. *No*, she thought suddenly. *No pretending. Start now.* The open notebook. Brand new, crisp lines. She would write something. A real Something. It would get attention and win awards and take her places. Already she felt sixty-four-year-old Denise pressing in, looking back, mourning the splintering versions she could become, each version asking, screaming, the same question: *Did you use your time well? Yes*, Denise wanted to answer. *I made Something.* But first, she had to name this character.

"Lucy girl?"

Bruise. She was standing by herself in the wings of the *Dance Till You Drop, Juniors!! LIVE! REUNION!!!* set and dressed to the nines. Her suit jacket sparkled like the moon. Her hair was slicked back, makeup impeccable. I had ventured from the dressing room, and now I regretted it. In the dressing room, I had been suffocating. Alice kept reminding me of the plan, repeating my lines in a hushed tone: " . . . groomed by Bruise, and then recount everything you told me: the sleeping in the same bed, the oversharing, that time at the club." Meanwhile, everyone was staring at me. Moms, former dancers. Marcel, of course, wasn't attending. My mom had told the producers to fuck off, they told me, laughing, almost like I should laugh with them. Wonder was in her freshmen year at NYU Tisch. Taylör was engaged. The other moms all seemed somehow sharper and more lethal. "Lucy," they hissed. "You're gorgeous! How are you? Staying away from this fire—so terrible, isn't it? All the damage? What are you doing now?" As if they didn't know. As if I didn't look like Mom, same eyebrows, same moon face, same furrowed expression, exactly what they wanted.

I needed air and wanted to watch the intro dance with my own eyes, a callback to the most viral dance from *DTYD!!*—a season 3 piece that had dancers embody a baby in the womb. When Bruise recognized me, her mouth opened in faux surprise, faux joy. Or maybe not faux—I am tired of parsing it. Bruise came at me, arms open. "How are you doing? You've really fallen off the face of the Earth."

"You're the one to actually fall off Earth."

Bruise's face fell. "What?"

"Like—you went to space."

Finally, Bruise managed: "I miss you, Lucy girl. I miss you like crazy."

"How are things? San Francisco? Eres?"

"Good, he's good. We're stronger than ever."

"I'm glad you've found real peace."

"And you—are you still seeing . . ."

"No. I'm . . . you know."

We were silent for a long spell, watching the dance before us, young girls writhing on the floor, penché front-rolling into a wrinkled pink-red curtain, beyond a cool dark void.

"I do really miss you," Bruise whispered back. "Like . . . sometimes at night, when I can't sleep, I'll still want to text you, call you, talk to you. Eres wants kids, and I think I'm only open to it because I want what we had once. But I want the real thing, you know?"

"Why are you telling me?"

"Because we tell each other everything."

"Then what's your real name?" I asked before I could stop myself.

Her gaze tore from the dance to me. "After all this time, you never googled it?"

"Why would I look you up? You're right here."

Another beat. She kept staring at me, as if trying to fix me forever in her memory. She stared until a crew guy began counting her down to join her place on the live set.

"Lucy girl," Bruise said. "On camera, let's pretend we're still . . ."

"Still what?"

A sad, little smile. "Whatever we were."

I try, now, not to think of her. Most days, she never crosses my mind. But sometimes, viral songs reach my small universe. Her recent biography shines at me from the aisles of Target. Bruise is a real mother. With Eres Mårtensson, she had two kids, carried via surrogates because she was past the point of natural conception. But she has a son, a daughter. That's all I know because she didn't release their names or post their faces. In her biography, Bruise skirts around the topic of me, Charley, and her divorce by gushing about motherhood. *I've changed. They changed me.* I stopped reading. The darkest part of me wants it to not be true. It's awful, but I want her to be the same Bruise, to reign her children's days with the same sound and fury, signifying nothing. No. I just want her to post them. I want to stare into their faces and discern what kind of people they are beyond the camera.

When I came back to the dressing room that night, Alice immediately pulled me aside. "I forgot about Mercury Blues."

"What?"

"When I evacuated Bruise's place, I was thinking so much about this and our plan that I just—I forgot him."

"Not Bruise's place," I said, panic icing my veins. Bruise's abandoned mansion was in the evacuation zone—right in the wildfire's path. "But he can fly. He could be anywhere."

"He's there. It's on the GPS."

She held up her phone, open to the GPS app. Sure enough, his dot was square in the Hollywood Hills. The app also showed the progression of the wildfire. I could almost feel the heat on my face. The fire, slowly undulating toward him, the heat and embers first a reflection in his eyes, then all over him, his worst fear, his worst and only fear, and oh my God—he'd told me he was going to stay and face his fear and I didn't listen.

"He'll fly away at the last second," I assured her, though we knew my words were empty. We were quiet, sitting in our private dread, when production popped in. It was time for the season 1 alumni segment. We lined up, headed toward the set, moms beside dancers, me at the caboose. Too soon, we faced the live set—the old judges on these plush chairs, empty love seats waiting for us. Big Duck tearfully recounted the first moment he saw our little faces. One by one, the dancers strode onto set, a little package of their past selves playing on the television above, sound bites of their most famous lines, their highest highs and lowest lows.

Before me, Alice was slipping away, unnoticed by her mom, who was consumed by deep Yogic breaths. I watched her head straight for the emergency exit.

"No," I hissed, sprinting to meet her. "You can't—"

"He's going to die unless we get him!"

I grabbed her wrist, whispered: "He's just a parrot!" Trying to convince myself just as much.

Alice shrugged me off, insisting: "I can't just leave him!"

"What about this?" I insisted, gesturing to the set, where the dancers and the judges and the cameramen and the studio audience waited. "Our plan?"

"But," she croaked, voice pressed thin. "It won't make a difference."

"Alice, you wanted this."

She smiled sadly. "I forgot for a second. This whole charade—at the end of the day, it doesn't really mean anything."

She pressed the latch for the emergency exit door and fled to the other side, another liminal hallway.

Security heeded her trajectory. "Hey," they said, corralling her. "Hey, you can't—"

I started toward them, but a hand was on my shoulder. A crew guy, pushing me back toward the live set. "You're supposed to be on," he said, annoyed.

The host was introducing me, my package was playing above our heads—twelve-year-old Lucy, earnestly pirouetting, so fucking fast, could I ever move that fast? Could I ever leap that high, could I ever make a comma with my spine? That was all twelve-year-old Lucy wanted, and when did I—suddenly the video was playing a clip of Mom.

"Lucy is the best thing that ever happened to me," Denise Ward said fiercely into the camera. "She's funny and zany and kind and sure, she can dance, but most important, she's a really awesome human."

Security had gotten Alice—I heard her yelling, begging to move, please let her go past, she had to get out of here. They were trying to talk her down, insisting she couldn't leave, she hadn't gone on yet. I recognized Alice's mother's voice, too, asking her daughter what was wrong now—"Why is everything always wrong with you, Alice?"

Without further ado, the therapy host was booming: "Let's meet the grown-up version of Lucy!"

Then the crew guy was pushing me, and the lights were on me, and all the audience's faces, a thousand faces but it was only Bruise's I looked for, her warm, lazy smile, the smile I knew better than anyone's, a smile I knew would wash away, revealing something finally real the moment I accused her of grooming. From the couch, Bruise yelled, "Lucy girl! I've missed you!"

A producer behind the cameras, shrugging, mouthing to Bruise—*Sing for her.*

And Bruise was standing, her mouth opening—

No, she wouldn't—

But yes, there it was, the lyrics to "Escape"—

The crowd sighed and oohed and aww'ed, relaxing back into their seats. This was it—maybe I didn't even have to accuse Bruise. I could dance, what I was put on Earth to do. I would dance and they would love me again, they would accept that I was Bruise's girl still and from there I could be back, I could be—

Really awesome human—

My gaze turned back first. Then my feet, and I was running, running as fast as my old body would allow—sprinting down the hall, toward the exit. Toward all the security people and Alice's mother now vlogging everyone who was swarming Alice, pulling her back to set. At my back, camerapeople were chasing me, desperate to catch this action live. But the cameras turned out to be all the luck I needed, because when the security people looked up, they were unprepared for the onslaught of glittering eyes in their faces. They hesitated to grab me when I seized Alice's hand, and they hesitated still when we race down the hallway into the lobby and finally made it to the parking lot, where my stupid, Joel-painted van lay in wait. Gunning the engine, we sped without a second thought straight toward the burning, smoke-clotted hills.

Mercury Blues

There was a blockade on the road in front of us, just one street over from Bruise's mansion. Columns of flames swallowed the yellowed knolls. Fire trucks and police cars, sirens flashing red-blue-red-blue. Of course, Alice and I knew they wouldn't let civilians through an evacuation zone to save a parrot.

"We'll sneak in through backyards on foot," I decided. There was no time for any other decisions, if there was any time at all. I parked the van alongside an empty cul-de-sac just before the blockade. We raced down the street, darted into the first opened side gate, into a backyard like Bruise's, all lounge chairs and teal pool and turf and glass railings, which we hopped, hiking quickly up the stiff, dry scrubland. Our eyes were on the cluster of mansions ahead: Bruise's street. We curved along the ridge, the view of the city below hidden to us in all the smoke and haze. The fire seemed almost wet, spreading like an undulating wave.

"There he is," Alice suddenly shouted. "Blues! Blues!"

I looked up—

Bruise's mansion, thankfully, had not yet been torched. But the edge of the wildfire was just creeping on her neighbor's mansion, wisps upon the balcony cabana. Just across, on the flat, white-stone roof: Mercury Blues. A tiny silhouette against the haze. A shift of dark, oily smoke swept over him. Then it cleared—he remained. His yellow eyes were wide and locked in fear. Already, the fire on Bruise's neighbor's property was tilting in the wind, igniting the dry lawn.

"We need a ladder." Alice raced ahead and vanished through those big mahogany doors.

Frozen, I stared after her, wasting precious seconds. Looking back to Mercury Blues, I called: "I'm here, bud! Fly down!"

He trembled, but didn't move. Time was running out. I went inside after Alice. In the months I had neglected to visit, the place had fallen even further into disrepair—priceless artwork on the walls were pockmarked with animal teeth marks; dead leaves and Bruise's old costumes and cups and cereal boxes and gold-plated awards and cloudy martini glasses and nude paintings and napkins with discarded song lyrics. Bottles skittered as I tore down the stairs, through the long hallways, casting my eyes this and that way—for Alice, for something, a ladder?—to get up to that stupid roof. Finally, I ran into Alice hauling the wooden door from James Cameron's *Titanic*.

Oh my God. I'd forgotten that Bruise bought that the night Patrick Kons left for the millionth time. She drunkenly swore she would make love on it the next time she was in love.

Alice panted: "Could this help you up?"

I ran my hand along it. It had ridges and footholds. It would have to do.

We ran back outside and leaned the door against the side of the mansion. With Alice bracing it, I clamored to the top of the door and reached. My fingers just barely clung to the edge of the roof, but it was enough, and I pulled myself up.

"The fire's right here," Alice screamed.

My gaze snapped even with the horizon, the wildfire claiming house after house, yard after yard, hill after hill, down the knobby spine of Los Angeles. *Focus on the bird*, I thought to myself. The roof was rough on my hands and knees, but I clung to it, moving slowly. Mercury Blues had been at the far side, looking out over the backyard and all of the city beyond. There he was. I could see his little chest rise and fall. Waves of black smoke covered us, revealed us.

"Hey," I cooed. "Hey, I'm here."

His marble eyes struggled to focus. "Blue-Blue fear." He croaked. "All over."

I reached, held out my hand. "Come here."

The bird hesitated. "No more. No more."

Alice's hoarse voice pierced through the thick carpet of smoke: "Lucy? The house is on fire?" Over my shoulder, I felt before I saw—the dancing heat, the orange, the wavering air. There was no more time to think. My vision was choked in haze, but I knew this mansion. I knew the layout of the backyard with the olive trees and the patio and the oblong infinity pool, and the distance from the roof to the pool, and if memory served, the pool was still filled with water—brackish, green water, but still—a chance.

First, I had to get the bird.

Mercury Blues blinked one more time. "All over. All over."

"Shh," I cooed. "It's not too late to—"

"All—"

"It's never over!" I shouted and leapt forward, arms extended, hands stretched, fingers wrapping around Mercury Blues. His body—light and fragile, nearly air. But I got him. My chin clipped the shingles, and red ignited my vision and I couldn't inhale but my body was still—here.

Scooting on my butt, I angled myself to where I thought the infinity pool was just below. "It's not over," I whispered to the stupid bird. His eyes met mine. "Keep trying."

"Keep trying," Blues repeated. "Keep trying."

"Just—brace yourself." I launched my body off the roof.

One, two seconds of free fall, my legs pinwheeling, hands still clasped around Mercury Blues. I didn't have time to worry about dying before my feet slapped the lukewarm pool water, then the roar of the splash, then the murky, welcomed silence under water. A last thought: *Is this what Dad's salamanders see?* The world became warbled, slick, echoey. I was loathe to surface. But my body moved on its own, up and up and up.

The mansion was an impressionist's vision of red and orange and black. I tried to pull myself out of the pool with my one free hand.

Then Alice had her hands on me, pulling me up, crying, sputtering, asking if I was okay.

I pushed the wet, smoldering parrot into her chest.

"He's fine," I choked. "Now, let's get the fuck out of here."

And then we were struggling to get to the van. I don't remember how we made it back. Vaguely I sensed there were birds fluttering overhead—ravens, pigeons, gulls, sparrows, all cawing and screaming. They seemed to make an arrow in the gray sky, which we blindly followed, zigzagging through the smoldering brush and abandoned backyards and side gates. The van was still parked on the empty street. Stinging hands found the keys. The AC rattled on, and for a brief spell, we just stayed there, stunned, breathing hard. Alice spoke first.

"That was like a movie."

"How's Blues?"

"Breathing," Alice said. "I don't know if he'll talk again."

"But he's alive," I wheezed. "Victory."

"Victory," Alice echoed. "We're alive."

When we had recovered enough to drive home across the 405, we got to talking about what would come next. "Come home with me," I said. But Alice shook her head and asked to be dropped off at her mom's house in Coto de Caza. She was only fifteen and though she had unofficially moved out into the Hoopla House and then Bruise's place, she still technically lived there, making enough appearances to satiate her audience and her mother. But the near-death experience had made her think about her baby half-siblings: how she'd never gotten to know them. How they might need someone half-sane around like she did.

In her Orange County driveway, faces blister-red, we hugged goodbye. "I'll text every day," I promised, "with updates on Blues." Alice insisted I take him—she couldn't forgive herself for forgetting him. We agreed his best bet of recovery was getting far away from this place.

Alice nodded, mouth tight. Her hand stroked the side of Blues's head. Then, the front door was opening—blond toddlers spilled out onto the yard, chirping, "Al's home!" and Anna Bell was clopping down the driveway, camera in her hand, all fake-sweet and asking, "What happened, honey, where did you go?" I could see the clickbait title already: ALICE HAS PANIC ATTACK AND RUNS AWAY DURING LIVE SHOW!!!

"Alice," I said suddenly, fiercely. "Soon, it'll be your life."

Taking in one final look at Blues, Alice whispered, "Vet school. Off-grid farm. Something else. Who knows?"

I know. Great things, Alice, great things. A tiny cabin in Vermont. A failed year in vet school—couldn't handle euthanasia. A new dream: a sanctuary for old animals in need of a good retirement. Each time I visit, she has acquired a new acre and a dozen more arthritic creatures. Each time, she tells me to try texting Rey, whom she has gotten back in touch with. Who knows?

But I'm getting ahead of myself. Driving back to Joel's apartment along the highway, I could see the fire still raging on the hills. Scarlet heat consumed the whitewashed walls, boiled the infinity pools, melted cars and outdoor grills and Grecian statues.

The fire's hands grasped white lounge chairs one by one. Only in the Valley did we seem protected and safe, partaking in the spectacle. By the following day, the wildfire would recede deeper into the mountains and canyons, follow the spine of hills into the backcountry, where it would last only a few more days before burning itself out, a startlingly brief disaster.

Mom, Again

Five weeks later, Joel and I pulled into the driveway. Just that familiar sight hitched my lungs—the canary clapboards, the rusted basketball hoop, the frazzled shrubs. It was nearly Christmas, but no snow had fallen yet. To someone else, it might've been a dreary sight, all the brown and skinny trees and wet blue tarps. But not to Joel, and not to me.

"You ready?" Joel asked, cutting the engine.

I fed Mercury Blues a red grape. "I cannot be in this van another second."

The front door was unlocked. I hadn't been home in three years, but it was like no time had passed: same blankets on the sectional, same TV, same Micah on the floor tinkering with snowshoes. As soon as Joel came barreling in, it was the same scene: my two brothers, sparring like bears, clubbing each other's backs, Micah asking if we'd visited all the national parks he'd suggested, Joel booming about how awesome each was, "Lucy lost her mind at Zion. Did you know she's afraid of heights?" Me insisting that I wasn't, it was just that Angels Landing is actually one of the deadliest trails, and then Micah coming in with the same story about how he hiked it on shrooms and Joel and I calling him out because that couldn't be real, literally, you would die—

"Micah? What's all that hullabaloo?"

Dad came through the screen door. He looked so much older, cheeks apple-red, his hair actually white. Why did the skin under his eyes look paper-thin? But still, he was wearing the same mucking boots, the embarrassing kind that went up to his armpits. Must have been outside, watching over the salamanders.

When he saw Joel and me, his face broke into a slow smile: "How was the drive? Car give you any more trouble?"

Joel had been texting him every time the van made a weird sound—and it made a lot of weird sounds across the last five weeks.

I told Dad I had a Christmas gift, and when he started going on about how I didn't have to, I gently coaxed Mercury Blues from my shoulder to Dad's outstretched arm.

"This is Mercury Blues," I said. "He has depression like you."

Behind me, Joel snort-laughed and Micah punched him. But Dad was absorbed in the parrot immediately, gently questioning his origins, why his plumage was so alarming. "He's a rescue," I explained, and that was really all there was to it. Off Dad went, crooning sweet nothings to Mercury Blues.

Mercury Blues now lives as a retired parrot, perched atop my father's shoulder across many educational hikes into the Leominster woods. It's doubtful anyone knows he's a movie star, but I think that's how Mercury Blues likes it. He doesn't talk, and I don't think he wants to, but the silence feels full enough with him and Dad out there on the lawn, staring contemplatively at the swirling ink of the vernal pool, late-summer sunsets buttering his new feathers, the shrill of cicadas and crickets and other bird sounds enough—he doesn't need more lines. He's a great singer, though.

Joel tapped me on the shoulder. "I hear Mom in the kitchen," he whispered. "Let's go say hi."

He took me down the wood-paneled, dead-wife-mom picture-framed hallway, where I could hear Mom's podcast, the one about *dying . . . well,* the soft Ira Glass–type voices blending in with the clang of pots and dishes and the beep of the timer.

I was born in this kitchen a few days after Christmas 2003.

"You just showed up," as Mom likes to tell the story. She'd assumed, despite her medical training, that at forty-seven she was too old to be expecting and was experiencing menopause until I made my grand appearance on the kitchen floor. It's a story my brothers like to recount too: the screaming (Dad, not Mom), the blood, the collecting of the towels, the cats still weaving around their legs and begging for dinner, and just the suddenness of another person in the room with you—me. Until today, I hated the story. I thought it was the most white trash way to enter the world, and it embarrassed me. Part of the appeal of Bruise's kitchen—the glossy countertops, the seamlessly slanted sink, the golden faucets—was its contrast to the kitchen I was born into, with its yellowed linoleum and cereal boxes crowning the fridge, the electric stove coils sheathed in dulling aluminum.

"And so the prodigal daughter returns," Joel whispered.

"God, shut up," I retorted. "Hardly."

He flicked my forehead. "Hey—no one said there was an age limit on prodigy."

"I thought that was literally part of the definition."

"Not in my definition," Joel said with a smile. Oh, Joel. Tomorrow he'll get up and look back at the failed pitch bible, highlighter in hand. Lifting things that stick, dashing overcomplications. "Simplify," he'll murmur a lot, hunched over fresh paper. He won't give up. Pivot and retreat, sure, but he's not quite ready to give up. And what he's coming up with now, I have a good feeling about. Great things, Joel, great things. Shapeless afternoons spent in the garage-studio, Joel doodling character designs, me . . . well. Sometimes I'll write out a new storyline for *August 8*. Sometimes I'll rehearse a random Shakespeare monologue, joking I'll really apply for that theater degree. Once in a while, I'll even dance.

Mom's voice in the kitchen: "Joel? You made it home?"

"Not just me," Joel shouted back, and yanked us both in. For a moment I stood off to the side, my fingers finding that familiar peel in the countertop that I had been working on since I was six, digging my nails into the flaking wood. Right before I was cancelled, Alice made Rey and me watch this YouTube video essay called "The Importance of Place" and the title got lodged in my brain. The importance of place—how ominous it felt stepping into this kitchen after being reminded I was born here, like literally here. Like I could hear the screams and laughs and the call for towels and the cat mewling. Like one wrong step and my present foot would go through my past-baby self on the stained linoleum, the first place I ever occupied.

There are eleven dimensions or something like that—I'm butchering this—but in one dimension you see a snail's trail of past selves going through all the spaces you've occupied; like in the four-year journey to Los Angeles and around the world and back home, I've created an entire army of past selves frozen from one moment to the next. Anyway. I was thinking about that—how my entire snail trail of past selves would start and end right here, in this place, my childhood kitchen, with my mom, listening to Joel regale her with the story of the trip. Besides chirping yeah and no a few times, I kept quiet, eyes roaming around the same counters, same oven, same sticky table. Before long, Joel was grabbing a lime seltzer out of the fridge and hightailing it back to the living room, where he continued to jab Micah about his fake shroom story, leaving me alone with Mom. Looking at me, waiting for me to break.

"Is Alex in *August 8* based off Dad? Like, your first date?" I blurted out. "And why did you name me Lucy?"

Mom blinked. "Whoa, partner. Hi, how are you?"

"Sorry—I read *August 8*. And it's good. Obviously. And I have questions."

Mom gestured to the kitchen table. "Come on, sit, at least."

She was making dinner. Mom—cooking! Some things had changed. As she shook out a box of noodles into boiling water, she started talking about how *August 8* had grown with her, from a play following many on the last day, to just Lucy. One of the last big things added was the ending date with Alex, their mesmerizing conversation before the sudden curtain fall. "It wasn't based off anyone. Just a conversation I had with myself, a long time ago."

I took my seat and asked, "When did you have it?"

"Oh," Mom said. "It was after my first bad shift as an EMT. I went to an art museum by myself, but couldn't stop thinking about dying, how sudden it must seem."

"Why was the shift bad?"

"Oh," she waved her hand. "I don't remember."

"C'mon," I teased. "You remember everything."

"Honey, it's too sad. Not right now."

"I'm sorry," I said, too quickly, too forcefully.

Mom just looked at me, her face like I had never seen it before. Not sad, not happy, just . . .

"I'm sorry," I said again, a line I couldn't quite get right. "I'm sorry."

"There's nothing to be sorry for, kid."

"There is. I was awful to you, and selfish, and I literally ran away from home."

"I missed you. Can we just start there?"

"Okay."

A beat. Mom started on a salad—chopping carrots, breaking open a bag of croutons, shaking out the old Caesar dressing. There would be time to really say what we meant, the want behind the want. To really break down all that went wrong, all the repairs that must be made. Right now, we were just warming up.

"The guy really wasn't based off anyone?" I prodded again. "Not Dad?"

Mom shook her head. "Someone—an old theater director, I think—once told me that performing is a mirage of a mirage. I always liked the tint of that saying. Like, the script is a mirage of one person, and the actor saying those lines is conjuring a mirage of a mirage of a person."

"And so Lucy—I mean, the character Lucy—is a mirage of . . ."

The oven dinged. Mom took out a tray of meatballs, saying, "Honey, I just liked the name. And when it became clear the script was going to live in a drawer, I thought you should have it."

"It's going to get made," I said, fiercely.

She tilted her head. "But it got made—I made it! I had fun making it. I was glad Joel read it. I'm glad you read it." Her eyes were bright and shimmery like she might cry, but before I could tell, Mom turned to whack a jar of red sauce against the counter and twist the lid.

"Wait! I have one more burning question . . ."

"Yeah?"

"What was up with the crazy upstairs neighbor?"

Mom threw her head back, laughing big. "God, that wasn't a mirage, I really had a neighbor who believed aliens would return any day, so he . . ." and she started on the story, leaning against the kitchen counter, me sitting at the table, mouth widening in shock at each new revelation. My brothers were in the other room, play-argument escalating, Dad nagging them to be quiet, because the parrot was overstimulated. Soon they'd join us for dinner, where Mom would retell the story with more flair and detail.

It's not like I don't think about Bruise, like I don't habitually stalk Rey or Charley or even my own name. It's not even like I know my next step. A year off after graduating high school late and the gap year became two and I'm twenty-two and just coming up for air. "But you're still so young," Mom says. We sit at the kitchen table lots of nights and talk. I weigh the best way to reconnect with Charley and apologize. We trade horror stories of LA and NYC, and endlessly workshop versions of future-Lucy—college? Writing with Joel? Acting again? Maybe nursing school . . . "Stop it," Mom says, wagging a finger. She tells me another sad death-doula story she's collected over the years, some funny-sad and others just . . . but I can't get enough, like future-Lucy is banging the door, begging me to take it all in. Mom is sixty-eight. How many years left? When I do the math of the time I missed—*But there's still time*, I tell myself. *You still have time. You're here.*

Mom set everything on the table. She called my brothers, my father. My eyes burned, laughing from something she'd said. The same bichon frise wall clock. Same artisanal saltshakers from Rockport. The dead wife's Fiestaware plates. Clatter of silverware and flat Diet Coke being poured. I inhaled the immediacy of home, the familiar things, the familiar people around me, here, now. Exhaled—we're still here, it's still now.

"Okay," Mom warned. "There was a recipe, but I took some creative liberties. Ready to dig in?"

Okay. I'm ready.

Reading Group Guide

1. Though Lucy is a fictional character, many of her experiences are inspired by the real world. What stories of childhood fame and notoriety came to mind as you read this novel?

2. *Lucky Girl* plays with columns and script formatting throughout the narrative. Why do you think the author Allie Tagle-Dokus chose to format certain scenes in these ways?

3. Author Kiley Reid says that "*Lucky Girl* is remarkably precise in its meditations on art, youth, sacrifice, and obsession." Would you agree? If so, are there particular moments from the book that come to mind?

4. *Lucky Girl* is richly populated with a memorable cast of characters. Is there a character you connected with most, or a character who really surprised you?

5. Parents and parental figures play critical roles in *Lucky Girl*. How are they portrayed in this novel and to what end?

6. How does being a younger sister to Joel and Micah shape Lucy's early identity? How would the novel be different if she didn't have siblings?

7. How would you describe the point of view throughout this novel? Why do you think the author chose to have a retrospective narrator?

8. Animals appear throughout the narrative—did you have a favorite animal in *Lucky Girl*? Why do you think the author uses animals at key moments in Lucy's life?

9. How do you think things turn out for Lucy after she returns to her family at the end of the novel?

10. After reading *Lucky Girl*, how would you define the concept of "success"? Are there ways in which your own conception of it differs from the one presented here?

Personal Acknowledgments

To my editor Alyssa, I'm deeply grateful for your sharp eye in making *Lucky Girl* its most authentic, brightest, and truest self. To Beth Steidle for creating a cover that I will never stop staring at—you actually made my dreams come true. And to everyone at Tin House, I am enormously fortunate to have Lucy's big debut with your guidance. At all points, you have exactly gotten the core of *Lucky Girl*, sometimes before I could even articulate it!

A billion thanks to my agent Lauren Scovel and the team at Laura Gross Literary Agency for first believing in *Lucky Girl* and helping me get her in tiptop shape. Without you, Lauren, this book would still be a massive word document on my computer.

I would not be the kind of writer I am today without working with other writers, and I am indebted to all the writers and teachers both at Emerson and Iowa whom I've sat with at a workshop table. Just know I loved your work and am probably still in awe of you today. Especially grateful for Kiley, Claire, James, and Maria who answered my frenetic emails about this process.

Particular thanks go to my early readers—Andy Schlebecker, Jake Schwartz, Andy's dad, and Ryann Tagle. To my friends—thanks for being so funny and loving, you made me funny and loving. To the Parker community and especially my Div 2 AH coworkers—thanks for keeping me afloat. To my students—thanks for being goofy goobers, making each day fun, and giving me purpose beyond the success of this book. To my family—I hope you see yourself in that final scene. I'm so lucky I get to come home to you.

Lastly, *Lucky Girl* is dedicated to Stephanie Weymouth, my cousin. She passed away in 2024. In many ways, she was like Denise: the most talented performer and dedicated playwright. She was a gifted singer who deserved the biggest and brightest stage. You were lucky to know her. I wish you could have met her. You can still hear her sing on Instagram at @songsbysteph_ and support her at the Stephanie Marie Weymouth Foundation (http://www.smwcharitablefoundation.org/) where we continue her legacy, seeking to elevate accessibility to performing arts through scholarships, funding, and mentorship.

ALLIE TAGLE-DOKUS is a writer and high school teacher. She received her BFA in writing, literature, and publishing from Emerson College and her MFA from the Iowa Writers' Workshop. She currently lives in Gardner, Massachusetts, with her husband and dog.